THE GiRL U WANT

Elaine Reed

HAGERSTOWN, MARYLAND

"Hey! Naughty girl!"

Sue Douglas stooped forward as a pair of hands landed—with the full weight of the person behind them—on her shoulders. Righting her posture, she automatically held up a black sticker emblazoned with "#naughty" in bold white text, along with a postcard advertising the radio station's next free show.

"Thanks, love." The interloper took the items and pushed off her shoulders to launch himself back into the swarm of concertgoers enjoying the balmy spring night.

"Can I have one too, please?" A petite girl with an apologetic expression stood before her.

Sue smiled and held out a different sticker in each hand. "Naughty or nice?"

"Naughty." The girl giggled and blushed.

Sue gave her the sticker and matching postcard. For every hyped fan who jumped on her, at least two shy people mumbled requests. She wanted them all. Even more, she wanted them to bring their friends to the next concert her station hosted. The only thing that kept management from flipping the switch and turning the small rock station into another pre-packaged "lite music" destination was advertising. Big attendance numbers at these events kept advertisers happy. That gave Sue the leverage she needed to get more budget to do better events. It boosted her reputation in the industry and kept at least fifty people employed.

The drum beat from the stage guided her as she zigzagged through the crowd, giving out stickers on her way to the afternoon drive time DJ. On her cue he would transition the free show in the nightclub's back parking lot to the ticketed concert inside. Sue gave away her last sticker and put an intern in charge of the postcards before she pushed through the final crush of music lovers.

"Axel!" She waved. "Hey, Axel!"

The scruffy blond DJ turned and beckoned her. "Sue! You got any more T-shirts? The black ones. I wanna hook these girls up."

"Yeah, I've got some in the van. Gimme a minute." She nodded toward the women. "Listen, Ax, when these guys are done—"

"I know." Axel flashed his palm with *naughty* scrawled across it in pink ink. "Text 'naughty' for Pink Slip and 'nice' for Derelicts."

"Exactly. Perfect." She blew out a breath and pushed her hair off her face. "Don't mix it up."

"You already pounded it into my head, woman!" Axel grinned and threw an arm around her neck, giving Sue a half-hug. "This is a cool thing you created. It's only May and we're already selling tickets for the Halloween show *and* the Christmas concert."

"It's what I do." Sue turned her attention to the people waiting and almost laughed. The "girls" were the wives of two prominent baseball players from the Washington Nationals. She smiled at them. "Come on, I'll get you shirts."

The women followed her through the groups of people piled around the temporary stage. While Sue climbed into the van to find the stash of black shirts, Axel addressed the concertgoers.

"Let's hear it for Derelicts!"

The crowd roared, having multiplied since the first band got on stage about an hour before. Now a sea of bodies filled the parking lot. She took a beat to appreciate how many people she'd drawn out.

"If you like these guys," Axel shouted, "make sure you text in your vote! Tonight's winner plays against two other bands at our Bag of Bones Halloween party. That winner opens our big Naughty or Nice Christmas show with The Presidents of the United States of America!" When the fans settled into a steady hum of energy, he spoke again. "If you wanna see Pink Slip, what're you gonna text?"

"Naughty!" the crowd thundered.

"If you want to see Derelicts?"

"Nice!"

"You got it! Text us now! Voting closes when the main event starts."

Axel reminded the crowd where to line up for the

indoor show before getting them into one more chant of "naughty" and "nice," then he left the stage.

No sooner had Sue given the women T-shirts, than Axel showed up with a crowd of guys.

"Hey, Sue." He jerked a thumb over his shoulder. "These guys say they're the opening act, but security won't let them in without tickets. Too many people in line already!"

Sue shoved the stickers she held in her back pocket, then looked past Axel. A familiar mop of hair—so black it was almost blue—ruffled in the breeze.

"Oh my God, Tom!" She jumped into the lanky man's arms, giddy with laughter. "I figured I wouldn't see you until this was over!"

"Wow!" Axel pulled his chin back. "I don't get treatment like that, and I approve your expense reports."

Sue laughed again, an arm still around Tom. "This is my cousin. We grew up on the same street."

Tom tousled Sue's hair. "It's been a while since we've seen each other. Axel says this melee is your fault."

Sue surveyed the crowd again. "With anyone else I'd be humble, but hell yeah, this is my fault!"

"We left to eat and came back to all this. Now we can't get in."

"I'll get you in under the stage." Sue grabbed a flashlight from the van and pulled the door shut. "Follow me!"

She directed the guys along the perimeter of the lot. When they got to the rear corner of the stage, she slid aside a piece of black-painted plywood and flicked on the torch. She dipped her head under the framework of the stage and shone the light toward a door just past the opposite side. "We're going this way." Partly crouched to avoid bumping her head, she led the group through the maze of stage supports.

"What are we doing?" a voice called from somewhere behind her.

"I don't know," someone else answered. "Follow the chick in the tight pants."

"Sweet," said a third voice.

"Hey!" Even though Tom only spoke one word, Sue recognized the tone in his voice.

Sue interrupted before her cousin could threaten his friends. "That's not how you vote! It's either naughty—"

"Or nice!" a few of the guys chimed in.

Sue chuckled and opened the stage door, where she greeted security. "Hey, Jabba, I've got Words Fail Me. They won't let them in the front door."

The security guard let out a throaty chortle. "Don't blame 'em. Rockers are the worst kind of riffraff. Come on."

They filed in, two tall guys with long hair—one dark blond, the other with a silky black mane—a stocky Asian guy with punk-rock spikes, and finally one with a ruddy complexion and the wardrobe and gait of a skater, each flashing their passes as they went.

Skater guy talked to her chest as he crossed the threshold. "Tits and ass really do open doors."

Sue put a concert flyer in his face. "Keep moving, bud."

"Shut the fuck up, Chris." Tom pushed the guy into the club.

Sue smirked at Tom. "Thanks, but I can handle myself."

"You shut up, too."

Sue lifted her eyebrows and he blushed.

"Okay." Tom held out a flyer. "This contest is cool."

"Thanks!" She beamed. "This is the first year we're doing a Christmas concert. It's the same weekend as the big Baltimore station's, so we needed a hook."

"Your hook is a contest that involves six bands and four shows?"

Sue calculated it in her head. "Yeah."

"And this is the first show."

"Yes."

"There's a couple hundred people crammed into that parking lot."

"The venue holds a thousand," Sue said. "I was shooting for at least half."

Tom squinted at her. "You should work for us. We need a good promotions manager."

"Sure, Tom." Sue shook her head. "I've gotta count the votes. We have to announce the winner before the show inside is over."

"What are you doing after?"

"I have to clean up all this." She gestured to the outdoor stage. After the bargaining and cajoling she'd had to do to get management to approve this contest, the last thing she needed was the venue complaining.

"After that."

"Hanging with you and passing out for about fourteen hours."

"Meet me at the station after-party. You have a pass."

"I never go to that stuff. I have to clean up and pack the van."

Tom held up a hand. "You have interns for that. After-party."

"This is my event. I'm responsible for—"

"Your interns are trained to within an inch of their lives. Put aside your control-freak tendencies for one night and come to the damn party."

"*You're* calling *me* a control freak? Really?"

Tom crossed his arms. "I'm tour manager. That's the job."

"Easy excuse."

"Come on, Sue. After-party."

Sue mentally reviewed the long list of things that needed to be done before she could party, and wrinkled her nose. It might be dicey. Still, she hadn't seen Tom in ages, and she knew Axel would help her do a final check. "Okay."

Before Tom could celebrate, she pulled her vibrating phone from her back pocket, read the screen, and laughed. "I have to go. Axel's trying to count the votes without me, and he thinks he broke the program."

Tom winced. "That's not good."

"He can't break the program. The votes come to my phone. And my email. And the texting company. I got backups for my backups. We're in good shape, Tommy."

Sue ducked to go back under the stage when Tom called out, "Station after-party. Be there!"

"Don't spend too much time talking to girls," Tom said. "Get to the party so I can make introductions."

"Sure thing." Brad beat his thumbs against his thighs, still riding the adrenaline high from playing in front of an amped crowd. The set they'd played was straight fire, and the show Skein put on after them had dumped a shit ton of fuel on it. The people hanging around pulsed with the same energy. He wanted to meet this girl with all the ideas and make some decisions, capitalize on the momentum.

"Hold on." Brad's bass player threaded a padlock through the latch on their instrument trailer.

"I got this, man." Brad jutted his chin at the venue. "Go get her."

Tom flashed a thumbs-up and jogged toward the club.

Chris finally finished locking the trailer and turned, rubbing his head. "You guys wanna hire the chick in the tight pants? You can't be that hard up, man."

Brad waited a beat to make sure he didn't visibly bristle at Chris's comment. "We should consider it. Did you see the crowd outside? The stickers? Those bands playing in the back lot? That was *all* that chick!"

"How do you know?" Chris spared Brad an occasional glance as he checked out the women loitering near the club.

"Tom and I were talking to the DJ who emceed the outside show. He said she invented the whole thing to promo their Christmas concert."

"The radio station in Bum Fuck, Maryland is big enough to have a Christmas concert?"

"Exactly!"

"Whatever. A chick shouldn't be following us from gig to gig. Unless you need a piece of ass on standby."

"Seriously, dude?"

Chris rubbed his chin. "It could come in handy. And she doesn't look used up yet."

Brad grabbed Chris's shoulders, giving him a light shake. "A little respect, man. She's Tom's cousin."

Chris knocked Brad's hands away. "She had one good idea. That's no reason to bring her on tour."

"You wrote one good bass line and we let you in the band."

"Fuck you. That's *not* how it went down." Chris glared, but Brad held his ground. "What the fuck ever, Brad. Do what you want." He smirked. "Might be fun to use up a girl together."

Brad snarled and pushed past him, taking long strides toward the club.

Post-concert, the building had a very different look. It still smelled like beer and smoke, but the illuminated house lights revealed its length. Most of the space resembled a long, wide hallway leading directly to the stage. Alcoves on either side contained bars and a few love seats. The party gravitated around the bar at stage right. A worker pulled over couches from the other side, containing the party in a more intimate space, while a few women danced to the house music.

Brad recognized the tight jeans at the other end of the bar with Tom. They looked like they'd been made specifically for her firm ass and hips. Her T-shirt hugged her curves and stopped right at the edge of her pants. He wished she'd raise her arms and give him a peek at her bare waist. Auburn hair hung loose down her back, tantalizing him. In a room full of blondes and brunettes, that hair qualified as exotic.

She turned her head and smiled, instantly upgrading from hot girl to knockout. When she faced Tom again, Brad took one more long look at her ass. He'd be a goner if she had a sense of humor, too. He muttered to himself, "Come *on*, personality like sandpaper!" He ordered three longnecks and joined Tom and the woman, offering the icy bottles.

"Thanks, Brad. I want you to meet Sue. Sue Douglas, Brad Gowan."

Brad had a smile ready when she faced him and gave her a beer instead of shaking her hand. "Nice to meet you, Sue. Axel brags on you a ton."

"Brags, or promises free stuff?" She reached past Tom to put her empty on the bar and gently swirled the new bottle.

"Definitely bragging. It was right after the votes were tallied."

"Yeah, he would've been happy then." Sue smirked and sipped the fresh beer. "The votes were five times the number of people that can fit in the club."

"Nice!" Tom clinked his drink against hers. "How'd you manage it?"

"I had four DJs talking about this show for two months." Sue took another pull on her drink. "And people could vote more than once."

As he and Tom laughed, Brad scrutinized Sue and her easy nature. Instinct said she could help his band. He needed the questions to ask to prove it. Chris walked in, his arm around a woman, and inspiration struck.

"My bass player wants to know how a radio station in Nowhere, Maryland got a Christmas concert."

"I asked for one."

"What do you mean?"

"I mean, I asked management for one," Sue repeated. "I have some seriously talented DJs and a few local bands who want more attention. They feel like there isn't room for them in Baltimore or Philly, and they aren't getting traction in Pittsburgh. So, I surveyed the listeners. A lot of them said they can't always get to Baltimore for music and they want more here. I took it to management. They gave me a Christmas concert."

"They gave her a Christmas concert, all right. Along with a big *fuck you*," Axel interrupted as he joined the group, closing it to a few people who'd been openly watching Brad.

Sue punched him in the arm. "Shut up."

"They did!" Axel narrowed his eyes at Sue, then turned to Tom and Brad. "Management didn't want to break their dull but profitable format. They set our Christmas concert the *same night* as the big rock station's in Baltimore, and our headliner is D-list. Obviously, they wanted it D.O.A. so they wouldn't have to consider making this an annual thing."

"The Presidents are not D-list." Sue put a hand on her hip and gestured with her bottle. "Kitschy? Sure. But fun! And great for our demo."

Tom collected the empties and put them on the bar behind him. "Didn't you mention Baltimore has Green Day? Most people choosing a '90s nostalgia band for Christmas are making the drive."

Axel signaled one of the bartenders for another round. "That's what you'd think. But Suzy here is already moving tickets."

"It's May." Brad finished the second half of his beer to hide his surprise.

Sue pursed her lips. "Yeah. I only have a few more months to sell it out, or no Christmas concert next year."

"She got The Presidents excited about this contest." Axel put a hand on the back of Sue's neck and gave her a tug. "They're hoping to swing a surprise visit to the Halloween party, which *is* sold out."

Sue shook off Axel and scanned the room. "Axel! You better hope no one overheard that. If it gets back to tonight's bands and it doesn't happen—"

"Relax! I know. I scoped out the area."

She elbowed him and finished her drink, then checked the room again before she spoke. "Technically, it's not sold out. Only the tickets we released are." She traded her empty bottle with the bartender, still with one eye on the partygoers.

"Sue, if the station would've let us release all the tickets for the party, they'd be gone by now. Or damn near it. We get regular calls for those tickets."

Sue seemed ready to protest when Axel shot her a look. She gave him a sharp glare instead.

Tom squinted as he regarded Sue. "She's putting you guys on the map."

"Yep," Axel said. "Our little Podunk station is becoming more than a training ground for first-year DJs."

Sue rolled her eyes. "Says the guy who's been doing afternoon drive time for five years."

Axel shrugged. "My wife likes it here."

"You're making DJs famous?" Brad asked.

"You wanna be famous?" Sue tilted her head, holding his gaze. Hers brimmed with confidence. "I'll make you famous."

She'd caught him off guard. "Man! That had some heat!" He tore part of the label off the bottle and rolled it between his thumb and forefinger. "I'm already famous."

"No. You're the most popular barfly in Detroit. You have a decent following in Michigan, but get away from the Great Lakes and you're just another guy with a guitar."

Brad clutched his bottle to his chest. "This woman is mean, Tom."

"Sue is painfully honest," Tom said.

"And she knows her shit," Axel added. "She researched tonight's bands weeks ago. She knew exactly how to promote you before your names were even on the marquee. It's too bad this isn't Baltimore or Philly. Sue's twenty-five and she's already sent three DJs to top-tier markets. She could run radio if she wanted to."

"You just want to be famous. I"—she pointed at herself with both hands—"can make you the disdain of parents the world over."

He didn't even try to stop the grin. Instead, Brad pushed Axel out of the way to put an arm around Sue. "Come work with us. I don't want to be famous. I want to be super famous. I want to be the enemy of every father and more than a few husbands. Tell me how you'll do it."

CHAPTER 2

Sue set a cup of fresh coffee on the café table for Emily, then dropped into a seat. She should be exhausted after hanging out with Tom and Axel until practically sunrise. She thrummed with adrenaline instead. "I was visiting with Tom, and the next thing you know, this hot rock guy draped himself all over me, and I convinced him I'd make him famous." Sue blushed and waited for Emily to stop giggling. "Shut up, this is serious!"

"Tom plied you with drinks, didn't he?"

"I only had two be—wait. Shit. I started a fourth beer."

"Feeling good after two, bold after three..." Emily said.

"Thank God I didn't finish the fourth. I'd be running for governor by now."

"Not waking up with the hot rock guy?" Emily lifted her eyebrows before sipping her coffee.

Sue waved the suggestion away. "Absolutely not. Never work guys. Not even fuck-hot musicians."

"Fuck hot, huh?"

"His charisma on stage is electric. He's striking, too. Native American, complete with high cheekbones and hair like silk." Sue shook her head, erasing the image she'd conjured. "Anyway, hard pass. Business plans before boys."

"But this boy is a benefit of the business plan."

"Nope. I don't mess around with guys from work. There's enough drama in publicity."

"I get it." Emily sat back.

Sue lean forward and grinned. "Have I told you how proud I am that you passed the bar exam?"

Emily crossed her arms. "Especially now that you need to register a business and write a contract?"

"Exactly. Plus, I need to make sure I'm not breaking any rules in my contract with the station. And I was proud of you before I created this whirlwind situation for myself."

"I'm a little surprised you're leaving the station in the middle of your holiday contest. Especially since the buzz you get them keeps them afloat."

Sue played with the tag hanging from her hot tea before answering. She had mixed emotions about walking away from what she'd built. Taking this job was a risk, and so was turning it down. "Axel says I'm too young to pass on a good opportunity for a job that doesn't give me an equity stake."

Emily's eyes popped. "Wow. Axel's a really good friend."

"Yeah." Surprised by sentimentality, Sue blinked back tears and cleared her throat. "I'll make sure my replacement is ready to hit the ground running. There's an assistant producer on the midday program who'd be good."

"The station expects you to replace yourself?"

"No. I'm not leaving Axel high and dry, though. He's always been my biggest cheerleader. Besides, radio is a small town. You may not know everyone, but you know *about* them. I gotta stay on the up and up." Sue sipped her tea and sat back. "I can't believe I'm creating my business already."

"You've been working on the business plan since sophomore year of college. I'd say it's about time."

"I can't screw this up, Em. I barely have anything saved and going back to entry-level radio would be humiliating."

"You'll be okay." Emily patted Sue's hand and smiled. "I'll build in safeguards for you. And you can always sell your house."

"I'm not ready for that. I never planned to stay there forever, but I finally finished the remodel. I want to enjoy it for a bit."

"Ha! Enjoy it from their tour-bus window!" Emily straightened and finished her coffee. "I have to get to the office. Give me the details you worked out and forty-eight hours."

Sue handed over a copy of her radio contract with a bright sticky note on the cover page. It had a short list of items, including the salary she and Tom had discussed. "You have twelve hours. Otherwise their record label is gonna assign someone from corporate."

"Jeez, Sue, why can't you pick a low-pressure job once in a while?"

She shrugged. "Too boring."

<hr>

ST. LOUIS, MISSOURI

Two weeks later, Sue pushed open the door to the dressing room at Mississippi Nights and looked around. The room damn near overflowed with trunks, duffel bags, and equipment. Hairbrushes, razors, and bottles of sprays and creams covered spaces that didn't already have clothes on them. Flyers and pictures were taped to the mirrors, and a bottomless garbage can hung from the wall with balled papers littering the counter, floor, and luggage around it. She'd seen messy dressing rooms from the concerts the station sponsored, but they'd rarely been disorderly from ceiling to floor and wall to wall. If these guys were sending a message, they'd have to try harder. She didn't care if their shaving cream got left behind.

To her right, directly behind the door, a man's bare foot hung over the side of a grossly overstuffed couch.

"Hey, rock star, how about helping a lady through this mess?"

Brad peeked from behind a copy of *Metal Edge* and

grinned. "Hey, Sexy Sue! When the door opened, I figured the next thing I'd hear was Tom bitching about amplifiers being expensive tables. I was hoping to blend in."

In one fluid movement, Brad dropped the magazine, stood, and scaled some gear to get to Sue's side. He took her messenger bag and kissed her cheek.

Sue grinned at his easy affection and cataloged the mess in the room again. Part of her job would be to help keep track of all the equipment. "You unload a lot of stuff for an eight-hour stop."

"The guys made it look worse for you. I don't think all this is even ours. How was your flight?"

"I don't know, I drove."

"Why? Hagerstown to St. Louis is like twenty hours. It's storming out there! How are you even awake?" Brad steered her through the maze of gear to the couch, almost pushing her into a speaker.

She cursed under her breath and freed herself of his direction. "It's twelve hours, the rain stopped this morning, and I'm not sticking exactly with the tour. I've got some meetings in Austin and I want to get to New Orleans before you, so I'm skipping the Houston gig."

"We would've rented a car for you in Austin and flown you to New Orleans."

Hadn't Brad seen the details of her contract? The record label wasn't exactly thrilled with the band's decision to use a third-party PR agent. They'd written all kinds of extra billing and payback requirements into the agreement, making something as simple as acquiring a plane ticket seem like quantum physics by the time all the forms were completed. Sue had negotiated a higher rate and decided to use her own resources instead of wasting time on red tape.

"That's sweet, but I don't mind driving. It gives me time to think in peace."

"Peace on a rock tour *is* a novelty."

"I won't drive all tour. The show in Charlottesville is about two hours from my place. I'll drive home from there and catch a flight to meet you guys in New York."

"That still leaves you driving across half the country."

"I like to drive." Sue managed to make it to the couch and grabbed the copy of *Metal Edge* Brad had been reading. "How far did you get in this?"

"Not far." He scratched his bare chest. "I think I was still in the letters to the editor section."

"Cool. Check this out." Sue thumbed through the magazine. She found the page she wanted, folded the rest of the pages back, and tossed the whole thing to Brad. "Bottom of the middle column."

What would the title of your life story be?
"I'm very pleased and terrified to be here."

—Brad Gowan, Words Fail Me

"You did this? You got us in here?"

"Yes, sir." Sue smiled and pushed a few stray hairs over her ears, then rested her hands on her hips.

"I can't believe it! Tom's been trying to get us in this rag for months!" Brad nimbly climbed over the equipment between them and wrapped her in a huge bear hug.

Laughing, she indulged him for a moment, then stepped out of the embrace. "Just doing my job. Tom gave me the quote and I stayed on the phone until I knew it was set." Then she made sure the record label saw the pickup along with the proofs for the next issue. She made sure she mentioned that the whole thing happened within forty-eight hours of executing the contract. It was more than a solid start toward fulfilling the publicity requirements.

"You're awesome." Brad's gaze floated between Sue and the magazine.

"Did you quote *Hairspray* on purpose?" Sue asked as she sat on the couch.

"We did the play in high school and I had it bad for the chick cast as Penny Pingleton. I felt that way pretty much every time she spoke to me. And when we signed our record deal." Blushing, Brad sat sideways on the couch, facing Sue.

"Penny was hot, huh?" Sue grinned, amused by his reaction.

"For a high school girl." Brad smirked.

Sue rolled her eyes. "Okay, Romeo. I wanna officially meet the other guys. We have a lot to discuss before we get to Austin."

"Like what?"

"We're taking full advantage of the opportunities at Indy Showcase. I scheduled interviews and I'm hoping for a small photo shoot, too."

Brad stood and rooted around the room until he found a T-shirt and put it on. His face stayed blank, though his eyes were dark. "How many interviews total?"

Sue recognized his concern but carried on, figuring it was better that he knew more. "Not sure yet. A few people agreed to interview you guys at the same time. One is only interested in Darryl since he produced your album. He can do that on his own while you guys talk to someone else."

"Are any of these gonna be live?"

"No. They'll all be recorded then transcribed. The bloggers may post some of the audio, but they'll tighten it up so they only have the witty parts on their sites," Sue explained.

"They'll edit us? Are they allowed to do that?"

"Yeah, so they can post the best parts of the inter-views. They'll want something unique and cool. If anything, the people who interview you together might fight over the best moments."

Brad smiled. "They'll fight over us?"

"It's a strong possibility."

"I love it when you talk rock star to me." His smile overtook his face, and his brown eyes danced.

Sue sat up and smiled back. His enthusiasm was contagious despite her road weariness. "You say that now but wait until I sit your ass in a room to interview for a couple days straight and then throw some photo shoots on top of it. We'll see if you like all the rock star talk then."

"I have a feeling you'll be able to get me into it."

"I certainly hope so." Sue stood. "Where are the rest of the guys? I want to meet them before the show."

"Yeah, we need to talk about that." Brad's expression sobered. He worked his way back to the couch and pulled Sue down next to him.

"What's up?" A small wave of fatigue hit her. Not from the drive, but from nerves. She'd been on pins and needles ever since she'd accepted the band's offer. Negotiating with the record company hadn't been a walk in the park, either. Her agreement to work as both tour support and publicist was unconventional but justified her joining the tour and made it possible for the band to afford her. Plus, it gave her an opportunity to prove her mettle in several ways. The record company had insisted on unusual clauses that put them all over a barrel. Sue was determined to prove she was worth it, and more importantly, that the clauses were unnecessary.

"They're kinda pissed that Tom and I vetoed them. They think a girl on the bus will change the dynamic of the tour and the whole 'what happens on tour stays on tour' thing."

"'What happens on tour stays on tour?'"

"Women." Brad looked sheepish.

"Huh. I figured I'd be a buzzkill making them talk to reporters. Being a cockblock never occurred to me."

Brad's eyes went wide. "They're worried about the work part, but Tom and I got them past that. We need the attention. We'd have to work for it no matter what. So...yeah. Women are still an issue."

"Okay." Surprised that sex was their biggest concern, Sue tightened her ponytail and her resolve. "That's no big deal. I don't care who you guys sleep with. It only matters if someone tries to confirm rumors with me. In that case, the less I know the better."

Brad frowned and raked his fingers through his hair. "Be prepared. They may be vulgar for a while, and they'll probably try to pull some shit on you."

"Hazing and vulgarity. I can handle it." Sue bobbed her head once.

"You sure? You're not scared?"

"Scared? No. Wishing I went to the Cleveland gig and negotiated with the band in person? Yes. Chalk it up to a lesson learned the hard way." Sue took the magazine and played with the edge, hoping he wouldn't see her frustration over her own eagerness to close the deal instead of doing her due diligence.

"I'm sure they won't do anything worse than teach you a few new curse words. Besides, Tom and I got your back."

Sue smiled at Brad and tossed the magazine back in

his lap. "Good. Where's this unruly band of yours?"

CHAPTER 3

"Hey, guys! Sue's here," Brad shouted as they crossed the stage.

Sue walked a few steps behind, taking in the space. The rest of the band sat in the first two rows of the venue with gushing female fans scattered around them. The band harassed the men arranging the headliner's gear, throwing paper wads and food at the stage.

"We aren't up to meeting another one of your groupies," the guy with punk-rock spikes shouted back. Vibrant tattoos covered his arms.

"Yeah, man. How are we ever gonna keep them all straight?"

The guys laughed as though Brad and women were a running joke. The ladies around them all fidgeted. Suddenly, an M&M headed straight for Sue's face. She caught it neatly in her mouth and swallowed.

"Nicely done." The guy sitting in the front row stood. "I'm Justin Arnold. I drum."

Even with Sue on the stage, Justin had enough height that she barely had to lean over to shake his proffered hand. The stage lights highlighted a strong jaw and made the glossy light brown and blond strands of Justin's long hair shine. "Nice to meet you."

"You sailed past test number one," Brad whispered as she straightened.

Sue didn't have time to process that little success before she went back on high alert.

"Hey, you should be on TV. Stupid Human Tricks!" The guy with spiked hair gave her a big grin, still sprawled in his seat, one foot propped on the chair in front of him.

"That's not my speed, but thanks." Sue smiled and tried to relax despite her cold hands and tense neck. She knew it was better that she hadn't done more than reapply her deodorant after twelve hours on the road, but she still wished for the armor of fresh clothes and neat hair.

Still on his feet, Justin shook the chairs near the other two. "Come on, stand up, assholes. That's Darryl Black, rhythm guitar and keyboards." He pointed to the spikey bottle blond, then jerked his head over his right shoulder. "The cue ball behind me is Chris Lorenzo, bass."

The young woman sitting next to Chris cocked her head as though waiting for her introduction. Justin didn't appear to notice.

Before Sue greeted the other guys, Brad jumped off the stage and showed them the blurb in *Metal Edge*. Justin took the magazine and evicted the woman sitting between Darryl and Chris, holding the pages open so they could all read the blurb together.

"Damn." Justin slapped the armrest. "*Hairspray* goes pretty far back, man."

"Yeah." Brad buried his fists in his pockets and ducked his head. The fan who'd forfeited her seat to Justin pinched Brad's cheek, her other hand on his bicep. Brad brushed her away.

"Where are the quotes from the rest of us?" Chris didn't speak to her chest this time.

"When I called Tom, you guys were shooting a video and Brad was the only one around. The editor agreed to save space in an upcoming issue to feature all of you." Sue crossed her arms and rocked on the balls of her feet while she waited for their response. She didn't like feeling vulnerable, especially as the stage lights shone on her with random strangers sizing her up.

"Brad was the only one available for comment, huh?" Darryl exchanged glances with Justin and Chris.

The three of them launched a full-scale food attack at Brad, pelting him with their snacks.

"Hey!" Brad scrambled back onto the stage and tried to gather some ammunition of his own. "Watch it!"

"Yeah, watch it." One of the women shook out her hair.

Still ignoring the women, the guys kept a steady stream of M&Ms, puffed cheese, and pretzels going in Brad's direction as they clamored onto the stage and chased him.

"Guys, you're supposed to trash the stage *after* the show!" All movement stopped as Tom stepped into view, tapping a tablet against his leg. "Besides, you know how Brad gets when shit sticks in his hair." Tom greeted Sue with a half-hug. "How're they treating you?"

"Better than they're treating Brad." She relaxed by a few degrees.

"Good. Saw your work in *Metal Edge*. You don't waste any time."

"It was nothing."

"Sure it was. Have you checked into the hotel?"

"No. I wanted to meet everyone first. I figure as soon as I get to the room, I'll pass out."

"You should've flown in."

"You think I can't make my car fly?"

Tom rolled his eyes. "Everyone knows you're here?"

She gestured toward the band.

"I mean your squad. They know you made it?"

"Oh!" Sue laughed. "Yeah. Emily called me a few times along the way to make sure I didn't decide our devil's deal was too much and change my mind. I texted Amy and Robin after I pulled in. Robin's jealous of some of the tour stops. He says it's been a while since they played in a beautiful, intimate space."

"Echo Chamber can write their own ticket. Tell them to do a fan club event at a place like that."

Sue flashed her eyebrows. "I have. They're considering it after the festival circuit."

Tom crossed his arms, his tablet tucked against his chest. "Why aren't you doing Echo Chamber's PR? You'd build the business faster."

"I consult sometimes and arrange media for Robin's art, but they've had a great team in place forever. You don't mess with a good formula."

Tom shifted his gaze to the band, still having a food fight on the stage. "Have you told them about Indy Showcase?"

"Only Brad. Wanna break it to them now?"

"Hey, guys!" Tom shouted. "Stop torturing the crew and come here! Sue has some news for you."

Justin sauntered over, draped his arm around Sue, and smiled. "Notice how you're the only person not covered in cheese shit?"

"Yeah." Sue braced herself, expecting him to grab Darryl's bag and dump whatever remained on her.

"There are two ways to stay that way. One: never spend time alone with Darryl. Two: make him think he's famous. Otherwise, I hope you like orange." Justin smirked and gave her a salacious once-over, lingering on her breasts longer than necessary.

Sue wove her fingers into the hand that hung carelessly from her shoulder and moved her head to look Justin straight in the eye. "I'm not gonna make him *think* he's famous, Justin. I'm going to make him famous. Will that work?"

"Uh... that'll do it." Justin's smile faltered under

Sue's gaze, but he kept his stance. When she looked away, she felt him exhale. When would this part of the gauntlet end so she could do the same?

"Ladies," Tom addressed the fans. "Can you give us a few minutes?"

"Seriously?" Chris crossed his arms. "PR chick is here ten seconds and already they have to go. Real nice."

"We're about to have a business conversation. It stays between us. Like always."

Chris glared, but Tom signaled to one of the roadies to show the women out.

Not wanting to make the tension worse, Sue waited to speak until Tom nodded to her. "We've gotta spend some time together over the next few days. I've set up some interviews at Indy Showcase, and I want to go over the types of questions you guys might get and—"

"Wait, wait," Chris interrupted. "We're gonna be interviewed in Austin?"

"Yeah."

"By who?" asked Darryl.

"The local radio station, a few magazines, and some blogs."

"Real magazines or a paste-up job out of some dude's garage?"

"Real magazines. *Sound Spectrum* and *Spin*. Maybe something bigger, I haven't been able to confirm yet. That may be a blog thing."

Justin looked her in the eye. "So, when you said 'some blogs,' you didn't mean random fan sites?"

"No. These are legitimate music blogs. Some are tied in with magazines and others are independent, but none of them are run out of someone's mother's basement," Sue said.

"And the radio station? Is it real or a podcaster?" Chris asked.

"Two stations, both real," Sue confirmed. "The rock station out of Austin and their sister station in Dallas. Plus, the *Song Exploder* podcast, which I'm sure we all agree is legit." She grinned as she took in the happy and surprised expressions on the guys' faces.

Tom chuckled. "You're the only woman capable of rendering these guys speechless. Even strippers have a hard time getting them to shut up."

"Thanks for that one," Brad grumbled.

"Hey!" Darryl quirked his lips. "Can we make fun of Maroon 5 during the interviews?"

"Not if you want to perform with them any time soon." Tom tapped his fingers against his tablet.

"What?" Justin looked from Tom to Sue and back again, the neat ponytail at his neck slapping his shoulders. Shock covered his chiseled face.

"I'm working on getting us into some festivals later this summer," Tom said.

"And regardless of who you'll be sharing a stage with,

don't say anything publicly about anyone unless it's how great they are," Sue added.

Darryl flushed and smiled, then elbowed Chris in the side.

"Hot damn." Justin tightened his grip on Sue's hand and spun her around the stage. "You're gonna keep us mighty busy, Sue! I like it. I think you're gonna be my new best friend."

She laughed while trying to keep up with Justin's frenzied twirling. "You may want to hold off on that."

"Nah. You're a lot hotter than Brad. Besides, I've known him since we were seven. It's time for a change."

Brad loped around Justin and Sue, singing what Sue imagined was an ancient Native American song.

"Wait!" Chris shouted. "Calm the fuck down!"

All the action on the stage stopped, and everyone faced Chris. Brad stepped toward Sue and put a steadying hand on her waist as she regained her balance.

"It's only a few interviews. We don't even know how they're gonna pan out. It doesn't mean she can get us more after that." Chris dropped a bag of pretzels on the floor and stomped on it, sending the remaining food and crumbs across the stage toward Sue's feet.

Justin stared at Chris. "What's your problem? A minute ago you were so fuckin' happy you looked like your head was gonna explode!"

"Nothing." Chris kicked at the pretzel bag.

"You sure about that?" Justin growled.

"Look, I know she can *tune my guitar*"—Chris grabbed his groin and pursed his lips—"but can she—"

"What the fuck, man?" Justin stalked toward Chris.

Without hesitation, Darryl stepped between the two, facing Justin. "Let it go, Just. He's freaked out."

"He needs to get over it." Justin stared at Darryl. His six-foot-four-inch frame towered over Darryl's shorter, stocky build, but Darryl stood his ground. "She's trying to help us."

"Then let her do her job." Everyone's heads swiveled toward Tom. "Since Skein is the headliner on this tour, I suggest you clean the shit off the stage." Tom turned toward Sue. "Let's go back to the dressing room."

She skirted around them, hoping Tom really had ended the confrontation.

Darryl and Justin patted each other on the shoulder and broke out of their death stare stance.

"Sorry," Chris said with a bowed head.

"Yeah." Justin exited the stage.

Relieved, Sue followed Tom out to the equipment trailer, ready to take on the next challenge.

Normally, Sue liked to hit the ground running. In this case, that meant learning how to pack the gear into the band's trailer. It was part of her contract with the record label, after all. But Tom insisted that she wait in the dressing room. He said they played this venue frequently and already had a solid system. Sue made a valiant attempt at arguing with him, and when she interrupted herself with a massive yawn, Tom pushed her into the armchair and left. As she sunk into the overstuffed seat, her eyes fluttered closed, fatigue finally overpowering the burst of adrenaline she'd had when she first arrived. She roused herself when the guys finally settled into the room.

"How'd you like the show?" Justin asked. He sat against a cooler of beer on the floor, tossing trash at the garbage can, making more shots than he missed.

Sue opened her eyes, then stretched. "Loved it. You guys are great live."

"Sure we are. She can't even look you in the eye, Just," Brad said.

"I hit a big wall of tired." Sue shifted in the chair and forced her eyes open. "But you were great. The audience responds to you. They can tell you're having fun on stage."

"Isn't that the point?" Chris asked.

"Shut up and get her a beer. I need her awake long enough to tell me how cool I am." Darryl reclined on the couch, his head propped in such a way that his spikes didn't impale the furniture. He tossed a tennis ball above his chest, stopping occasionally to drink from his own beer.

"Darryl." Sue stretched in his direction. "You are so cool on stage that it makes a girl willing to risk her life with those spikes. I saw it in the crowd. The women wanted you. They were out there practicing how they'd hold you once your hair punctured the artery in their arms."

"You know, if I didn't think you'd eat it like that M&M before, I'd throw this ball at you."

"Keep your balls to yourself," Chris muttered as he shoved Justin away from the cooler.

"You are so funny!" Justin grabbed some ice and mashed it into Chris's face.

"Fuck you, man." Chris scowled. "If the girls want us so much, where the hell are they?"

"I asked security to keep them away," Tom chimed in from the doorway. "I wanted you all to have a chance to unwind before the T and A comes through."

All the guys fidgeted at the comment, but Sue was too tired to do anything more than hide a smile behind her hand.

"Don't worry. I'm sure there are plenty of women waiting at the bar," Tom added.

"Thank God for that." Darryl feigned wiping his brow.

"Seriously, Darryl," Sue said. "Your hair hasn't moved at all since this afternoon."

"I know! It's this awesome mohawk glue my sister got me. It's hair cement."

"You'd better hope someone doesn't put Nair in it one day." Justin threw a paper wad at the garbage can.

"Please, we all know Brad's the one who'd shit if that ever happened. I'd paint my skull or something," Darryl said.

"You guys are too much. I want you to talk like this in your interviews." Sue finished her statement with a yawn. If they hadn't been in the room talking with her, she'd be out cold.

"Seriously?" Brad sat across from her on a trunk. Again, he only wore jeans. The combat boots he wore during the show sat on the floor on either side of him. One sock hung off the garbage can/basketball hoop, the other on the floor near it. His T-shirt lay folded across one of his legs.

"Yeah. Don't you want your fans to like you for who you are?"

"I want the fans to like our music." Chris gave Sue a long neck, then perched on the counter behind Brad.

"Who writes your music?"

"We do." Darryl sat up on the couch.

"Where do your ideas come from?"

"People we know, things we've done." Brad shrugged.

"Then it's safe to say that your music is personal." Sue took a swig of beer.

"I guess." Darryl tossed his ball.

"Definitely." Justin punctuated his answer with an empty water bottle clattering against the garbage.

"Sometimes I feel a little removed from the songs, but it all depends on the subject," Darryl added.

Brad leaned toward her, his hand extended. "My history is in each of our songs. I live these songs every day. Even before the band. I'm meant to play this music." Brad stared at Sue.

Sue held his gaze for a moment, then focused on Chris. "And you?"

"I'm with Brad." Chris kept his eyes on the beer bottle he held in his lap.

"You're all intricately woven into your songs. Your fans feel a connection to the music. You shouldn't put on an act when you're talking about it. The most important thing is to be sincere when you're talking about the music, because you're actually talking about yourself." Sue paused and sipped her beer. She winced at the taste and read the label. She didn't recognize the brand. "Your fans became interested because of the music. They'll be fiercely loyal because of you."

The guys were silent for a minute.

"I guess this means the world'll find out about my

hair obsession." Brad raked his fingers through his glossy locks.

"Count on it, buddy," Justin answered with a wicked grin.

"Sue, as soon as you leave this room, Brad's gonna beg Tom for security so we can't put Nair in his shampoo." Darryl sank back into the couch.

Brad spun around on the trunk and threw his shirt and empty water bottle at Darryl as everyone laughed.

"What type of beer is this?" Halfway through it, Sue's instincts screamed that the taste and texture wasn't right.

"It's cheap shit." Chris tasted some from his bottle and made a face. "Skein makes us drink it since we're the openers and regularly trash the stage."

"Ahh." Sue tried another sip. "Are you sure that's it? It seems a little... skunky."

"You get used to it. The other girls don't have a problem with it."

"Chris." Tom shook his head.

Sue waved off the comment, then took another swallow, grimacing at the taste. She dropped her head back on the chair and closed her eyes.

"Are you ready for the hotel?" Tom asked.

"Yeah." Sue chugged the rest of the beer, then stood. She wasn't sure if her weariness or the drink had made her woozy. She regained her balance and surveyed the room, trying to figure out where to put the bottle. All the garbage littered the floor around the broken can, so she took aim. The bottle hit the back rim, then fell through, landing among the paper balls.

"Didn't even break the glass. Nice," Darryl said.

Sue gave him a small smile and turned toward the door, looking for the easiest path out of the room. All of the instruments and equipment from earlier had been packed away, yet somehow a huge mess still remained.

Tom tapped a finger on the back of his tablet. "I don't even know how you got in here."

"Neither do I," she admitted as she made her way to him.

"Did you bring in any stuff?" Tom asked.

"Shit." Sue pointed at her messenger bag, tucked into the farthest corner of the room.

"I'll get it!" Darryl hopped off the couch and climbed over everything, including Brad, to get the bag.

"Thanks, Darryl."

"Sure thing." He bounced out of the room with Chris close on his heels.

"I'll be back soon, guys." Tom held the door open.

Sue waved at Brad and Justin as Tom directed her out of the room.

"Is the rest of your stuff in your car?"

"Yes."

"Give me the keys, I'll drive you." Tom put an arm around her.

"Let's hurry. I think chugging that beer was a mistake."

Sue made a beeline for the bathroom, barely lifting the toilet seat before she retched. She purged so much that she didn't have the energy to move. Thankfully she'd made it to her hotel room and didn't have to.

The next morning, she woke to the room phone jangling. With one arm wrapped around her sore stomach, she crawled the few feet from the bathroom to the phone. Stretching to reach it made her abdomen ache even more, so she pulled the whole thing into her lap. She answered with a hoarse croak.

"Are you okay? Your phone went straight to voicemail." Tom sounded frantic.

"I was sick last night. I didn't charge my phone, sorry." Every word tore at her throat. "Hang on." She pulled herself up and trudged to the bathroom to gulp water from the sink. It tasted tinny, and swallowing hurt as much as talking. "I'm glad you called. Band meeting soon, right?"

"We'll do it later. Stay in bed until we head out."

"No." She shook her head at the phone. "There's too much at stake. We have to do this before the show tonight."

"You sound like shit. I'm not gonna let you beat yourself up. The drive was bad enough." Tom paused.

"Besides, Uncle Glen scares the shit out of me, and if this tour kills you, I'm the one who has to tell him."

Sue tried to laugh, but her throat hurt too much and she coughed instead. "Come on, Tom. Dad is all bark and no bite."

"Maybe to you."

"Chicken." She forced more water down. "Gimme a half hour to get ready. Bring some water or juice with you. Please. I promise I'm fine."

"I'm telling the guys to take it easy on you."

"Yeah, that'll be a huge help." Sue sighed as she hung up. She put the phone on the floor, took a deep breath, and waited to see if she would throw up what she'd drunk. When her stomach stayed calm, she got in the shower.

Thirty minutes later she pulled an oversized Aerosmith tour T-shirt over her head when there was a knock on her door. The guys crowded the entrance, all looking like they'd had much better nights. Tablet tucked under his arm, Tom held a six pack of water and a tray of food that Sue eyed warily. She stepped behind the door to let them in.

Tom barely set down the food before Chris and Darryl raided it. Brad loitered by the door and scrutinized the space.

Justin closed the door behind him and stopped next to Sue. "Not that I'm complaining, but were you planning to maybe put on some pants?"

Sue froze, caught Tom's eye, then looked down at herself. She immediately buried her head in her hands. "I didn't realize... I can't... I'm sorry." She knew she should move, but she couldn't. She didn't know if embarrassment or the fear that she might vomit again had her stuck.

"Nice legs." Darryl pointed up and down.

"Stop." Tom walked over to Sue and shielded her. "She's sick. Sue, are you sure you're okay?"

"I don't know. I tossed everything I've ever eaten in my life. I think I lost part of my brain, too."

"How long have you been puking?" Darryl asked.

"All fucking night," Chris said.

Tom furrowed his brow. "How do you know?"

Chris pointed toward the bathroom. "My room is downstairs. I heard all that mess. Sounded like a heroin party was going on up here."

"Yeah, that's not what happened." She shot Chris a dirty look. "I got sick right after I got into the room, and a million heaves later, I fell asleep next to the toilet." She ran a hand through her damp hair before she continued. "Now my stomach feels hollow, my body aches, and my throat is killing me."

"You still feel bad?" Chris asked with wide eyes.

"Are you sure you want us here?" Justin gave her arm a quick squeeze.

"I'll be fine. I just have to figure out how to soothe my

throat." Sue went to her duffel bag on the dresser and dug for a pair of jeans.

"What you need is some hot tea with honey in it." Brad took the little coffee pot from the dresser and filled it with water in the bathroom. "The heat soothes the irritation and the honey coats the throat."

"That's such a mom thing to know." Darryl plucked a grape from the food tray and popped it into his mouth.

"Shut up, asshole. I'm a singer. It comes with the territory."

"Sure," Darryl drew out the word as he grinned at Brad.

"Let's do this later." Chris walked to the door, looking uncomfortable. "You're sick, we should leave."

"I'm fine," Sue said. "Lemme put on some pants and drink some tea. I'll be fine."

———

Sue didn't look fine. She didn't look sick or hungover to Chris, either. But she also didn't look like the woman who'd bragged about all the press she'd get them when she got to town yesterday. She carried a pair of jeans into the bathroom and pushed the door closed. A phone in the doorjamb kept it propped open enough that if she heaved again, they'd hear it. Maybe even smell it.

"She does have great legs," Brad said under his

breath. Figured that fucker would check her out, even when she was sick. Hell, he'd hold her hair back to cop a feel when she finished puking.

Tom flicked the perv in the back of the head.

Brad rubbed the spot, then rooted around the coffee setup, actually making a fucking mug of tea, probably hoping it'd get him into Sue's pants. And they gave Chris shit for going after women. Whatever. At least he didn't play games. A girl was down to fuck or she wasn't.

Sue emerged fully dressed, her hair in a ponytail, and nudged the phone out of the doorway. She glanced up. "Ready?"

Chris slid down the door and sat. This stupid fucking meeting wasn't getting more than the bare minimum from him.

Tom gestured at a small table as Darryl and Justin took the couch. "I got the so-called suite for you so there'd be some space." Tom pulled out a chair. "Sit."

Brad served Sue a mug of tea as she settled at the table. "No honey, but the heat'll help." He moved an empty chair next to her, facing everyone.

Sue brought the mug to her lips, making Chris wince. "Are you sure you wanna drink that?" he asked. "If you can't keep anything down, you should wait."

"You afraid of a little puke, Chris?" Tom settled on the edge of the bed, his omnipresent tablet balanced on his leg.

"No."

"He'd better not be, considering how often we got him drunk last tour," Justin said.

"Yeah, *that* was a lotta puke." Brad chuckled.

Chris rolled his eyes. He'd been taking their shit for years. It wasn't his fault all those assholes were older. He wasn't taking it today. He didn't want to be around Sue in general, and he sure as hell didn't want to be here if she might spew again. What fucking media training involved his band trotting out all his dirt, anyway?

"Tell me about last tour." Sue took a small sip of tea.

"It was a blast," Darryl said. "It was the first time we had to drive more than an hour or two for a gig."

Brad beat a thumb on his thigh. "And my sister wasn't the only one in the audience."

"Chris doesn't remember most of it," Justin added. "He turned twenty-one right before we hit the road and didn't have much experience with alcohol."

"We educated him." Darryl tossed an orange from hand to hand.

Chris decided to get this shit over with and cop to it all. Maybe she'd be so disgusted by them that she'd bail. "I can name a hundred and twenty-seven different tequilas. I probably drank all of them."

Sue lifted her eyebrows but kept going. "So, it was a giant party the whole time."

"Better than a party," Brad said.

"It had elements of a party, but it was more than that." Justin gestured as though describing a big fish.

"A lot changed for us on that tour," Darryl said.

"Like what?"

She'd shifted them right into interview mode and no one else even noticed. Some fucking media training. Chris scrubbed is palm against his scalp. "Well, for one thing, instead of getting drunk and going home to puke, I hurled in every club parking lot between Boston and Miami."

Puking nightly had gotten old fast. But something about that tour—their first time down the East Coast as a band that made a little money—had them celebrating each show as though it had been their first or might be their last. Chris hoped they never lost their enthusiasm for the job, just the retching.

"There's a few places we can't go back to." Brad pointed his chin at Chris. "At least not until they forget all that."

"I'm the king of projectile vomiting." Chris knocked the side of his fist against his chest. "I know the perfect blend of beer, tequila, and pretzels to achieve optimum distance and velocity."

"He's pretty good with accuracy, too," Justin said. "A couple times he said he'd hit something from a few feet away and he made it."

"We tried to get people to bet on it, but there weren't many willing to stick around and watch." Darryl sucked on an orange slice.

"Do you blame them? I don't like being there when I puke." Sue blanched.

The guys laughed again, and Justin and Darryl seemed to relax. They looked loose to the casual observer, but they'd both been tense since hiring Sue. They thought they hid it by fucking up the dressing room and teasing her about her pants, but growing up with these guys, Chris knew better. Justin cataloged everything. And Darryl, as laid back as he was, would be the first to yank back his trust. Chris counted on that. He needed Sue to have one big fuck up so he could win them back and replace her with someone who wasn't an outsider. Brad stretched behind her, taking grapes from the food tray. Stupid bastard believed women automatically dropped their panties for him when he got close. Sue shifted away from him. Chris coughed to cover his snicker. Served the horny asshole right.

"Seriously though, what changed for you on the tour?" she asked.

"Everything became real," Justin said.

"How?"

"Until the tour, we all had other jobs. Chris was in college. Going on tour meant *this* was our job."

"Yeah," Brad agreed. "Until last summer, when people asked me what I did, I told them I was in a band and they would say, 'no, really, what do you do?' As annoying as the question was, I always had an answer. Now when people ask me, they're shocked when they realize the band is my only job."

People constantly offered job advice. Chris didn't

give a shit about their advice. He wanted them singing along. "Boring ass people always say to me, 'gee, it must be fun to be in a band in college,' and then they ask me what my major is." Chris rolled his eyes.

"What is it?" Sue asked.

This time Chris gave a genuine grin. "Music."

She returned the smile.

"Now tell her your minor." Justin thrummed his fingers on the arm of the couch.

Fucking smart ass. "Network programming." Chris hated the burn in his cheeks.

"At least you have something to fall back on." Darryl mimicked the phrase they often heard in a high-pitched, scratchy voice.

"You can still kill that." Sue sipped more tea.

"How?" Chris asked.

"Tell them programming is your minor because you want to learn Industrial from the inside out and be the next Trent Reznor."

"Okay, I want you all to know, Tom" —Darryl leaned forward and looked at him— "I'm officially cool with you hiring this girl. She's quick."

Brad patted her knee and gave her a thumbs up. She drained her tea and tipped the mug to him. She wasn't flirting, but Brad fucking winked at her anyway.

Justin crossed his arms and frowned. "Are we gonna

talk about this interview or what?"

"We were." Tom leaned back on his elbows.

"Huh?"

"Fucking dense assholes," Chris muttered.

"We were," Tom said. "Sue was asking the type of questions interviewers will."

"She was, wasn't she?" Darryl narrowed his eyes and smiled. "You little minx!"

Sue tipped her head and took a banana. "Since you haven't done a lot of interviews there'll be some genuine interest about how you guys got together. I know one of the DJs well. He loves history. Don't be surprised if he compares you to another band in that respect."

"I hate comparisons." Justin thumped a foot. "It ruins people's impressions, especially when they don't know who we are."

"Then don't let them do it," Tom said.

"How?" Brad asked. "I don't want to sound like an asshole when I tell someone I don't care how other bands do it."

"Ignore it." Sue swept her hand as though pushing the question away. "Say something like 'yeah, a lotta bands do that' and move on."

They were finally getting to the part of the conversation Chris wanted, and Sue's solution was to ignore a question right in his face? The bitch was crazy. "They'll force us into a conversation about it."

"They usually won't. If it does come to that, shift it into a conversation about that band. If you don't know the band, get them onto a band you do know. By the time they figure out you're off topic, they'll have other questions they'll want to ask."

"They'll only want to talk about music, right?" Darryl asked. "I mean, we're not famous enough for them to ask personal stuff."

"Mostly." Sue shifted in her seat. "Music, where you're from, how you guys got together."

"Basic shit," Darryl said.

"Yeah. But journalists from bigger outlets will have done more research. They'll want to know more."

Brad beat his thumbs against his thighs. "Like what?"

Sue turned her attention directly to Chris. "Do you think you'll go back to school?"

"Yeah," Chris said.

"*Dumb and Dumber* over here"—Darryl pointed to Brad and Justin—"reminisce about their college days about every ten seconds. Of course the kid wants to go back."

"You three went to the University of Michigan, right?" Sue asked.

"Yes," Brad and Justin answered in unison.

"Together?" Sue asked.

"Yes," they said at the same time.

Sue laughed. "What were your majors?"

Brad and Justin stared at each other, neither answering. After a few seconds, Justin slapped the arm of the couch. "Mechanical Engineering."

"Damn." Sue widened her eyes.

"Yeah. I like being a drummer better."

"He still won't hesitate to remind us that he could be off improving green energy, or more likely building a sex robot, instead of being in a band with our sorry asses," Chris said.

"Damn straight," Justin responded.

"What about you?" Sue turned to Brad.

"Elementary Education. You'd think it'd come in handy with these guys."

Sue snickered as everyone, even Tom, groused at Brad and his way-too-easy joke.

Chris studied each of his bandmates. It annoyed the shit out of him that they accepted this chick so easily. They put her in charge of moving them from garage band to a legit rock outfit and no one seemed concerned that she came from Podunk radio. Why wasn't anyone else nervous?

Sue squirmed and pressed a hand to her stomach. Mother fuck.

"You doin' okay over there, Sue?" Darryl asked.

"Yeah. I ate too much."

"You barely ate anything." Justin pointed at the half of the banana she hadn't finished.

"It's all relative." Sue shifted in her chair. "Let's get back to the interview. They might ask what some of your songs mean."

"You're wiggling a lot, Sexy Sue." Brad poked her arm.

"I'm fine." Sue shifted again. "One minute." She hopped up and bolted to the bathroom.

"Oh shit," Chris whispered. She was gonna hurl again. He knew it.

The door closed and the bath water came on.

"Shit, shit, shit!" Why hadn't she puked it all out already? He knocked the heel of his hand against his forehead. What bullshit. This shoulda been done and over with.

"What the hell?" Darryl asked.

Tom waved at him. "What's wrong with you?"

With all eyes on him, he had no choice but to confess. "Pretty sure it's my fault she's hurling."

"Your fault?" Tom asked. "People get sick."

Justin walked over and crouched to his level. "You look feral, man. What'd you do?"

Chris stood. "She's not sick." He stalked to the far end of the room. "I might've poisoned her."

"What?" Tom shouted.

"Where the fuck'd you get poison?" Darryl asked.

"Tell me you're lying," Justin said.

Brad's hands balled into fists. "What in the ever-loving fuck?"

"I put ipecac in her beer. It was in the first aid kit. I didn't think it worked when she didn't puke right away. It was supposed to be funny!" Chris looked to the ceiling and shook his head. Of all the fucking pranks to backfire. Hands on his hips, he finally looked at the guys. Better to see the blows coming.

Besides angry, they all looked confused. Chris dropped his hands and focused on the bathroom. Was the water still running? Was she dry heaving? Did they need to take her to the hospital?

Finally, Brad spoke. "Can ipecac really hurt her?"

"Not too much, right? It was in the first aid kit," Justin said.

They needed to shut the fuck up and let him listen for her. This day had already pushed him to the bleeding edge of his patience. "She could die!" he barked out the words and crossed his arms. There. They all knew the worst. Time to fix it.

The guys all turned toward him, silent, with varying expressions of rage.

"I googled it. If you give someone too much..." Chris shook his head to clear it of the warnings he'd read the night before. All he'd wanted to know was why she hadn't thrown up right away. The horror stories were a gross surprise. "It's the fucking internet—"

Tom's face went dark red, and he shoved Chris. "Why didn't you call me?"

Chris squared his shoulders. "I didn't know it was her until we came up here. And I didn't think it worked!"

"How much did you give her, dumbass?" Darryl tapped away on his phone.

Chris squinted and stepped back. "Maybe half the bottle?"

"Was that too much?" Justin asked.

"I don't know." Tom dashed to the bathroom door and banged on it. "Sue! Are you okay? I'm coming in!"

"NO!" she yelled and flushed the toilet.

Chris took her answer as a good sign. At least she hadn't passed out.

Tom looked back at the guys, held his breath, and went in anyway.

"Close the door!" Sue shouted.

After Tom closed the door, Brad went to it, pressing his ear against the wood. Chris headed for the main door. She was speaking, she was fine.

Justin stopped him. "What were you thinking?"

Chris rubbed his head. "That it would be funny to

watch her puke. Take her down a peg or two.”

“Why the fuck does she need to be taken down a peg?” Darryl threw a tissue box at Chris.

Chris caught the box and threw it back hard. “She’s too confident.”

Brad spun and glared. “Did it ever occurred to you that confidence is really fucking important for a publicist?”

Chris pursed his lips and continued toward the door.

“Calm down, Brad,” Justin said.

“You’re okay with this?”

“No. But let’s find out how bad it is before we beat him.”

Justin had a point. As much as Chris didn’t want to deal with this shit, he *did* want to know if he’d caused her real harm. He wanted her gone, not hospitalized. He slumped against the door.

Brad sat on the bed. “If we have to take her to the emergency room, Tom’s allowed to rough him up.”

Justin nodded. “Fair.”

“I’m in the room, assholes,” Chris said.

“Fuck you, dumbass,” Darryl said.

Tom burst out of the bathroom and made a beeline for Chris, pushing him away from the door long enough to open it and shove him into the hallway. “We’re gonna have a little chat.”

Chris faced Tom head-on. “Is she okay?”

“What the fuck do you care?”

“I wanted to embarrass her, not kill her.”

Tom punched him in the stomach. “She had to pee, fuckwad.”

CHAPTER 6

MEMPHIS, TENNESSEE

"We're only three songs in!" Sue had finally gotten to watch a whole Words Fail Me set from the floor and had been excited for Skein, but one of their roadies had come to pluck her from the audience.

"Sorry. Tom looks scrawny, but he'll have my balls in a vise, especially if you puke again."

Once backstage, Sue turned for the dressing rooms, but the roadie nudged her.

"This way." He deposited her on the side of the stage for a truly amazing view of Skein. "You get the best seat."

"Wow!" Sue tore her gaze away from the stage long enough to grin at the man. "I owe you one!"

He flashed a thumbs up as he made his way into the bowels of the venue.

Skein took the frenzy Words Fail Me had built to a whole new level. Their lead singer, Zen Dave, pumped energy into the audience like a true rock legend. He wasn't what Sue expected from someone people referred to as "Zen Master."

She couldn't help comparing the lead singers. Zen Dave worked the crowd like a cheerleader, yelling into the mic while gripping it tight, splitting his attention between his ax, the mic, and the crowd, seeking their approval. Brad invited the audience to join him. He held the mic stand with a light teasing touch and hovered over it, his mouth close like he was whispering in someone's ear. Brad seemed content to simply play. Zen Dave led the charge for an adventure.

When Zen Dave noticed Sue on the side of the stage, he pointed to her and winked. Usually immune to rock star swagger, she shocked herself when she giggled, clapping a hand over her mouth. He launched into the next song, and she fell under his spell.

"They're amazing, aren't they?" Brad said into her ear.

"They're great." Sue kept her focus on the stage.

Brad stayed behind her, standing close as he spoke. "No one would ever know that a year ago, all this guy knew how to play was 'Stairway to Heaven.'"

Still enthralled with the music, Sue didn't look away from the stage when she spoke. "I can't believe he wasn't born playing a guitar."

"He used to be a roadie. Then their original singer, Roger, quit a month before the European tour. Their bass player watched Zen Dave play 'Stairway to Heaven' during soundcheck for Roger's last show and convinced the rest of the band they needed him. They spent their entire month off teaching him their catalog."

"That's insane." Sue glanced briefly at Brad, eyebrows raised. "It works, though."

Brad stood close enough that she felt him moving with the music. She was tempted to dance with him but didn't want to take her eyes off the show. "How'd he get the name Zen Dave? This is a totally different energy level than I expected."

"His full name is Zen Roadmaster Dave. Before this he was a legendary crew manager. They say his bands were only ever late on stage if they were watching TV. There was nothing that happened on a tour that Dave wasn't prepared for. Lost gear, fires, bad control boards. He could solve anything and cruised through it like a walk in the park."

"Nice." Sue continued, still watching the show. "How did he go from chill park man to rock's biggest cheer-leader?"

The song ended before he answered. "I'm not supposed to talk about this. You have to keep it between us."

"Okay."

"He confessed to me that he's worried he'll cost Skein fans. They taught him their songs, but he paid a private instructor to give him lessons during off hours and even brought the guy on tour so he'd get good on guitar fast. The band told him not to sweat it, that any loss would be Roger's fault. But we're talking about one of the top rock bands in the world. They could be playing stadiums right now, but they're doing these small gigs to get close to their fans again. Dave doesn't want to lose a single one. He feels responsible for the whole organiza-tion—the band, the roadies, their families, everyone. He said if he doesn't bring it, they all fail with him. So, he busts his ass every night to win over Roger's fans."

"No shit. Good on you, Zen Dave." Sue immediately felt a kinship with the man. She understood exactly what it meant to be responsible for other people's livelihoods. She thought about Words Fail Me and all the people she'd left behind at the radio station. She sent up a silent prayer that the plans she'd put in place before her departure had kept things running smoothly there. Zen Dave caught her eye again, and she gave the man a salute. He blew her a kiss and she giggled again, covering her burning cheeks.

Brad chuckled and put his hands on her shoulders. "How you feeling?"

"Great." Sue's impulse was to move away. She was too emotional after learning about Zen Dave and needed space to collect her thoughts, but Brad blocked her exit.

"Sorry about the ipecac. I don't think Chris understood what he was doing."

Sue shrugged. The ipecac *had* pissed her off, but she was too stubborn to let it stop her. That didn't mean she wanted to talk about it.

"I guess he figured since we used to make him puke—"

Sue wiggled her shoulders, shaking Brad's hands off her. "I get it. Besides, I can't blame him for wanting me to quit before there's a real risk to the next album."

"Why would you quitting put the album at risk? We already wrote half of it."

Her stomach dropped at Brad's clueless expression. Did he not know about the do-or-die clause the record company threw in at the last minute? If she didn't damn near make them a household name, that clause could cost the band their future. How did he not know? Did Tom hide it? She refocused her attention on the stage and tried to stay calm. "The whole chick on tour thing."

"Nah." Brad squeezed her shoulder again, but her reflexive twitch knocked his hand off. "You sure you're okay?"

"Yeah." Sue backed up a few steps. "Yeah. I've gotta find Tom."

CHAPTER 7

Sue pushed open the band's dressing room door. Skein still had about thirty minutes left in their set. Once they were done, everyone would be busy, moving and packing gear and selling merch. She needed to talk to Tom alone, and soon. "Where's Tom?"

"I don't know," Justin said. "What do you think now that you're wide awake?"

"I loved it." Despite her angst over Tom, Sue gave Justin a big, genuine smile.

"Really?" Chris asked.

"Really. I even met a few ladies who're into Darryl. I got their numbers for you, man."

"You did?" Darryl appeared both shocked and hopeful.

"No," Sue said.

Darryl shook his head. "That's cold, girl."

She smiled and lifted a shoulder. "Do you know where Tom is?"

"He's coming," Brad said as he entered the room. "He and Skein's road manager are talking about when we're all leaving and the hotels and stuff in Oklahoma."

"Okay." Sue sat on an amp, hiding her aggravation. He hadn't returned any of her texts and had a roadie manning the merch booth. She needed to find him and figure out if her suspicions about the clause were true.

"Do you want a beer?" Chris asked.

She gave him a withering glare. "Not from you."

Chris rolled his eyes.

Tom stuck his head through the open doorway and motioned for Sue to join him in the hall. Finally.

"Sue, Mark, Mark, Sue." He gestured between her and a tall man with stringy brown hair. "Do you have your room confirmed in Tulsa?"

"Yeah, why?"

"I want to add it to the itinerary," Mark said. "I like to make sure everyone on tour is accounted for. Do you have the confirmation number?"

"Yes." Sue pulled her phone out of her pocket and scrolled through her email. "As long as I have you both here, I got the official confirmation. Words Fail Me is playing at the zoo benefit in New Orleans. Does that take us off the tour for the night or the week?"

"The week. We already had a break planned to shoot a video. The timing works."

"This is Amy's benefit?" Tom asked.

"Yeah, with Echo Chamber." Sue still searched through her emails.

"Nice," Mark hissed.

Sue grinned. "Thanks. I don't see the hotel confirmation here. I have a printout in my laptop bag."

"Do you mind getting it for me?" Mark asked.

"Sure. It's in my car."

Tom stuck his head back into the dressing room. "Guys, we'll be back in a few minutes."

Before they moved away from the door, Darryl ran past them. When they got outside, they found him trying to break into the trunk of Sue's car.

"What're you doing?" Sue asked.

"Nothing. Can I borrow your keys? That would make this easier."

"Darryl, what's going on?" Tom asked.

"It's not a big deal."

"So, spill. What did you do?" Sue had one hand on her hip, shifting into high alert as she had ipecac flashbacks.

Darryl stepped toward them. "I did this last night, *before* the ipecac. It was supposed to be funny."

"Like the ipecac was supposed to be?"

Darryl held his hands out in front of him. "No. No way. Go back inside, and I'll bring the laptop to you."

Sue tossed him the keys and crossed her arms. "No."

Darryl hung his head for a second, then slid the keys into the lock.

"Should we step back?" Tom asked.

"Nothing'll fly out at you." Darryl lifted the trunk lid.

When Sue peered in, she found her laptop bag decorated with lube and condoms. Some of the condoms were inflated and stuck to the bag like balloons. Others were tied to the strap.

"Is that...used?" Sue asked, pointing to one hanging from the zipper.

"No. It just looks that way. They're lubricated."

"Mark," Sue said, "I can't get you that confirmation right now."

Lips pressed together, Mark nodded. "Pass it along when you can."

"Will do." Sue looked at Darryl. "You have a favorite instrument or anything?"

Tom snickered.

Sue whirled on him. "Don't you laugh, Tommy. You're in trouble, too."

"What did I do?"

"It's what you *didn't* do." She leveled a cold glare at him and turned back to Darryl. "So, favorite instrument?"

Darryl didn't answer.

"Okay, well, let me know when this is clean." Arms crossed, Sue stared at Darryl until he started plucking condoms off the bag. She watched him remove half of them before she went back into the building with Mark and Tom.

"Sue! I'm really sorry!"

"I know," she called out.

After Darryl's prank, Tom had managed to evade Sue. She'd hoped to get him alone in her car to speak freely about her contract. But Tom being Tom, he had a perfectly logical excuse to ride with Skein. Once at the hotel, she went after him again, only to discover all their rooms lined up in a row. Sure, Tom wasn't sharing a room, but Sue didn't want to risk being overheard. Noticing a small gym near the lobby, Sue decided to use it to her advantage.

She knocked, then leaned into Tom's room as soon as he opened the door. "I need to work out. You wanna work out?"

"Huh?" Tom looked like he could sleep standing in the doorway.

"You heard me. Workout. Let's go." Sue gave him a bright smile and tilted her head toward the elevators.

"It's three a.m. and you slept on a tile floor last night.

Don't you want to sleep in a real bed?"

"Nah. I'm wired. Let's go!"

Tom scrunched his forehead as though he had to force himself to stay awake and think. "I'm not dressed to work out."

"It's a hotel gym. No one'll care." Sue grabbed his arm and yanked him out of the room, then dragged him down the hallway.

"I don't have my phone."

"Trust me, it's better that way." Sue pushed him into the elevator and pressed the lobby button, her body vibrating with tension. She didn't speak again until the elevator opened on the ground floor. She gestured toward the lobby. "After you."

Tom shuffled into the exercise room. "Not much here."

Sue closed the door behind them and leaned against it. "Had an interesting conversation with Brad tonight."

Tom turned to her, clearly confused. "Okay."

"They have no idea about that clause, do they."

Tom paled. "It's not a big deal."

She balled her fists and ground her teeth before she spoke, fighting her urge to yell. "Lying to your best friends, your business partners, *me* is not a big deal?"

"You're the right person for this job."

"No, Tom. I'm a fucking shill. You made me a shill, and you're betting their future. What the fuck!"

"I'm not betting anything." Tom grabbed a tuft of hair near his temple and stalked away from her. "What did Brad say?"

"Huh?"

"When you mentioned the album, what did he say?"

"You're worried about what Brad said, not whether their album gets canceled?"

"Motherfucking fuck! Sue! What! Did he! Say!" Veins pulsed in his neck as Tom yelled, now wide awake.

"He asked me why the album would be at risk. I made an excuse about having a girl on tour."

"Thank God." Tom sank onto a weight bench.

"That he didn't find out you lied to them?"

Tom glared at her. "They don't need another distraction on this tour and making them think the album's in danger is exactly that."

"Excuse me? Are you kidding?"

"No. Everything's fine." Tom stood and walked around a giant exercise machine, resetting pins as though he planned to use it.

"Like hell! If I don't hit the label's goals, they have to pay back my salary or forfeit the album. Did you forget that part?"

Tom spun around. "I didn't forget. You have no idea the threats I made trying to keep that clause out of the contract."

"Yeah, I'm sure the wet-behind-the-ears manager of a band with one radio hit really has a lot of sway."

"Fuck you, Sue." Tom sneered. "It's two hits. And you have no idea."

Sue cackled. "I've spent the last three years clawing my way out of the trenches of corporate radio to make something of myself and I have no idea."

"They need you!" Tom kicked at a treadmill. "The label wanted to assign some asshat who works with boy bands and was more interested in getting them fucking designer perfumes than actual media attention."

"Maybe perfume would be good for them!"

"Are you listening to yourself?" Tom pressed both of his hands to his skull. "The label wanted to invest nothing in this band. Less than nothing. We need you. We need your take-no-shit guerilla tactics. We need someone who has a stake!"

"So you decided the best way to get someone with a stake was to gamble their future and lie to *all* of us about it?"

"It's not a gamble!"

"I appreciate your confidence, Tom. But yeah, it's a fucking huge gamble."

"I have the money!" Tom's face reddened, adding

menace to his feral expression. "I could've hired you my damn self."

Sue reared back. "What?"

"You know our inheritances from Nan?"

"You used it for college."

He dropped his hands. "I had roommates. I've always lived cheap. It's sitting in a money market account. I subleased my place when we hit the road. I have practically no expenses. I have the money, and I have easy access to it."

"All the money. Even hotels, airfare."

Tom paced the room, digging his fingers into his hair.

"So help me, Tom, if you lie to me again, I will kill you with my bare fucking hands."

"I have the money for your salary. If I keep my expenses low while we're on the road, I'll be able to cover the rest."

Sue banged a fist against the door. "You are such an asshole!"

"How? I found the best person to help my band. I gave you an amazing opportunity and I have your back! Financially, emotionally, all of it!"

Sue's body shook. Now that she knew everything, she had no idea how to keep herself together. "Because if you have to pay it out, you'll be broke!"

"I won't have to pay it out!"

Usually Tom being her biggest cheerleader warmed her. Now it tormented her. Sue threw her hands in the air. "If you're so sure, why did you lie?"

"Because they don't know you like I do, and we need you, Sue. We need you."

"That wasn't your decision to make alone. We need to come clean to them, but what will that do to you?"

"You can't tell them." Tom leaned against the giant weight machine. "If it gets out, people'll think you had a part in hiding it, too."

Sue shook her head. "Yeah. It'll end us both in the industry." Tears welled in her eyes. She wanted this job, this career, but not at his expense. Yes, it would be a hit to her integrity, but she could pivot and do PR in a new industry—probably a boring one, but still, she'd be working. She may not even have to go back to entry level. But Tom, his job was perfect for him. The balance of details, comradery, wanderlust—it hit all his high notes. He had a degree in finance, but a job in an office? Wearing a suit? No. That wasn't him. And losing the trust and friendship of the band would be an even deeper blow. Why did he put all of this on the line? Sue was as confused as she was hurt and angry.

"This is why I didn't tell you. Shit, Sue! Why didn't you trust me when I said Chris didn't prank you to get you to quit? Huh?"

Sue broke into hysterical laughter. "Surely you see the problem there. I trusted you with *everything*, and now not only could it take us both down, it could end the whole fucking band! What the fuck is wrong with you?"

Tom walked away, lifting a free weight and banging it back into the rack. "If you'd shut the fuck up and keep working, it's a non-issue! That's why they don't need to know. It's a non-issue."

She wiped tears from her cheeks and crossed her arms. Hurt and angry, she was done with the conversation. "You built a house of lies and you expect us all to live in it. No one knows what's at stake."

"You've never taken a big chance, Sue?"

"Not one that could ruin other people with me." Sue wiped her face again and walked to the door. "If this doesn't work out, it kills me in this industry. I accept that. If this doesn't work out for you, it might kill the band, it will end you in the industry, but mostly, it ends the family you guys have. And frankly, right now, you and I are on shaky ground." She pulled the door open.

"Sue."

"I can't. Not tonight."

"Please." He sighed. "Keep this between us." The wild fell out of his eyes, leaving sadness and fear.

Exhausted and wrung out, Sue dropped her head without answering and went to her room. Would Tom land on his feet if this went sour? Who knew? She could make sure the dumbass didn't wind up destitute, though. She took out her phone and navigated to her money apps. She needed to get her shit in gear and make a plan.

The agenda for the next morning was simple: check out of their rooms on time, hit the road, and avoid Tom. Since she was packed and ready to go with an hour to spare, Sue hoped to take advantage of the downtime by prepping the guys for their interviews. She hadn't decided whether to tell them about her contract, but until she figured it out, their media training would be her top priority.

Getting them comfortable with the press was a skill she could leave them with no matter what happened with her, Tom, and the damn contract.

She found Justin in the hotel lounge, playing air drums while he watched TV.

"Hey, you busy?"

"Nah, it's not a good practice session unless I can drum to *Jerry Springer* reruns."

She laughed. "Is that how you guys got your band name? That look on someone's face right before a fight, when they lose all reason?"

"Ha!" Justin hit another silent combination. "Maybe that's what we should tell people. The real story is probably only amusing to us."

Sue leaned a hip on the couch she stood behind. "Now

you have to tell me."

Justin pulled his hands together and shook the sticks in a silent drum roll. "We got the name from Brad's sister." He dropped his hands to his thighs, stilling the sticks. "We had a ton of songs and were getting ready to record an EP, but we didn't have a name. We were sitting around Brad's Mom's kitchen trying to think of one. Annabelle kept coming in, claiming to get drinks. She's two years younger, and for some reason she thought we were cool. I'll be honest, I like flirting with her. It annoys the shit out of Brad. Totally innocent. Annabelle likes pissing off Brad as much as I do."

Sue laughed. "I get it. I used to flirt with Tom's friends to make him twitch."

He grinned. "Anyway, since she was hanging around, we asked her opinion on some of our options. Darryl liked 'Stout,' Chris wanted 'Against the Ocean.'"

"That's about right coming from Chris."

"Right?" Justin sat back. "Annabelle hated them and asked what our lyrics were about. Brad writes most of them and he wasn't comfortable telling his baby sister that most were about sex. So I decided to do my buddy a solid."

"Uh oh."

Justin resumed the posture he usually took behind his drum kit and started another silent combination. "I leaned in real close to her, mouth right by her ear, and said, 'how about Wanton?' She lost it. Her eyes were wide like plates, she made a weird squealing noise girls make, and said 'words fail me.'" Justin slammed his imaginary cymbals.

"She nailed it."

"Yeah." Justin blushed. "We speak best through our music. Good luck getting us ready for the press."

Charmed by Justin and the story, she knew the opposite would be true. They'd have journalists eating from their hands. "I'll manage."

"You wanna sit? I promise I won't drum you."

"Thanks." She sat on the couch catty-corner to him. "Where's everyone else?"

"Darryl's asleep on the bus, Chris is somewhere, and Brad's still waking up."

"Darryl slept on the bus?"

"Yeah. Now that we get hotels sometimes, Tom orders wake-up calls and Darryl hates it. If we have to leave before lunch, D crashes on the bus to skip the call. It works out for Chris, too. They usually share a room."

"Chris gets alone time and Darryl gets to sleep."

"I doubt Chris is alone. At least, he hasn't had a whole lot of alone time lately."

"Lately?"

"Chris got a lot bolder with women when Tom told us you were joining the tour." Justin silently pounded out what could've been a thunderous punctuation.

"He's that happy about the arrangement, huh?"

"He's young."

"What makes it worse? That I'm a woman, or that I'm related to Tom?"

Justin froze for a moment before answering. "Figured that one out, huh?"

"I had my suspicions, then I overheard his drunken rant to a groupie last night."

"Dumbass."

Sue didn't argue. "He lets loose when he's drunk."

Justin waited a beat then quirked his lips. "He's gotta get it out of his system. He'll come around. I don't get why the cousin thing is a big deal. Maybe he's obsessing over it so he doesn't overthink the good things happening for us."

"Maybe."

"Hey, you want a travel companion?" Justin thumped his foot.

Sue looked at his foot, then his face. "Are you gonna kick me?"

Justin grinned and shook his head. He gestured in front of himself, making the shape of a drum. "Nah. You'd make a terrible bass drum."

Sue smiled and ran a hand through her hair. "Okay. But my car doesn't offer the comforts of the bus."

"If you think the bus is comfortable, you haven't spent enough time on it."

"My mother taught me nice girls don't get on the bus."

Justin chuckled. "I've managed an invite to more than one apartment with that very line."

Sue laughed. She'd had the right idea when she decided to talk to Justin away from the rest of the guys. She could sense his mood shifting when they were around, like he always needed to be ready for something. But the two of them fell into an easy camaraderie when they were alone.

Tom rushed toward them from the parking lot, stress stamped on his face. "Where is everyone? You were all supposed to be down here or on the bus by now!"

"D's on the bus," Justin said.

"Brad?"

"Probably doing his hair."

"Chris?"

"Your guess is as good as mine."

"Damn it!"

"Damn what?" Brad made his way over from the stairwell, holding a small duffle bag over his shoulder.

"We don't know where Chris is," Tom said.

"Oh." Brad's voice was heavy with significance. "He's on his way."

"What does that mean?" Tom vibrated with irritation.

"Keep your eye on the elevators. You'll see."

Justin shook his head. "Great."

The elevator dinged, and Chris, accompanied by a giggling, half-dressed woman, spilled out. Her hair hung in damp clumps, and the seam of her skirt lay crooked over her hip. She dragged a purse and a backpack behind her while she hung onto Chris. He adjusted his pants in an exaggerated fashion as he walked toward them, a wicked grin on his face.

"Hey guys!" Chris raised a hand in greeting.

"Hi." The woman gave a small wave and a giggle.

The guys shifted silently. Sue gave her a small smile, not sure what else to do. Tension rippled off Tom and Justin, though Brad looked more amused.

Chris cleared his throat. "Well, sweetie, I gotta get on my way." He smacked her ass and stepped away from her.

"You said we'd have breakfast!" she whined in a baby voice.

"If we had time. We don't. I gotta go."

She leaned forward and slipped her hands in his pockets. "Miss me?" She leaned up on her tiptoes and moved to kiss him.

Chris snaked his head away. "I don't do dick breath, sweetheart."

"Whoa," Sue whispered.

The woman reared back and slapped him. "Asshole."

"Yeah. And?" Chris smirked and rubbed his cheek. He took the backpack dangling from her arm and slung it over his shoulder as he turned away and shoved his hands in his pockets.

The woman stomped toward the exit as best she could on acrylic heels.

"Wait," Chris called out. "What's this?" He waved a pair of panties that were little more than ribbons and a small triangle of fabric. "Did you think I wanted this?"

The woman turned and her face crumpled.

Chris flicked the panties toward her. They landed in the middle of the lobby.

She took a timid step forward then paused. She stood straighter and a fierce gleam lit her eyes. "You're an asshole and a shitty lay."

Chris laughed. "That's not what you said in the elevator. But it's okay, sweetie, do your thing."

The woman growled and stormed out the door.

Chris turned toward the couches where Sue, Tom, Brad, and Justin waited. "We ready?"

Tom glared and curled his lip. "Yeah."

"All right, then." Chris made his way toward the door, strolling right past the panties.

Brad and Justin both pointedly avoided eye contact with Sue. Dazed, Sue let Brad pull her to her feet and hold her hand as they all walked toward the door. She turned to Tom, silently asking if this was normal. If it was, she had no intention of sticking around.

Tom's jaw ticked, and he shook his head. As they passed the woman's underwear, he swept them up on his fingertips and deposited them in the small garbage can next to the door.

Chris hopped on the bus without a glance back.

"Sue, I'll ride with you." Tom veered toward the back of the bus, where Sue had parked her car that morning.

"Actually, I'm gonna ride with Sue," Justin said, stopping Tom in his tracks.

"You?" Brad asked.

"Yeah."

Sue ignored them and climbed up the first step of the bus. She'd accepted the ipecac as a prank gone wrong, but this was too much. She wouldn't let Chris treat women like garbage. "Chris! Come here."

"What?"

"Come out here." Sue waited until he approached, then stepped off the bus.

Tom raised his eyebrows, and Sue responded with a glare that made him visibly shiver.

"'Sup," Chris hung out of the doorway.

Sue leveled her gaze on him. "Don't take your beef with me out on the women you meet."

"Huh?"

"You're not that stupid, and neither am I. Deal with me. Don't take it out on random women."

"You think me hooking up has to do with you?" Chris bared his teeth in a vicious smile.

"No. I think your public display of assholery was a demented message aimed at me. And *I know* if you piss off the wrong woman, it'll wind up in the press, and the whole band will take the fall. I have no patience for that shit."

Sue noticed Tom flinch out of the corner of her eye.

"It's your job to make me look good in the press. So do it." Chris sneered and pulled himself back into the doorway of the bus.

"This will all be easier if you have me on your side."

"Are you my mom now?"

"You wouldn't be acting like such an asshole if I was."

"Fuck off." Chris stomped the rest of the way onto the bus and flicked a bird from one of the windows.

Tom grabbed Sue's forearm before she could follow. "You have directions and the address in case we get separated?"

Sue had to force her attention to Tom in order to answer. "Yeah. Yeah, I do." She didn't miss his silent plea to let it go.

"I'll call when we're getting ready to stop for gas."

"Okay."

Brad gave her a quick kiss on the cheek. "That was awesome." He bounded onto the bus.

Tom smiled, waving as he followed Brad.

"I hope Chris's mom doesn't find out you insulted her like that," Justin said.

Sue flushed. "Oh my God, I didn't mean that *she* had made him an asshole!"

Justin threw an arm around Sue. "I know. You did good."

Chris leaned against the wall, trying to stay out of Justin's way as he stacked their equipment cases into a tiny alcove. They'd spent the last ten minutes bickering about Justin giving Sue a tour of the bus while everyone else arranged gear on the stage. Aside from Justin's kit being a bitch to set up, the last thing Chris needed was this woman in *more* of his life.

Since Sue would eventually wind up on the bus with them, they'd come to an uneasy truce: Chris had to be less mean to her, and Justin would keep her clear of Chris's stuff. He wasn't thrilled with having to reel it in, but Chris needed his space.

He looked down the length of the hallway, counting the cases they still had to stow, and found a gawky guy with what could only be described as a pompadour mullet talking with Sue. He glanced at Justin, then back at Sue. "Hey, do you think she knows him?"

Justin looked over his shoulder. "Doubt it."

Chris rubbed his head. "He must work here."

"She's coming." Justin pushed Chris out of his way, picked up another box, and added it to the stack they'd created.

Chris stared at him, unsure of what to do.

"Are you guys done, or can I help?" Sue asked.

"We're finishing up," Justin answered.

"Who was that guy?" Chris asked.

"Smooth," Justin said under his breath.

"Mike."

"You know him?" Chris asked.

"Just met him."

Justin almost knocked over a gear box, but Sue stepped in and held it steady.

Chris stared at the pompadour guy. He looked super awkward. Sure, Sue was pretty, but she ruined it as soon as she opened her mouth. All bitch, all the time. "You just met him?"

"Yeah." She acted like this type of thing was normal.

"Over there by the merch table?" Justin asked.

Sue slowly raised her eyebrows. "Yes. He asked me out for drinks later."

"What?" Aggravation replaced Chris's initial shock. Did Sue seriously think she could go around picking up men when she had a job to do?

Justin smacked Chris in the stomach.

"I didn't say yes. We're working."

"Good." At least she remembered why she was here. Sue letting some weirdo fawn all over her made Chris wonder if she'd worked for a tiny radio station instead of one with an actual audience to get laid easier.

"I told him I'd put his name on the list, though." Sue flashed a quick grin.

"Why?" Justin asked.

"Why not?"

"Wait." Justin held up a hand. "If you have to add him to the list, he doesn't work here. How'd he get in?"

Sue glanced toward the merch table. "That's why I walked away. If he doesn't belong here, security can deal with him."

Justin thumped his foot. "Good call."

Chris squeezed his head. "Is he on the list or not?"

"No." Sue rolled her eyes. "I'm fucking with you."

"You want security to get rid of a guy you picked up?" Aggravated even more, Chris didn't understand how Justin seemed cool about their publicity person trolling for dick at work. Especially after all the shit she gave him over his last hookup. "You can't go picking up guys at our shows."

"I didn't pick him up."

"You know what I mean," Chris said. "You can't go meeting guys in a bar or a club."

Sue put her hands on her hips. "Where should I meet them? Especially since hooking up backstage like you do appears to be off the table."

Chris narrowed his eyes. "We do not pick women up backstage."

"A week after Tom offered me this job, I flew out to Montreal with contracts. Why didn't the whole band meet with me?"

Chris shrugged. "Some girls offered us a tour of the city."

"Shut up, man!" Justin said.

Chris scowled and stomped his foot. "We didn't pick them up!"

"Okay." Sue rolled her eyes. "Whatever. What's next?"

"Soundcheck." Justin stalked away.

"Wait." Sue grabbed Chris's wrist and dragged him as she jogged after Justin. "Hold on. Is this bothering you guys for real?"

"No." Justin bent down and fiddled with his shoe.

"Yeah." Chris snapped his wrist out of Sue's grasp.

"Justin?" Sue pulled him up by the shirt.

"I forgot we're all single. It threw me for a minute."

"I'm gonna meet men. The situation is ripe for it."

"You work for us," Chris said. "You don't have time to date."

"First of all, I'm your PR rep, not your concubine. Second of all, if you have time to fuck the groupies who come your way, Chris, then I have time to get a drink with a guy."

The balls on this bitch were infuriating. How did she get off thinking she could do whatever she wanted? Chris pushed Justin toward the stage, but Justin gazed at Sue as though she'd turned into fucking Wonder Woman. Chris wanted to call this girl out for the things she said about him, especially now that it was clear she wanted to get some ass, too, but he knew Justin would throw their deal in his face. Better to give her a piece of his mind when Brad or Darryl was around.

"Okay, hold up." Justin looked at Chris and Sue in turn. "We weren't prepared to see you talking to some guy who's not somehow involved with us."

"Yeah." Chris went with Justin even though he was in the dark. Justin was a smart fucker. He logic'd his way out of all sorts of shit.

"You're on our team. You're kind of becoming one of us," Justin continued. "Sometimes when guys see strange dudes talking to their people—cousins, whatever—we get weird."

"Yeah, you belong to us now." Chris crossed his arms.

Sue barked a laugh. "I belong to you? Is this the third world?"

Justin punched Chris's arm. "You're such a fuckin' dork."

"Whatever." This was why Chris had no business giving interviews. He couldn't even have a conversation with people he saw every day.

"We wanna make sure you're not hanging with ass-holes." Justin exchanged a look with Chris.

"Yeah." This argument appealed to Chris. Having Sue around was bad enough. He didn't need whatever uptight nerd guys she liked getting in his way, too. "You can't be polluting backstage with lame shits."

Sue crossed her arms and studied both men. "Lame shits like your buddy who screen-prints T-shirts for you in his parents' basement?"

"That dude makes some serious coin," Chris said.

"Whatever." Sue dropped her arms to her sides. "I'm capable of separating the assholes from the men worth my time." She glared at Chris.

He raised his eyebrows. "You sure about that?"

"Positive."

"Care to wager on it?" Chris asked.

Justin thumped his foot again. "Hell yes."

CHAPTER 10

Sue checked the time and stifled a sigh. Nine-thirty. She'd been dealing with this guy, Mike, since around six. Chris, wearing a smug smile, had deposited the man—and a brand new all-access pass—at the merch table where she'd been working with instructions to "have fun." She'd hoped Justin would intervene, but he'd left her high and dry, predicting Mike would run out of energy before ten.

"Skein isn't done yet! You can't go! There's so much going on!" Mike tried to wrap an arm around her.

She moved away, uninterested and wishing he'd finally move on. He never stopped talking—as she tried to sell shirts and CDs, throughout all of Words Fail Me's set, when she tried to get security to take him off her hands. Always talking and fluffing his big hair.

"I know. They're the best part of the show." She grinned when Justin made a stabbing gesture at his heart. "You can stay as long as you'd like. I still have to go. I'm sorry."

"Can I get your number?"

Sue cringed inwardly. The way Chris had encouraged this guy to take a chance on a dead end was bad enough. She didn't want to add to it. She also didn't want this guy talking at her any more. "I gave it to you already."

"You did?" Mike fumbled with his phone.

"Yep. I'm in there!"

"Okay. I'll call you tomorrow?"

"I'll be at a conference. I won't be available much." Sue hoped the warning would dissuade him long enough that he'd forget about her and never catch that she'd lied about putting her number in his phone.

Mike's shoulders curved in on his lanky frame as he flicked his mullet away from his neck.

"Hey, Mike, have you ever been on a tour bus?" Darryl showed Sue some much-needed mercy.

"No, never."

"Wanna see ours?"

"Yeah! That'd be neat!"

Darryl led him away, and Sue let out a deep sigh of relief. "Wow, I almost feel bad."

"For Mike?" Brad asked.

"No, Darryl." Sue couldn't suppress her grin. "I got him back for the condoms on my laptop thing, but he doesn't know it yet."

"What'd you do?" Justin asked.

Sue swallowed an excited giggle before she spoke. "It's better if you wait for it."

Justin grinned. "You really going to the hotel now, or

trying to shake the love of your life?"

"I'm going to the hotel. I'm leaving early tomorrow so I can see most of the trade show in Austin. I'll be on the road before you get a chance to kick your latest conquest out of bed."

"Speaking of women, Mike's been slowing me down." Justin shook his head.

"You mean you don't want him to be your wingman?"

He laughed and gave her a fist bump.

"Tom'll be pissed if someone doesn't walk you to your car." With a hand on the small of her back, Brad guided Sue toward the door. "Especially if that guy comes back."

"Oh, thanks." Sue did a quick mental check to make sure she had all her things. She'd rather leave under her own power, but Brad's reminder that Mike might return at any moment was enough to get her to speed up her exit.

Justin elbowed Brad out of the way and gave her a hug. "You're a good sport. Have fun in Austin."

"Thanks. Have fun all over Texas and Arkansas. Tell Chris and Darryl I said bye."

"Will do." Justin gave her a wave and went in the opposite direction.

As they walked to her car, Brad tried to get Sue to confess her revenge against Darryl.

"Trust me. Let it happen. It'll be funnier that way."

They stood next to the driver's door of her car, Sue grasping the handle, when Brad enveloped her in a huge bear hug.

"Uh, thanks?" Sue tried to pull away.

"Mike's coming."

"Oh."

She couldn't see Mike, but he spoke loudly, telling Darryl he wanted to make sure he said goodbye before she left. Brad moved so that he stood between her and Mike, his back to the man.

"Tell me when Darryl gets him inside."

Sue peeked over his shoulder. "Shit." She ducked her head.

"There she is!" Mike said.

"I don't think that's her," Darryl said.

"No, it is. Those are her shoes."

"Are you kidding me?" Sue whispered to Brad.

"Follow my lead, okay?"

Sue gave him a quick nod, figuring he'd shield her long enough for her to get in the car.

"Sue?" Mike called out, getting closer.

"You'd better go before everyone finds out about us," Brad said in a loud voice.

"Yeah." Sue turned back to her car and pulled on the

door handle.

"Try not to pick up any more guys before I can get my hands on you again."

She gave Brad a skeptical look. What the hell was he doing? He knew Darryl could hear him, too, right?

He goaded her silently with wide eyes.

Why was he making shit up? "I have to go," she said.

Brad turned as if to go back to the building, giving Sue a glimpse of Mike. She hesitated a second, upset that Brad had chosen a cruel way to get Mike out of her hair. Brad wrapped an arm around her waist and pulled her close, pinning her arms against his chest. He pressed his mouth to hers, not quite kissing her.

Sue twisted her face away from his as she pushed against him.

"Go with it," Brad whispered, chasing her mouth.

"Oh." The sound of Mike's cowboy boots clicking on the pavement retreated.

Darryl coughed loudly.

Brad pulled Sue closer and moved his head, putting his mouth against her throat. His hot, fast breath against her neck made her skin crawl. This was wrong, no matter how ardently Brad might've claimed it was fake.

Brad loosened his grip, gave her a loud smacking kiss on the mouth, and twirled her toward the car. He opened the door for her. "Drive safe, baby."

Sue hopped in and looked around Brad as he closed the door behind her. Mike took long strides toward the club, head bowed. Darryl stayed at his side, obviously talking nonstop. She glared at Brad.

"That was mean!" Sue smacked the steering wheel.

"It worked." He jogged toward the venue before Sue could say anything more.

CHAPTER 11

AUSTIN, TX

"I can intro you to Jim Diamond and Russ Cage. That's Dallas and Chicago." Sue sipped her Manhattan, trying to look casual as the tiny brunette with a pixie cut considered her offer. After close to six hours on the road to get to Austin, an afternoon on her feet at the tradeshow, and a twenty-minute power nap before she changed her clothes and came to this event, she was wiped out. If this gambit didn't work, she'd have to prowl the ballroom in the last few minutes before the conference's awards ceremony to find an "in" to meet more DJs and continue to schmooze when she desperately wanted to fall into bed.

"Seems like a lot just to meet Carter." The pixie tapped a finger against her glass.

Sue swirled her drink. "I like the way she puts together stories, and I've got an up-and-coming band that could use a good one."

"She's gonna grill you about whether you actually know those musicians."

"I've got the audio to prove it."

The woman chuckled. "I can check her schedule. See if she has time for an intro."

Sue grinned. "I'll do you one more, either way."

"What's that?"

"I need a photographer for at least one of my band's sets and maybe a few candids at interviews. I hear you have someone hot."

"Budget?"

"Market rate."

The woman threw back the rest of her drink. "If you're willing to take a shot on an unknown with a good eye, I'll make sure you get ten minutes with Carter."

"I can't say yes without samples."

The woman texted a link to Sue, and they hunched over her phone, reviewing photos. Sue tapped the screen, zooming in on one. "This is exactly what I want for their sets. Is she already here?"

"Yeah, I'll go get her." The brunette gave Sue a big smile and walked toward the ballroom.

Sue ordered another Manhattan, then stepped away from the bar after it was delivered. Her phone lit up with a call from Tom. Perfect timing; he'd be excited about the new photographer. "Hey!"

"MY BUNK? YOU HAD TO GO AFTER MY BUNK?" Darryl greeted her.

Pleased with his reaction, though sorry she couldn't see it, Sue didn't bother with a hello. "You would've done the same thing."

"That's not the point!"

"Did you know you can buy vats of lube?"

"Huh?"

"At warehouse stores." Sue's voice shook as she tried to hold back laughter. "Vats of lube! Who needs vats of lube?"

"A reckless redhead who likes to declare war!"

"It's good you don't have a car on tour, too."

"I may not have a car, but I. Am. Fucking. Creative!"

Sue gave into her laughter as something rustled and Darryl cursed in the background.

"You were right, Sue." Justin took over the call. "It was much funnier waiting for it to happen."

"Right? Is he mad?" As much as Sue had enjoyed putting together the prank and making the point that she could play on their level, she hadn't meant any harm.

"No. He's smiling now. I think he's annoyed with how good you got him."

"She did not get me good!" Darryl shouted in the background.

"She did, man," Tom said, sounding closer to the phone.

"Listen, Sue," Justin said. "When we get to Austin, make sure your stuff is locked up and don't spend a lot of time alone with D."

"Of course. Let him know I left clean sheets on the top shelf of the cabinet next to the fridge."

Justin repeated the instruction and added, "She planned this shit out. This is way better than what you did."

"Thanks, Just."

"Credit where credit is due."

Sue sidestepped toward the bar to avoid a cluster of people headed to the ballroom. "I've gotta go, this awards show is about to start. Stay safe."

"You, too. And hey"—Justin paused for a moment—"there's no shame in duck and cover if it comes to it."

Sue laughed. "Thanks for the advice. See you soon." She ended the call and sent Tom a quick text asking if anyone had gotten pictures.

"I wish a woman would look like that after a call from me." A guy in a backward newsboy cap with a tidy beard approached Sue.

She slid her phone into her purse, the smile dropping from her lips as she realized he'd taken her picture. "I'm sorry, do I know you?"

He held up a laminated badge. "I'm one of the event photographers." He dropped the badge and held his camera out to her, preview screen up. "That's a great snap. You gotta sign my photo release."

Still wary, Sue read his badge, now partially tucked into his vest, and confirmed he was who he said. This man might come in handy if other photo connections didn't come through.

"Sue!" The pixie she'd negotiated with earlier leaned out of the ballroom doorway. "I got Carter and the photog!" She gestured for Sue to follow.

Sue held up one finger then addressed the guy. "I have to go back to work. Find me when this is winding down. I'll sign your release." She waved, then joined the woman in the ballroom.

The banana Sue grabbed on the way out of the hotel that morning hadn't been the robust breakfast she needed for her marathon day. She had people to meet, interviews to confirm, and best of all, for her anyway, one of the band's shows had been canceled. That meant they had more time for interviews. She intended to use every moment.

But first, lunch. As soon as Sue had more than five minutes to spare, she found the taco joint everyone at the conference had been talking about, picked up a sturdy to-go container, and set to making herself an assortment of small tacos: steak, chicken, pork, and shredded beef. Everything smelled so good, she decided to taste it all.

She'd finished building the bedrock of her tacos when her phone rang.

"Did it occur to you that we might want to see some of the music at Indy Showcase and not fucking talk all day?"

"I promise you will have plenty of time for music, Chris. How's the drive? You making good time?" Sue selected cheeses and guacamole for each of her tacos and moved on to the refried beans.

"The drive is fucking great. Luther's game to stop any-fucking-where and hang out so I can skip your bullshit schedule."

"Aw, you'd miss all that music just to avoid me? I'm flattered, Chris."

"Fuck you, Sue."

With the phone balanced between her ear and shoulder, Sue rubbed the space between her eyes before taking in the salsa options. "Tread lightly there, Chris."

"You fucking tread lightly. You have more at stake here than I do."

Chris had no idea how right he was. She flung salsa onto her tacos. "You should know by now that I'm not gonna march you in front of reporters without being prepared. How many talks have we had about interviews and how to get out your message?"

"Seriously? Some conference calls while we're on the bus is prep?"

"We've done much more than that. Plus, I've vetted all of these people. We're only talking with reporters who're interested in what you have to say." As Sue replaced the serving spoon, she noticed someone waiting in the corner of her eye. She gave him a small smile and backed away from the bar. Once she had more space, she faced him and mouthed "sorry" as Chris continued to rant in her ear.

The man gave her a friendly nod and picked up the spoon. As he scooped food, he looked over at Sue.

She knew she should leave and deal with Chris in a more private place, but damn it, she wanted hot sauce, and she wanted to know what her options were. She glanced over the variety of bottles and picked up a packet that promised to light her ass on fire.

She wanted to light Chris's ass on fire. She wasn't about to dress him down on the phone, though. She'd do that face-to-face.

"You try to make them all happy. I'm not some ass-licker about to make a reporter's day."

Sue rolled her eyes. Chris's view of publicity was seriously off. Where did he get this shit? She adjusted the phone and almost lost her tacos.

Fortunately, the guy she'd cleared the line for took the hefty box from her. Sue smiled and mouthed "thank you."

"You have a plan for controlling these fuckers, right?"

"Listen to me. I won't let anyone interview you without me there to moderate. And you and I will work together beforehand."

"Don't give me more notecards. That shit makes me look like a dork."

"You will not look like a dork." She rolled her eyes again, and Taco Guy laughed quietly. His smile was familiar. Where had she seen him? She refocused on Chris, who was ranting again. "If you don't want to do this, it's fine. The rest of the guys—"

"You need to keep these reporters off my ass. Dust off your dick-sucking skills and make yourself useful."

Sue squeezed her fist so hard her nails dug into her palms. Hot sauce sprayed all over her. She willed it to be a figment of her imagination, but a splatter marred her dress—a favorite and the only one she'd packed. She raised her eyes to Taco Guy, her cheeks burning with both rage and embarrassment. He held up one finger and ran off. With her lunch. Damn it!

"Don't ever talk to me like that again," she growled into the phone.

"Like what? A realist?"

"Like you're garbage." She shook her hand in front of her, the sauce already tingling her bare palm.

The guy returned with her food and a stack of napkins. He put everything on a nearby counter, produced a wet napkin, and took her hand in both of his. He plucked the exploded packet from her and cleaned her hand, carefully wiping both sides twice. He followed with a dry napkin, then dumped them all in the trash nearby. The tender kindness calmed her, her hand tingling from him instead of hot sauce.

Chris had continued talking, though she didn't register a word he said. All her attention was focused on Taco Guy.

"Chris, we'll work it out when you get here. I gotta go."

"What?"

"I gotta go. Bye."

She ended the call and pinched the bridge of her

nose, mostly to give herself a second to not swoon over the man in front of her. When she finally looked at him, he offered another napkin.

"I can't believe I did that." Sue accepted it and dabbed at her dress.

"It could happen to anyone." Taco Guy gave her a warm smile.

She immediately returned it, then studied the mess on the light gray sheath. She sighed. "I love this dress."

"Can you move this to help cover it?" Taco Guy pointed at her oversized asymmetrical collar.

"No." She twisted her lips. "I have to change."

He offered to take her dirty napkins, but Sue balled them up, dropped her phone in her purse, and took her lunch, tucking the box flaps closed. "Thank you for the extra set of hands. Sorry I screwed up your place in line."

"No big deal." The guy smiled and picked up his own plate. His massive steak tacos looked almost as good as he did.

"You look familiar," Sue said. "Were you a speaker at the media conference?"

"No."

Sue openly stared at him. His dark hair was cut close on the sides. He had a lean build and a light tan. He looked like he spent time outside, maybe a ball player? "Where have I seen you?"

"Could've been anywhere." He slipped his free hand into his pocket. "I've been in town for a few days. At the conference."

Sue stared again. He glanced down at his food, then back at her. Finally, she placed him. "You're the guy from *Sports Mecca*. You won the Best Content award last night."

He gave her a shy smile. "Yeah, we did."

"Congratulations." That's why he looked like he spent a lot of time outside. He spent most days on fields, talking to athletes. Sue gave him one more quick once-over. She'd bet he played on those fields sometimes, too.

"Thanks. I'm Adam Fletcher. You are?"

"Sue Douglas. I love how you made your editorial team get on stage to accept the award."

"*Sports Mecca* wouldn't be this good without them."

Sue beamed. Now that she knew who he was, she appreciated his comment even more. He founded *Sports Mecca*. He could've taken all the credit. She caught herself mid-swoon. She should be drooling over lunch and interview schedules, not a man. Even if he did save her meal and keep her hand from pepper burns. "They're waiting for you, right? I'll let you go. Thank you for the save."

"I'm on my own. Join me?"

His offer tempted her, even though she'd planned to eat in her hotel room. She needed to prepare background sheets on all the interviewers for the band. Plus, her abdomen tingled from the sauce seeping through her dress. "I'd love to, but I have a packed day, and now I need to change. Thanks for the assist." She gave his arm a light squeeze and drew away.

He blinked at her. "It was my pleasure."

"And thanks for not laughing." Sue gestured to her dress.

"Why on earth would I laugh?"

Sue looked back before she left. She smiled again and waved. Damn her timing.

CHAPTER 13

Tuesday evening, Sue looked out her window as the band's bus pull into the hotel parking lot. She expected the guys to run off the bus as soon as it stopped. Instead, Tom and Chris crept out. Sue met them in the lobby as the receptionist gave Tom room cards.

"Hey!" She peered around a pillar.

Chris looked up from where he reclined against the counter. "Darryl was pissed the entire way to Lubbock."

Sue stepped out from behind the pillar. "Does he have his revenge plotted?"

"He has about eighty scenarios ready." Tom counted the room cards and thanked the receptionist.

"How was the trip?"

"The usual," Tom said.

"Dull as shit," Chris added.

Sue pointed her thumb at the restaurant behind her. "You wanna get a drink or dinner or something?"

"Yeah. Let's put these cards under their pillows, then grab a bite." Tom headed toward the parking lot.

They quietly boarded the bus and tucked room cards into hands and pockets and left a note on the dry-erase board on the door.

We're either in the hotel restaurant or our rooms.

Tom – 514 Chris – 519 Sue – Text her.

"Not taking any chances, are you?" Tom asked as Sue finished writing the note.

"He'll have to work for it if he wants to get me back."

"Let's go before they wake up." Chris pushed the bus door open and jogged ahead to the hotel.

"He was pretty relieved when I told him you canceled the interviews for tonight," Tom said, his voice low.

"No interview is better than a bad interview. Especially since I need him to talk to a lot of people." Sue let Tom open the hotel door for her. "The extra prep time won't hurt. I'm hoping to have him at least somewhat relaxed by the time we have the big press night for the benefit in New Orleans."

"Thank you for being patient with him."

"It'll get better."

They'd caught up to Chris in the restaurant and waited until they were seated in a U-shaped booth and had placed their orders before picking up a new conversation.

"Did you accomplish what you wanted these last few days?" Tom scrolled through the calendar on his tablet, reading the list of events Sue had lined up for them.

"More than what I wanted." She wiped some salt off her margarita glass and licked her finger. "We've gotta make sure everything fits in the schedule, but I think it will. You guys'll be excited when you see it come together."

"Why?" Chris sipped a margarita out of a giant glass that had an umbrella, a slice of lime, and a miniature parrot perched on the rim—all in keeping with the restaurant's kitschy beach theme.

"I've been working on some fun stuff to give you more exposure. I don't want to talk details until everything's confirmed, though."

"Like what?" Chris pulled the parrot off his glass and tossed it at the conch shell centerpiece.

"The benefit for the New Orleans Zoo."

Chris sat back and crossed his arms. "The Jack Ragnar thing?"

"Yep." Sue resisted giving him a smug smile. Jack Ragnar was one of the biggest names in rock; it wasn't possible for Chris to be unimpressed by her connection.

"It'd be worth it if we met him."

Sue mirrored his posture. "I'll arrange something."

Chris looked away from her. "You do that."

Tom laughed. "Sue knows Jack personally. She and

his wife have been best friends since grade school."

Chris dropped his head on the back of the seat. "Of all the dumb luck—"

"It's luck if we happen to be in New Orleans when they need a band." Sue swiped more salt from the rim of her glass. "This is seizing an opportunity. The press will be fantastic."

Chris chugged part of his drink, then leaned on his hand. "I have no idea what to say to reporters, and now the ultimate rock god will be there. 'Hi, Jack Ragnar, nice to meet you. Please excuse me while your whole event makes me squirm.'"

"Just be yourself." Tom took his own drink and drained half of it.

"Eh. I'm not the main attraction in this band." Chris thumped his hands on the table.

"That's not true." In fact, Sue had tons of requests for interviews with Chris. Rumor had it that he made his own instruments, plus several of the guitars Brad played. People were curious. Everything the guys used on stage looked like top-of-the-line professional instruments. How did he do it?

"It is true. And I don't mind. Let Brad have the spotlight. I'll be in the back, making music."

Tom nudged the giant margarita glass toward Chris. "People want to talk to you, whether you stop playing while they interview you or not."

"You say that now, but wait 'til some asshole know-it-all-reporter gets pissed because I don't give the answer they expect. One curve ball and bam! The whole article focuses on what a dick you are." Chris made a jerk-off gesture.

Sue exchanged a look with Tom, then took a long swallow of her margarita. She needed to find whatever article Chris was talking about and figure out how it had gone sideways.

"I can protect you from that. I can only allow print articles that follow—"

Chris waved at Sue and talked over her. "Nope. Sorry, reporters with so-called integrity print what they want."

"No." Sue leaned forward. "Reporters with integrity print what we give them."

Chris scoffed. "Yeah, okay."

"I'm teaching you how to handle interviews. How to only show the cards you want to play. You don't have to worry about bad interviews. I won't let you give any."

Chris stared off into the distance, twisting the stem of his glass between his fingers.

Sue pulled a folded page out of her pocket, flattened it against the table and slid it toward Chris. She produced a pen and placed it on the page.

"What's this?" Chris poked at the corner of the page.

"Let's call it a study guide."

Chris rolled his eyes, then read the page and shoved it back at Sue. "Looks like one of those social media twenty questions bullshits."

"That's what an interview is, Chris," Tom said. "Sometimes more in-depth. Sometimes not."

"What drew you to playing music?" Sue asked.

Chris furrowed his brow. "We're doing this now?"

"Yeah," Sue said.

He rubbed a palm over his head. "Um, I guess I got into it in elementary school. Music hour. It was an escape from all the shit at home."

Sue lifted her eyebrows at Tom, and he shook his head. Chris carried on without Sue flagging his "shit at home" comment.

"I'd always try to get an instrument to play instead of singing. Even if it was only the triangle."

"You must know how to play a lot of instruments."

"Nah. I know bass and guitar. I'm okay on the piano. I dabble with drums to piss off Justin. I'd like to learn how to play more weird stuff, like the talk box. That thing sounds so cool in Sweet Emotion. Gives the song edge."

"Are you an Aerosmith fan?"

"No, but Tom Hamilton is my hero."

Chris's grin shocked Sue. She'd become accustomed to his smirks and sneers. She smiled and tipped her drink to him.

"See? You can do this." Tom tossed a drink garnish at Chris. "This is easy."

"Because she's asking. I know her agenda. What happens when there's a microphone in my face?"

"That's what the pen is for." Sue gestured toward the pen and paper.

"Huh?"

"We're gonna go through these questions, and you're going to write down the answers. Then when you have a microphone in your face, you're going to think about the paper and remember your answer."

"You're funny." Chris shoved the paper and pen toward Sue.

She slammed her hand over the page before it made it to the middle of the table. "I'm a fucking riot. Conference calls on the bus aren't prep. Remember?"

Chris's gaze hardened into a cold glare. "Everything I say is used against me, huh?"

"You make it that way." Sue sat still and held his eye contact. "Writing helps you remember. It's science." She nudged the paper toward him.

"Someone finding this and posting it online is technology. I'm not doing this."

Sue produced a lighter and set it near her on the edge of the table. "Once you have it memorized, I'll burn it."

"Holy shit," Tom whispered.

Sue didn't even look Tom's way. She was too interested in the expression Chris was trying to cover with his frustration. She'd surprised him, and he clearly didn't want her to know. She tapped the lighter on the table. "What got you interested in music? Write it down."

"I'm not gonna forget that memory." Chris crossed his arms and sat back.

"I'm not interested in the memory. Write down the answer."

Chris's eyes lit as he made the connection. He reached for the margarita and drank a good bit before setting it aside. "I'm not writing it all out."

Sue stayed silent, not willing to budge.

"I might jot down a phrase or two, though."

Tom cleared his throat. "Will that be enough to trigger the memory?"

"It's not what I want," Sue said.

"Do you want to fight all night, or do you wanna set some shit on fire?" Chris asked.

Sue raised her eyebrows, sitting back. "Fire."

Chris clicked the pen and pulled the paper toward him. "Gimme the lighter."

Sue slid it to the center of the table.

Chris picked up the paper and kept his gaze on it. "What time do we have to be in the radio booth tomorrow?"

"You won't be in a booth." Sue glanced at Tom, surprised by the question. "The interviews aren't live. We're doing them in a lounge. It'll be like hanging out in someone's house."

Chris inhaled and let it go when the server appeared with their food. He put the page facedown next to his fork and kept his hand on it as their plates were set out.

"Can I get you anything else?"

"I'm gonna need a great big margarita." Chris held his hands out shoulder-width apart.

"Bigger than that?" Tom pointed at the fifty-two-ounce glass in front of Chris.

"As big as they got."

One hour, six normal-sized margaritas, four questions, and a lot of eye rolling and passive aggressive comments later, Chris, Tom and Sue were well on their way to getting completely trashed. Sue sighed in relief when she noticed Brad, Justin, and Darryl trudging sleepily toward the booth. She hoped they'd stay and run some interference.

Darryl's eyes narrowed to slits. "You." He waved a finger at Sue. "You're lucky I'm too tired to throw a blow-up doll at you."

"Um-hmm. Sure, Spiky." Sue sipped her drink. "You should go ahead and give in now."

"No way. It took damn near two hours to clean up!"

Sue giggled. "Good! It took a long time to set up."

"How did you even get in there?" Frustration marked Darryl's face, setting Sue into a fit of giggles.

She wasn't sure if she was punch drunk or drunk drunk, and she didn't care. She was relieved to not be arguing with Chris for a few minutes.

"Shut up, D." Justin nudged him. "We're here to figure out how much longer we can sleep."

"Tomorrow until three," Tom said.

"What's at three?" Brad rubbed his eyes.

"The first interview."

"Margarita!" Chris barked, his eyes searching for the server. "I need another margarita!"

"Huh?" Justin wrinkled his brow.

Sue closed her eyes for a second to avoid rolling them. "Don't ask."

Justin nodded. "You wear that Aerosmith shirt a lot, Sue. You got a thing for rowdy old dudes?"

She squinted. "Rowdy old dudes?"

"Steven Tyler. You into old guys with scarves?"

Sue leaned her head against her fist. "No. No, I'm not. Just the music."

Tom snorted. "Liar."

"What?"

"Sue's been into Joe Perry since her mother first warned her about bad touches."

"What the fuck, Tom?" Sue threw lime rinds at him.

"It's true." Tom threw one back at her. "She watched the 'Rag Doll' video over and over and over. I could get dementia, and I'll still remember Joe Perry playing guitar in the middle of the street."

Elbows perched on the table, Sue covered her burning face with her hands. "Shut up, Tom! Do we need to talk about you and Natalie Imbruglia videos?"

"Natalie Imbruglia?" Chris asked.

Brad jutted his chin. "'90s chick music. Interesting. But let's get back to Sexy Sue and Joe Perry." Brad slid into the booth next to Sue and draped his arm along the back.

"Yeah," Justin smirked. "I had no idea you went for grandpas, Sue."

"He's not *my* grandfather." Sue scooted closer to Tom and leaned forward. She'd drunk more than she meant to, and the last thing she wanted was to pass out against Brad.

"Sue." Darryl leaned on the table. "You need to stop pranking and start focusing on Viagra suppliers."

Sue knocked Darryl's hand off the table. "Let's focus on what's important here."

"You needing a defibrillator nearby if you ever hook up with your dream man is pretty important," Justin said.

Sue rolled her eyes. "No! What's important is that twenty years after Aerosmith's heyday, chicks are still walking around with the band's name across their tits. You want that magic? You fellas better be nice to me."

"Shit." Brad dropped his hand on her shoulder. "That's a good point."

Sue shimmied out of Brad's grasp and moved closer to Tom.

"It hasn't been twenty years." Tom shook his head. "Forty years. It's been forty some years since their first album. That is a kick-ass goal."

"I'd be good with young girls throwing themselves at me forty years from now," Chris said.

Sue leaned forward. "I'm awesome, but I'm not promising miracles."

They broke into laughter, and Sue sat back with a satisfied smirk. There might have been a little too much tequila running through her veins, but them all laughing together did a lot to soothe some of her stress.

"Do you need menus?" The server interrupted with more than a hint of annoyance.

"I'm good," Darryl said. "Going back to bed." He pointed to Sue. "Sleep with one eye open, prankster."

Sue waved him off.

"I'm out of here, too." Justin drummed on the table. "Tom!"

Tom swung his head toward Justin, widened his eyes, then focused his gaze. "Yeah."

"Make sure you and Sue eat. Clean your plates. Got it?"

Tom saluted. "Got it."

"Behave." Justin looked at Brad, then each of them in turn before leaving.

"What's going on here?" Brad shifted toward Sue and Tom.

"We're trying to help Chris feel better about the interviews." Tom elbowed Chris.

"He's super nervous," Sue added.

"Ooh." Brad craned around Sue and tapped the back of his fingers against Tom's shoulder. "Did you give him the stage-fright talk?"

"We can't do that." Chris shook his head. "It won't work."

"Sure, it will." Brad picked a fry off Chris's plate.

"No, don't even waste the time."

"Wait!" Sue said. "What's the stage-fright talk?"

"It's when we point out all the dumb things we've done in front of people." Brad plucked another fry from Chris.

"So we remember that we won't look that dumb in public ever again." Chris waved as if to poo-poo the idea. "It never works. I always find a way to look dumb in front of people."

"Like when you wanted to fight Justin because I set up an awesome interview schedule?" Sue asked.

"Not helping!" Chris said a little too loudly.

After telling countless embarrassing stories about each other, Brad shepherded his drunk friends toward the elevator. Sue lagged behind a few steps, playing with her phone. When Brad glanced back, some hipster bearded guy with a camera and a newsboy cap swooped in.

"There she is!" The guy put an arm around Sue and kissed her cheek. "We're going to Palm Door. Come with."

Sue shook her head. "I'm on the clock."

The guy looked up and locked eyes with Brad. Brad gave him a glare that should've sent him running. This bastard pulled Sue closer and said, "How about later? I might need you to sign another release."

Sue smirked. "I'll text you if I'm free."

The guy landed a kiss near the corner of her lips. "I hope you text real soon."

With a hand on her waist, Brad guided Sue toward the elevators, where Tom repeatedly jabbed the call button. When she got a few feet ahead, Brad snarled, "She's with me now."

The guy crossed his arms. "Sure, buddy."

Brad strode back to Sue and draped his arm around

her, not bothering to look back at the asshole.

Chris leaned against the wall, his head hanging to the side. It looked like it took a force of nature for him to focus on Brad. He opened his mouth, but the elevator arrived. Chris grunted and dragged himself into it.

Tom batted at the buttons for their floors as the doors closed again. "I'll walk you to your room, Sue."

"Nah. I drank a lot of water. I made it back down to tipsy."

"You look full-on drunk to me." Tom barely covered his mouth as he burped.

"That's cuz *you're* full-on drunk."

Brad threaded his fingers through Sue's. "I'm in better shape than him. I'll walk you."

The elevator lurched to a stop and opened at Sue's floor.

"I'm good. You guys'll pass out in the hallway. That'd be a terrible first article for me."

"You sure?" Brad tried to follow her, but she put her hand in the middle of his chest and held him back. He covered it with his own, following her to the hallway.

"I'm good," Sue said as she pulled away.

Brad watched until she let herself into a room, then backed into the elevator.

"I'm going to puke soon, so I can't keep an eye on you." Chris raised a crooked finger, the grimace on his face giving the impression that he fought off a wave of nausea. He wobbled, even though he leaned against the wall with a white-knuckle grip on the railing, and lifted his chin, making eye contact with Brad. "I got her drunk. You better not take advantage of her." Chris may have been drunk off his ass and barely able to stand, but he delivered those words loud and clear.

Tom cocked his head and shifted his whole body to face Brad. "Huh."

Brad hadn't drunk as much as Tom and Chris had, but the warm, loopy sensation he'd cultivated instantly disappeared. "What're you talking about?"

"Don't fuck her." Chris spat as he spoke. Color leached from his skin, and his eyes flickered closed. "I know you want to. But if you fuck her and you piss her off, she'll fuck our careers. So don't fuck her."

Brad stared at Chris. He wouldn't look at Tom lest he recognize Tom had the same suspicions. No one spoke until the doors slid open again, this time at their floor. Tom wrapped an arm around Chris's waist and pulled one of Chris's arms over his shoulders. Brad assumed the same position on Chris's other side. Together they dragged Chris to the room he shared with Darryl. Brad stopped in the doorway, ready to go on to his own room, when Tom asked him to wait while he deposited Chris in the bathroom. Tom closed the door behind him and stood there for a minute, studying Brad.

"You like her?" Tom asked.

"Yeah." Brad didn't make eye contact.

"You want to sleep with her?"

"I'm dealing with it."

Tom put his hands on his hips, and blew out a noisy breath. He walked down the hall and gestured for Brad to follow. "I hope the way you're dealing with it is by convincing yourself it's the worst idea you've ever had."

"The thought crossed my mind."

"And if you tried to do this, not only would you be compromising her integrity, you'd be putting everything she's working for on the line. She risked a lot to come here, and you could make it blow up in her face."

"She can always get another job," Brad grumbled.

Tom stopped and pushed Brad into the wall, hard. Tom's face made it clear that they were both surprised by his force.

"I won't try anything." Brad finally looked Tom in the eye to show his friend his sincerity.

"You guys are like brothers to me. It's my job to protect this band and do what's best. But I'm telling you right now, you cross that line—you hurt her or her business—I'm with Sue." Tom stabbed his fingers through his hair, pulling on it before dropping his hand again. "I didn't hire her so you could have another piece of ass. I hired her because she is the best possible person to do this. If you ruin it, I'm gone."

"Tom, I—"

"I don't want to hear it. She's an adult. If she wants you, that's between you and her. But the second you fuck things up for her, I'm out."

"Okay," Brad whispered.

"I'm gonna be sick." Tom stormed the last few feet to his room and slammed the door behind him.

Brad lingered in the hall for a minute, dazed, before he continued to his room. When he finally swung the door open, he slammed it into the wall.

Justin stopped brushing his damp hair. "I was about to see if you guys wanted to hit some bars. Looks like you want to hit something else instead."

"Sue and Chris are too drunk to do anything. Tom is puking." Brad flung himself on one of the beds and stared at the ceiling. He didn't know how to process Chris and Tom's threats and had forgotten Justin would be here.

"Tom is sick before Chris?"

"Might be a draw."

"What do you want to hit?" Justin asked.

"Chris."

"Too drunk to make it worthwhile?"

Brad shrugged, embarrassed to admit he wanted to hit Chris for figuring him out.

"What's up?"

"You know how Chris is when he drinks." Brad pushed up on his elbows.

"Doesn't stop talking."

"Yeah."

"And?" Justin asked.

"He told me not to fuck Sue." Brad hoped he sounded irritated, but shit, he was surprised Chris had picked up on anything. That guy was usually too busy hating on her and hitting on chicks to notice anything else.

Justin rubbed his mouth. "Staking a claim?"

"Doubtful. Then Tom threatened me." Brad sat all the way up.

"Wow, staking a different claim."

"I guess." Brad hung his head, thinking and avoiding Justin in case that joker decided to threaten him, too.

"Obviously this ruined your buzz. Let's go to some bars." Justin walked toward the door. "You coming?"

"Yeah, what the hell."

They made it out of the hotel, in and out of one bar and into another, keeping the conversation casual the whole time. Brad had almost convinced himself that Justin would let Chris's comment go, but he knew better. He knew Justin rode with Sue between tour stops to keep Brad from having an excuse to be alone with her. That knowledge burned at him. He wished they could all fight it out and be done. Instead, they danced around it.

A harried bartender with pink hair and nipples hard enough to break glass served them fresh long necks, then moved to the next guy down the line.

"You think it'll work with Sue?" Justin asked.

"Huh?" Brad acted startled.

"You heard me. You going for it?"

"What makes you ask that?"

"That bartender is exactly your type, and you didn't even give her rack a second glance. That means you're preoccupied with someone else. I think you've been into Sue ever since she gave you those naughty and nice stickers in Maryland."

Brad turned his back to the bar and set his gaze on the crowd in front of him. "That long?" He chugged his beer, then tapped the bottle against his leg. "Fuck."

"So." Justin poised his bottle in front of his mouth. "You think it'll work?" He sipped his drink.

"I think she sees me as the one guy in the band who hasn't tried to torture her yet."

"Yet."

Apparently being supportive wasn't in Justin's wheelhouse.

"Tom's right, she's risked too much. I need to stay away, let her prove herself." Brad banged a fist against the bar. "Why did Tom have to find the one good-looking woman with a brain *and* a personality to hire?"

Justin laughed. "He can't help who he's related to. Besides, like the rest of us, Tom doesn't like boring women. Even if he's not going to bed with them."

Brad beat his thumb against his beer. Women were the one thing they all had in common. When it came to those they had a real interest in, they all preferred women who had something to say. Even Chris.

"She works with us," Justin said. "You can't do it."

"I'm trying to keep my distance."

"It's been pretty obvious." Justin lifted his bottle to the bartender for more beer.

"I figured that out." Brad beat his thumb against his thigh. "Which makes it even worse because it's obvious and she's ignoring it."

"She's got a job to do. Besides, she's in PR. She's supposed to control the story. If she dates you, she *is* the story. It's not fair to put her in that position."

"I know." Brad pulled out cash to pay the bartender. "I'll get over it."

"You know a great way to get over a woman?"

Brad shook his head, defeated and surprised. Encouraging casual sex wasn't Justin's usual MO. "I'm not into the idea of a random hookup right now."

"Yeah, but there's a cutie staring at you." Justin gestured to a perky blonde with a ready smile. "And a little conversation never hurt anyone."

Brad gave it his best effort, but despite a few inebriated offers to stay elsewhere, he and Justin went back to their hotel as dawn broke.

"You remember how Sue met that mullet guy in Oklahoma City?" Justin asked as they made their way to the elevator.

"Unfortunately."

"Chris and I weren't expecting her to meet someone, which amused her to no end."

Brad pushed the elevator call button and racked his brain for a way to change the subject.

"It got me thinking that maybe she should have someone to hang with."

"Yeah?" Brad raised an eyebrow.

"Carlo's flying in the day after tomorrow for the Latin music events. I'm gonna introduce them."

Brad's gut clenched. "Okay."

"You sure?"

"Nope." Brad beat his thumbs against his thighs. "But I'll deal."

Leave it to Justin. Carlo could lift an eyebrow and women came running. Brad had seen it happen before, and it gutted him to imagine Sue reacting that way. He couldn't compete with that.

If Sue and Carlo met and hit it off, that door would be closed to Brad forever. Fuck Justin for knowing him so well.

Sue woke at two in the morning and tossed and turned for a few minutes before she figured out the pounding came from her door, not her head. She stumbled out of bed, looked through the peephole, and opened it with a sigh.

"Sue." Darryl pressed his head against the small opening, making her jump. "I dreamt about the interviews and it freaked me out."

"How did you find my room?"

"Chris said you were four doors from the elevator. Now focus." Darryl knocked on the door one time. "My dream."

"Ugh. I was dreaming about Joe Perry." She pushed Darryl's head back, unlatched the door, and opened it, motioning him in. As soon as Darryl closed the door, Sue climbed into bed.

"I'm nervous about the interviews and I can't get back to sleep."

"I'm sure you can get some sleeping pills from the front desk." Sue burrowed into the bed.

"I hate pills. I wanna talk about this. Please?"

"Darryl, *I* need to sleep."

"You don't have to talk. Besides, there's plenty of time for you to recover, Miss Margarita."

The more Darryl talked, the more her aggravation grew. He'd handled the few interviews the band given in the past, and he'd done well. She didn't believe for a second that Darryl had any nerves. "Yep, and if I go back to sleep now, there's a good chance Joe Perry'll be waiting for me."

"Naked?"

"That'd be nice, wouldn't it?"

"Pleasuring you with those guitar-playing fingers," Darryl said in a low voice.

Sue smiled and sank further into the bed, humming as she pulled the blankets tight under her chin.

"So," Darryl leaned closer to Sue, his voice even lower. "Is fondling his wrinkles part of your foreplay?"

Sue sat bolt upright, almost butting heads with Darryl in the process.

"Out!" She pointed to the door. "Get out!"

He fell back, laughing.

Sue shoved at him with the soles of her feet.

"Come on, take a little walk with me." Darryl patted her foot as his laughter subsided.

"No." Sue sat back with her arms crossed.

"Please? I didn't mean it about the wrinkles. I'm sure

he doesn't have many."

"Keep digging, D."

"I'm sorry. Joe Perry is awesome. Forgive me and take a walk with me."

"No. Get. Out. I need to sleep."

"Chris said some guy was all over you in the lobby. You getting your freak on? Is he hiding in here?"

"We are not having this conversation." Sue kicked off the blankets and got out of bed. She put her hands on her hips and paced. The guy in the lobby—her backup photographer—had been there and gone in a blink, but it shouldn't surprise her that Chris had noticed. He was a pain in the ass, even drunk.

"There's nothing wrong with getting a little on the road, Sue." Darryl leaned on his elbows and smirked.

She dug through her duffel and yanked out a cardigan. She put it on over her tank top and stepped into sandals. She had no intention of changing out of her yoga pants. This wouldn't be a long walk. She gestured toward the door. "You wanted to take a walk?"

"Oh yeah!" Darryl hopped off the bed.

"I'm gonna book photo shoots for you for every spare moment you get." Sue closed the door and jiggled the handle.

"I deserve it."

"It's not even the least of what you deserve." Sue didn't speak again until they got to the lobby. "My head's spinning. I need some water."

Darryl found a vending machine and bought them each a drink.

"Looks like there's a light breeze out there." He gestured toward the patio. "Might be nicer."

Sue followed him to a set of lounge chairs past the pool, at the far end of the patio. She let the breeze wash over her, taking away some sleepiness.

"How were the shows in Little Rock and Lubbock?" She gulped from the bottle, the cool water staving off the parched feeling in her throat.

"Great. We used the new opening and the crowd went wild."

"It's a cool way to open the set." Sue stretched her arms over her head, alert now and engaged in the conversation. "I'm sorry I missed it. You guys put on a good show."

"Serious?"

"Yeah. Why are you surprised?"

"I know you're a rock chick, but you're here for business. When the suits from the label come out, they stand there dead-eyed. They're counting ticket sales and how many T-shirts we move. They never even tap their toes."

"I'm not one of the suits."

"You're right," Darryl said. "Sorry to lump you in with them."

Sue picked at the label on the bottle. She understood why Darryl had called her a suit. She still didn't like it. She'd chosen this profession because she loved music. Record labels and corporate radio limited what people heard; she wanted to get more music out. She needed to make money, but it wasn't her primary motivation. Words Fail Me made great music, and the world deserved to hear it. Her job was to make sure that happened.

She didn't need to rehash that with Darryl. She'd given them the sales pitch back in Maryland. She pushed her hair off her face. "It's not only me. The crowds love you guys. It's fun watching everyone get into it."

"That's so cool."

"You earn it every night."

"I can't believe the way things are happening for us." Darryl sat back and crossed his legs at the ankle.

"Why not? You work hard."

"The realist in me thought it was all a fantasy." Darryl chugged some water. "Plus, you hear all these stories from other bands about how they went after it for years and years before they got their break."

"It took you guys a while to get one."

"Only a year after we got serious. We didn't get regular gigs until a few years ago when Brad and Justin graduated. About nine months later, we were invited on a summer tour."

"It is fast, but you're good. And it's not like the band is new. You've been together for a while."

"Yeah, I guess." Darryl got up and paced. "We didn't even have a full-length album out when things started happening for us. Maybe we should've."

"Why?"

"There's always the one-hit wonder fear. Two-hit wonder for us. And I don't want to read about my life, you know?"

"Like in the tabloids?"

"Yeah."

Sue couldn't do anything about his fear or the concerns they both had about their respective careers, but she knew all about the tabloids. "I'll control them. All you'll ever read in the rags is how we had to hire a security team to fend off women."

Darryl laughed and sat on the end of his lounge chair. "That'd be nice, I think. I like the attention, but I don't wanna be a groupie magnet. I don't want my mom hearing that."

"Wow." Sue pulled her sweater closed. "I thought easy sex was a big motivation to be a rock star. You broke the stereotype."

"I'm a simple guy. I love the music I play and the guys I play it with. If I become a star in the process, it's a fringe benefit."

Sue leaned forward to study Darryl. He reclined in

the lounge chair and watched the stars with a small smile. He was telling the truth. If he stayed this relaxed and sincere during interviews, journalists would love it. Sincerity made great articles. Seeing the press treating his buddy well might assuage some of Chris's concerns about the media's agenda, too.

"So, simple guy, if you weren't in this band, what would you be doing?"

"I'd still be working at the recording studio back home, saving money to open a music shop."

"A music shop?"

"Yeah, a place full of axes and drums and all kinds of funky, cool instruments. I'd let people come in and play as long as they wanted to unless they tried playing 'Stairway to Heaven.'"

Sue laughed and stretched. "Sounds like a nice life."

"Yeah. I still plan to do it one day."

Sue closed her eyes for a moment. "Cool."

"Thanks." Darryl patted her leg. "You look genuinely tired. I'm sorry!"

"Eh. I had to get up at some point." Sue drained her water bottle, then scrunched it.

"Come on, you should go back to bed." Darryl stood and offered his hand. "And Joe Perry."

"I'm not gonna argue." Sue put the cap on her water bottle, made sure she had her room key, then took Darryl's hand. The next thing she knew, she was airborne, about to land in the pool. She pulled her legs close and held her breath before she hit the frigid water. She surfaced, spitting and cursing. "You son of a bitch!"

Darryl laughed and pointed at her from the poolside. "Don't bring my mom into this. She could kick your ass!"

Sue snarled as she swam to the ladder. Darryl played dirty. Getting her out of bed and keeping her off guard only to toss her into a pool? He'd pay for this. Dearly.

"Thank you, ladies and gentlemen, thank you very much." Darryl waved and bowed to an imaginary audience.

"That was so cheap!" Sue threw her water bottle at him, then tugged her sweater over her chest. The pool was fucking cold.

"Those are the breaks!"

"Ooh, you have no idea how bad it's gonna get." Sue climbed out of the pool. She'd find a way to pants this asshole while he was on stage. Maybe she'd arrange something when they got to New Orleans.

"Aww, how bad, Suzy?"

"One of us may drown before this ends." Sue rung her sweater out on Darryl's feet.

"Bring it."

Sue's alarm went off at nine. She texted Tom, then went to the hotel gym to burn off some nervous energy. She'd gotten them some press before she'd joined the tour, but this was the first round of interviews, the first time they'd watch her handle journalists. The first time they'd see in person what she could—or couldn't—do for them.

Sue got off the treadmill twice before she finally finished her workout. Concerned about Chris and Tom having hangovers, she delivered water and sports drinks to their rooms. The second time, she picked up donuts and left a box at each of their doors, relieved to see they'd each brought the fluids into their rooms. She needed them ready to go, or it wouldn't matter how she handled the reporters. The last time Sue stepped on the treadmill, she cranked up the volume on her MP3 player and zoned out for more than thirty minutes.

Once she had a grip on her nerves, she went to her room to get ready. She'd originally planned to wear her gray dress for the interviews, but sadly, her attempts with stain remover and a sponge hadn't salvaged it from the hot-sauce fiasco.

Instead of the dress, she paired fitted jeans with a belted tunic and a suit jacket. She rolled up the sleeves and slipped on a pair of black pumps. Something about a formal shoe always made her feel more professional, no matter what she wore.

Sue arrived at the club before the band. She wanted to check out the space ahead of them. Couches lined the perimeter of the small room with a tiny stage in the corner diagonal from the door. A narrow staircase ascended the wall to her left, behind a small bar. A few staffers lingered; one stocked the bar, another swept the stage, and a third arranged chairs of varying sizes and styles.

The sound engineer greeted Sue and led her up the stairs. He directed her to a room at the front of the building with windows overlooking the street.

The walls were decorated with photos from on-site performances and shots of the city. It was enough to give people something to look at without being distracting or intimidating. Two big armchairs with ottomans sat with a rocker and an overstuffed couch arranged in a circle by the windows. A beat-up trunk served as a coffee table. Several bottles of water sat on the center of it. A counter with a few high-backed stools lined the wall behind the couch.

The engineer showed her a collection of small body microphones, explaining how they worked and assuring her that he'd be there all day, making sure the recording equipment worked properly and the interviewers left with their audio.

Happy that the area looked more like a coffee shop than a radio booth, Sue had one final touch to add. "Can we have some music in here?"

"Sure, we can pipe in the house music. All I have to

do is flip a switch."

Sue appreciated the suggestion, but she didn't want music that might distract the guys. "I have a playlist on my MP3 player. Can we bring it in at a low volume?"

"Not on your phone?"

"And be separated from my lifeline?"

The engineer chuckled. "Never. I can pipe in the MP3 player."

Sue queued up a carefully curated playlist, set it to loop, and handed over the device. Satisfied that they were ready to go, she went downstairs to wait for the guys.

The guys all walked in together, talking. Darryl and Justin seemed like their usual selves. Chris sipped on a bottle of water but didn't look hungover, a good sign. Brad's faraway gaze suggested he was someplace else mentally. His finger movements looked like he played chords in his head, even though he didn't have his arms in "air guitar" position. Tom, pale on the best of days, had the glossy pallor of someone about the hurl. Whether from nerves or a hangover, she wasn't sure. If Tom had the only hangover in the group, she'd handle it.

When Sue joined them, they immediately stopped talking.

"Hey." She gave them a big smile. "Do you guys want to hang out here until the DJ shows, or do you want to get settled in upstairs? It looks a lot like a living room. You'll like it."

"Home-field advantage," Darryl said. "Let's go up now."

Sue led the way up the stairs, explaining that their first interviewer, a DJ who went by the name Jimmy Diamond, had worked with her in Hagerstown. She told them a little bit about his personality—a friendly guy, and first and foremost a music fan—and the types of questions he usually asked.

The band lingered for a minute near the doorway of the interview room, but Chris immediately walked all the way in, pulled an ottoman over to the trunk, and sat down. He put his water bottle on the floor next to him and made himself busy studying the photos as his right leg shook enough to power the entire building.

Once everyone was settled, Sue stepped out to greet the interviewer.

Jimmy smothered Sue in a hug the moment he saw her.

Sue swallowed a nervous giggle as she squeezed him back. "I take it you missed me?"

"Of course! You were the best promotions manager I ever worked with. You always got me the cherry concert hookups."

"Remember that while you're putting my boys under the microscope." Sue smiled at Jimmy. Back when she'd helped him get a lucrative promotion, he promised her the moon and stars. Luckily, when she'd called in her favor, he hadn't forgotten.

Jimmy tried to ruffle her hair, but she ducked out

of the way. "Hey, for their first radio interview, you couldn't have picked an easier mark."

"I wouldn't call you easy." Sue elbowed him. "This is my first interview, too. I wanted it to be friendly."

"You did so much to shine my star, I'll always help you out."

"Nah." Heat rose in her cheeks from both pride at his confidence in her and how she was capitalizing on it. "I just made sure the whole world heard your show."

"Let's break these boys in." He grinned and gestured to let Sue enter the room first.

For the second time that day, as soon as the guys saw Sue, they all stopped talking.

"Meet Jimmy Diamond. He's the host of the late-night show in Dallas. Jimmy, this is Words Fail Me."

They all shook hands and settled into their seats. The sound engineer mic'ed up everyone except Sue and Tom and ran a quick test. Jimmy sipped some water, then signaled for the recording to start. He went through a brief intro, then dove in.

"What's your favorite song on this album?"

As soon as Jimmy finished speaking, Bob Marley poured out of the recessed speakers, loud enough to be recognized, though soft enough not to overtake the interview.

Sue watched Chris as the music played. During her mock interviews with him, she'd asked a lot of ques-

tions about music. The playlist she built only had songs
she knew he loved. As the first song ended and the next
one began, Chris released the death grip he had on the
coffee table. He leaned back and smoothed his palm
over his head, a small smile forming on his lips. Sue
took her first full breath of the day when he stretched
his arms out before him and tapped his foot to the beat.

Once the first interview was under their belts, the
rest of the afternoon was a breeze. They did two more,
with Darryl ducking out of the last one for an exclusive with a special interest magazine. She knew the
next day would be equally effortless now that they had
some experience. She didn't worry about having to split
them up to cover all the press. She just hoped she had
planned it right so they wouldn't have to cut an interview short before their show.

While the guys said their goodbyes before leaving for
soundcheck, Sue stood at the bar with her laptop, going
over the next day's schedule.

"Hey." Tom dropped his tablet on the bar next to her,
interrupting her concentration, and crushed her in a
bone-shattering hug.

"Whoa!"

"Thank you," he said without letting her go. "I can't
believe how well today went. I know the music was your
idea. You had them ready, you got them relaxed. Thank

you. I never could've done all this."

"You're welcome," she whispered. She blinked back tears, finally feeling accomplished.

Sue planned it so the band didn't have time to do a postmortem on their first round of interviews. They had a set to play. About halfway through the opening song, she got a glimpse of a euphoric look Brad gave his guitar. She made a note to get a photo next time—it'd make a great meme for the band.

When the set ended and the gear had been handled, Sue left the merch table and went to the dressing rooms, where she found Darryl with his head practically in the sink and a towel over his shoulders.

"Good show. Where are the guys? We're going dancing, right?" Sue tapped her toe expectantly. After a great day of interviews, Sue was taking a victory lap on the dancefloor. She'd even changed into her favorite pants and a vintage Adam Ant concert tee.

"Of course we're dancing!" Darryl said, his head still in the sink.

"What're you doing?"

"The stage was an oven, so I dumped water on my head. Some of the goop in my hair ran into my eyes. I'm trying to rinse it off."

Sue sauntered over, knowing this was something she could easily solve. "I've helped many girls in my college dorm with dye. I am excellent with heads in sinks."

Darryl laughed and righted himself as Sue approached. "I can handle it, thanks."

"I promise I'm good at this." She opened the faucet and put her fingers into the water to gauge the temperature.

Darryl closed the tap. "After last night, I figure I shouldn't be anywhere near you and water."

"I have no idea what you're talking about."

"No idea? You seemed pretty sober after I tossed you into the pool."

"No witnesses, never happened." She had been sober when she climbed out of the pool, and she would be sober when she enacted her revenge—some other night.

Darryl's eyes widened a fraction. "You're hardcore."

"No, I want to freaking go dancing and not have to worry about you for a night." Sue turned the water back on and moved Darryl toward the basin. "Now get your head in the damn sink." She pushed his head under the faucet and worked soap and water through his spikes. It only took her about two minutes to get all the paste out.

Darryl finger combed his wet hair and grinned. "Nice job!"

"I told you. Always trust a girl with thick hair. We know all kinds of tricks." Sue gave him the towel she had used to dry her hands. "Are you gonna spike it again?"

"Not the way I normally do," he said. "It'll only take a

minute."

"Cool. Mine needs a brush out." Sue pulled a comb out of the wristlet she carried. "Where is everyone?"

"Brad's in there." Darryl pointed to a door near the sink. "Taking a shower. Justin's watching Skein. I don't know where Chris is. Probably on the bus sleeping."

"Chris wears himself out, doesn't he?"

"Sometimes. He gave up a lot to chase this thing. He forgets he can always go back."

"Going back isn't always easy." What did she have to go back to? A half-furnished townhouse and a low-paying job she'd been sure to fill before she left.

"Maybe a better way to put it is that he can always start over. You know, finish college, carve out a normal life." Darryl poured a mountain of gel into his hands. He shook them, making the gel jiggle, then wiggled his butt before closing his hands together.

"Did you leave school or anything?"

"Nah." Darryl swirled his hands through his hair, occasionally pulling them out, making strands poke out, then swirling his fingers back in. "I took classes at community college and worked at a recording studio."

"Why didn't you go to the University of Michigan?"

Darryl shrugged. "My sister's the smart one in the family. She's working with NASA to make prosthetics. Real *Iron Man* type shit. I never had the drive for any of that. All I really want to do is make music." Darryl picked up a wide-toothed comb and selectively combed sections of his hair, pointing all his spikes in one direction. "I took some business classes so I could figure out how to open a music store. Mostly I hung out at the recording studio, jamming with anyone who'd let me." Once he threw the comb back on the table, his hair looked like small spikes about to take flight.

Sue liked it.

"I'm ready, what about you?" Darryl gave her a once-over. "Nice pants. You're rocking that crystal belt."

"Thanks." Sue pulled the loose end of the belt through her hand. "I bought it for my friend Robin. He won't mind me taking it for a spin. Should we text the guys? Invite them again?"

"Why not?" Darryl pulled out his phone and sent a message. Another phone chirped near the sink. "Oh yeah, Brad's still in the shower. Hang on."

Darryl knocked on the door to the bathroom and cracked it open as Sue bent at the waist, flipped her hair over, and brushed furiously.

"Sue and I are about to head out to the clubs, you wanna come?"

"I don't know." Brad's voice echoed out of the small bathroom. "I'm kinda tired."

Sue stilled the comb in her hair to hear them better. She hoped Brad stuck with his excuse. She didn't want to treat him differently, but given his crush, some distance was good.

"We don't have anything until like four tomorrow. You can sleep all day."

Darryl's feet shuffled against the floor as he re-entered the room. Brad's boots thumped after him.

Sue straightened out, cocking her hip for balance, and flipped her hair back. She ran her fingers through it as it settled around her face.

"I, uh, let me grab a shirt." Only wearing jeans, Brad walked to a pile of duffel bags, obviously forgetting the shirt he held.

Darryl grinned and walked over to Sue. "I think Brad likes your pants, too."

Sue rolled her eyes.

Darryl laughed and patted Sue's back. "You're all right." He turned to Brad. "Come on, dickhead, put on whatever's in your hand and let's go."

"Huh?" Brad glanced at the shirt, then pulled it over his head.

———

Brad acted casual, using Darryl as a buffer between him and Sue as they walked to another rock club. The band had been good and the beers ice cold, but when the band took their break, some asshole queued up boy bands on the jukebox.

Once back on the street, Brad asked, "Where to now?"

"Are there any good Latin clubs?" Sue asked.

"Oh, yeah." Darryl jerked his head to the left. "Follow me."

Habana's was a different world. The house lights were low, and colored spotlights swirled throughout the club. People spun, shook, and laughed all over the club. Skirts and scarves fluttered nonstop. The sounds of horns and guitars drowned out most everything else.

As soon as Sue made it past the bouncer, she got on the dancefloor, pulling Darryl behind her. Brad took advantage of the unguarded moment to openly watch her. She showed Darryl a few steps, and the two of them let the crowd engulf them. Sue's concert tee and Darryl's Hawaiian shirt made them stand out from the other patrons, who were more formally clothed in airy dresses and tuxedo shirts. Then again, Sue would still stand out. She brought light wherever she went.

Brad found a seat at the bar and enjoyed the view. He hadn't known Darryl to be much of a dancer; the guy mostly bopped his head and tapped his toes. But D could obviously follow instructions or else he'd be flat on his ass with the other dancers running right over him. Sue blew Brad away.

She danced as though she'd been born doing it. She never looked at her feet, her body moving in perfect time with the music. If she made a mistake, it was impossible to tell. With frequent bouts of laughter and a smile planted on her face, she worked her way around the dancefloor, her hips, legs, and shoulders in constant motion. At one point she danced around Darryl with her hair gathered up and held to her head while she pretended to hold a skirt with her other hand.

One song bled into the next, never leaving a moment's pause. Eventually Darryl said something to Sue that had her shooing him away. She kept dancing and spinning until she wound up with another partner. Brad envied both the man's fortune on the dancefloor and Sue's confidence to stay out there without knowing another soul. She gave herself to the music in a way he couldn't unless he was playing an instrument.

"Why aren't you out there dancing?" Darryl signaled to a mustached bartender for two bottles of water.

"I don't know how to dance to this."

"Neither do I! But damn, it's fun! Ask her to show you a few steps."

"I'd look like an idiot. I'd stomp all over her."

"There's a ton of people out there. Do you really think she's gonna notice how you dance? Or if you step on her feet?" As Darryl spoke, the floor opened up, and they got a clear view of Sue and her current partner. The guy was about an inch taller than her, wearing black pants and a white button-down shirt that stuck to him from perspiration. The guy tried snaking his arm around her waist, but she stopped him, yanking his hand away and pushing against him.

Sue shook her head at the sweaty beast. The asshole laughed and rested his hand on her waist again, this time without trying to drag her against him. Her knee coming dangerously close to his groin might have had something to do with that. Brad indulged himself with a fantasy of tossing the dipshit out the door.

Brad motioned to the bartender for another beer. Coming with them had been a bad idea. The dancing Sue had done during those moments between Darryl leaving her and another partner stepping in had seared itself into his brain. That wouldn't make it any easier for him to get past his emotions, and he needed to.

"Pardon me." A six-foot tall, slender Latin beauty stood next to Darryl, her hand on his biceps.

"Hola, señorita," he replied with a wide smile.

"Dance with me." Without waiting for his answer, the woman pulled Darryl toward the dancefloor.

He grinned at Brad. "If you're not gonna dance, at least bring Sue some water!" He pointed to the bottle on the bar near Brad's elbow.

Brad glanced at the drink, then back at Darryl, already in the middle of the dancefloor with his beautiful new friend, a smile on his face as electric as the music that pulsed through the club.

"He's right. Take her the water," the bartender said. "It can get hot out there. You'd be her hero."

Brad gave the bartender a long look, grabbed the bottle, and headed for Sue. It took him a few minutes to navigate through the tide of dancers. When he finally got to her, he put one hand on her shoulder and touched the cold water against her neck. Sue leaned her head back against it.

"That feels so good!" she shouted.

Her dance partner tried to grind her hips again.

"Not you!" she said, then spun around.

"Thirsty?" Brad asked, showing her the water.

Sue gave him a huge smile and twined one arm with his as she grabbed the water. "You have perfect timing," she said into his ear. "I'm dying of thirst, and I thought that guy would never let go!" She kept one arm around Brad and drank most of the bottle in one shot.

Intimidated by their physical closeness and not knowing what else to do, Brad put a hand on her hip, gently rubbing the soft leather of her pants, and stared down her former dance partner until the guy finally paired up with someone else far away. "Glad to be of service."

"It's about time you got your ass out here!" Sue picked up her dance, one hand on Brad's shoulders, the other holding the water bottle.

"I can't dance." Brad stepped back, managing to keep his fingertips on her hip. "D was gonna bring the water to you, but he got kidnapped." Brad pointed out Darryl in the arms of a woman a good three inches taller than him, grinning like the cat who ate the canary.

Sue laughed. "I'm not gonna steal him back. You're getting a crash course!"

"What?" Panic like he'd never experienced before set in. He couldn't dance, and he definitely couldn't dance with her. Not when he was supposed to be getting over her. "I can't!"

Sue laughed. "It's just a dance!"

Brad finally understood that she wanted what Darryl had given her. He assented.

Sue showed him some steps, which he forgot the moment she put her hands on his waist and had him move with her. After a few minutes of forcing himself to concentrate on Sue's feet and not how close they were or where she touched him, Brad finally caught on. She let go of him and they danced.

The first three songs were fast paced and fun. He'd almost forgotten his panic when he figured out how to keep up. They danced together and with other people in the crowd. Once he got comfortable, he tried to impress her, which only made her laugh. Even though he was acting ridiculous, he enjoyed himself. During the fourth song, the bartender passed through the dancers with a tray of tequila shots. His nametag read "Victor."

Brad slid the man cash as he and Sue each took a glass. "Thanks, Victor!"

Sue clinked her drink to Brad's before swallowing the shot and returning the empty to the tray, staying in constant, sensuous motion.

The fifth song was a merengue.

Brad begged ignorance of the dance and moved toward the bar. Sue grabbed him by the belt loop and pulled him back, her lips right next to his ear, her breath raising goose bumps along his neck.

"It's easy, all in the hips." She let go of his belt loop and squeezed his sides. "You can learn as you go. Let the music guide you." She moved him into position and picked up the dance.

Brad's head spun, hyper aware of Sue's body. He couldn't tell her how he felt, but did she sense the weight of his stare? His pulse speeding up when she danced closer? Would she notice—and please, please—react to his nonverbal cues? Despite his fervent wishes, she seemed engrossed in the music. He was an idiot. She wanted to dance. She'd told him that from the start. He should've believed her. Her sudden laughter jarred him from his thoughts. "What?" Brad asked, afraid that he had messed up the steps.

"Look." Sue pointed out Darryl.

Enraptured with his new friend, Darryl struggled to keep up. Under different circumstances he'd be doing well, but next to the young woman's elegant figure, Darryl's shorter, stocky build looked clumsy. The lucky fucker didn't seem to care. He and the woman were lost in each other.

Sue pulled Brad's hand over her head and spun. He trailed behind her on the floor the way the other men did with their partners and resolved that this would be the last time he looked at her with interest. Her hair looked like dark copper silk swirling around her shoulders. Her leather pants clung to her hips and thighs and calves. He slowly lifted his gaze, certain she would stop turning soon. Halfway up her body, her crystal belt sparkled and shone in the light, setting off her waist with reflections of the different colored spotlights that hit them. With her arms extended, her shirt slid up and revealed a taut pale stomach. He stretched his fingers out along the edge of her pants to feel her muscles as she moved.

Another couple bumped Sue, and she fell against him. Instinctively, he put his arms around her waist, one hand in the center of her back to help her regain her balance. He froze, not sure what to do next.

"I'm so sorry! I'm sorry!" a petite blonde said. "Are you okay? I didn't know how close I was!"

"Oh, I'm fine." Sue straightened out of Brad's arms and smiled at the clumsy dancer. She smoothed her hair off her face and glanced toward Brad.

He kept his hand on the small of her back. "You sure you're all right?"

"Yeah." Sue gave him a wide smile. "I'm thirsty."

Brad directed her toward the bar, letting her move away from his hand and making a conscious effort not to touch her again.

"Two waters, please!" Sue called out.

Victor gave her two icy bottles. Sue handed one to Brad and put the other on the back of her neck.

Victor filled a plastic bag with ice. "Put that on your neck, drink the water."

"Thanks!" Sue said.

"Sit!" Victor motioned to stools that were emptying as the music picked up. Sue hopped on one and patted the seat next to her.

"You hungry?" Victor asked. "I've got chips and

salsa."

Sue's face brightened. "That sounds great!"

Victor rapped on the counter and stepped away.

"You're not bad for a beginner." Sue nudged Brad with her elbow.

"It's easy to fake it in a crowd."

"Aw, come on, you were great out there."

"Thanks, I guess. You made it easy."

Sue gulped some of the water. "It's all the music."

"Here you are!" Victor returned with a huge plate.

"Thanks!" Sue grabbed a chip and scooped some salsa.

"Tell me," Victor said, leaning on the bar, "who taught you to dance?"

"I learned some in school, and my *abuelita* taught me the rest."

"*Abuelita*? You are Spanish?"

"On my mother's side," Sue said. "My dad is Irish."

"That explains it." Victor smacked the bar. "You move like a Latina, but you don't look like one."

Sue held up her hands and shrugged.

Victor chuckled. "Some of the best things are surprises!" He picked up Sue's left hand and kissed her knuckles.

"Hey now." Brad kept his tone light, but he wasn't about to watch another man hit on Sue. Again. "It's gonna take more than salsa and compliments to get her attention."

"What're you worried about? You're the one she's been dancing with." Victor rolled his eyes and moved down the bar, taking drink orders from other people.

Sue grabbed more chips, then pushed the tray toward Brad.

He dug in. "Does that bother you?"

Sue swallowed. "What?"

Brad scooped salsa onto a chip. "That you don't look Spanish."

She circled a chip in the salsa. "It bothers me that I don't look like my mom."

"Why?" Brad nudged her and waited for her to meet his gaze. He wanted to see her face when he shared this tiny piece of his feelings. "You're gorgeous."

She rolled her eyes and pushed his hand away. "My mom has mahogany hair that falls in waves, her eyes glow, and her lips are naturally ruby red. Her skin has a golden undertone." She drank some water, then continued. "When I was five, we moved to a very wealthy suburb. People who didn't know us said shitty things about her being my nanny."

"Why would they even care?"

"Because that breed of rich people—old money—they think their opinions are important. Critical."

Brad grunted, pushing salsa onto the chip she'd dipped into the edge of the bowl, then shoveled a heaping helping into his mouth.

"I always wanted to look like my mom because she's the most beautiful woman I've ever seen. As I got older, I wanted to look like her to shut those assholes up." Sue sighed. "Plenty of Spaniards have red hair."

"Sue." Brad rubbed her lower back, at a loss for what to say.

"Does it bother you?"

"Nothing about you bothers me." He gave her an overly dramatic wink.

Sue laughed and shifted away from his touch. "No, that people might not know that you're Native American."

"Ah." Brad stared into his beer bottle and swirled the liquid. She didn't want him to touch her off the dancefloor, but this woman was asking him soul-deep questions. It was a difficult combination. "Not in the way you'd think."

"Then how?"

Brad straightened his posture on the stool, grabbed his hair into a loose ponytail, then pulled his hand down the length. "I'm afraid it'll get lost. It's vital to me, but away from my family, my life is *so* white. I don't want my identity to get lost in all the whiteness."

Sue widened her eyes and dropped the chip she'd been holding.

Overwhelmed that she finally saw him, Brad turned his gaze to the food. He fished out her abandoned chip, loading it with salsa. "Annabelle looks like a fucking Native American warrior goddess. I stick close to her and it's all good."

Sue gave Brad a small smile and squeezed his arm.

Awe caught his voice. That she knew not to speak after his confession struck him.

"More chips for the dancing lady!" Victor refilled the tray with multicolored chips and produced a little tub of cheese dip.

"Thanks, Victor!" Sue tried the dip, then pointed a thumb at Brad. "Did you know this guy is in a band?"

Brad's emotions seesawed again. Victor saved him from his emotional overwhelm, but Sue pimping him while he sat next to her was another heady experience.

"He is?" Victor eyed him.

"Yeah! They have a show tomorrow night. Brad's the lead singer."

"Obviously it's not a Latin band, or he'd be a better dancer."

"Does your boss get pissed that you talk so much?" Brad took a swig of water.

Victor smiled and gave him a beer.

"Come on, Victor, be nice. He was pretty good out there."

"At least he didn't knock you over like that *gringa* did!" Victor gestured toward the blonde, still stumbling on the dancefloor.

"Seriously, do you do any work back there?" Brad asked.

Sue carried on as though Brad hadn't said a word. "Brad's in a rock band called Words Fail Me."

"The ones who sing *Midnight Mountain*?"

"Yeah!"

"I love that song!" Victor leaned back and took in Brad. "You guys are great! You should've told me you were in a band. I would've been nicer to you!"

Brad smirked, then tipped his bottle to Victor before taking a drink.

"They're about to get a new song on the radio." Sue nudged Brad with her elbow.

"Which one? I downloaded the album," Victor said.

"You did?" People told Brad this all the time at their gigs and in various bars in Michigan. But here? Finding a fan in a place completely unrelated to the rest of his life was a high he hadn't expected.

"Yeah. You guys are big out here, man!"

"I told you." Sue patted Brad's shoulder.

He wanted to grab her hand, grab her *and* squeeze her, share this thrill. He kept his hands to himself, though, not willing to risk a rejection when he was so elated.

"Are you in the band, too?" Victor asked Sue.

"No, I'm their PR rep. I'm making them famous."

"Teach them how to dance. That'll be a big help." Victor saluted, then gave his attention to another customer.

"I can't believe that guy knows us." Brad tapped his hands against the bar, withholding the enormous *whoop* he wanted to let out.

"By the end of your show tomorrow, all of the Midwest will know you."

"Right." Brad sipped his beer. He needed to temper his ego. Victor was a random one-off.

"You guys get tons of downloads after your shows."

"Yep." Brad reached for more chips.

"I'll get the numbers after tomorrow's set. You'll see."

After they finished the chips and another round of beer, Sue declared that she wanted to hit the dancefloor again. She stood before Brad, tempting him with her swaying hips.

"If I go back out there, you're gonna make me pass out." He held back the fact that he wasn't sure if the exhaustion would come from trying to keep up with her or not being overwhelmed by being so close to her again. Not to mention that he liked her about a million times more now that he knew she saw him.

Victor leaned over the bar. "If he won't dance anymore, you can always dance with me."

"Really?" Sue had her hands on her hips, looking at Brad with her eyebrows raised.

"Yeah," Victor said. "I'm due for a break."

Brad smiled at Sue and gestured toward the dancefloor, encouraging her to go.

"Come on."

Victor skirted the bar, then offered Sue his arm. The two of them danced their way into the middle of the crowd toward Darryl, who still danced with the woman who'd kidnapped him earlier.

After a few songs Victor went back to the bar. Sue stayed on the floor, dancing with Darryl and his partner. Victor told Brad she was his wife's sister, Lena. After two more songs, Darryl joined Brad and Victor. The women continued to dance.

"Look at them!" Brad gestured toward the dancefloor once Darryl sat.

Sue and Lena danced with their right hands on the other's left shoulders, heads close as they talked. They moved in perfect rhythm with each other.

"They're something," Darryl agreed with a big grin.

"You hit the jackpot, D."

"I hope Sue doesn't tell Lena I'm a player or any-thing."

"She'd never lie about you, man." Brad clinked his beer bottle against Darryl's.

Lena and Sue stayed on the dancefloor until Darryl and Brad dragged them off. The music became tranquil, and the house lights came up, but the women managed to con one more dance out of them. After a few minutes of watching Darryl try not to get out of Lena's arms, Brad suggested they find a diner for an early breakfast.

CHAPTER 18

"You sound comfortable with that answer," Sue said.

"Any reason I shouldn't be?" Justin countered.

"No." Honestly, why Justin had avoided interviews flummoxed her. He was a natural, almost as good as Darryl and Brad. "Keep that confident tone during the actual interview and you're golden."

He beat his fingers against the café table. "Got it. Next question?"

"That's it, you answered them all."

"We completed my entire dossier?" Justin gave her an exaggerated look of surprise.

Sue fought back her chuckle before answering. Chris wasn't the only band member with pages of questions. She'd created interview prep documents for each of them, and for every interview they had scheduled straight through New Orleans. "For now, yes."

"Chris is gonna be so jealous. He said he has like a hundred pages to go."

Sue rolled her eyes. "Feels like it." She tapped her laptop closed and sat back. "I don't want you guys surprised by anything. If a reporter manages to slip something past me, I want you all comfortable enough to answer it on the fly or know what you'll say to shut it down."

"Solid plan. This interview will be easy, though. I've been reading this mag since I bought my first set of drumsticks. I'm ready."

"That's good to hear," Tom said, joining them in the small restaurant. "We have to head that way in about ten minutes."

"Not now?" Justin asked.

"Nope." Tom put his tablet on the table and surveyed the restaurant. "That guy looks a lot like Barry."

"What guy?" Sue asked.

"The guy with the '90s-era Bluetooth on his ear and the stick lodged up his khakis." Justin leaned forward and nodded toward an uptight-looking man walking the perimeter of the room. "That *is* Barry."

"I thought Carlo wouldn't be around until later tonight," Tom said.

"Carlo?" Sue asked.

"Giáncomo. From Cáceres," Justin said. "We toured together for about a month last summer. I invited him to join us."

"Justin, you should've told me you wanted to have lunch with Carlo; we could've prepped earlier." Sue checked her watch. "Now you only have enough time to say hello and goodbye."

Justin smirked and crossed his arms. "I didn't invite him to have lunch with me. I invited him to have coffee with you."

Sue scowled. "Don't be ridiculous. I have your interview in a few minutes, too."

"Nah, that's why I'm here." Tom shot her a grin. "Justin said you might want to skip this one. Now it makes sense."

"What? No!" Sue pushed back from the table and slid her laptop into her messenger bag. No fucking way. She had planned this whole week down to the second, and no way were these dopes gonna fuck it up, especially not with something like this. Not happening. Sue stood. "We're going. Now. You can apologize to Carlo later. Or have him meet you after the interview."

Tom tugged on her arm. "Come on, Sue. Don't be rude."

She let out a menacing laugh. "You're unfuckingbelievable, Tom. Everything we have riding on this, and you tell me not to be rude. Are you kidding me?"

Tom flinched, the color draining from his face.

"What's the risk?" Justin thumped a hand on the table. "It's a magazine I've been reading for years, and I'm not Chris. I can talk to people."

Sue sat and pushed her hand through her hair. Mentioning stakes was a serious fuck up on her part. She wasn't worried about Justin—not much, anyway—she was worried about whether or not the interview would get published. She needed as much proof as possible to show the record company that their stupid clause had been unnecessary. "I'm sorry, Justin. You're right. It's not you. I'm trying to get you guys as much good press as possible while we're here so we can get more and bigger press opportunities. I know you'll be great. I don't want to take that for granted."

Justin reached across the table, clapping a hand on her shoulder. "I won't let you down, Sexy Sue, but be nice to my friend. It's not his fault I didn't think through my timing."

Sue gave Justin a weak smile. "You're right. I'll be nice."

"What's taking Barry so long?" Tom asked. "We're running out of time. He's gotta get Carlo in here."

"He's probably triple checking that no one here has a press pass," Justin said. "Barry hates having reporters around Carlo when it's not something he's planned and has control over."

"Sounds like my kinda guy." Sue leaned forward and tracked Barry through the restaurant. He was short and slicked his hair back like a mobster. Hopefully he was nice. "Why aren't you setting me up with him?"

Tom tapped his tablet. "He's an abrasive dick."

"And he dates men," Justin said. "No interest whatsoever in womenfolk."

"Is he interested in Carlo?" Sue asked.

"Even if he was, they've worked together too long for Carlo to hold any appeal for him." Justin rested his arms on the table and leaned toward Sue, a glint in his eye. "And Carlo is extremely interested in womenfolk."

"Speaking of that interest, why are you setting me up with a man who lands a new woman every night?" Sue pointed at herself. "I'm into exclusivity."

"I can tell you from personal experience, Carlo doesn't spend time with groupies, nor does he date women who openly throw themselves at him. So be on your best behavior. Don't get all googly-eyed with the Latin lady killer."

"Please." Sue sipped from her water glass.

Tom knocked on his tablet. "Here he comes."

Carlo walked toward them, unaccompanied and smiling broadly.

Justin stood and Tom followed suit.

"Justin, Tom, it has been so long!" Carlo shook each man's hand.

"Good to see you again," Justin said. "I'd like to introduce you to Sue Douglas, our new PR person."

Sue stood and shook Carlo's hand. "Nice to meet you."

Carlo wore well-fitted slacks, a black button-down shirt that was open at the collar with the sleeves rolled up, and a leather cuff on his right wrist. His thick hair was brushed off his face.

"Tom and Justin speak highly of you," Sue said.

"All lies. They know too much." Carlo laughed.

"Carlo, why don't you take my seat. I have an interview to get to." Justin held his chair out.

"Actually," Sue said before Justin moved away from the table, "we all need to go to this interview. You're welcome to wait here or walk with us." Sue offered her sweetest smile as Justin's glare bored into her.

"You know, I had a very long flight. I would like to move around a bit." Carlo offered Sue his arm.

The gesture was a bit over the top, but she slung her messenger bag over her shoulder and accepted his arm. She'd promised Justin she'd be nice, and this man was rolling with the punches.

Carlo steered Sue through the restaurant and held the door for her. "I take it you showed Darryl Twitter?"

"I did. He's been tweeting a lot."

"Yes. In fact, he and I have tweeted back and forth quite a bit on his personal profile."

"Mmmm." Sue directed them toward the location for the interview, keeping her eyes in front of her. She'd had no idea Darryl had a personal Twitter account. When the fuck had that happened? How did she miss it? She didn't want Carlo, or anyone else, to know she'd been caught unaware. She pointed toward an office. "This is us."

Carlo held the door again, and she entered with Justin and Tom on her heels.

"How's it goin'?" Justin asked her in a low voice.

Sue rolled her eyes. "Amazing, we're already

engaged. I need you to focus on this interview."

"I told you, it's in the bag."

Sue tilted her head. "Prove it."

The journalist came out and introduced himself to everyone, including Carlo.

"This is quite the entourage you have," he said to Justin.

"Carlo's not here for the interview." Sue held out an arm to shield him. "He's visiting with Justin and not on the record."

Sue hadn't noticed Barry had followed them until he spoke. "All questions have to be pre-approved."

"Thank you, Sue, Barry." Carlo offered Sue a smile and glared at Barry. "I am certain the focus will be rightfully on Justin." He focused his attention on the reporter. "Justin should have your full attention. Pretend I'm not here."

"Not even to talk about collab you guys did?"

Justin pointedly looked away from Carlo. "That was more than a year ago."

Sue took his lead. "That's not—"

"If there is time at the end, perhaps." Carlo smiled and offered a hand to the man.

He shook it, then ushered Justin to another part of the room. Sue gestured for Tom to follow them, then turned to Carlo and Barry. "I appreciate your offer, but you don't have to do this. In fact, I'm certain we can find a private space for you if you'd like to wait. If you don't have time, I understand."

"He's not doing it." Barry's tone was brusque. "He has twenty minutes."

"Barry." Carlo's voice was firm. "I am right here and well aware of the schedule." Carlo glared at Barry for a moment, neither man giving an inch. Eventually Barry stepped back. "Sue, I would like to sit with you, even if it is only to listen to Justin's interview. We'll decide on questions if it comes to that."

"Okay." She led the way to Justin, who'd already established a comfortable rapport with the journalist.

Sue listened intently, jotting a few notes as the men talked. Carlo stayed at her side, quiet. A few times he nudged her and smiled when Justin had particularly good answers.

"You prepped him well," Carlo whispered toward the end of the interview.

"Thanks," Sue whispered back. Something about his expression made her confess. "I want them to succeed."

"It shows." Carlo squeezed her knee, his hand lingering until the interview ended and they all got up to leave.

Conveniently, Carlo's schedule got pushed back. Justin found a reason to leave, and Tom distracted Barry, allowing Sue and Carlo to sit and chat in the restaurant where they'd met earlier.

"Justin and Tom are great friends." Carlo moved the box of sweetener from the far edge of the table to the center. "But subtlety is not one of their strengths." He gave Sue a big smile and she laughed.

"They could learn a thing or two." Sue relaxed a bit, despite Justin blindsiding her and Carlo making himself familiar at the interview. She saw what made him an international heartthrob. His eyes twinkled when he laughed, and he had a natural charisma. Sue had noticed each time he touched her, yet she was comfortable with it, even though she'd just met the man. Did his fame lower that barrier, or was it simply him?

"How do you like life on tour?"

She considered her answer. "It's different from what I was expecting. I mostly like it."

"Mostly?"

"Days are topsy-turvy," Sue said. "Sometimes we're going almost twenty-four hours. Other times we go a few days barely seeing sunlight. It takes some getting used to."

Carlo nodded, then sipped his espresso. "It does. Though it seems to suit you."

"Thank you, but the jury is still out on that one. Ask me again as we wind down this tour."

Carlo gave a deep chuckle. "Darling, none of us have kind things to say about this life as the tour ends. Other than good riddance."

"And you all still do it over and over."

"We are like sharks." Carlo flashed bright white teeth. "If we are still too long, we die."

"Mind if I interrupt?" Tom pulled over a chair and sat, sliding his tablet onto the table. "Great interview, Sue. Justin nailed it."

Sue eyed him. "Do you really think I would've let you guys get away with this"—Sue gestured between herself and Carlo—"if I hadn't already known it'd be a slam dunk?"

Tom blushed and fiddled with a sugar packet.

"Well." Carlo adjusted his cuffs. "In your absence, we discussed favorite colors, foods, movies and pets."

"Did you?" Tom accepted the ribbing.

"Yes. We'd moved on to people we'd most like to shake." Sue gave her cousin a lethal glare.

Carlo leaned back and laughed. Joy looked good on him. His broad smile reached his eyes, and once again, Sue was charmed.

Tom held his hands up. "In my defense, this was all Justin's idea. He meant well."

"We know you both did." Carlo patted Tom's shoulder. "Next time you must be more discreet."

"Lord help them if there's a next time." Sue crossed her arms.

Carlo laughed again, and getting swept up in his mood, Sue laughed with him.

Tom cleared his throat. "How's Tony?"

"Ah, thank you for asking." Carlo bowed his head. "He's doing well. Focused on the fight."

"Fight?" Sue asked. She'd been doing a lot of that lately—fighting with Chris, fighting for connections, for interviews, for freaking photographers. She'd love to actually hit something and release some of her tension.

Tom wiped his tablet with a napkin. "Tony has a big one coming up."

"If you ask Tony, they are all big ones." Carlo raised his eyebrows.

"As big as the Heavyweight Championship this week?" Sue had purposely left that night open in their schedule so she could hole up in her hotel room and order the pay-per-view special.

Carlo looked surprised. "You follow boxing?"

"Follow boxing?" Tom raked his hair off his face. "Sue took lessons until she joined the tour."

"Not hardly, Tom." Sue refocused her attention on Carlo. "I have a friend who's an amateur boxer. Sometimes we worked out together. And yes, I like boxing."

Carlo narrowed his eyes. "You do boxing workouts?"

"Kind of?" Sue raised her eyebrows. "I hate exercise, but I like sports. Boxing was fun this past winter when the snow got out of hand. But the jump rope, bleh." She shivered.

Carlo laughed. "My brother says the jump rope is his

form of meditation."

"That's a level of dedication I will never achieve."

"Do you know who Tony Azzuré is?" Carlo leaned forward.

"Of course. He's about to be Heavyweight Champion. He practically dances when he boxes." Sue bit back the desire to talk about Azzuré's technique and how she thought he'd beat his latest challenger. Between keeping the guys in line and Tom boasting about her boxing workouts, she didn't want Carlo thinking she'd kick his ass. She probably could. He didn't need to know that, though. "I'd love to go to that fight."

"You would?"

"I've only been to amateur fights. Seeing a pro fight in person would be amazing. Especially an Azzuré fight."

"I have ringside seats." Carlo laughed when Sue's eyes got big. "Come with me."

Sue didn't know what to react to—his cherry seats, his invitation, or the fact that he laughed at her. "Are you kidding?"

"Of course not. I would love to take you," Carlo said.

Sue stared, certain she was having an out-of-body experience. Or vertigo. Or both.

Tom chuckled. "When's the fight?"

"Friday," Sue and Carlo answered.

"I can't go." Sue wilted. Even though she didn't entirely believe that Carlo had prime tickets, it didn't matter. She had a job to do.

"Why not?" Carlo asked.

"Wait." There were too many things she needed to know. "I know you're an A-list celeb, but how'd you get tickets? The match has been sold out since they announced it. Your name hasn't been on any of the who's-who lists when they talk about attendance."

"You are missing a key detail." Carlo folded his hands in his lap and grinned. "Tony is my brother. He uses our grandfather's name."

Carlo mimicked the stern face Tony made at every weigh-in, and the blood rushed from Sue's head. She saw the resemblance. Tony was wider and shaved his head, but their faces were similar, their postures, too.

"I think she might pass out." Tom snickered.

Sue sent him another glare but was too overwhelmed to arrange her racing thoughts into a retort.

Carlo leaned forward. "Come with me. I already have the flight arranged, and I'll put you on a plane the next morning so you can get right back to business." Sue hesitated, and he followed up with, "It'll be a night you'll never forget."

Sue slumped and rubbed her temples. Would she ever have another opportunity to go to a major fight like this? She had no idea. She did know she only had one opportunity to succeed with Words Fail Me.

Nope. She was staying put. Her pay-per-view plan was solid.

"Go." Tom looked her in the eye, his expression sincere. "The guys have a free day on Friday, and you can be back in plenty of time for the set on Saturday. Go."

"I have to follow up on interviews." Sue twisted her fingers in her lap as she agonized over what was at stake in her job, along with Chris telling her she didn't have time to date. Surely leaving the tour with a man she barely knew would register as a ten on Chris's Richter Scale of Drama.

"Your follow-ups are all phone calls. You can do that anywhere," Tom said.

"I need to send emails, too." Sue shook her head again, trying to send Tom a telepathic message.

"It's a chartered flight," Carlo offered. "You can email from the air."

"Chris?" Sue looked directly at Tom. She didn't dare speak of the payout clause hanging over their heads. Not even a hint after her earlier flub with Justin.

"I'll get him drunk. He won't even notice you're gone."

Sue let out a soft chuckle. Drunk or not, Chris would notice. He'd noticed a ten-second exchange while he was too drunk to stand and dished it to Darryl between heaving and passing out. That kid missed nothing.

"Chris'll be fine. He's coming around," Tom said.

Sure, Chris hadn't said anything to her about the guy in the lobby, but he'd still said something. Sue shifted tactics, not wanting to badmouth Chris in front of one of his friends. "The hotels are all booked."

"Tony has a dozen rooms reserved." Carlo grinned.

Sue faced Tom directly. Time to go there, damn it. "The stakes here are too high."

Tom tilted his head. "You already had the day off. We're on solid ground. Go."

Sue closed her eyes for a beat, grateful for his confidence but still not convinced. She dug deep for one last argument. "I don't have anything to wear, only jeans and T-shirts and a dress covered in hot sauce." Sue gestured down the front of her blouse.

Tom sighed. "You can take my credit card and buy something when you get there."

"Tom. You're willing to part with money so I can go?" Sue put a hand over her mouth, feigning shock.

"It's a sign. You must come." Carlo reached across the table and touched her hand. "The fight will not be the same without you."

Sue giggled. The Latin Lady Killer hadn't gotten to her, but the idea of seeing a title fight up close and personal sure had.

Carlo glanced at Tom.

Tom rolled his eyes and gave Sue an impatient look. "You're going?"

"Hell yes! I'm not missing the Heavyweight Title match, are you kidding me?"

Carlo laughed and patted Sue's hand again. "I'll call Tony and arrange for your room."

"Shit." Tom tapped his tablet. "Now I have to give her my credit card."

CHAPTER 19

During their flight, Sue sent interview confirmation emails while Carlo told her about building Cáceres as his brother made a name for himself as a boxer. His stories captivated her. Maybe Justin's instinct had been right.

She stepped off the plane in Las Vegas, surprised by the quiet at the executive airport, and climbed into a waiting town car with heavily tinted windows.

When they were both settled, Carlo asked, "Are you ready for the first real taste of how insane my life is?"

"It doesn't look so bad." Sue gestured to the empty airfield.

"You might change your mind about that in a minute."

The town car drove off the tarmac and around the airport building. When they got to the driveway leading to the street, photographers, news cameras and reporters crowded the sides of the driveway, snapping photos of the car.

"How do they know this is you?" Sue angled her body toward Carlo to focus on his answer, not the flashbulbs going off around the car. If Carlo had tricks to get press lined up—aside from tipping them off to his whereabouts—she wanted them.

"They don't. A lot of people are flying in for the fight. The regular airport is covered in press, too. If I lower the window and wave, they'll follow us back to the hotel. Where more press is waiting."

"Is this a regular day for you?" Sue ran a hand through her hair, considering what it would take to manage packs of media day in and out.

"No. We had coffee yesterday without a single snap of a camera."

"Sure, but the club last night had tons of reporters."

"Yes. That is exactly what I wanted. Cáceres lured them in and blew them away with fresh talent." He laughed and shook his head. "Sometimes the press is fun."

"You're right about that." Winning over journalists with a good hook was the high that had gotten Sue into Public Relations.

"Shall we stop at Neiman Marcus so you can spend some of Tom's money?" Carlo eyed her messenger bag, the only luggage she'd brought with her.

Sue pulled the bag close. "No, thank you. I'm good."

"Are you sure?"

"Yep."

Rather than deliver them to the portico at the front of the hotel, the driver pulled into the parking garage and stopped at a bank of elevators. Several photographers and cameramen waited on the other side of the car.

"Get ready." Carlo squeezed Sue's knee, then opened the car door nearest the elevators. Flashes immediately went off and questions were lobbed at him. He smiled for the cameras and gave a brief wave, then offered his hand to Sue.

"Carlo! Is Tony ready for this fight?" someone shouted as Sue got out of the car.

"Of course," Carlo answered, a smile plastered to his face. "He's been ready since we were twelve. I have the scars to prove it."

"Who's your friend?" another disembodied voice called as the elevator doors chimed.

"A fellow boxing fan."

The elevator doors slid open, and Carlo and Sue quickly entered. Carlo gave one more wave as the doors closed, blocking out the press.

"I'm sorry about that." He pressed a button that sent the elevator up. "I didn't prepare you very well for it."

"It wasn't too bad." Sue patted him on the back.

"No, but Barry will be waiting for us when these doors open again."

Sue didn't react, though like Justin and Tom, she found Barry overbearing.

Carlo chuckled softly. "I know. He's difficult. So difficult it might make you want to walk through all that press again."

She laughed. "I can handle Barry."

The quiet of Sue's hotel room was a nice change from the hubbub she'd grown accustomed to after only a few weeks on tour. Even so, her curiosity about the prep and the pre-fight activities made her restless. She distracted herself with work for as long as she could, then she paced her room, dressed and ready a full thirty minutes before Barry would take her to meet Carlo.

She wore a rich black silk dress that fell just below the knee. It had a modest cowl neck and whisper-thin straps over her shoulders. While conservative in the front, the dress left her back bare all the way to her hips, where the subtly shiny fabric gracefully wrapped around her and draped down. To set it off, she wore her hair in a loose chignon. She'd pulled out a few strands around her face and curled them so they came up to her jaw. Square aquamarine studs graced her ears and one silver bangle with crystal scrolls brightened her wrist. Her strappy heels were barely noticeable next to the dress.

She mindlessly flicked through the channels on the TV until ten of six, when there was a light knock on the door. She did one last check in the mirror before answering it to find Barry talking to someone on his Bluetooth. He barely acknowledged her before speaking.

"You look nice. Are you ready for Carlo?"

Sue nodded, trying not to bristle at what his tone implied about being "ready for Carlo."

"Let's go." Barry strode off ahead of her, still talking.

Sue didn't know if he spoke to her or someone in his ear. He turned his head slightly in her direction before he said, "I told Carlo to stay in his suite until his arrival time. I'm taking you there for now."

"Okay." Sue walked briskly to keep up.

Barry led her down the hallway and past the main bank of elevators to another hall with an elevator that required a key. They rode in silence. When the doors opened, they found Carlo waiting.

"What are you doing out here?" Barry half yelled. "I told you to stay in the room!"

"Tony's manager is on the phone. It is too loud."

"I don't care. I don't want the press up here." Barry glared at Carlo.

"Security will keep them away." Carlo kept his voice firm and held Barry's gaze when he spoke. He paused for a moment, then went to Sue. "You look lovely."

Barry huffed and entered the suite, holding the door open long enough for Sue to clearly hear one half of a conversation.

She widened her eyes for moment, acknowledging the loud talk. "Thank you, this is my favorite dress."

"Spin and let me see it." Carlo made a twirling gesture with his finger.

Sue raised her eyebrows, surprised by his forward request, then turned slowly on her heel. She laughed when he let out a low whistle.

"I think this is *my* favorite dress, too. But are you sure you won't catch a chill?"

"Isn't that what your jacket is for?" She playfully tugged one of his cuffs.

His lips quirked in a smile. "Turn again."

Sue narrowed her eyes, gave a half smile, and complied. If this was all she was to Carlo—window dressing—she'd play the part. If he was disappointed later when she didn't accompany him to his room or invite him to hers, well, that was his problem. She liked feeling pretty and desired. She didn't like being an accessory.

"Did this work of art go on Tom's credit card?" Carlo gestured to her dress.

"No. I asked my friend to overnight it."

"That explains it. I worried you would dress like a skimpy ring girl when you refused to shop on the way from the airport." Carlo put his thumb and forefinger on his chin. "This is much better."

Sue chuckled. How would he have reacted if she hadn't looked elegant? "Thank you. You look rather dapper, as well."

He fussed with his collar. "What do you think of this?" Each side of his bowtie had three points instead of two, adding a little panache.

"I like it. A twist on a classic." Sue made a minor adjustment to straighten it after his fussing set the tie askew.

"Much like the back of your dress."

She chuckled. "We match!"

"Yes." Carlo offered his arm. "Let's go before Barry comes back."

"You don't have to ask me twice." She threaded her arm through his.

They rode the elevator to the second floor, then took the stairs. When they got to the bottom, Carlo wrapped her in a hug. "I'm sorry about Barry. He can be extremely...tense. I hope he didn't behave rudely."

"I can handle him."

"Barry is not good with people. However, I have never been late to anything unless the planes were delayed. It is important I have that."

"I understand."

"This is where we meet the car. We'll drive around the block, then walk the red carpet."

"I've never walked a red carpet before." Sue smoothed her dress. "I didn't realize they'd have one here."

"Darling, they have red carpets wherever they can get celebrities to congregate."

Before Sue responded, Carlo had the door open. A limousine waited for them. As Carlo had explained, they drove around the hotel and were dropped off at the business end of the red carpet, where a valet opened the door for them. Carlo climbed out of the car, waved, then offered his hand to Sue. Once she stood by his side, he whispered, "smile" into her ear, wrapped an arm around her waist, and started down the carpet.

Shutters flickered all around them. As they worked their way to the entrance, Carlo stopped several times to pose for pictures, answer questions, and even sign autographs. Sue marveled at how normal he made it look. Even though no one knew her and most likely didn't care, she had butterflies in her stomach. She tried to act natural throughout the ordeal, posing when Carlo asked her to and staying a step back when he talked to reporters and signed autographs. She smiled the entire time and appreciated the less chaotic seats pay-per-view would've offered.

When they finished the red carpet walk and were out of sight of the cameras, Carlo pulled Sue out of the line, headed to the ring, and took her up an inconspicuous staircase.

"This is the best place to be before the fight. All the tension, and no one fussing over seats." Carlo opened the door to a plush room with a wall of windows that provided a bird's-eye view of the boxing ring. Groups of people were scattered around the space. "These are the hardcore sports writers. They'll act like they aren't interested in anything except the fight. Then as soon as they file their stories, they'll call the gossip columnists to give them a minute-by-minute breakdown of what I said, what I wore, and on and on."

"Does that bother you?"

"No. At this point we are all friends. This is their job. And more often than not, they treat me like everyone else, which is nice. They want to know more about Tony and angle for insider information."

"Do you ever give it to them?" Sue asked.

"They want the small details. They never ask a question they don't already know the answer to."

"So, they don't ask much about your life."

"No. Nor do they editorialize when they pass info to their gossip columnists, either. I give them credit for that." Carlo offered one of the men a small salute.

As they worked their way through the room, more people acknowledged Carlo. It started with a few hellos and pats on the back, a handful of random questions about Tony, and then reporters swallowed him up. Sue quietly ducked away, signaling that she'd be at the bar.

Adam entered the press room ready for a drink. His flight had been late, his tuxedo arrived without a tie, and his best photographer fell while collecting gear from the airport luggage carousel and sprained an ankle. Having done his best to fix everything, Adam made a beeline for the bar. The first pull of the Manhattan helped unwind some of the stress knotted in his neck. He faced the room, knowing representatives from each boxing team would come out soon to answer questions before the fight began.

A woman leaned into the safety rail of the window wall as she looked down on the ring. She wore a backless dress that showed off acres of naked skin. Certain she'd be another heavily made-up, empty-headed trophy date, Adam moved toward her. Trophy dates were often superb sources for scoop.

She must have seen him coming because she turned and flashed an easy smile as he approached. Her fresh face and welcome expression surprised him. A moment later recognition hit, and he stopped dead in his tracks.

"You're the woman from the taco bar."

She studied him for a second, then blushed. "You recognized me without hot sauce on my dress. Impressive."

Adam grinned. "You clean up nice."

"Thank you." She glanced away briefly and sipped from her martini glass. "Adam?"

"Yes. Adam Fletcher." He hesitated for a moment, thrilled to see her again, yet flustered. Her name was on the tip of his tongue. "You're...Douglas? I'm sorry, that can't be right."

She nodded. "Sue Douglas."

Relieved that he hadn't totally fumbled it, he smiled. "It's a pleasure to see you again, Sue."

He enjoyed the flush returning to her cheeks.

"Do you think Tito will use the fractured rib as an excuse again if he loses the fight?"

Adam cocked his head and took her in. Here stood the woman from the taco bar, the same creamy skin and almost red hair, but with something different. She'd been tense at the restaurant, distracted. Here, in the middle of the press, waiting for the most anticipated Heavyweight Championship fight since Foreman/Ali, wearing a dress that put her flawless back on full display, she embodied calm. Even talking about the fighters didn't get her worked up.

"You're covering the fight?" Adam drank his Manhattan.

"You didn't answer my question." Sue took the toothpick out of her glass, pulled the olive off with her teeth, and chewed it slowly.

Adam chuckled, stepped toward her, and took the bait. "That injury's been healed for at least six months."

"After his last fight, Tito's trainer tried to say it was re-injured. It's only been two months."

Adam put a hand on the railing next to her. "If that was truly the case, Tito would've asked Azzuré to postpone, and Azzuré would've. He's always said he wants to fight Tito when they're both at their peak." Adam leaned closer to her, his mind going a mile a minute between her skin, her smile, and the conversation.

"Yeah, but maybe there's a pride thing there. Tito shut down the rib story." She angled her head toward him.

He inhaled deeply. As her scent washed over him, he forgot what they were talking about for a moment. He took another long look at her before he answered. "It was spin to get Azzuré wondering what he'd be walking into."

"Come on, we all know Azzuré doesn't care." She pushed a tendril of hair over her ear, rested her hand next to his on the safety rail, and leaned toward him.

Keeping his gaze on her, Adam took another swallow of his drink before he answered. "Azzuré doesn't care. His people do. I've never seen you at a fight before. What outlet are you with?"

"Adam! How are you?" Carlo came from behind Sue and wrapped an arm around her waist, blatantly shifting her closer to him.

She rolled her shoulders but didn't shake him off.

Adam also stood straighter and took half a step back. "I'm doing well, Carlo. You?"

"Excellent." Carlo's smile went from fake to gracious after Adam's retreat. He focused on Sue and pointed his head toward the door. "Shall we?"

She nodded.

Adam held a finger up to stop them. "Wait, I was about to ask Sue what outlet she works for."

Carlo moved his hand to the small of Sue's back, already directing her away.

"I don't work in sports. I work in rock and roll." Sue looked back and sent Adam a dazzling smile.

He smiled back, speechless.

Hoping he'd timed it right, Adam took the stairs two at a time. When he got to the landing, he stopped for a moment to steady his breathing. He opened the door, peeked into the hallway, and grinned. Sue leaned with her arm against the wall next to a door on the far side, a few feet from him, her back enticing him to touch her. He savored the view for a few seconds until she glanced over her shoulder and noticed him. She seemed only mildly surprised.

Adam let the door close behind him as he entered the hallway. "The woman Tony Azzuré and Carlo Giáncomo are fighting over returns to her room alone? Scandalous!"

Sue chuckled. "I'd hardly call sharing a toast fighting over me." She shifted toward him with a tired smile, one shoe in her hand. "But you're the lucky guy who gets to break the story."

"I'm not looking for a story. Just you."

Her smile brightened.

Adam came to stand in front of her and took her shoe, noticing a room card partially stuck to the insole. "You glue your key to your shoe?"

"It's hairspray. It's pretty much a guaranteed way for me not to lose it." Sue pushed off the wall and held her arms out. "No pockets."

Adam took advantage of the invitation to ogle her, then peeled the card free and handed her the shoe. "I'll have to pass that tip along to my sister."

"Please do." Sue leaned on his shoulder and took off her other shoe.

Surprised by the comfortable gesture, Adam seized the opportunity to put his hand lightly on her hip. When she wobbled, he stepped closer and slipped his arm around her waist. The half embrace momentarily dazed him. Her skin was softer than the silk of her dress, and despite the overflowing bottles of champagne and Carlo hanging on her all night, she smelled as she had before, like roses with a deeper, woodsy undertone.

She caught her balance and met his eyes.

He pulled her tighter and almost kissed her.

"Thanks," she murmured and stepped out of his grasp. She leaned back against the wall next to the door and held out her hand.

Adam placed the card on her palm, then held her hand. "Don't go. Talk with me for a minute."

Sue pulled her hand away and smiled. "Okay."

"Did you like the fight?"

Her smile grew, and she pushed her hair behind her ears. "It was great. Nothing like I was expecting."

"What did you expect?"

"I don't know." Sue lifted and dropped one shoulder. "I'd only been to amateur fights. The atmosphere was different. Like those guys had something to prove."

He loved the idea that this woman knew about boxing and hadn't come to the fight simply for the fanfare. "Tito and Tony had something to prove."

Sue shook her head. "No. They each had something to lose."

"Tony didn't."

"Oh." Sue's voice dropped an octave and hit him in the gut. "He did. Or don't you know about the athlete's ego?"

Adam smirked. "Touché."

"Tito had the belt, but Tony had the bluster. If he didn't win tonight, he would've had to blow up like Kanye." Sue shrugged. "That hardly even works for

Kanye anymore."

Adam laughed. "Then no offense to Tito, but I'm glad Azzuré won. I'd hate for such a nice guy to take that kind of turn."

"He is a nice guy."

"You've known him long?"

Sue looked toward the ceiling. "Umm, for about three hours now."

Adam chuckled again and slipped a hand into his pocket before he propped it against the wall next to her.

"How long have you known them?" she asked.

"I've been following Tony Azzuré since he was an amateur boxer working to qualify for the Olympics. Tito I've known a few years."

"You can go jogging with them whenever you want, huh?"

Adam lifted an eyebrow. "Maybe. I'd actually finish the jog, though."

Sue lit up. "In better shape than Norman Mailer was?"

"You read *The Fight*?"

"Yeah." Sue straightened her posture. "It was no *Fever Pitch*, but it got the job done."

Adam squared himself as if preparing for a blow. "Book or movie?"

"The book!" Sue looked at him like he'd been ridiculous to even ask.

"Thank God." Adam pushed a hand through his hair. "You like sports stories?"

"I like *good* stories."

Adam glanced at his shoes, fighting the urge to ask if she read *Sports Mecca*. "Top five books, lay 'em on me."

"Nice Hornby reference." Sue's eyes sparkled as she spoke.

"Well? What are they?"

"You want to talk about books after that amazing fight?"

"Is that wrong?"

She shook her head.

He desperately wanted to know more about this woman—his buddies in the press corps only had the bare minimum on her—and whether she thought his stories were good. There were a few things he needed to know first, before he went after her approval. "So, Miss I-Work-in-Rock-and-Roll, you represent Words Fail Me."

"Yes."

"They got invited to play the New Orleans Zoo benefit, right?"

Sue wrinkled her brow. "Yes. Are you an investigative reporter?"

"It wasn't hard to put together. Carlo talked to a lot of people about you."

"Did he now?"

Adam ignored her question, his jealousy rising at her wry smile when she asked it. Instead he focused on her eyes and getting the answers he needed. "You know Carlo through the band?"

"Yes."

"You're here with him?" Adam stepped forward and put his hand on the wall next to her head. He leaned in, his eyes serious as he waited for her answer.

"Well…" Her voice had become husky. "He invited me."

Adam paused to let her voice sink into his brain. "So separate rooms to distract the press." No longer asking questions, Adam needed her confirmation, even though he didn't want it.

Her expression morphed into one of disgust, and she straightened her posture. "I should go." She pulled his arm down and moved against the wall toward to her door.

Adam flinched at her touch, then realized he almost had her caged in. Not wanting her to feel threatened, he stepped back. "I'm sorry. I interview guys with head injuries for a living. Sometimes I forget my manners."

She visibly relaxed and paused, her hand hovering near the doorknob. "Why are you up here, anyway?"

"I told Barry you dropped your room card on the way out of the party. I'm not sure he believed me, but the idea of having one less reporter around Carlo was probably too appealing for him to pass up."

Looking into the distance, Sue said, "I don't think Barry likes me around Carlo, either."

"I never thought I'd have something in common with Barry."

Sue locked her gaze on him. "Really."

"Sue, if you're dating Carlo, I will never cover another Azzuré fight. Especially if you continue to wear dresses like that." Adam visually feasted on her body, memorizing her, bare feet and all, before he made eye contact again.

Sue rubbed her finger along his lapel. "Or go to another media conference?"

"That, too."

Sue tsked at him. "That would be a terrible shame."

Sensing her shift to a playful tone, Adam stepped closer and lowered his voice. "I'd never give up the taco bar, though. That place is too good." He beamed when Sue laughed. "How long are you guys in town?"

"Are you hoping I'll throw more food on myself?"

"Something like that."

Her lips quirked in a half smile. "I don't know how long Carlo will be here."

Adam tilted his head at her incomplete answer. "And you?"

Sue pulled his untied tie from around his neck and flicked it at him. "I fly out in the morning."
He grinned and let her keep the tie. "Why so soon?"

"Still so many questions?"

"It's my nature." Adam rolled his shoulders back, never taking his eyes off her. "Why not stay longer?"

"Work."

Adam cocked his head. "Does that bother Carlo?"

"That I work?"

"That you're leaving tomorrow. Does *that* bother Carlo?"

"Doubtful."

Recognizing he had already pressed his luck, Adam took Sue's room card. When she lifted her eyebrows, he held one hand up and offered the card back. "Just opening the door for you. Trying to be polite for a change."

Sue pushed a strand of hair behind her ear. "Okay."

Adam tapped the card against the lock and twisted the knob, but held the door closed. "Do you have time for breakfast in the morning?"

"No. Early flight."

Adam heard regret in her voice and swallowed a

smile. He pushed the door open and returned her card. She moved into the open doorway, eyes on him.

He didn't want to let her go. "You know..." He leaned toward her again. "If you call room service, they'll pack a breakfast for you. It's much better than airport food."

Sue stepped forward and brought her mouth tantalizingly close to his as she draped his tie around his collar. Then she dropped her hand over his on the doorknob. His brain faltered and restarted.

"Thank you for the tip." She turned, her hand still on his, bare back displayed to him, and entered the room.

Adam fought an impulse to run a finger down her spine. "I hope you had fun tonight."

Sue looked over her shoulder with a mischievous glint in her eye. "I did."

Adam slowly pulled away and stepped back, fighting more primal instincts.

Sue faced him again, holding the door against her and offering a slow smile. "Did you?"

"Yes." Adam leaned toward her again. "I'm going to the zoo benefit, too."

"Maybe I'll see you there."

"Count on it." Adam grinned, then walked toward the elevator.

They'd all agreed to meet in Tom's hotel room by noon the day after the fight to review plans for the next two days. Brad arrived early, eager to see Sue. He and Tom were drinking coffee when she arrived.

"Hey, Sexy Sue. You made it back in one piece."

"I did." Sue smiled. "Carlo is a man of his word."

"How was the fight?" Tom had been pacing the room but perched on the air conditioner as he spoke.

Sue's face lit up. "Amazing. So intense."

"Who won?" Brad asked.

Sue furrowed her brow. "You don't know?"

"Hello." Brad pointed to himself. "Rock star. Busy drinking, partying, trashing hotel rooms. I've got no time to follow up on scores."

Making Sue laugh would've been the highlight of his day if she hadn't just returned from a night away with one of his friends. Had she slept with Carlo? Would she tell if she had? Brad's stomach roiled while he faked a grin, waiting on the information that would make or break his hopes.

"Okay, big shot. Azzuré won. Of course." Sue tossed an envelope at Tom. "Those are your winnings,

Tommy."

Tom smiled and counted the bills.

"Tom!" Brad sat up in his chair, not bothering to hide his surprise. "You gamble?"

Tom shrugged. "You don't know everything about me."

Sue shook her head at Brad. "Don't get too excited. He bet a hundred bucks that Azzuré would win. He made chump change."

"You did better?" Tom stood and slipped the envelope into his back pocket.

"I bet three hundred that he'd win before the fifth round."

"When did he win?" Brad drained his coffee.

"Barely into the third with a knockout that almost tossed Tito out of the ring."

"Where'd you get three hundred bucks?" Tom paced the room again. "Aren't you on a budget?"

Sue pulled Tom's credit card out of her back pocket and held it between two fingers. "You said I could buy something when I got there."

Despite his nerves, Brad gave into a belly laugh as Tom snatched away the credit card.

Sue gave him a big grin and three hundred-dollar bills. "That's to cover the charge."

Tom scowled. "I should get a cut of the rest."

"I'll buy you a few beers tonight." Sue sat on the foot of the bed. "Hell, I'll buy you a top shelf drink."

Tom shook his head, even though he grinned as he answered Justin's drumbeat knock on the door.

"Hey, Sue, how was the fight?" Justin craned around Tom as he entered the room.

"Excellent." Sue leaned back on her elbows and smiled at Justin.

Was she smiling because of the fight? Because she liked Carlo? Both? Brad needed a way into this woman's head. Waiting for answers was killing him.

"Did you have fun with Carlo?" Justin asked.

"Yeah." Sue sat up and patted the bed. "I didn't get to spend much time with him, though. Barry sequestered him before the fight."

If Brad hadn't already been seated across the room, he would've raced Justin for that spot. Instead, Justin sat next to her and shot Brad a look like he was Sue's bodyguard and knew exactly what Brad was thinking.

"Cool." Justin flicked her ponytail. "I hope you at least dressed up for the da—fight."

"Duh." Sue pulled her ponytail tight. "How much did Chris complain about me being gone?"

"He didn't." Like everyone else, Brad had been braced for a nuclear reaction when they told Chris that Sue went to Vegas with Carlo. Instead, Chris had said "good for Carlo" and shot-gunned a beer.

"Really?" Sue asked with wide eyes.

"Yeah." Tom rapped on his tablet. "Darryl introduced him to Lena, and the three of them spent most of the day together. Lena must intimidate Chris. Darryl said he behaved like a gentleman. D even used the word 'gentleman.'"

Sue grinned. "Lena is like ten feet tall and stunningly gorgeous."

"Yeah," Brad seconded, eyes on Sue. "I'm impressed she went for D."

"Impressed or jealous?" Justin teased.

"Both." Brad ran a hand through his hair, hoping for a reaction from Sue, some kind of insight. Her face didn't belie the slightest bit of jealousy, awkwardness, or even discomfort. This woman proved over and over that little could rattle her.

Darryl burst into the room, Chris right behind him. "What are we doing today? Hey, Sue." He plopped down on her other side.

"Hey." She looked directly at Chris.

"I saw Azzuré won. Did you have any money on the fight?" Chris asked.

Sue gave him a wide smile. "I did."

"*My* money." Tom snarled.

Brad laughed again, still amused by how easily Sue

got under Tom's skin.

Tom knocked on his tablet, bringing everyone's attention to him. "Show tonight. We go to Dallas tomorrow, Houston the day after without Sue, then we head to Louisiana." Tom acknowledged each of them as he spoke. "We have two full days off in New Orleans before the press stuff. Show night is Thursday, and the benefit's on Saturday. We leave for Alabama on Sunday."

"Sweet!" Darryl stood. "Can I come back here after Houston? I wanna spend some more time with Lena if she's cool with it. I'll catch a flight to meet up with you guys."

Everyone in the room looked as shocked as Brad felt. Darryl? Fly back? To hang with a girl? Something must have tilted in the universe. Usually D was the one helping Tom keep them on track.

Tom checked his tablet before answering. "What if your flight gets delayed?"

"I can fly in Wednesday to be safe."

After a stretch of silence, Sue spoke. "I'll double check that we're clear until Thursday. If that holds true, I can pick you up at the airport on Wednesday."

"Thanks, Sue!" Darryl squeezed her as though she were one of their sisters, then faced the guys. "We cool?"

Justin thumped his foot. "If Sue's in, I'm in."

"I met Lena. I get it." Brad lifted his coffee mug to Darryl. "Have fun." Brad would move heaven and earth for time alone with Sue. He wouldn't block Darryl from Lena. Sure, D had his share of hookups on tour, but the guy never looked back. If this woman—a nursing student who taught salsa dancing lessons at Habana's—caught D's eye, she was something special. Plus, the lucky bastard didn't have anyone breathing down his neck, making threats because he liked her.

"Damn it, D." Chris pounded the floor next to him.

"What?"

"If you stay behind, Sue's gonna try to get me on Twitter again."

"I'll tweet from here." Darryl answered without missing a beat.

"Okay." Chris stood and walked toward the door.

Tom went through the revised plan, let everyone know when and where to meet for soundcheck, and ended the meeting.

"Hey." Justin followed Sue into the hallway with Brad close on his heels.

Brad knew Justin was at least as curious as he was. Better yet, Justin could get away with asking all the questions Brad wanted answers to.

"Did Carlo fly back with you?"

"No," Sue said. "He had a thing this morning. He'll be back tonight."

A thing this morning? Did Carlo tell her that as they woke up together? Damn it, he needed answers.

"Do you know when?"

"No idea." Sue shook her head.

Brad kept his face neutral, even though he was dying to know. Did she have no idea because she didn't care? Was Carlo's day packed so full that he only knew the time it all started? Both?

"You spent twenty-four hours with the guy. How can you not know this?" Justin gave voice to Brad's frustration.

"I didn't spend all of the twenty-four hours with him, and we didn't talk about our itineraries when I *was* with him."

"Not much talking at all, I hope." Justin leered.

Brad smacked his friend's arm. Yes, he wanted to know how well she and Carlo had gotten along, but Justin didn't have to talk to her like she was Tom or Darryl.

"Please." Sue rolled her eyes, then continued down the hall toward the elevators.

"We're not gonna get anything out of her." Justin sighed.

"Nope," Brad agreed, frustrated and not at the same time. He could still hope until he knew for sure. "Did you call him?"

"Already left two messages."

"He'll call." Brad clapped a hand on Justin's back.

"Hey, guys!" Sue called from the elevator.

Brad looked at Justin, who was already wide-eyed before they both faced Sue.

Justin cleared his throat. "Yeah?"

"I'm not one to talk about my private life."

Brad grunted, about to lie to defend himself, when Sue held up a hand.

"And you know Carlo won't talk, either," she said.

Justin stepped forward. "Sue—"

"But I will give you this: Carlo is a nice man. We had a nice time. I stayed in a very nice hotel room." She put a hand on her hip. "Alone. Don't push so hard." Sue stepped back, and the elevator doors slid closed.

Brad stood in silence for a full minute. *Alone.* She'd spent the night alone! No sex with Carlo! He still had a shot! He had to get his shit together before Justin lectured him.

"She likes him. She had fun." Justin held up his fist.

"And she didn't sleep with him." Brad bumped Justin's fist, smiling wide.

"Yet," Justin added.

Brad shrugged. *Yet* meant he was still in the game.

"You got a pen?" Justin waited as a woman with a slight hippie vibe dug into a knit bag. After the band meeting, they had all gone their own ways—Darryl off with Lena, Brad and Chris to a club, and Justin stayed in the hotel, taking in the impromptu jam sessions that broke out in the areas around the lobby every few minutes. This woman had caught his attention when she'd started talking about the influences she heard in each original song. She handed him a marker and he smirked. She may have known a lot about music, but maybe she was more interested in being a muse. "Like autographs?"

She gave a small shake of her head. "I teach kindergarten."

Justin pulled her hand to him. He ran his thumb across her open palm, then wrote "WFM" across her wrist. He signed his initials, then made eye contact with her as he blew on the ink, noting a slight tremor from her. Yeah, they could inspire each other. "If that doesn't get you in the door tonight, ask for Tom. He's our manager. He'll take care of it."

The woman smiled.

He put the marker in her palm. "Find me after the set."

Her tongue darted over her lips. "Definitely."

"Justin!"

He looked up at the sound of his name. Carlo approached from across the lobby. Justin acknowledged the man, then brought his focus back to the woman, not wanting to be rude.

"Should I bring a friend?" she asked.

"The guys can fend for themselves."

She flipped her hair and slid the marker into her bag, eyes on Justin. "You busy now?"

He would've preferred to say no, but this week was important for them. He stuck with the responsible answer. "Gotta go to soundcheck."

"And talk to me." Carlo jerked his head toward an empty alcove near the elevators. "Come on."

Justin grunted. "And talk to him. See you tonight?"

"Yeah." The woman smiled.

He walked backward a few feet, flashed his eyebrows, then turned and followed Carlo. "Congrats on Tony's big win."

"Thanks, I couldn't be prouder." Carlo glanced around like he'd buried a body and needed a getaway. "Barry will be here any second. I have to make this fast."

"K. S'up?"

"Can you put me on the list for your show tonight?"

Justin rubbed his hands together, hopeful he had made a good match. "Sure. Excited to hang with Sue again?"

Carlo adjusted his wrist cuff. "I need to make sure she likes me."

"Of course she does. You don't think so?"

Carlo scanned the area outside of the old phone alcove. "It never occurred to me that after achieving this level of success, I would hide in a corner to talk about a woman."

Justin knew better than to laugh. "It happens to the best of us, man. What happened?"

"Is she around? Sue made me agree to tell you *nothing* about the trip. Payback for the blind set up."

Justin snickered. "She's at the club. You know I won't talk."

Carlo winced before he spoke again. "She met someone last night."

"Huh?"

"I wanted to impress her, so I took her to the press box." Carlo stalked to the back corner of the alcove. "It has a great view, a huge bar; it's almost as nice as the suite where Tony had his victory party. A few reporters pulled me away with questions about Tony. The next thing I know, she's talking to Adam Fletcher." Carlo practically spit the name. "They looked like they were in a private moment. If I could have, I would I have decked him, thrown her over my shoulder, and taken her away."

"What *did* you do?" Justin asked.

"I interrupted and took her to the ring. Then I flaunted her as my date the rest of the night."

"That's exactly what you should've done." Justin grinned even though Carlo's frustration seemed to grow.

"I was an ass. You know flashy isn't my style."

"So don't be an ass around her anymore. She told us she had a great time." The noise in the lobby grew as two guys with guitars settled in for a performance.

"I don't know." Carlo tapped a foot, glaring toward the crowd forming around the musicians.

"Did she say anything or act annoyed?"

"No. She was perfect. She let me take her into the ring after the knockout, she stayed by my side at the party, and we danced. I thought she had a good time."

"Dude." Justin blocked Carlo's view into the lobby. "What you're saying makes no sense. If you'd fucked up, there's no way she would've been cool the rest of the night."

"She didn't let me kiss her goodnight." Carlo leaned against the wall and ran a hand over his hair.

"Was Barry there when you left the party?" Barry was the ultimate buzzkill. If he fucked up this fix up, he'd learn *all* about karma.

"No. Well, Barry got her out of the party. Too much press." Carlo shook his head as though the light finally dawned on him.

"She's not gonna kiss you in a room full of cameras. She controls the press for a living. She doesn't give them anything she isn't in charge of."

"You're right. I sent flowers to her room today, though, and I haven't heard a word from her."

"She probably wants to thank you in person. She knew you were coming back to Austin." Justin let the silence hang between them for a moment before he spoke again. "Do you like her?"

"Yes, but she obviously liked Fletcher." Carlo pressed a fist against the wall.

"Did she talk to him again after that?" Some other guy horning in could be an issue, and Justin hoped Carlo had put a swift end to it.

Carlo barked a quick laugh. "You think I would give him another chance?"

Relieved, Justin gave his friend a confident smile. Seeing how much Carlo liked Sue meant Brad would stand down. "Go back to doing whatever it is that makes women giggle and pass out around you. Pretend the night went exactly the way you wanted."

"You're sure?" asked Carlo.

"Yeah. Come to our show. Sweep her off her feet. You'll have fun."

CHAPTER 22

For their last night in Austin, Sue spent her time before the set in the club talking up the band to reporters and other musicians, hoping for more press as well as collaboration opportunities.

She settled in to watch when the guys hit the stage. After a few songs, Barry appeared and pulled her to the edge of the crowd. He brought Carlo to her.

"Hey!" Sue gave Carlo a side-hug. "Did you get my texts? The flowers are beautiful!"

Carlo raised his eyebrows. "I didn't get any texts."

Sue dug her phone out of her pocket, hoping she hadn't forgotten to hit "send" after typing the text. Thankfully, her phone indicated that it had gone through. She showed him the message, which included photos of a lavish bouquet of roses and lilies. "You can smell the lilies all the way to the elevator."

Carlo beamed. "You like them?"

"Yes! Thank you so much!" The flowers were a lovely surprise during a busy week, but they worried her. Carlo making a fuss over her being his arm candy at the fight had killed her romantic interest. She needed a kind way to tell him that wouldn't hurt the band's relationship with Cáceres.

"Perfect. Are you having fun?"

Sue smiled. "This is the best part of the night. After this I have to network more."

Carlo put an arm around her waist and pulled her close. "I am an expert networker."

"Let's enjoy the music now." Sue laughed and put space between them, determined not to encourage him. "Rub elbows later."

When the guys began their final song, Sue excused herself and headed backstage to help them get their gear out, as had become her habit on tour. Her contract required that she oversee merchandise and sales, which she did, but her determination to show her value turned up in other areas, like clearing the stage fast, too.

After everything had been packed, Sue focused on the people hanging around between the bar and the merch table. CD sales were surprisingly good, especially since all the band's music could be downloaded or streamed, but T-shirts barely moved. CD sales meant people were interested, but she wanted cities filled with people wearing Words Fail Me tees—spreading awareness about the band through silent endorsement. She chatted up some of the buyers to figure out why shirts weren't moving.

Carlo followed her for a while, until he and his bodyguard became a distraction. He moved back toward the stage.

As the next set began, Sue worked the crowd, giving out postcards and talking up the band. She took a fan photo and had them sign digital releases for social media, then she surveyed the room for her next opportunity.

Adam stood near the doorway, watching her. Her stomach flipped, and she finally recognized her nerves when she saw him had nothing to do with the circumstances and everything to do with him.

She smiled, and another thrill surged through her when he crossed the room to her. He looked great, comfortable and sexy in jeans and a plain fitted shirt that showed off his physique. It was clear the jostling club-goers wouldn't throw him off balance.

Adam gave her a broad smile when he stopped next to her. Sue positioned herself to talk directly into his ear. The loud music gave her an excuse to stand close. He smelled good, fresh. Not like cigarettes, beer, or sweat like so many of the people around them. She figured her hair reeked of smoke, but the opportunity to get into this man's space was too tempting to pass up.

"I thought you were a sports writer," Sue said.

"I am. I came back for the ballgame tomorrow."

"I read *Sports Mecca*. I don't recall you guys covering amateur softball games at tradeshows." She'd been following the site for a few years. They never boiled the athletes down to statistics, injuries, and inspirational quotes. They told real stories, and they told them well.

"We're branching out," Adam said, his voice husky. He put a hand on her hip and squeezed, sending sparks through her.

Sue pulled back to study his face and consider. His

eyes glimmered, though his expression was calm. She leaned in again. "What brings you to this particular club?"

"Oh, I love..." Adam gestured at the stage. "Music." He squeezed her hip again. "I heard Words Fail Me was headlining tonight. I hoped you'd be here." He tilted his head back, catching Sue's gaze, then smiled.

Sue returned it and squeezed his arm when she stepped closer to answer him. "It's good to see you again, too."

"I was thinking...since we're both going to the zoo benefit, we should go together."

His breath tickling her ear and neck gave Sue goosebumps. Instead of hiding it or shying away from Adam, she leaned closer, almost brushing their chests together. "I like that idea."

"Good. If you have some time while you're in New Orleans, we could have dinner together, too." Adam shifted closer as swarms of people moved around them.

The band on stage must've finished their set. Sue didn't care. Her attention was divided between what he was saying and her plotting to get his other arm around her.

"I like the way your mind works." She leaned in even more. "When were you thinking we'd do this?"

"I'm sorry she's not hanging on you, man." Justin wiped his forehead with the sleeve of his shirt. He'd changed right after their set, but the club was packed. He couldn't cool off. "She's got it in her head to find us new collaborators before we leave Austin."

"She's smart." Carlo ran a hand down each arm, smoothing his shirt. "Don't worry. I've been paying attention. When she has moments by herself, I seize them." Carlo didn't look at Justin; instead, his gaze darted around the club. "Ah, maybe I'm about to get another. She's stopped." Carlo pushed through the crowd toward Sue.

Justin didn't envy Carlo. He wiped his head with his shirt again to make sure his deodorant hadn't failed. The humid club reeked; the smell was so pervasive Justin worried it had rubbed off on him. No way would he be confident going after a woman if he thought he stank. He mentally gave Carlo points for dedication, then turned and accepted a pen and CD when someone asked for a signature.

"Love your drumming, man," the guy said as Justin scribbled his name on the liner notes.

"Thanks." As Justin handed back the CD, the woman from that afternoon came up beside him and hugged him.

"Great show, Justin."

He smiled. "Hey! Glad you made it. Want a drink?"

"Yeah!"

"Justin!"

He looked up, searching out Carlo. He lifted his eyebrows when he caught Carlo's eye, only a few feet in front of him.

Carlo waved. "Come here!"

The woman sneered. "Always this guy. Seriously?"

Justin smiled. "Cut him some slack. He's trying to date my friend. Come on." He wove their fingers together, keeping her by his side.

When Justin got to him, Carlo pointed his chin at Sue. "There."

She talked with some guy—tall, broad shoulders, didn't look sweaty—his hand resting on her hip as she leaned against him, tapping on a phone she held against his upper arm. She smiled a deep, warm smile. When she stopped tapping, she didn't step out of his embrace. She slid the phone down the guy's arm, never breaking contact as she put it against his hand. He stopped touching her long enough to shove the phone into his pocket. Then he reached for her hand, playing with her fingers as he talked into her ear. When she answered, she pulled her shoulders closer to him.

Justin thumped his foot. "That's the guy."

Carlo nodded.

Mother fuck. Justin had set Sue up with Carlo because Brad wouldn't interfere. But some guy with decent hair and no pit stains in this dank ass club shows up and turns her head? Brad would see it as a challenge. Hell, Sue's lack of interest in Carlo was the perfect excuse to go after her. Justin'd seen Brad do some sneaky shit to win over girls. Why the fuck couldn't Sue fall for Carlo?

"Lemme buy you a drink, man."

A shirtless guy with a Words Fail Me sticker on his back brushed past Sue, leaving her with a mix of emotions. She held in her sigh and practically rested her chin on Adam's shoulder as she spoke. "I hate to do this, but I need to get back to work."

Adam brushed his lips against her ear. "Okay. Will you be at the game tomorrow?"

This time she did sigh. She'd let him tease her with his lips at her ear and fingers against her waist all night, save for work. Damn job. "Travel day."

"I'll call you when I get to New Orleans."

"Be sure that you do." Sue leaned back and aimed her best knee-melting smile at him.

He hugged her, giving her an extra squeeze before he loosened his arms. "I will. Safe trip."

Her skin tingled and her head swam for a moment. She wanted another hug and a kiss. She really wanted to kiss, but she had a job to do. "You, too." She wrapped her arm around his shoulders, giving a squeeze. She pulled away quickly, barely letting her hands linger on his biceps before heading for the bar. As much as she

enjoyed touching Adam, she needed to lean on something else to get her bearings back.

CHAPTER 23

When her phone rang the next morning, Sue answered it without checking the screen. "Getting impatient for me to text you back?"

"I didn't text you." The gruff voice sounded nothing like Adam.

He'd texted her a few times since they'd traded numbers the night before. Opting to shower first, Sue hadn't answered his most recent message. She figured this call would be from him.

Sue read the screen and didn't recognize the number. "Who is this?"

"Barry. Tom says your day is empty until two. I set up brunch for you and Carlo in fifteen minutes."

What the fuck? Where did Barry get off making plans for her? "Carlo can invite me to breakfast himself. And I can say no."

"Carlo's in the shower and we leave soon. He said he texted you, but something's wrong with his phone. We're expecting you in the lobby."

This asshole had some serious nerve. How many women went along with this bullshit? "I require more than fifteen minutes notice for a date."

Barry huffed. "This is the life. If you don't want it, do

something about it. Be there in fifteen."

Sue sneered, wanting to give Barry a piece of her mind, but the man had a point. If she wanted to be treated differently, she needed to lay down the law. "Next time Carlo delegates date requests to you, tell him I decline. I just got out of the shower. I'll be there when I'm ready. In more than fifteen minutes. Pretend you're happy to see me." She hung up without letting Barry respond.

When Sue finally arrived at brunch—forty-five minutes and a handful of texts with Adam later—Carlo, impeccably dressed and groomed, looked like he'd needed more time. Green around the gills and eyes at half mast, he clearly had a wicked hangover.

"I don't know why I try to keep up with Brad. He always drinks me under the table." Carlo rubbed his fingers over his eyebrows, then massaged his temples. He gave Sue a pained smile. "I have no idea how he recovers so quickly, either."

"He must have a secret remedy." Sue pursed her lips, suppressing a laugh.

Carlo dropped his hands into his lap and slowly tilted his head to the side. "I amuse you."

"You do."

He grunted and guzzled a glass of water.

"Being amusing isn't a bad thing." Sue smiled, then dropped it when he rolled his eyes, then pressed his palm to his forehead. "Are you okay?"

Carlo sighed. "I will have this headache for three days."

Sue signaled to the waiter and requested more water and a large orange juice. "You need sugar and grease. I want you to chug some OJ and order breakfast with a big side of bacon."

"I promise I won't be like this when we get to Europe. I'm extremely disciplined when we have so many shows stacked up."

"You don't have to promise me anything." Sue pushed her own glass of orange juice toward him.

"Because I amuse you."

She tilted her head. She saw nothing wrong with amusement.

Carlo drank half of the juice. "I amuse you, but you don't want to date me."

Sue let the silence hang between them while he finished the pulpy beverage. He set the glass down with a *thud*, and his bloodshot eyes met hers for the first time that day. While Sue didn't like having this awkward conversation when Carlo felt ill, she refused to lead him on.

"I'm sorry. I like you, Carlo. But I don't see a romance for us."

He looked away for a moment and rubbed his hands together. "Greasy food? That works?"

"It does for me." Sue kept a close eye on him, expecting more than his quiet acceptance. He could've made the meal more uncomfortable, even stormed out of the room. Instead, he ordered another side of bacon after declaring the first had helped him feel better.

Despite the awkward beginning, the meal ended well with them parting as friends. Sue had learned her lesson, though, and had no intention of answering her phone again without having a better idea of who had dialed her.

When it rang again an hour after brunch, Sue girded herself, expecting Barry or Justin but hoping for Adam. She made a mental note to give Barry his own special ringtone. Seeing Darryl's name on the screen, she answered without further hesitation.

"Hey, D, what's up?"

"I need to talk to you about something. Can I stop in? Are you decent?"

"Yeah, I'm packing. I'll open the door for you." Sue propped the night latch between the door and the frame and resumed her task, listening for Darryl.

When he arrived a few minutes later, he knocked as he entered.

"Hey, what's going on?" Sue asked.

Instead of immediately making himself comfortable as he usually did, Darryl stood in the middle of the room and bounced on the balls of his feet. "Well, first I wanted to say thanks for backing me up yesterday about coming back for Lena."

"No problem. I like her." Sue tucked the charging cord into her computer bag.

"Yeah, I like her, too." Darryl paused and smiled. "I hope I can ask you for another favor in that regard."

Sue slid a notepad into her bag, zipped it, and faced Darryl, hands on her hips. "What do you need?"

"You look like Wonder Woman when you stand like that." Darryl mirrored Sue's posture. "Now I see why Brad's a mess."

Sue narrowed her eyes and dropped her hands. "How is Brad a mess?"

"He gets nervous about the interviews, and then you do something like—" Darryl gestured toward her. "Wonder Woman and he worries that you'll kick his ass if he disappoints you. It's distracting."

"Does it distract him enough that he stops worrying about the interviews?"

"I guess?" Darryl shook his head again. "Anyway, I already talked to Tom about this last night. He's cool with it. Now I need help on Lena's side."

"Okay, what's going on?"

"I want to take her to the benefit." Darryl tilted his head slightly, as though he'd delivered bad news.

"That's great! Have you asked her?"

"Yeah."

"And?" Sue sat on the edge of the bed and studied

Darryl. She'd never seen him uncomfortable before. Did he not like asking for favors? Or did Lena, and how he felt for her, make *him* nervous?

"She wants to go, but she said her sister and brother-in-law, Victor, are very…protective. She doesn't think they'd let her go on a trip like this without a chaperone. Lena and Imogen, her sister, are from a pretty conservative family. Even though their parents are still in Brazil, they expect the girls to follow the family ways." Darryl blushed a deep scarlet.

"Do you want me to get extra tickets for Imogen and Victor?" Sue asked. She loved this idea. Who better to chaperone than a bartender? They'd seen it all. Plus, Victor was fun to talk to.

"Not exactly." Darryl shook his head.

"Then what?" Sue leaned back.

"I want *you* to be her chaperone." Darryl hit her with another unexpected answer. Did he do it on purpose to manipulate her? Did he hope she'd look the other way or lie for him? Neither of those options seemed like things Darryl would do. Then again, Sue hadn't expected Chris to dose her with ipecac or Justin to set her up with a celebrity, either.

Sue lifted her eyebrows. "I don't know, Darryl, I have to work while we're there. I can't be around you guys all the time."

"I know." Darryl paced the room. "It doesn't have to be that intense. If you'd share your room with her, that's all it would take."

"I don't mind sharing my room."

Darryl stopped pacing and beamed at Sue.

She considered before she spoke again. She needed to know Darryl's true intentions. She didn't mind doing him a favor, but she wouldn't let him walk all over her, nor would she lie for him. "So...I never thought I'd have a conversation like this with any of you."

Darryl knotted his eyebrows together and gestured for Sue to go on.

"If we tell Lena's family that she and I will share a hotel room, then she has to sleep in that room. I have to be in the other bed. And you can't be there."

"Yeah." Darryl held out his hands. "That's the whole point."

"You wouldn't try to sneak in after she thinks I'm asleep?"

Darryl's face twisted in horror. "God, no, I'm not Chris."

Sue swallowed her chuckle at Darryl's expression. "I didn't mean to imply that. I want to make sure we understand each other."

"Let me lay it all out." Darryl plopped down next to Sue. "Lena will fly into New Orleans with me. We go back to the hotel, and you two share a room. I stay in my room all night. She stays in your room all night. She keeps a low profile when we're doing press stuff. She comes with me to the benefit. After the benefit, she goes back to your room and stays there with you all night.

When it's all over, I take her to the airport and put her on a plane back to Texas. Then the rest of us drive to Alabama."

"It's that simple, huh?"

"Yeah," Darryl said. "I like being around her. This arrangement is how I get to do that."

Sue's heart warmed. "Okay. Let's do it."

"Thank you so much!" Darryl jumped off the bed. "There's one other thing—can you come with me to Habana's to tell Victor?"

"Sure. When?"

"Now."

Sue gasped and checked her phone. "Brad's interview is—"

"In two hours. You'll be back in plenty of time. Please?"

Not accustomed to Darryl's anxiety, she gave in. "Let's go."

CHAPTER 24

NEW ORLEANS

Sue's decision to drive through the night to New Orleans was personal. The hotel wouldn't be ready in the wee hours of the morning, but her best friend, Amy, waited with doors wide open, no matter the hour. After the last few weeks, she craved that comfort.

Sue parked on the street outside of Amy's Garden District home just after five a.m. She had one foot on the curb when the long, gangly form of another friend, Robin, loped across the front yard. Sue's road weariness lifted, and she ran to him until they almost collided. He stopped short, scooped her up, and spun her around.

"Why are you awake?" Sue clung tightly to Robin, even though she'd rarely felt safer in another pair of arms.

"Jack and I finished a song, and I was too pumped to sleep knowing you'd be here about now. I've got starts on a few more songs."

Sue hugged her friend again. "Play them for me."

Still carrying her, Robin walked back to the porch. He bent his knees and she twisted the doorknob as though he carried her all the time. He didn't, but they knew each other's needs better than their own. "The first one goes like this." Robin hummed a melody, adding a few ba-dums and drumbeats as he went.

"Mmmm, sounds like a hit." Sue laid her head on his shoulder, considering whether to have him put her down or to continue to let her body unwind as he walked through the dark house. "Amy and Jack are sleeping?"

"Yeah. Jack said you knew where to find the spare key, but I wanted to greet you." Robin carried Sue into the fish room—a room done in sea colors with a floor-to-ceiling saltwater tank making up one wall. He set her in the middle of a plush royal-blue rug, then collected a variety of throw pillows. He arranged them on the floor and pulled her down with him.

When they were curled on their sides, facing each other, Sue smiled. It had been months since she'd seen Robin, but he looked exactly the same: willowy tall with perceptive eyes and the kindest face she'd ever seen. Her body relaxed as though she'd been holding her breath all this time and finally had fresh air. "What's going on with your hair?"

He'd shaved his head but left bangs and odd little tufts of hair at random around his head.

"I was trying something. It didn't work the way I expected."

Sue wrinkled her brow, then shrugged when he didn't elaborate. He'd tell her eventually. He always did. "Sing me the song again."

He immediately hummed the melody.

Sue closed her eyes and listened.

"Hey, woman, now you're getting mail at my house?"

A thick, oversized envelope landed with a *thwack* next to Sue's head.

She moaned and stretched. "I figured you wouldn't mind. Especially since I sent you gooey butter cake from Missouri."

"Um-hmm." Amy tapped her foot and crossed her arms. "You know we've got like eight huge beds in this place. Why'd you guys sleep on the floor?"

"We like it down here." Robin sat up and scratched the back of his neck.

"You ruined it, Robin. You guys looked like a lopsided yin-yang." Amy grinned.

"Sue needs longer legs." He stood, then pulled Sue up next to him. "See? She's a wee woman." Robin patted the top of her head.

"Wee?" Sue put a hand on her hip.

"I figured you'd prefer that to squat."

"Ugh." Sue rubbed her eyes and pushed her hair off her face. "You're lucky I love you, you strange giant of a man."

"Yep." Robin grinned and nudged the envelop toward her with his foot. "What's in that?"

Sue bent and picked up the package, feeling the weight. It had to be more than one copy. They wouldn't send multiple copies if the mention was bad, right? She got up and hugged it to herself. This wasn't her first print placement for the band, but it was the biggest so far. "My victory."

"Sounds exciting." Amy backed toward the doorway. "Let's read it in the kitchen. Jack's making omelets."

"*The* Jack Ragnar making us breakfast? Now *that*, my dear, is a victory." Robin pushed Sue toward the kitchen.

"That home-cooked food smells good!" Sue made a show of inhaling as she entered the room. She dropped the envelope on the island and gave Amy's husband a side-hug as he sprinkled cheese into an omelet pan. "If the guys even believed that you cooked me breakfast, Jack, they'd die of jealousy."

Jack snorted and pulled away, then folded the omelet in half. "A guy's gotta eat."

"That's right, boss man." Robin had made himself comfortable on one of the stools at the island. "When's the grub gonna be ready?"

"Forget the grub. I wanna know what's in here." Amy held the envelope by two corners in front of her, a broad smile on her face.

Sue took it and sat next to Robin. She closed her eyes for a moment, then answered. "It's an advance copy of *Rolling Stone*. We got a blurb."

Amy, Robin, and Jack all cheered, but Sue held up a hand to quiet them. She didn't want to get swept up in their excitement only to be crushed if the story criticized her band.

"I don't know if it's good or bad."

"Why would it be bad? It's your victory!" Amy took glasses out of a cabinet and lined them up on the counter.

"We only got a blurb. Who gets an advance copy on a blurb?" Yes, Sue had Jimmy Diamond championing her, but maybe he'd insisted that the reporter send it so Sue'd have a warning of bad news.

"You do." Robin fiddled with the pull tab. "Now open it, or I'll do it for you."

Sue narrowed her eyes at Robin, then ripped away the tab. She covered the opening and looked at each of them. "I get to read it first."

Once they all agreed, Sue pulled out the magazine. She slowly turned each page until she found a photo of Brad from one of their Austin shows alongside a paragraph in the upper left-hand corner. She held up the magazine and read, then put it down and sat back. "It's good. It's really, really good." She cleared her throat and read aloud.

"Many bands get a chance to play more than once at Indy Showcase. Most of those bands squander the opportunity by playing the same songs each time. Not Words Fail Me. The ambitious Michigan ensemble offered three sets as different as fingerprints during their time in Austin, and all with original music. It was a big risk to take, and they rocked it. Each set brought the crowd to a frenzy and drove people back to the merch table to load up on CDs. Strong lyrics and tight hooks have us looking forward to hearing more.”

Amy crossed the kitchen and hugged Sue. Robin jumped off his stool, whooping and smacked Jack on the ass. “You got any champagne, boss man?”

Jack laughed and pointed to the refrigerator. Robin rooted around until he found a magnum and popped it open. “A toast to my favorite lady! May you always kick ass!” Robin passed Sue a tumbler with champagne, clinked the bottle against it, then chugged directly from the bottle.

After breakfast Amy and Sue stayed in the kitchen and caught up while Jack and Robin went to the studio above the garage. Deciding that more than enough attention had been paid to her already, Sue demanded that Amy bring her up to speed on the benefit, her work as a local journalist, and life in general.

“Honestly? I want to talk about you.” Amy paged through *Rolling Stone* as they talked. “This isn’t the first time we’ve done a mammoth event and it won’t be the last. I want to hear all about your new business.”

“I don’t even know where to start.”

“How’s the bus?”

“Don’t know yet. That’s coming next week.” Sue rubbed her temples. Thus far they’d stopped at hotels or she'd been driving separately to get to tour stops ahead of the band, so she'd been able to skip sleeping on the bus. That would end soon enough. They had several overnight drives coming up, and Sue had no excuse to miss them. That meant she'd have to give into a compromise she'd made with Tom her first night on the tour. They'd take turns on the overnight drives, with her sleeping on the bus the nights that Tom drove her car, and they'd each drive with a companion—one of the guys or a roadie from Skein's crew.

"At least you got that mild reprieve. How about sales?"

"Inconsistent. CD sales are steady, which is remarkable in the age of streaming. Downloads spike on show nights. But T-shirts, hats, pins." Sue held up her hands in frustration. "It's all touch and go. I want those walking endorsements out there. Plus, that's the stuff that puts money in their pockets in real time."

"How are the designs?"

"Okay. There are no real standouts. Everything sells equally slowly. I have some concepts I want to run by you and Robin."

"That's easy. Hell, Robin might even screen print a few for you. You know he loves that shit."

Sue smiled, remembering all the custom T-shirts Robin had made for her throughout college. He would surely be remembered as one of the great guitarists of his time, but he was a classically trained cellist as well as a gifted sculptor, photographer, and painter. He loved art and tackled new mediums with fearless curiosity.

"Thanks, Ames. You guys are getting a ton of ink on this event."

"We are. Maybe you can leverage this for a few more inches in *Rolling Stone*." Amy flashed her eyebrows. "They'll be here, you know."

Sue smirked at her friend. As if she'd skip an opportunity. "I do know. How's Jack dealing with all the attention?"

"He's been great. He knows how to play the media game, and he likes that all of this is happening for a cause. He likes that it's bigger than us."

"My favorite part of this whole event is that it pumps money into the community *and* the zoo." Sue rested her cheek on her fist.

The music playing in the background shifted from classical to heavy metal, and Sue let out a low chuckle.

"What?" Amy asked.

"Justin would think this is weird."

"The benefit?"

Sue shook her head. "Going from the Brandenburg Concertos right into metal. Except for the few times I've left ahead of the band, Justin usually rides with me. He gets all discombobulated when I leave my MP3 players on shuffle."

"I hope you've been educating him."

"Oh, I have. Don't worry." Sue closed her eyes for a moment, breathing in the fading coffee scent in the room. "This is the most relaxed I've been since Tom showed up at that concert last month."

"I thought you were excited about the new gig." Amy hopped off her stool and added champagne to each of their glasses, then topped them off with orange juice.

"I am. Extraordinarily excited. And beyond stressed out." Sue twirled the stem of her champagne glass between her fingers. "I have a lot to prove."

"To?"

"Them, myself, their record label, probably a big pile of other people, too." Sue rolled her head along her shoulders, wishing she could shake off the tension that consumed her whenever she thought about the strings tied to her work with Words Fail Me. "I didn't tell you about the insane deal Tom accepted from the record label to bring me on."

Sue gave Amy the details of her contract, spending extra time on Tom's scheming. As she finally got it all off her chest, she felt some more of the tension she'd been holding leave.

When she finished, Amy chuckled and shook her head. "Classic Tom."

Frustration boiled to the surface, and Sue slammed her hand on the counter. "Not helping, Ames!"

"Okay, let's step back a little bit. How is Tom?"

"Aside from this craziness, he's great. A little over-protective, but obviously supportive and completely swamped."

"Of course. Tom's always been a detail man." Amy returned to her stool. "You don't have anything to prove to him."

"I don't want him to have to fire me and go broke to pay back the label." Sue took a generous swallow of her mimosa. She wasn't worried about proving anything to Tom. She worried about making him homeless. She worried about him losing his career and his friends over a gamble. She knew that no matter what, Tom would forgive even her worst transgressions and sing her praises the rest of the time. But would the band forgive Tom for risking their career along with his own?

Amy let out a loud, exuberant laugh. "I sincerely doubt that Tom would ever have to fire you. Even if he did, I bet he'd be too scared to break the news to you."

"He always has been a little afraid of me." Sue smiled despite her fears. Maybe the levity was good for her. Maybe Amy needed time to process this mess to help sort it out.

Amy opened a nearby drawer and pulled out her phone. "You've given me bits and pieces. Now let's go over this list you sent last night." Amy flashed the phone at Sue, then read a text out loud. "'*Chris thinks I'm a cockblock, Brad likes me, Justin tried to set me up with Carlo, Darryl met the love of his life in Austin, and I have a date for the benefit.*'" Amy arched an eyebrow. "Is your date Brad or Carlo?"

"No."

"Then you do have a lot to tell me."

Sue groaned. Those things were petty. She could figure them out with a few minutes to herself. Should she
come clean to the band? Was it wrong for her to remain
silent? Was she obligated to keep the secret? *This* was
where she needed help.

"Hey, you gave me the list, chickadee. Let's start at
the top. Chris thinks you're a cockblock. That's fun."

Sue launched into the story of the tour so far, filling
in all the little details that never made it through their
regular text conversations. She'd barely finished talking
about her date with Carlo, when Jack and Robin reap-
peared.

"Ladies," Robin said with a bit of a flourish. "Please
excuse the interruption, but we have some brilliance
you must hear."

Jack snickered as he plugged a flash drive into a small
stereo on the counter.

"You finally finished the song?" Amy asked.

"I think so." Jack nodded.

"Cool!" Sue hopped on her stool and patted the one
next to her.

Robin immediately plopped down and pulled her
against him. "Once this is over and you tell me how fantastic it is, you have to tell me everything. I've missed
too much."

Sue shifted in his arms and craned her head up to

look at him. Even seated, Robin seemed eight feet tall. She smiled at his sweet face and hugged him. "I will. After you tell me what inspired this patchy shaved head."

Music flooded the room, preventing his answer. Sue settled against him and listened, tapping out the rhythm with her feet. Jack replayed the song several times at Sue and Amy's request before returning to the eclectic mix.

"Please tell me your new album will be out soon. That is amazing, and I want to hear all the songs that go with it." Sue squeezed Robin's arm and smiled and Jack. "Preferably in my car and extremely loud. Until you tour on it."

Amy bounced on her seat. "Oh! Private show!"

Jack snickered. "I'll give you a private show."

"Dude." Robin rolled his eyes. "No sex talk in front of the kids." He leaned his head against Sue's. "You really like it?"

"I love it."

"We'll make sure you get a mix before you leave." Jack promised Sue.

Sue smacked a kiss on Robin's cheek and blew one to Jack.

Her phone rattled with a text. Sue checked the message—Tom checking that she was safe and sound—and sent him a quick response that she was with Amy and Robin and would be until the band arrived. Tom's quick acceptance surprised her. She figured he'd want more details or insist she check into the hotel.

"What's up?" Robin massaged her shoulders.

"Tom didn't try to boss me around." Sue didn't try to hide the shock in her voice.

"You're on a tour break."

Sue put a hand over Robin's. "I figured he'd be upset because he hadn't heard from me since my text that I got here."

"He knew you were here."

Sue smiled, happy to have Robin's unwavering confidence, and leaned against her friend. "This is nice. I've missed you guys."

"That's why you're gonna stick with us today." Robin pulled her off her stool.

"Perfect." Sue wrapped an arm around Robin's waist.

"But you must shower. I look gorgeous after crashing on the floor." Robin fluffed his bangs. "You look absolutely hideous."

CHAPTER 25

Sue accepted Amy's offer to shower and change at the house. After the hot water from the fancy multi-head shower pummeled her muscles to jelly, she climbed out and wrapped herself in oversized plush towels. She gathered her dirty clothes from the floor and slid her phone out of her pants pocket. The message indicator flashed.

Adam: Should I get you a corsage for the benefit? What color is your dress?

Sue grinned and replied.

This isn't prom. No corsage.

Her phone dinged almost immediately.

Adam: Then I guess I don't have to match my tie and cummerbund to your dress, either.

Sue giggled.

S: Hell no. And don't pick me up in a white limo.

A: Look who's too cool for school!

S: Everyone's cool in NOLA.

A: You there already?

S: Yep

A: Lucky. I'm outside the Cubs locker room.

S: Getting any good scoop?

A: Too distracted deciding whether to buy you a corsage anyway.

Sue laughed again.

S: No corsage.

A: What if I want a boutonniere?

S: I'll swipe a flower from a centerpiece.

A: Perfect.

Sue rolled up her clothes and went to the guest room, still smiling.

"Robin, leave her shit alone! Sue's gonna be so pissed if she catches you!" Amy pushed clothes back into Sue's bag as Robin lifted them out.

"I'm taking inventory. She shouldn't own clothes as awful as what she was wearing when she got here. I have to fix this."

Overwhelmed with affection for her friends, Sue leaned against the doorjamb. "Robin, while you're going through my stuff, hand me a pair of jeans, please?"

"How are you not mad at him for this?" Amy pushed her hair behind her ears and glared at Robin.

Sue dropped her dirty clothes by the door. "He's

Robin. He's immune to dirty socks and boxes of tampons."

Robin continued pulling clothes out of her bag and tossing them on the bed. He shook out the dress Sue had splattered hot sauce on and held it up. "What happened to this?"

"Bad day at a taco bar. I've been trying to work it out but haven't had a lot of time for stain fighting."

"Did someone shake a bottle at you or something?" Robin scratched at the fabric, smelled it, then touched his tongue to it and grimaced before shaking the dress out.

"Sort of." Sue took the dress and studied the midsection. Though the stain wasn't as dark as it had been, it had spread the way a bruise does as it heals. "I was on the phone with Chris, holding a packet of hot sauce. He made me angry. I squeezed it too hard—"

"And your dress paid the price." Robin shook his head and tsked.

"It was embarrassing. That was the first time I met Adam."

"Not at the fight?" Amy found the box of tampons Sue had mentioned and waved it under Robin's face.

Robin ducked around the box and pulled more clothing from the bag.

"No, that was the second time." Sue put the dress down and tossed two T-shirts she knew were dirty onto the floor.

"Does he remember the saucy incident?" Robin batted away the box Amy continued to wield and looked at Sue, eyebrows up.

"Yeah." Heat rose in Sue's cheeks, and she focused her gaze on picking through her clothes. "He mentioned it at the fight."

"Nice," Robin and Amy said at the same time.

Sue closed her eyes and shook her head. She'd been mortified that he remembered and thrilled that he stuck around and talked with her anyway. "Embarrassing."

"No, nice." Robin returned his focus to the dress. "Ames, you have a good dry cleaner?"

"Oh yeah."

Robin tossed a well-worn jean skirt to Sue, then rifled through the rest of her clothes. He plucked a T-shirt out of the pile, shook it out, and gave that to her as well. "Cool, we'll drop it off and go shopping."

"No. Shopping feels like work. Too many decisions. Let's walk the Quarter and maybe do Rock'n'Bowl." Sue wrinkled her nose at a pair of jeans and threw them on the floor with her other dirty items, then pushed all the clothes within reach back into her bag. She took the strand of rhinestones she'd bought in Austin out of a side pocket and draped them over Robin's shoulders. "For you, sir."

Robin pulled the glittering rope through his fingers. "This is perfect for my current sculpture."

"I know," Sue said, happy to give him something.

Robin beamed, then snapped to attention. "I refuse to spend any more time with you in baggy jeans, so deal with it." Robin handed Sue her makeup bag. "Besides, I owe you from that concert when Cherise spilled beer on your silk skirt."

"That *was* a good skirt."

"Yep. I have to replace it. Go." Robin pushed Sue toward the bedroom door. "Get dressed."

"I'm shaving those tufts of hair off your head before we go anywhere."

"I was saving that job for you. Now go!"

<hr>

Sue let Robin drag her into a high-end boutique. A peppy zydeco tune they'd heard buskers playing stuck with her as Robin and the salespeople dressed her in a wide variety of clothing. Robin let her nix a few outfits, but he had a good eye, and she didn't say no to much. After letting him pick clothes for her for close to ten years, Sue knew Robin would only select things that were both comfortable and flattering. When it came time to pay, she stepped aside to count her winnings from the fight, pleased she had some extra money to play with.

"What're you doing?" Robin asked as she thumbed through the tags on her selections.

"Adding."

"Why?" Robin rubbed a hand over his freshly shaved head.

"To make sure I have enough cash." Sue looked at him as though he should know better.

"Uh, no. I owe you. We already talked about this."

"One skirt, Robin. You already covered it with this ingenious black thing you found." Sue passed him a matching top and skirt.

Robin held the hangers at arm's length and smiled. "It is spectacular. I wouldn't have let you say no."

Sue returned his grin. "I'm glad." She thumbed the tags of the other items she wanted and closed her eyes to add.

"Stop." Robin gave her a quick squeeze, then gathered all the clothes. "Please let me do this."

"I have the money, Robin, it's okay."

"I brought you to this store; I picked these clothes. I never intended for you to spend a dime."

"Yeah, and I wouldn't have spent nearly as much time letting you dress me if I didn't recognize that I packed terribly for this trip."

"Hallelujah!" Robin raised a hand in the air and let out a whoop. "Save your dirty gambling money and let me spoil you." He strode toward the checkout counter with the clothes.

Sue trotted behind to keep up with his long gait.

"What're you wearing to the big dinner on Saturday?" Robin gave the clothes to the salesclerk, then faced Sue.

"I happen to have my black silk dress carefully tucked away in the car."

"I do like that dress." Robin smirked. "But it's a black-tie event."

"I've worn it to black ties before." Sue put her hands on her hips in defiance.

"Yes, and now you've been photographed in it. You can't wear it to another public event."

"How do you know?"

"You made TMZ, baby." Robin grinned like he'd won the lottery.

"I what!"

"Don't freak! It was just the website. You were listed as Carlo's companion. No name." Robin rolled his eyes. "A damn shame if you ask me. They should've printed your name. You looked great."

Sue couldn't hide her smile. "Thanks. I put a lot of effort into it that night." She shook her head. "That's not the point! What if Chris sees it?"

"Besides me, how many guys do you know go to the TMZ site?"

Sue twisted her mouth while she considered. "A lot. And what if someone else picks up the picture?"

"No one in the band will see it." Robin gave the cashier his credit card. "Even if they do, they'll be too distracted by how good you looked."

"Chris won't." Sue narrowed her eyes. "He's such a whiny pain in the ass."

"Then tell Chris to fuck off. Let's go, I have more styling to do on you."

CHAPTER 26

Justin spent his first afternoon in New Orleans walking. Grateful that Sue and Tom had orchestrated time off in a vibrant city, Justin seized the opportunity to explore it. Eventually, Sue and Tom texted with details on when and how to get into that night's benefit show. After two po' boys and a beer, he went to the designated spot and entered the club with the rest of his band as the headliner, Bloody Maggots, finished their soundcheck.

"Wow." Chris stopped short, eyes glued to the stage. "Is that Jack Ragnar hanging on stage with those guys?"

"Looks like it," Tom said.

"More importantly, who are the girls in those jeans?" Brad asked.

"Probably Amy and Sue."

Justin laughed and clapped a hand on Brad's shoulder. "Now we know you're not only attracted to her brain."

Chris and Tom laughed along with Justin.

Brad glared. "Ten bucks says that's not her."

"You're on." Chris stood next to Brad and extended his hand sideways to shake.

Justin pulled out his wallet. "I'm in."

Tom collected their money, then cleared his throat. "Hey, Sue!"

The women standing near the stage stopped talking and turned.

"Hey, guys!" Sue's face lit up when she recognized them. "Come meet everyone!" She gestured for them to come to her.

"Motherfucker," Brad hissed.

Justin counted the money Tom gave him, smirking at the extra five.

"Pleasure doing business with you." Chris clapped Brad on the back as he headed toward Sue.

Brad snarled.

Tom followed Chris to the main part of the club.

Justin studied Sue for a moment. "She does have a nice ass."

"Shut up."

"She hasn't worn tight jeans since that night in Maryland. It could've happened to any of us," Justin said.

"But it didn't."

"So what? Chris and Tom are gonna blow right past this. Sue never has to know."

"I spent almost two days away from her. I hit on some

pretty great-looking women. Thought I was past it. Then she has to…" Brad paused and curled his fingers into fists. "She only wears baggy clothes on tour, and the night I'm gonna prove I've moved on, she has to wear *those* jeans."

Justin chuckled but cut it short as frustration twisted Brad's face. "That makes tonight even better. She looks great, but you don't care. This club will be full of great asses in about an hour. No problem."

Brad shook his head. "I do care that she looks great. And it's not only how she looks."

Justin raised his eyebrows. Brad's efforts with women the last few days had not gone unnoticed. This morning he'd even traded numbers with someone staying in their hotel. How was this still an issue? "Then what is it?"

Brad scrubbed the heels of his hands against his eyes. "Most girls don't get past the guitar and the hair. She sees *me*. We talk about real stuff."

Justin studied Brad until the man looked away. Justin had been joking when he made the comment about Brad liking Sue's brain. It had never occurred to him that Brad's interest could be emotional rather than strictly physical. "She does that with all of us."

Brad shook his head, beating his thumbs against his thighs. "Not the same."

Justin narrowed his eyes, considering his response.

"Hey, Justin, Brad!" Sue called out. "Come on! I want to introduce you to Amy, Jack, and Robin."

"One sec!" Justin turned to Brad and forced eye contact. "Wanna get shitfaced? We have tomorrow off. You can be hungover and fix yourself. Then you move forward. Because Wednesday we go back to work."

"Yeah." Brad tapped his fingers against his legs. "Shitfaced sounds good."

He and Brad drank shots at the bar before joining Sue's group near the stage. Justin regretted his hasty suggestion to get drunk as soon as introductions were made. He and his bandmates all idolized Jack Ragnar and Echo Chamber. Brad should savor this moment, not drink through it.

As the club filled with people, Justin hung with Robin and paid attention to how the famous musician responded to fans asking for photos and autographs. Robin impressed by seeming genuinely thrilled to talk with everyone who recognized him. When people came by as the house lights dimmed for Bloody Maggots, Robin remained gracious but gave the band his respect. He quickly signed tickets, declined a photo, and redirected their attention to the stage.

Bloody Maggots immediately sucked Justin in with the energy they pumped out. Even Brad was entranced, never leaving for another drink. Justin mentally tipped his hat to the band for keeping his friend's attention. As soon as the band left the stage, Justin turned to Brad and went down a quick list of things he loved about the show. Eyes bright, Brad added to the list, giving Justin hope that maybe he'd moved on from the earlier crisis.

"Bloody Maggots, ladies and gentlemen." Jack Ragnar's voice came from the dark stage, surprising Justin and, based on the reaction in the room, everyone else. Jack summoned the band for another bow.

Once the house noise lowered, Amy joined Jack and thanked everyone for coming out. Brad hissed when Jack slung an arm around his wife and kissed her temple. They were the picture of a happy couple.

"Gonna get a refill." Brad disappeared in the crowd.

Justin chastised himself again. He needed to find a better way to help Brad cope with his emotions or the whole tour would suffer.

***

Jack gave Sue a lot to consider when he joined Bloody Maggots at the merch table, trading autographs for donations. T-shirts moved at lightning speed. Was that the way to get Words Fail Me shirts out there? Could the band afford to donate potentially their entire stock? Could she convince them it'd be a worthy investment? Her mind reeled at the possibilities as she catalogued the enthusiastic response from the fans.

Brad shuffled over, clearly drunk. He waved his full glass at the merch table. "Why the big deal? Jack's one of those guys who can't be bothered with autographs?"

"No." Amy bristled, always protective of her husband. "He likes to have more control over meet-and-greet situations. He's shy."

Brad barked a laugh while sloshing his drink. "Yeah, Jack Ragnar, King of Rock, is shy. Okay."

Sue put herself between Amy and Brad, shushing him. Whether Brad joked or was serious didn't matter. His tone implied criticism, and her friends didn't deserve it.

"You would be too if complete strangers thought they knew you inside and out." Amy sneered at Brad.

"Yeah, that'll be the day." Brad slurped his drink.

"Brad, please. Be nice," Sue said quietly. She didn't get why he went after Jack and Amy. They'd given him a huge opportunity, and more importantly, they were her *friends*. She leaned against his arm, trying to push him away from Amy.

"Why? No one cares who *I* am. Not even you." Brad spit as he talked.

Sue stepped back and glared. So this was why. He spit venom at people she loved to get to her. A poor choice. "Wow. You're stupid drunk."

"And?"

"I wish you weren't. I like you when you're sober and fun and not a complete asshole." Sue again tried to push him out of Amy's hearing.

"Whatever," Brad scoffed and stepped away. "You go play with your A-listers, and when you're ready to slum again, come find me. I'll be the nobody at the bar." He turned and lurched through the crowd.

The words landed like a slap, but Sue followed him, her anger growing with each step. If he wanted to get drunk and be an ass, he was welcome to do that somewhere else. Taking his shit out on her and the people who invited him wasn't an option. When she knew they were well away from Amy, Sue grabbed his arm, forcing him to stop. "Is that really what you think of yourself?"

"Don't you?"

"No." She didn't recognize how deeply Brad's words stung until he gave her a sloppy grin and downed the rest of his drink. Even if she had liked Brad the way he wanted, this immature manipulation would've killed it. She admitted to herself that if she'd been in a similar state, it'd be easier to deal with the emotion Brad wore on his sleeve. She struggled for what to say next. "Brad, I'm—"

Robin and Tom nudged her out of the way. They sandwiched Brad and practically carried him through the crowd and to the stage door. She stood in place, shocked as tears welled in her eyes. Had Brad spoken his mind? Had the liquor made him melodramatic?

Justin appeared out of nowhere. "Did he stomp all over you again?"

Sue glared at him but quickly bowed her head, knowing Brad deserved the dirty look. "In a manner of speaking." She wiped her face, willing herself not to cry.

"Hey, hey, that was supposed to be a joke. Like two left feet, you know." Justin crouched, making an extra effort to catch Sue's gaze. "What'd he say?"

Sue glanced away again, deciding which part of her

exchange with Brad weighed on her most. "Does he seriously think I'm slumming with you guys? Does he think that little of *all* of us?"

"No. None of us think that."

"Is he usually a mean drunk?"

"Not even close. He's working through some stuff."

Sue gave him a half-hug. "Okay. I'll be all right. He took me by surprise."

"You sure?"

"Yeah." She took in the crowd again, hoping Justin wouldn't catch the lie. She felt guilty. Brad's mood probably had to do with her, but she didn't know what to do about it without causing more trouble.

Justin put an arm around her shoulders. "If it's any consolation, he'll remember all of this tomorrow."

"That does make me feel better."

"Atta girl." Justin tightened his arm around her, and they worked their way back to Amy, who stared wide-eyed at Jack as he collected donations and signed autographs.

Sue tugged on her friend's arm to get her attention. "I'm sorry about Brad."

"What are *you* apologizing for? Brad's the dick." Amy gave Sue a quick hug, still watching Jack.

Justin laughed and gave Amy a high five.

Sue smiled in spite of herself. "He's not a dick."

"Yeah, he is," Justin said. "I've known him most of my life. I'm uniquely qualified to make that call." He held up his hands, offering a bashful look.

"He's raking it in, Ames!" Robin came up behind them and gripped Sue's shoulders.

"I know! My knight in shining armor!" Amy's smile overtook her face.

Robin cupped a hand around his mouth. "Jack, you're totally getting laid tonight!"

Jack smiled. He lifted his eyebrows at Amy, who immediately dissolved into giggles.

"It never occurred to me that *Jack Ragnar* would have to do anything to get laid," Justin said.

"He's a man in a relationship. He's gotta work for it like everyone else." Amy crossed her arms, still smiling.

Justin grunted. "That sums up why I'm single."

"Here, here." Robin offered a fist bump.

"Ames," Sue said. "Who works harder to get laid? Married Jack or Single Robin?"

Before Amy could answer, Robin bellowed, "Enough drooling over the hot rock star! How about some Rock'n'Bowl?"

Sue gave a little bounce at the suggestion. "Yes!"

"I'm in," Amy said.

"Let's do it!" Justin thumped his foot.

Sue surveyed the crowd of autograph seekers. "Let's find Tom and Chris."

"Tom's got his hands full, but there's Chris." Robin pointed him out.

"Snag him. I'll text Tom in case he can join us later." Sue pulled her phone out of her pocket, not feeling any guilt over excluding Brad.

Chris fidgeted as he sat alone on Bloody Maggots' tour bus. He'd been there ever since he'd gotten the text about hanging out with them and Echo Chamber. He hated looking eager, especially with anything that involved Sue, still he had to admit, she had a great hookup. Bloody Maggots were a hot new band and they put on a good show, but he'd been listening to Echo Chamber, the band he waited on now, since he was thirteen and they were in heavy rotation on the college rock station. Echo Chamber grew into the biggest band in the world, and Sue was tight with them. Figuring out how she managed to get these connections in that Podunk town she lived in kept him up at night.

Sue hadn't said as much, but he figured accepting her invitation to go bowling with his heroes would cost him. It was worth it. He'd sneer through whatever interviews this obligated him to.

Chris fiddled with his phone, needing to look busy. He smirked when a photo message from an unknown number came up. Tom would tell him not to download it.

"It might be a virus," he'd say.

By now, Chris knew better. If it was a virus, there'd likely be a gratuitous T-and-A shot with it. Another chance worth taking. He loved horny cock chasers.

He downloaded the message. Oh yeah. A beautiful rack with tight nipples, followed by a perfectly rounded ass. The third and last photo was a tease. A shot down her pants that made it clear she waxed thoroughly but didn't give him a glimpse of lip. He sent a message back.

Chris: Love to, honey, got a band thing. You around later?

Girl: I know you're with Echo Chamber. Show them. They'll let me in the party.

Chris blanched. He knew these women used him as much as he used them, but this was the first time one of them was so unabashed about it.

No dice.

He deleted her messages and photos.

When the bus door finally opened, the chatter outside bled in. Sue climbed on, glowing with laughter, followed by Justin. Of course that fucker was friends with her. He could be friends with anyone.

Robin's long legs ate up the steps, and he pushed the other two farther into the bus. He surveyed the space, then hung his long body out the door.

"Come on, dickfaces! Bus rolls in three minutes!" Robin came back in and flopped onto the bench next to Chris, gesturing toward his phone. "Any good texts?"

Chris smirked. "A few."

"Nice." Robin drew out the word and offered a fist

bump.

Chris schooled his features to hide how giddy he felt over chatting with someone he admired.

Sue caught his eye, wearing a giant smile. "Anyone you want to bring along?"

Sue was willing to let him bring a girl? No. The price would be too high. Besides, the girl who texted him was obviously a star fucker. He wasn't about to compete with her for attention from Robin or anyone else. Especially if he wasn't likely to get laid afterward. He shook his head.

"She'll wait."

Sue looked toward the front of the bus, where Amy boarded. Jack followed right behind her with Bloody Maggots, the band he'd personally selected to open the first night of his week-long benefit, on his heels. Lucky fucks.

Robin slung an arm along the back of the bench he sat on. "Danny, Nate, and Ali coming?" he asked, referring to the rest of Echo Chamber.

Jack shook his head. "Ali's laying low since he finally kicked the flu. Nate's shacking up. Danny's playing a midnight gallery show."

"Sweet." Robin jutted his chin at Sue. "Tom?"

Sue checked her phone. "He's holding back Brad's hair. He'll hang tomorrow."

"Road managers always get the shit end."

"Chris." Jack settled into a seat across from Chris, Amy on his lap. "Nice save with the T-shirt markers."

"Huh?" Chris looked up from his phone, surprised Jack remembered his name, let alone addressed him directly.

"For signing the shirts. Those markers came in handy. Didn't smear at all." Jack grinned and held up his left hand, pointing out the lack of ink along the edge.

"Oh." Chris hoped the blush that burned his cheeks wasn't too bright. "Yeah, my mom gives me a pack of laundry markers before every tour. I don't know why. It's not like the guys are gonna steal my shorts."

Jack chuckled. "They were great tonight. I'm gonna have to find out if they make them in metallic colors since all our shirts are black. Less mess than paint pens."

Chris nodded, too self-conscious to know what to say.

Robin clapped his hands, getting the other people into their seats. "All right, let's ride!"
The engine growled as the bus crawled forward. Chris took in the people around him, fighting the urge to take pictures. How did this become his life? He stopped questioning it and soaked it all in. He'd worry about Sue calling in this favor later.

Once at the bowling alley, Chris stood next to Justin, his arms folded, and jerked his chin toward Sue, standing with Jack near the ball return. They were having an animated discussion, Sue demonstrating something with a bowling ball and a wide smile.

"Is she always this…" Chris held out a hand as he searched for the word. "Glowy?"

Justin glanced at Chris, then back at Sue. "Yeah. She dials it down sometimes. A lot, actually. But yeah, she lights up the room."

Chris snapped his gaze to Justin, worried that he was also into Sue. Justin was ogling the tits on the girl who brought two pitchers of beer to the high tops behind their lanes.

"Hey, Justin!" Amy shouted. "You're up! You'll be next, Chris!"

Chris went to his lane, seizing the chance to talk with Jack.

After the first game, Jack and the guys from Bloody Maggots went to check out a small arcade near the bar. Chris stayed put, not wanting to be a pest, even though he found the idea of watching Jack play *Space Invaders* infinitely appealing. Robin brought back a fresh pitcher of beer and summoned everyone to the table for refills and food.

Justin settled on the stool between Chris and Amy. After downing half of his beer, Justin turned to Amy. "I know you and Sue go way back. But how did you guys meet Robin? Through Jack?"

Chris immediately sat straighter. He'd been dying to know how they'd all met.

"No," Amy said. "I didn't meet Jack until Sue had known Robin for a while. She met him through an ex-boyfriend."

"Sue has terrible taste in men," Robin said.

"Not *all* men." Sue gestured toward Robin with her mug. "I hang with you."

"Yeah, but you had seriously poor judgment when you chose *that* man."

Sue dipped her head. "You got me there."

Chris smirked. The idea of Sue employing poor judgment tickled him. She didn't know everything after all.

"So what about this guy?" Justin asked.

Amy sat back on her stool. "Our senior year in high school, Sue decided to date this college guy, a bouncer."

"A bouncer? Really, Sue?" Chris didn't hide his skepticism. He made a point to not know much about her, but the idea that she liked bouncers didn't fit.

"I didn't know he was a bouncer when I met him. I learned that after a few dates." Sue sighed. "He was beautiful."

Amy nodded. "So beautiful. Tall and built. He had gorgeous chestnut hair—almost like a shiny mane. Total eye candy." Amy chewed on a nacho, obviously pondering something. "You know, he kinda looked like Brad."

Sue shrugged. "Yeah. I never thought about it. Anyway, Jon took me to an Echo Chamber concert. It was one of those nights when all kinds of things were passed around the stadium, and he decided it was his job to try it all."

"Did *you* try anything?" Justin asked.

Chris perked to the question, hoping he'd finally get some dirt on Sue.

"Nah."

Of course not. Sue avoided vices like someone planning to run for office.

She made a face, then continued. "By the end of the concert, he was in a state."

Robin laughed. "Who wouldn't be—drugs or no—after a classic Echo Chamber show?"

"This is true, Sue," Amy said with wide eyes.

Sue bowed her head, conceding the point.

Impatient with their punch-drunk banter, Chris prompted them. "So, what? He went nuts and tried to get backstage?"

Robin refilled his mug and topped off those near him. "He went nuts, all right, but he never made it backstage."

"Yeah," Sue said. "He kept talking about how the show was *transcendent*. At some point he fixated on Robin and what a quote 'beautiful creature' he is." Sue leaned her head against Robyn.

About to take another sip of beer, Justin said "Uh oh."

"Yeah. He was deeply apologetic as he explained that he had to leave me for Robin." Sue beamed at her friend.

Amy broke into giggles. Chris exchanged a glance

with Justin.

"He was gay?" Justin asked.

"I don't know. It didn't occur to me until that night." Sue sat upright. "I told him it was cool if he wanted to leave me, but he should find out if Robin was into men first. He didn't believe me about Robin being a guy."

"I had long braids at the time," Robin explained.

"That he wore in a ponytail on top of his head." Sue reached to put her hand on top of Robin's head and smiled at him, then everyone at the table.

"His second-skin latex shirt probably didn't help, either," Amy said, cheeks flushed. Chris couldn't tell if the color came from merriment or too much beer.

"I can't help that latex looks so damn good on me." Robin scooped up a nacho chip and shoved it into his mouth.

Chris rubbed his temples. Why did these people have to take so long to get to the point? If this wasn't Robin Fucking Jung, Chris would've beat it out of him already. "I still don't get how you met Robin through all this."

"I'm getting there," Sue said. "Jon was wasted and decided he had to go back to the stadium to get his love. He was too high to remember he was holding the belt loop over my left ass cheek, so he pulled me with him. I tried to get him to come back to the car, or at least let go of my pants. He walked maybe four steps before he tripped on a grate in the parking lot and fell."

"Oh no." Justin sat back and crossed his arms. "He

brought you down with him."

"Nope. But he took part of my pants with him." Sue slapped the table.

The image of Sue's ass hanging out of her pants in the middle of a parking lot was too much. Chris laughed, not realizing how hard or long until Justin elbowed him in the ribs as everyone settled down.

"As I recall from your rant, they were your favorite jeans." Robin lifted his mug as though he were about to toast.

Sue narrowed her eyes. "They were."

Robin laughed again. "Has Sue yelled at you guys yet?"

"No," Justin said.

Chris glanced toward Sue before answering. "Not really."

Amy snorted. "If you're saying not really, the answer is no."

"Ames is right." Robin pulled Sue against him. "This woman can make a sailor blush. She yells long and loud, and you'll never forget what you did to piss her off."

Sue blushed deeply and hid her face behind the glass she held.

Amy bounced in her seat. "You have to finish the story, Robin."

"This stoned guy is literally on his knees, begging Sue to stop yelling and help him find the love of his life. Sue is yelling that no way in hell is she gonna help him do anything with a good chunk of her ass on display." Robin patted Sue low on the back. "It was great."

Justin grinned. "And you had to help the damsel in distress."

"Naturally. We were getting ready to board the bus when I saw them. I couldn't resist checking out what was going on. And *that* is how I met Sue."

"We both got to reject Jon on the same night." Sue squeezed Robin's hand.

"Beautiful, stoned, and nowhere near as interesting as the woman yelling in the parking lot." Robin pulled Sue toward him and kissed her on the head.

The way Sue and Robin beamed at each other gave Chris a profound reminder of how much he missed Brad's sister, Annabelle. Darryl, Annabelle, and Chris were as tight as Sue, Robin, and Amy. Sure, he texted with her all the time, but it was different not having her on tour anymore. What made the moment between Sue and Robin even worse was the realization that Sue seemed to give her friends, and his whole band, every bit of care and attention that Annabelle did. He wasn't often lonely on the road, especially for a woman, but the pang for Annabelle made his whole chest throb.

Sue hugged Robin. "That was the night Robin started replacing my clothes."

Robin held up one finger. "Only the clothes I had a hand in ruining."

Sue patted her thigh. "He got me these jeans to replace the ones Jon ruined. He gave me leather pants two years later when another friend burned a hole in a different pair of jeans with a clove cigarette."

Robin gestured with his beer. "Those are the only two pairs of pants Sue's allowed to wear around me."

"Allowed?" Chris looked from Robin to Sue, remembering his flub a few weeks before when some guy had hit on her. When Chris told Sue that she belonged to his band, she immediately shut him down, all but calling him a fuckboy. Now she appeared unaffected by Robin's choice of words. Famous dudes got away with that shit around her?

Robin leaned forward. "Sue needs to show more leg. She danced for years. She should show it off."

The memory of the morning after Chris had spiked Sue's beer surfaced. She'd answered her hotel room door without pants. The eyeful of leg had been nice. Chris plucked a jalapeño from the nachos. "I get it. She does have good legs."

Robin threw back his head and laughed as Justin choked on his beer. Amy and Sue stared at Chris, clearly shocked.

"What? You *do*." Chris ate the pepper, giving them a minute to get over the surprise. Even though she was a bossy broad, he could concede that she was attractive.

"Wow." Sue looked dazed as she reached toward the food in the center of the table.

Amy stared at Sue for a moment before speaking to

Robin. "What did you guys get today?"

"I replaced her silk skirt from last time we hung out."
Robin addressed Chris and Justin. "A woman I was sort
of seeing dumped beer on Sue to get my attention."

"Who are these people you guys hang out with and
why do they hate you, Sue?" Justin asked.

Sue smiled and shrugged.

Robin put his elbows on the table and leaned toward
Justin. "I think she plants them so I have to buy her
clothes."

"*Right.*" Sue stretched out the word.

"He does upgrade you every time." Amy popped a fry
into her mouth.

"Wait till you see the skirt, Ames." Robin leaned back
on his stool and gestured to illustrate. "It hits her in
just the right spot to show off that line that goes up her
thighs."

Chris exchanged another look with Justin.

"Did you meet Jack through Robin?" Chris asked
Amy.

"No. Sue and Robin have been thick as thieves for
years. I didn't meet Robin until a few days after I met
Jack at a show in Maryland about three years ago."

"How is that possible?"

"Easy." Sue put down the nacho she had scraped
along the bottom of the platter. "I met Robin senior

year in high school. Ames and I went to different colleges. I never had the opportunity back then to introduce them, or believe me, I would've. She loves the whole 'I got dumped for Robin' story."

Chris turned to Justin, still puzzled. Justin topped off his beer.

Amy nudged Chris with her elbow. "It's okay, Chris. We got all the pieces together eventually."

"I'll drink to that." Sue raised her glass. They all clinked glasses and bottles together.

Chris admitted to himself that the dynamic between Sue, Robin, and Amy was genuine. He supposed that meant Sue was, too. But it didn't mean he'd be good when she finally cashed in on letting him hang out with Jack and Robin.

CHAPTER 28

Spending time with her friends and seeing things from a fresh perspective gave Sue new ideas on how to move more merchandise. The next morning, she outlined them at breakfast, then texted Tom to meet her in the hotel parking garage. His footsteps echoed through the space as she hauled a box of T-shirts out of their equipment trailer.

"If anyone else summoned me to a parking garage to talk, I'd be way more suspicious," Tom said. "And even though it's daylight, I don't like you being out here alone."

"I'm not alone anymore, Tommy." Sue flashed her eyebrows and shoved the box down the ramp. "Let's talk money."

Tom raked a hand through his hair. "This is a weird place for that talk. How much do you need?"

"Sweet cousin." Sue's heart swelled. "It isn't for me. It's for the band."

"The guys are asking you for money?"

"Merch sales."

"Ah. A new box of CDs arrived yesterday. More of those dollar pins, too. We're good."

Sue propped one hand on her hip. "We need to move

more shirts. They have a better margin, and they advertise the band."

"What's your idea?"

Sue grinned, glad he knew she already had something in mind. "I have a few, but they involve a small investment."

Tom crossed his arms. "I'm listening."

"I only want to bring two T-shirt designs to the show tomorrow night. A limited amount of the best seller, plus the one with the most inventory. We offer them both until a few songs before the show ends. Then we take down the popular shirt. When they start signing stuff for donations, we only sell the slow mover."

"No stickers or pins?"

"The pins are too small to sign, and the stickers don't have enough space for more than one signature. But I have an idea for that, too." Sue retrieved her laptop from the equipment trailer and flipped it open, pulling up designs with extra negative space. "Robin said he'd help me refine these and would even sign some to help bring in donations. Plus, he knows a printer who'll run them for us today at a decent price."

Tom took over the computer, scrolling through the images. "So, our investment is the cost of the T-shirts we trade for donations, plus the cost of the stickers."

"Yes, and I have a way to recoup some of it." Sue didn't want anyone walking around broke. Merchandise sales kept money in the guys' pockets and sometimes put gas in the tour bus's tank.

"Go on."

"The sticker quote is for five thousand pieces. We can sell them at the rest of our gigs. If the designs go over well, we can put one on shirts for a small run and see how they do."

"Would Robin let us put up a sign in the merch booth citing him as the designer?"

"I already asked. He said yes."

Tom shut the laptop and handed it to Sue. "I like it. We can swing the money, and if the designs are hot, we'll be in better shape in the long run."

"Exactly." Sue drummed her fingers against the laptop. "Are you sure the band can afford it?"

"I'm sure. I'll run the numbers before we explain it to the guys. They may wanna limit how many shirts we give away."

"Bloody Maggots donated 125 last night."

"Okay, I'll start there and add the sticker prices. We can afford it."

"Don't lie to me, Tom. 125 shirts will cost the band a thousand dollars."

Tom sighed and paced the length of the equipment trailer and back. "I'm not lying. I'll show you the ledger. We make enough money that we don't have to share hotel rooms anymore, even though we do. There's some slush."

"A thousand dollars of slush?"

Tom wiggled his hand. "Seven fifty would be safer. But yeah. A little over that, actually."

"Will they be okay with this?"

"Like I said, we may need to negotiate how many shirts we give away. Otherwise, they know they need to put some money out to get the return."

"Then why the secrecy about my contract?" Sue asked in a lower voice.

"We can always make more money. Risking music is different."

The full weight of what was at stake resettled itself on Sue's shoulders. She wouldn't let the next album get canceled. "Do the guys share rooms to save money for stuff like this? If they don't have to ask the label for an advance for merch, it looks like they're making more."

"Nope." Tom tapped the calculator app in his phone. "We do it for Renee."

"Darryl's sister?"

"Yeah. Renee is NASA-level smart, and she won a scholarship to some intense engineer program, but it only covered tuition. Mrs. Black wanted to take out a second mortgage, but Darryl stopped her. He asked Chris to bunk up so he could send most of his money home."

"D is a freaking unicorn," Sue said.

Tom looked up from his phone. "It made sense on a couple of levels. There're nights when some of us skip the hotel. Why pay for unused rooms?"

"That's very pragmatic, Tommy."

Tom rolled his eyes and went back to his calculations. "While Renee was in that program, we all kicked in. Now she's in some other program where she gets paid. We're all used to sharing rooms, though, so we do."

"Wait." Sue waved a hand in front of his face. "You all sent money home for Renee?"

Tom swiped off his phone and gave Sue his full attention. "Yeah."

"What did Darryl say?"

"He didn't know for a while. I do the payroll. D gave me the account he wanted the money to go to. Chris came to me first, then Justin and Brad. Everyone kicked in about sixty bucks a week on top of what Darryl sent, which was easily eighty percent of his take. His mom called, concerned he was either whoring himself or not eating because it was so much money."

Sue snickered. "I know Darryl doesn't get out there the way the rest of the guys do, but you know, rock tour."

"We don't talk to our mothers about that."

"Wise." Sue put her laptop back in the trailer and opened the shirt box. "You gave money to Renee, too?"

"Yeah."

Overcome, she hugged Tom. Her cousin had always been supportive of her and her brother. Seeing him treat the band and their extended family like they were his own hit her on a deep level. She both understood and hated why he kept her contract a secret. Tom had absolute faith in her that she'd deliver for these guys. She wouldn't let him down. After a few seconds, Tom patted her back, and Sue let him go. "And now you're all used to living on the cheap, so I can spend that money to make them famous. Thanks, Renee!"

Tom slid his phone into his back pocket. "Which one is the slow mover?"

Sue dug around in the box and pulled out a gray shirt with a muscle car on it.

"That's Justin's favorite."

"I'm not surprised. But it has lots of room for signing, and this will get more visibility on his beloved car. Isn't that still a win?"

"Save your bullshitting for Justin."

Sue swung the shirt over her shoulder, then pushed the box back into the equipment trailer. "I'm gonna meet Robin at the printer to get things rolling with the stickers. Wanna come?" Sue grabbed her laptop, then closed and locked the equipment trailer.

"Nah. I'll go explain all this to the guys. Keep your phone handy in case they have questions."

Sue and Robin spent a few hours finalizing designs. True to his word, Robin created an original drawing for a new T-shirt. When she sent the sketch to Tom, he immediately called her back with a budget for stickers and told her the band wanted a run of one hundred shirts featuring Robin's design, along with a sign for the merch table. Declaring the day a success, Robin picked up Amy and took both women out for a late lunch. They sat at an outdoor café, talking about their plans for the rest of the week.

"We have more people joining the fray tonight, right?" Robin lifted his eyebrows at Sue. "The Nomads, your California boys?"

Sue stabbed at a tomato in her salad. "I think so. Their show is tomorrow, Ames?"

"Yep." Amy sipped a bottle of water. "They just finished a few dates opening for Foo Fighters and have some time off. They're staying straight through Sunday, too."

"Nice exposure!" Sue sat back. "It'll be so great to catch up. I haven't seen those guys in about a year."

"It's been more than a year for me—since the wedding." Amy leaned forward. "Do you still fantasize about locking yourself in the coat check with Owen?"

Sue laughed. "No. Not lately." She hadn't thought about another man like that since she met Adam.

"That's a shame." Robin narrowed his eyes. "At least let me dress you tonight. Give Owen a taste of what he's missed."

"You want me in that dangerous black outfit you found." Sue dug around in her salad, smiling at Robin. This man would forever encourage her confidence, and she loved him for it and a thousand other things.

"Oh yeah. With a smoky eye."

Sue nodded. "I can go for that."

Robin sat back and clapped. "Yes! Now, Ames, on to you."

"Me?" Amy looked aghast. "Happily married!" She waved her left hand at Robin.

"Yes! And still gorgeous. We're gonna work that hour-glass of yours. Make Jack drool from the stage."

Sue tipped her drink toward Amy. She loved watching her friend bring Jack to his knees. "In for a penny, in for a pound."

Amy tapped her bottle against Sue's. "Who can say no to Robin, anyway?"

CHAPTER 29

With plans in place to hang out with The Nomads after the show, Sue dressed to kill. Her hair and makeup were perfectly arranged—courtesy of Robin—and she entered the club through the back entrance with an extra spring in her step. A quick trip backstage confirmed that Words Fail Me hadn't arrived yet. Sue stopped at the end of the bar, facing the entry, and dialed Tom to find out when everyone would get there. Before Tom answered, Brad walked in.

"Hey, Brad!" Sue canceled her call.

Brad lifted his chin when he saw her and walked toward the bar.

"How was your day?"

"Long and painful." Brad rested his elbows on the bar and quirked a small smile.

"Oh, yeah." Sue glanced at her phone, remembering how drunk he'd been the night before. "Bad hangover, huh?"

"That I can deal with. Justin yammering all day was torture."

"Yammering?"

"Yeah. He likes to talk my ear off when I'm hungover. He thinks it's fun to add to my headache."

"What does he talk about?'

Brad rolled his eyes. "Nothing. Sometimes he dramatically reenacts whatever's on TV or the radio. It's a real pleasure."

Sue bit back her laugh.

"Listen, before anything else happens, I owe you an apology." Brad ran a hand through his hair and looked her in the eye. "I've been, ah, dealing with some stuff. Last night getting drunk seemed like the best way to handle it. I never meant to be such an ass. I said horrible things that I didn't mean. I'm sorry."

He had looked away during his apology, and Sue waited for him to meet her gaze again before speaking. She needed to see his face to know if he apologized out of a sense of obligation, or if he felt like an ass. She hoped for the latter. He'd already been forgiven, but him feeling bad meant he'd be less likely to pull something like that again.

"Thank you. Now let's get one thing straight. I am not, nor have I ever been, slumming with you guys. If I thought even for a second that any of you were bottom-dwellers, I never would've wasted my time. Stop acting like it."

Brad gave her a deer-in-the-headlights expression, then blinked it away and straightened his posture. "Yes, ma'am."

"I mean it, Brad. You guys have something special going on. I'm lucky to be a part of it. Let go of whatever's bothering you and enjoy what's happening for your band."

His small smile didn't reach his eyes as he ran his hand through his hair again. "I don't deserve anything that you're saying, but thank you."

"As soon as you get your head out of your ass and see what I do, we'll all be much better off." Sue closed her eyes for a moment. She hadn't meant to lecture. She huffed then refocused on Brad, hoping her expression was casual. "Amy deserves an apology, too."

"Done." Brad leaned against the bar. "Can I buy you a drink?"

"Sure." Sue silently summoned the bartender and they ordered.

Robin emerged from backstage. "Hey, man, how's the shoulder?"

"A little sore." Brad rubbed his left shoulder and grinned sheepishly.

"What happened?" Sue asked.

Brad kept his eyes on his soda as he spoke. "Ran into a doorway."

Sue faced Robin. "I wonder how he ran into a doorway, Robin."

"I have no idea," Robin said, the picture of innocence. "You know how unstable drunk people can be. One minute we're walking toward the dressing room, and the next Brad pegged the doorway. It's lucky he didn't face plant."

"True." Brad pressed the back of his hand to his

mouth as his eyes danced.

"I'm not buying it." Sue swung her gaze back and forth between them. They were both in good humor, yet something more lingered. She wanted one of them to give it up.

"What?" Robin asked.

Sue stared Robin down. "Lucky he didn't face plant?"

"I am. Can't sing with a swollen mouth," Brad said.

Robin snickered. "Or play guitar with a busted arm."

Sue put a fist on her hip. "Are you guys reliving a fight?"

"I can honestly say there was no fight." Brad held up a hand as though swearing an oath. Then he and Robin laughed.

Sue wanted to ask them to clarify when her phone rang. Adam.

"I'll be right back." She waved the phone at the guys, then power walked to an adjoining room where it was quieter. She waited a beat before answering to make sure she sounded casual. "Hey."

"How's New Orleans?"

Sue leaned against a shelf, savoring his deep voice. "Amazing, as always."

"Good. I can't wait to get there."

"That will be?"

"Tomorrow night," Adam said.

Her pulse pounded. She'd get to see him sooner than she'd thought. "Do you want to come to the show?"

"I'd love to, except my flight gets in too late."

The obvious regret in his voice took some of the sting out of his dismissal. "We have a dinner thing after. Join us." Sue cringed, hoping she didn't sound desperate.

"As anxious as I am to see you again, I want you to myself on our first date."

Sue almost purred into the phone and turned to face the shelves to give herself an extra degree of privacy as she shivered at the possibilities his statement held. "Can't argue with that."

"Good. What about Thursday?"

"Sure."

"We can go to the Café du Monde for breakfast, then check out the city. Maybe go to the zoo since that's what's bringing us all there."

"I like it, but I have to do some things at the club that morning. Lunch?"

"Hmmm."

The sound resonated in Sue, putting her on edge as she waited for Adam's next words.

"Are you sure we couldn't at least grab coffee?"

Ready to say yes to damn near anything he asked in

that honey voice, Sue forced herself to be pragmatic. She was in New Orleans to drum up press for the band and build her business. Not for Adam. Adam was an excellent bonus, but still a bonus. Worked needed to come first. "Maybe."

"I'm gonna make that maybe a yes."

Sue clung to her last bit of resolve. "We'll see."

"I have to go. Talk with you soon."

As she blocked out Thursday afternoon on her calendar, her phone vibrated.

A: If I can get an earlier flight on Wednesday, you free?

S: Definitely maybe.

A: Tease.

S: You gotta get here first, big talker.

Brad waited at the bar for their drinks, regretting that he'd let Sue talk him into joining the late-night romp down Bourbon Street. He tried to focus on the house band as they played a kick-ass rendition of 'The Train Kept A-Rollin'' but he couldn't keep his eyes off Sue on the dancefloor, the skirt that barely covered her ass, and The Nomads singer, Owen, dancing with her. Jealousy burned a pit in his stomach.

"Jesus," Brad whispered. She danced with Owen the

same way she had with D. It wasn't worthy of jealousy. And yet... He scrubbed his fists against his eyes, only to open them to Owen's hands on Sue's hips. Brad turned to the bartender. "I know it's a big order—got anything I can take back to the table?"

The bartender lifted his chin and pushed a tray toward Brad. "One more martini and you can take this."

Brad drummed his fingers against the bar, waiting as the bartender carefully strained the mixed drink into a glass and dropped a toothpick with two olives into it. Brad took the tray with both hands and made his way through the crowd toward the long table Tom had managed to reserve for them.

"Want me to go back for the rest?" Tom asked.

"I'm good." Brad set the tray down and hustled back to the bar, relieved to have had a minute to focus on something else.

The bartender shoved another tray at him, this one full of water glasses. "Bring back the trays, and I'll have all your beers ready."

Brad saluted and trudged back to the table, narrowly missing Chris's date. If she wasn't drunk already, she looked close. Wobbly on her feet, Chris's arm around her kept her from crashing into Brad and his tray. Brad raised his eyebrows, hoping his friend wasn't about to take advantage of an impaired woman. Chris shrugged and gestured toward the oversized tumbler of water she drank from. Brad nodded and continued to the table.

"Yay, water!" Sue bounced on pencil-thin heels, her muscular legs damn near glittering from her ankles up, up, up to the edge of her skirt. When Brad set out the glasses, she took one and chugged.

He studied her hemline, a touch disappointed that it didn't creep up even a little bit.

A sharp pain in his ribs broke Brad's concentration. Tom glared at him, clearly ready to inflict more pain. Brad pressed his lips together and gave Sue's cousin his best silent apology.

"Unload the drinks," Brad said. "I gotta take these trays back to get all the beer."

"Lemme help." Owen reached around Sue and unloaded the trays. He grabbed one and worked his way around the table. Brad took the other and led the way to the bar.

"Who's rooming with Chris tonight?" Owen asked.

Brad grinned at the question. "Tom."

"He better hope you or Justin go home with someone so he's not sleeping in the lobby."

"Either way, we have him covered. We're making enough now that no one sleeps outside."

Owen offered a fist bump. "Feels good, doesn't it? Finally doing more than breaking even?"

"Yeah. How long'd it take you guys?"

"Felt like fucking forever. We've been on steady ground for about two years now. It's nice."

Brad passed Owen one of the trays of beer, then

picked up the other.

Already headed toward the table, Owen looked over his shoulder and called back, "Of course, we had some luck before that. With friends like Amy and Sue, we had soft places to land when we needed 'em."

Brad almost fumbled the tray but collected himself quickly. Even though he was behind Owen, he didn't want the man turning around and seeing his seething jealousy over Sue being a "soft place."

"You okay?" Justin appeared at Brad's elbow and took the tray.

"Yeah."

"You sure?"

"I'm jealous as all fuck of Owen dancing with Sue, but I'm dealing."

Justin passed the tray to Tom and faced Brad again. "You got this, man. Trial by fire. By the time we leave New Orleans, she'll be like a sister to you."

Brad barked a laugh. "Yeah, Sister Sexy Sue, the best thing to ever happen to a nun's habit."

"Will you punch me if I laugh?"

Brad gave his friend a genuine smile. "Nah. Sue'd have my ass for bruising your pretty face before a photoshoot. And not in a good way."

"You know it."

"I heard my name!" Sue shouted from across the

table. "That must mean one of you is ready to get back on the dancefloor. Who's it gonna be?"

"Me." Owen wrapped his arms around her. "Always me, baby."

The fire hit new levels in Brad's gut.

CHAPTER 30

Jack Ragnar had offered his studio to Words Fail Me for a practice session, and Chris wasn't going to be late. He had an hour to get this bitch up and out and get to the warehouse district. Chris jiggled his foot against the bed as he tied his shoe. He slammed his foot on the floor and pushed the other against the bed, jiggling again as he tied. He slammed his foot on the floor and checked the time on his phone. How long would it take to get this girl gone?

In retrospect, it had been wrong to shut off the alarm the second it woke him. He'd showered and dressed too quietly, too. This chick had been a fiend the night before—which had been fun after working up a good buzz on Bourbon Street—but he was done with her now. He flopped on the bed and shook her.

"Wake-up time, sweetheart. I gotta go."

She spoke into the pillow, so he grabbed her shoulder and pulled her onto her back. "What?"

"Do you have to be such a jerk?"

"I gotta go. Get up."

The girl glared, then stretched her arms over her head. "No need to rush. Let's get a shower first." She gave him a slow wink, making her smeared eye makeup look like a bruise.

Chris scrubbed his hand against his head. He might be an asshole, but he wasn't the kind who gave women black eyes. "Already showered. Let's go."

She sat up and pounded her fists on the bed. "I am not leaving here like this. I'm taking a shower."

"Fine, sweetheart. I put your clothes on the chair." Chris opened his wallet and threw a few bills at her. "Get yourself some breakfast after you leave."

He strode out the door, pulling it shut behind him. He addressed a maid with a cart. "This room's ready for service."

He took the stairs, not willing to stick around for any more antics from the groupie. When he got to the lobby, he ducked into the terrace to check for Brad and Justin. Sue was there with the guy who'd hung all over her last night. He made a mental note to rub it in with Tom when he collected on the bet they'd all made the night before about whether Sue'd bang the guy. Tom had been emphatic that she wouldn't. That fucker thought he knew her so well. Chris sent Brad and Justin a text that he wasn't waiting for their lazy asses to go to Jack Ragnar's studio, then set out on foot, letting the morning sun burn off the traces of his hangover.

About halfway there, he got a text from Tom telling him to cut the crap and let him into their room. Chris responded that he was almost at the studio and received a string of angry messages about the girl. Chris put his phone on silent and continued on. Tom handled all the tour hiccups. He could handle this, too.

Robin let Chris into the studio and showed him

around, inviting Chris to sit with him and Jack while they mixed a song. Chris spent every moment absorbed in their process, so much so that Jack startled him when he got up to answer the buzzer. Brad and Justin followed Jack into the room, joining Chris on the couch. The three of them sat with Jack and Robin for another twenty minutes before they went to the practice room to arrange their gear.

When Darryl walked through the door, Chris wanted to spill what he'd learned. He greeted his friend with a shake and a slap on the back. It was weird that D didn't make eye contact with him.

Tom stalked in behind Darryl, dropped Sue's laptop bag on a side table, and glared at Chris. "We had to get another room thanks to that chick you banged refusing to leave. You owe us one seventy-nine a night, man."

Chris smirked. "D's the one who needs the room-mate."

"Not being a douchebag is getting pricey." Darryl sat behind the keyboards and fiddled with the settings.

"Whatever." Chris rolled his eyes. "Split it?"

Darryl finally made eye contact with Chris. "I'll do fifty a night."

Chris scowled. "Eighty."

"Forty."

"Fine. Fifty." Chris shook Sue's laptop out of the bag. "That girl said she saw Sue online."

"Maybe." Tom sat on a nearby couch. "With all the events at Indie Showcase and her old job in radio, she could've shown up on a lot of sites."

"She saw Sue on TMZ." Chris sat on a stool and flipped open the laptop.

"Sue was on TMZ?" Justin stood from his kit, spinning a drumstick across his knuckles.

"She said there were pictures of her with Tony Azzuré at the fight."

"Go, Sue." Darryl played a few chords.

"Exactly what I was thinking," Chris said dryly.

"Let's see 'em." Justin pulled a tall stool toward Chris and gestured for the computer.

Brad fidgeted, then fell in behind Justin. "Where's Sue?"

"Robin's making her coffee. She'll be in here any minute." Tom eyed the door before lining up next to Justin.

Justin set the laptop on the stool and brought up the site. Chris directed him to the photos.

"I get why Carlo lost his cool." Tom leaned over Justin.

"Because his brother was all over his date?" Chris let smarm drip from his words.

"Toasting with Sue isn't being all over her. I meant the dress." Tom paced the room.

"What about it?" Asked Justin.

"It's completely backless. Her ass crack is barely covered. She wore it to her brother's New Year's party his freshman year in college. Gavin almost fought his buddy to keep the dude off her."

"Go, Sue." Justin grinned and fist bumped Darryl.

Brad leaned in closer to the screen. "She's facing the camera in all these pictures. Her smile is killer."

"Lame." Chris shoved Brad. "Do you think she was still lit when we had that meeting the next day?"

"No." Tom stopped pacing and looked directly at Chris. "Sue doesn't usually drink much unless Amy's around. Even then, they hardly ever get drunk. The glass she's holding in that photo is probably all the champagne she had."

"Jackpot!" Darryl stepped back from the computer, letting the image on the screen take center stage. Once again, the guys crowded around.

The photo had been taken when Sue and Carlo were at the end of the red carpet near the hotel entrance. Carlo stood in front of Sue, partially facing the camera, pointing at something behind them. Sue's body faced the hotel, with her head turned toward where Carlo directed. Their positions provided an unobstructed view of her bare back.

"Whoa." Brad shook his head and leaned closer to the computer.

"You're right, Tom. That dress barely covers her ass."

Justin moved toward his drum kit on the far side of the room. "And she wears it like it's no big deal."

"It's her go-to fancy event dress."

"That woman is scandalous." Darryl grinned as he went back to his keyboards.

"I'll say." Chris took D's place in front of the computer.

"Okay. That's enough. We have business to conduct here." Tom leaned over Chris's shoulder and closed the TMZ window.

Brad picked up a guitar and Tom resumed pacing.

"Hey, guys." Sue entered the room with a mug of coffee.

"How you doin', Sue?" Justin asked.

"I'm good." A pair of dark sunglasses perched on top of her head, but someone who didn't know better would have no idea she'd drunk her way down Bourbon Street the night before.

"How was your night, Sexy Sue?" Chris perched on a stool, laced his fingers together, and put his hands on his head.

"Not as exciting as yours." Sue pulled a folder out of her laptop bag and sat on a small couch across from their instruments.

"I don't know about that." Chris decided to both win the bet and get a reaction from Sue. "I saw you at breakfast with Owen."

Brad's head snapped up.

"Who's Owen?" Darryl asked.

"Sue's handsy date last night." Chris wiggled his eyebrows.

"Please." Sue rolled her eyes. "I had breakfast with Owen because I bumped into him in the hallway."

"Just in the hallway?" Chris asked.

"Tom?" Sue lifted her chin toward her cousin.

"Since you needed our room, Chris, I crashed with Sue. I woke up about five times to pee, and she was dead asleep in her bed, alone, every time."

"Doesn't mean she didn't get a little morning delight!" Chris licked his lips and rubbed his hands together, waiting for the moment when Sue gave in.

"Chris, unlike you, I don't need to fuck everyone I flirt with. Lay off." Sue's glare reminded him of a dour librarian.

Tom positioned himself sideways between Chris and Sue, like a referee. He looked at Chris. "D's back, Lena's here now. We have work to do."

"Here's a schedule for the next three days." Sue pulled a few pages out of her folder and passed them out, barely acknowledging Chris as she gave him one. So, he did get under her skin. Good.

"Friday's the worst day," Sue droned on. "Dinner interview tonight, your show is tomorrow night. Friday you have a photo shoot with the other bands and some short interviews in the afternoon. The Echo Chamber show is Friday night. We're all invited to it and the after-party at Amy and Jack's. Saturday you're free until six, when you need to dress for the benefit." Sue glanced up from the schedule. "I'm picking up your tuxes after we break here. You'll all need to try them on today in case you need different sizes."

Chris flicked his paper. The press stuff stressed him out, but being around these other bands was killer. Sue didn't need to know that, though. "We really have to wear tuxes?"

"Bitch to Amy. Personally, I love the idea. Who doesn't look good in a tux?"

"Chris," all the guys said in unison.

Chris rolled his eyes.

Sue walked around the room handing out glossy sheets of paper and markers. "These are the proofs from the shoot in Austin. I already selected three photos and gave them to the bloggers who requested them. We need to decide on some for the site and maybe some posters and stuff. Everyone pick five, and we'll go from there."

Chris hated looking at pictures of himself as much as he hated posing for them. He made a face and barely registered the images before shoving the proof sheet at Sue. "Here's mine."

"Thanks. Read this." Sue gave him two printed pages.

"What is it?"

"It's for *Sound Spectrum*. They've given us final approval. All of you have to read it."

"Seriously?" Chris asked. Reading this shit, keeping track of the journalists, that was all Sue's job. She needed to stop wasting his time and do what they were fucking paying her for.

"Seriously. You especially. Apparently, you hit on the reporter and she was less than charmed." Sue gave copies of the same article to the rest of the guys as they gave her their marked proof sheets.

Chris didn't even glance at the stupid fucking thing until he noticed everyone else reading. "What the fuck is this?" He jumped to his feet. "'*Chris Lorenzo, the band lothario, fancies himself a smooth mover. Too bad his weak lines, ruddy complexion and skinny arms have women hoping he'll introduce them to his more appealing bandmates.*' The fuck!"

Sue held up a hand. "I've already had them strike it—"

"Damn straight, they're gonna strike it!"

"It's done," Sue said in a calm voice. "I need you guys to understand how important it is to be aware of whom you're talking to."

Chris glared at Sue, then went back to the so-called article to see what other bullshit it held. The number of jabs the bitchy reporter managed to slide into two pages gave him nausea.

"This is fucking ridiculous. I'm not that bad." Chris threw the article at Sue.

Justin picked up the papers and pushed them into Chris's chest. "Yeah, you are, dude."

"I'm not! But even if I am, it's Sue's fucking job to keep this out of print!"

"I have. Relax." Sue held eye contact with Chris.

That she was so composed when he barely controlled his anger pissed him off even more. "No. I'm not gonna relax. I bet I had this interview while you were off in Vegas partying with Carlo and Tony."

"Excuse me?"

Chris made the picture of Sue toasting with Tony fill the screen, then turned her computer around. He crossed his arms and waited. When Sue finally looked away from the screen, the glare she gave him made his skin crawl.

"While you were off playing superstar, you let me fall on my face."

Darryl rounded the keyboards and gently pushed the laptop closed. "Chris, stop."

Chris ignored him. "What's your job, Sue?"

"Chris." Justin spoke louder than Darryl had and positioned himself next to Tom, forming a wall between Chris and Sue.

"No. I want to know." Chris put his hands on his hips. "What's your job, Sue? Letting me fall on my face when I asked you not to make me do interviews? Fucking around with the rich and famous?"

"Chris!" Tom got in Chris's face.

Sue yanked on Tom's arm and pulled him back.

Chris had her backed into a corner. She had to admit she only joined the tour for the perks. "I'm waiting for an answer, Sue. Are you a star maker? Or a star fucker?"

"Enough, Chris!" Brad said from across the room.

Sue gripped Tom's arm, her glare like laser beams.

Chris held himself steady, even though her reaction made no sense. She'd lost. She was the star fucker. Where was her shame? "Well?"

"Fuck. You," Sue said, her voice low.

"Huh? What?" Chris taunted.

"Fuck! You!"

Chris squinted and stepped back.

"Fuck you, asshole! Where the hell do you get off? I fucking prepped you. I held your hand through every damn interview. I canceled interviews and made everyone else do more to make up for your selfish, slack ass. Hell, I made Justin take one because you were too busy fucking groupies. How your dick hasn't turned green and fallen off by now is beyond me. I refused interviews where we didn't get final approval before the articles and transcripts went live. I edited copy to make you sound smarter, funnier, not like the asshole you are."

Chris pointed to himself. "I'm the asshole?"

"A massive asshole!" Sue stalked toward the stool that held her computer, pressing her fists into the seat, and got as close to Chris's face as the small barrier would allow. "I spent four hours overnight in an editing bay putting together an interview so it'd sound like you said more than you did. News flash, I snuck off to Dallas for that one. Didn't sleep that night. Thought about asking you to call the DJ to answer a few more questions because the guy was interested in you. But even *mention* a radio interview, and you shit a brick. I fucking twisted myself into knots for you, and for what? To get talked down to, insulted, forced to kick your hookups out of the hotel, and poisoned! What the *fuck* is with you?"

Chris shifted his gaze away from Sue and looked around, only to see each of his friends glaring at him. He burned with anger.

"Bitch, you—"

"No." Sue straightened, leaving her fingertips on the edge of the stool. "You do *not* get to talk. You know why?" Sue pointed at Tom. "You put this man through agony for hiring me. His *cousin*," she sneered the word. "You know why he hired me? Because any other PR agent would've bailed after the ipecac. I'm the only *bitch* crazy enough to stick it out with you fuckers. Every single one of you have given both of us grief. And everyone, *everyone* except you, Chris, has come around. What the *fuck* do I have to do to get you to understand that I am the best chance you have? You think I shouldn't have gone to the fight?"

"No! You shoulda—"

"Tough shit! I do not regret a single fucking second I spent in Vegas. Wanna know why? There weren't any interviews while I was away. That *Sound Spectrum* interview was the last one you guys gave before we left Austin. You, asshole, hit on the reporter the night before and didn't even fucking remember her the next day. I practically did that interview for you, feeding you good answers. And you screwed yourself when you didn't have the brainpower to remember just *one* of the many women who rejected your offer for a cheap fuck. Congratulations."

Sue pulled her car keys out of her pocket and threw them at Tom.

"I have to leave now and confirm another slew of interviews for you guys. Do me a favor, Chris. Don't try to fuck these reporters. They work with Amy, and they'll bite us all a lot worse. I fixed this. But don't fucking count on me to keep doing it if you're gonna keep going out of your way to be an asshole." Sue swept her gaze across the room. "That goes for all of you."

<hr>

After Sue's shitty outburst at the studio and the even shittier treatment from his bandmates, Chris waited to go to The Nomads show until the last minute. If he hadn't met some of the guys the night before, he would've skipped their show. But they were cool and had interesting ideas about music. He wanted to see them live—their whole set. He got to the club about twenty minutes before they were due to hit the stage and scanned the room for Sue. When he found her, he made a beeline in the opposite direction. He joined Darryl and Lena, keeping an eye on Sue as she talked with Owen and his drummer.

"She likes them better than us."

"Maybe she likes them better than *you*," Darryl said.

"I'm gonna get her flowers or something."

Darryl rolled his eyes. "Please."

"What?"

Lena reached past Darryl and pushed Chris's arm. "You are going to give her a sincere apology. You can give her flowers for her birthday."

If Chris hadn't spent time with Lena and D in Austin, or if he didn't know how much his friend cared about her, he never would've let her get away with that. Even worse, as far as he could tell, Lena was pure goodness. "An apology for what? She bitched me out. Flowers'll make her feel guilty."

Darryl crossed his arms. "You deserved every word she said. And she deserves an apology. Until you see eye-to-eye with me on that, you'd be smart not to mention it."

Let Sue fucking quit. Then they'd go back to the way things were. Let Tom handle the press stuff. Brad and Darryl were the best interviews. Chris didn't need some woman telling him what to do and putting her hands all over his gear. He turned to D, about to say as much, but noticed the firm set of the man's jaw.

Chris stalked off instead. There was no talking to Darryl when that muscle in his neck tightened up. Whatever. Chris decided to find a woman who only wanted to tell him what to do in bed. A woman who would give him the thrill of the chase while barely even producing a ripple on the other guys' radar. The way it should be. He hoped Darryl saw when he smacked the tight little ass that had been standing a few feet in front of them.

Chris loved every second of The Nomads show until the end, when Amy pulled Sue on stage to present the silent auction items. Of course Sue was tight with all these cool people he wanted to know. He tried to convince himself it didn't matter. So she got him into the room with Jack Ragnar. He could make his own connections.

Instinct had Chris seeking out Darryl again, until he remembered that D expected him to apologize. Darryl would have to learn to live with disappointment. Chris decided to give Brad a shot. Everyone got in his face during the fight except Brad. Maybe the guy saw beyond his libido after all. Some hot women were asking Brad to take their picture with The Nomads bass player. Even better.

"I can take a shot if you want to get in there." Chris gestured to take the camera phone.

"It's okay, they don't know us." Brad took the picture and gave the phone back to one of the women.

"Should we?" she asked.

Chris lifted his chin. "We play here tomorrow night. We're in Words Fail Me."

The girl gave Chris a broad smile. "This place is crawling with rockers!"

"The Nomads really bring it." Brad nodded toward the bass player, who smiled as he signed autographs.

"Hey, hot bass player."

Chris turned, confused because the voice calling "hot bass player" belonged to Sue.

"Hey, Sue, how goes it?" The Nomad they were with grinned at her. "I heard I missed all the fun the first half of the week."

"Woulda been better if you were here."

The man finished signing autographs for the women and gave Sue a hug.

"You're at table two, Jimmy. Brad, table four. Chris." Sue caught his eye. "You're at table three."

Chris crossed his arms. "Where's Jack sitting?"

"Table one. With Darryl."

"Nice," Brad said. "D'll enjoy that."

"Yeah. The two of you are the best interviews. Darryl

hasn't been able to spend any time with him yet, so I figured this would work."

"Totally."

"Chris, you're with Robin." Sue walked off.

"Pissed her off pretty good today, and she still gave you a sweet hookup," Brad said.

"Don't you start."

"Whatever insults are going through your head right now, she's still got your back. Dick." Brad followed Sue to the main area of the club.

Chris stayed near the merch table and watched girls pose for pictures and giggle over The Nomads. He wanted to mix in with them and find someone to take his mind off everything, but he knew he couldn't bring a girl he'd just met to dinner.

He didn't even want to go to the dinner, an exclusive interview session for a handful of high-profile publications, but Amy had found a way to make it appealing. All the bands participating in the benefit were there. Yeah, most of them were at the same level as his band—not huge, though big enough to have fans willing to travel to a destination city—and this event provided quality time for all the bands to mingle with the members of Echo Chamber.

Once The Nomads signed their last autograph, Chris followed them back to the dining area and found table three. He kept a close eye on Robin and managed to get a seat across from him, at the center of the long table. Sue turned up with Owen as everyone started to sit and took the seat next to Chris. Of course. Chris snapped the white linen napkin and dropped it into his lap. He gave her a quick glare, then picked up a bottle of red wine. He filled his glass to the rim, then offered the bottle to the guy sitting on his left.

"Ladies and gentlemen," Sue called everyone's attention to her. "Before we get into any deep conversations this evening, I need to let you know that anything Chris Lorenzo says is off the record." As soon as she said "off the record," the entire table quieted, and everyone turned toward her. "We'd be happy for you to include him in the conversation and even quote him in your articles. However, any quotes you use must be approved by me before publication. I've left my business cards on the table, or you can contact me through Amy Ragnar's agency." Sue sat back and looked up and down the table.

Chris shifted and caught her eye. He wanted to lay into her but couldn't with all the reporters and rockers around them. Sue gave him a slight tilt of the head as if to challenge him. He glanced away, hoping no one noticed the vein throbbing in his temple. She probably sat him at this table with Robin on purpose so he wouldn't react to her. He picked up his wine glass and sat back, holding it in front of his mouth. "Passive-aggressive, much?" he whispered.

"Ms. Douglas, does that hold true for the rest of Words Fail Me?" one of the reporters asked.

"No. You can speak with and quote them freely. These restrictions only apply to Mr. Lorenzo."

"Well—" Owen clapped once. "Don't let that hold ya

back. I'm an open book."

The table erupted in laughter, and the reporters got the ball rolling.

The entire dinner was an out-of-body experience for Chris. He mentally floated above the table, picking up pieces of great conversations and barely opening his mouth, certain no one would hear him. Robin threw him some sympathy and roped him into a few chats. Chris still felt like persona non grata. If he hadn't sat his ass smack in the middle of the action, he would've left.

As the dinner wound down, people moved around. A few couches were set up near the stage with video cameras. When Chris noticed Jack sitting on one of them, he wandered over to listen. Tom followed.

Chris kept his eyes on Jack as he spoke to Tom. "You knew about this no-comment bullshit?"

"Yep."

"What the fuck? You couldn't warn me?"

"Tried. You bolted after practice."

"Well, you don't have to babysit me. No one wants to fucking talk to me now, so you have nothing to worry about."

Tom sighed. "We're trying to protect you. All of you."

"What the fuck ever, man. Fuck off." Chris stalked away, catching Sue alone in a narrow passage to the back of the house. He grabbed her arm. "What was that about?"

Sue's gaze hardened. She glanced from his face to his hand and back. When he let go of her, she crossed her arms, her stare still cold. "I told you I'd protect you. That's what I did."

"By publicly excluding me from the entire event."

"You've made it crystal clear on more than one occasion that you don't want to do press, Chris."

"You had to get that out in front of everyone?"

Sue cocked her head and took him in for a moment. "I didn't coach you this morning, and I didn't have an opportunity to talk to them all before we got here. I wasn't trying to embarrass you."

"You sure about that?"

"If I wanted to embarrass you, it would've been far worse."

Chris didn't say anything, not willing to give her an inch. He crossed his arms, mirroring her posture.

"If any requests for quotes come in, I'll share them with you for approval." Sue waited another moment, then continued down the hall.

"Why are you doing this?"

Sue stopped and turned halfway, looking him in the eye. "I said I'd protect you. *Sound Spectrum* showed that I need to take more control."

"This is because I got pissed."

"No. I decided this before our argument. When I

made my calls this morning, some of the reporters
weren't available. I needed to give them the news
directly."

"If you're expecting me to thank you, you're gonna be
disappointed."

"No. I am, however, expecting to get all kinds of shit
from Amy. Thanks for your concern. Not everyone gets
to compromise business relationships and a lifelong
friendship in one day. I consider myself lucky."

CHAPTER 31

Sue took a long pull from the Hurricane in front of her. Even with the extra shot of bourbon she'd requested, the drink didn't do much to loosen the tight knot of tension in her back.

"Bandmates get into fights all the time, Sue. Why do you think we scatter as soon as the bus stops?" Owen bumped his shoulder against hers.

"To get away from the fart smell."

Owen laughed. "That, too."

She gave him a tired smile. "I'm not a bandmate. I was trying so hard to give them all, especially Chris, some space. I can't find a middle ground with him."

"You'll find it. Or he'll get a beating."

She furrowed her brow at the ominous promise, and Owen grinned.

"There can only be so much tension before someone gets punched. That's how it goes with guys. Give yourself a break and enjoy all of this." Owen gestured to the catwalk at the center of the room, where Robin danced with two drag queens. Despite Robin's tall stature, one of the performers towered over him in platform boots that easily gave the queen an extra foot of height.

"You're right." Sue tapped her glass against Owen's

and finished her drink, then waved money at the stage.

Robin sent over a very convincing Beyoncé look-alike, who took the cash, stuffed it into her cleavage, and gave Sue a loud, smacking kiss on the forehead. Before she left, Beyoncé batted her eyelashes at Owen and clucked him under the chin. She sashayed away, blowing a kiss to him over her shoulder. Sue couldn't help her laugh, especially at Owen's blush.

"Now you can say B's into you!" Sue pulled her vibrating phone out of her pocket. She went from exhausted to elated with the flash of Adam's name.

A: Flight landed. Officially in NOLA

S: Yay!

A: Where can I pick you up?

Sue giggled and tapped out a message to buy some time.

S: Last we talked I said maybe.

"Owen, if you were taking a woman out for a late-night drink, where would you go?"

Owen furrowed his brow, so Sue showed him her phone. "You said a woman, not you. That's a completely different thing."

"What does that mean?" Sue's phone shook with another message.

A: Did I wake you?

S: No.

A: Where should I pick you up?

Sue grabbed Owen's arm. "Seriously. What do I do here?"

"You asked me where I'd take a woman for a late-night drink, not where I'd take a woman I like. When I ask someone out late, it's so I'm not going home alone."

"You're right." Sue tapped on the screen to respond.

Owen signaled for another round. "Women have all the power. How you guys don't know that is beyond me."

S: What makes you think I want our 1st date

to happen at 2 in the morning?

A: You're answering my texts.

S: You asked me how I like my eggs. I don't like them before 8 a.m.

Reading over her shoulder, Owen nudged her. "That was good."

"Thanks." Sue gave him a nervous smile and sipped the fresh drink Owen slid in front of her.

A: You got me on a technicality.

Sue smirked and showed Owen the phone.

"Don't answer. If he wants to see you, he'll figure it out."

"Okay." Sue put the phone down and faced Owen.

"Distract me."

Owen sighed. "I can't believe I'm helping you with this. Did you and Amy ever have conversations like this about me?"

"The talks we had about you were much dirtier."

Owen threw an arm around Sue's neck and kissed her temple. "By far the greatest let down I've ever gotten."

Sue hugged him, grateful for his friendship.

He gave her a squeeze, then pulled back, nodding at the table. "He figured it out."

A: There's a breakfast place near Jackson Square. Best quiche I've ever had. Do you still like eggs at 8:30?

Adam spotted Sue the second he walked into the restaurant. She sat at a table near a window with a glass of orange juice. She'd warned him when they made the date that she couldn't stay long. He didn't care. When she smiled at him, it went straight to his gut. He didn't know how he made it to the table without knocking over people and furniture along the way.

He pulled out the chair across from her and sat. "Good morning."

"Morning. How was your flight?"

"Too long." Adam leaned forward on the table. "How has your week been?"

Sue widened her eyes briefly. "Action packed." She sipped her orange juice. "I'm sorry this has to be such a short date. We don't have any roadies for this show. I have to help the guys get their gear set up for tonight."

"I know you're here on business. I thought for sure you'd say no."

Sue gave him one of her megawatt smiles. "You're not the only one who wanted my maybe to be a yes."

Her admission gave him a nice boost, especially after the buckets of sweat he'd shed, worried that he'd pushed too far with his texts the night before.

They made small talk for a few minutes, then Sue gave him the club's address. They agreed on a time, and she left, taking his appetite and all the sunshine in the city with her.

Adam got a coffee to go and went to his hotel room, where he worked until the alarm on his phone let him know he could finally see Sue again. At least now he would have her to himself for the afternoon.

He arrived at the club exactly on time. After a minute he found Sue on a ladder on the stage, her head in a huge light fixture. "I thought you were in PR, not lighting."

She crouched, a smile brighter than the lights spread across her face. "Darryl's tweeting, Brad's blogging, Chris is chasing tail, and Justin's doing an email interview. Since they're all more or less doing what I've asked them to, that leaves me and Tom to do the dirty work." Sue climbed down the ladder.

"Need a hand?"

"No, we're about done."

Sue's hair fell out of a messy ponytail, and her Words Fail Me tour T-shirt hung almost to the knees of her faded jeans. The shirt must've been a size XXXL. Her unkempt hair and baggy tee begged him to steal her away for a weekend. Had she been dressed like this at breakfast? He hadn't even noticed. He'd been too distracted by her smile.

"You still up for an afternoon out?"

"Oh, we're going out." Sue's eyes sparkled. "Let me

shake off the dust from the lights and change my shirt, and I'll be ready. In the meantime, hang with Tom. Tom! Can you come out here, please?"

Tom appeared from the depths of the stage, wearing an identical outfit to Sue, except his shirt fit. Adam kept his face neutral despite his fantasy being stomped out. He mentally shook it off. They must be crew member shirts. They were important for security. Yeah.

Sue made introductions. "Can you keep Adam company while I change?" She pulled her hair out of the ponytail. "It'll only take a minute."

"Sure thing."

Sue walked backward toward the wings of the stage and pointed at Tom. "Don't make him work."

Tom shook his head and turned. "She thinks since she can order the guys around, I'll fall in line, too."

"Yeah?" Adam asked, one eyebrow raised.

"You're a sports writer?" Tom changed the subject.

"Yes."

"For a website?"

"SportsMecca.com."

"Any money in that anymore?" Tom scrunched his face.

Adam tried not to smirk. "I do all right."

"Yeah, that's what we all say." Tom directed them to

a table nearby. "You travel a lot?"

"A fair bit."

"Must make it difficult to have a life."

"When I want a break, it's not difficult to orchestrate." Adam tried to keep it light, but keeping his answers from sounding defensive against Tom's accusatory tone challenged him.

"Where do you live when you're not traveling?"

"I have a place in Boston."

Tom narrowed his eyes. "You don't have a Boston accent."

They stood next to the table, Adam waiting for Tom take a seat. "I'm originally from Colorado. I went to Boston College, liked the area, and decided to stay after I graduated." Adam waited a beat. "You have a bit of New England in your accent. Where are you from?"

Tom waved away the question. "Think you'll ever move back to Colorado?"

"Maybe."

"Do you write about sports because you're not coordinated enough to play them?"

That one hit a sore spot. Reminding himself that Tom worked with Sue, Adam straightened his posture and checked his ego. "I write about sports because I like them."

"Still, you know. Those who can, do. And those..."

Adam crossed his arms. "Who have knee surgery midseason lose a lot of playing time."

"So you live vicariously through the guys who got to go pro." Tom straightened his posture and lifted his chin.

Adam cleared his throat. "I created another opportunity."

"Think you'll stay in sports, or evolve into something else?"

"Think you'll evolve into something other than rock 'n roll?"

Tom barked a short laugh. "Who'd want to evolve beyond rock 'n roll?" He slid into the booth and gestured for Adam to do the same.

"Whatcha talking about?" Sue asked, perching next to him on the edge of the booth.

Adam flinched. How long had she been listening to him and Tom posturing?

Tom shook his head. "Nothing. Getting to know each other."

Adam grinned at Sue. She'd changed into a lightweight cardigan with a V-neck that dipped low enough to stoke his imagination, even though it conservatively covered her. A massive improvement over the crew shirt. Tiny buttons were closed all the way down the front except for the one at the bottom where the sweater touched her jeans. She'd taken her hair out of the ponytail and pulled it back with a barrette. Her face was fresh and open, and she glowed. As usual. "Ready?"

"Yes." Sue stood and moved back, letting Adam slide out of the booth.

He gave Sue another once-over. When would he be allowed to touch her?

"Will you be back for the set tonight, Sue?" Tom asked.

"Yeah. I've set up an interview with a podcaster, and one of the editors from Metal Edge will be here. I'll definitely be back."

"You'll be here too, Adam?" Tom asked.

Adam shrugged, hoping it looked casual. "I don't know. Don't want to intrude."

"You know, I just assumed you'd come." Sue tilted her head. "Do you wanna see Words Fail Me?"

"Yes." Adam tried not to look as eager as he had in his texts, though it thrilled him when she invited him.

Sue smiled. "Add him to the list, Tom. That's F-L-E-T-C-H-E-R."

After the dark of the club, the light of the balmy New Orleans afternoon made Sue uncomfortable. Being alone together in the daylight and not having to dash away made this long-imagined date very real and stoked her nerves.

Adam directed her to a gray sedan. He held the door for her, and as she climbed into the car, Sue's stomach fluttered. She'd gotten so used to trying to fit in with the guys that she'd forgotten what little niceties, like having a door held for her, were like.

He slid into the driver's seat, started the car, and pulled into traffic. "Are the guys adding anything to the silent auction?"

"Yes. There's a CD pack, and we came up with a unique T-shirt that Justin'll wear at the show. Brad's donating the guitar he's playing tonight. The guys'll sign the shirt and the guitar while they're on stage."

"That's cool."

"Yeah, it's tough to pick stuff because they aren't at the level where anything they toss out will garner interest. The things that do are still expensive for them to give up," Sue said.

"Like the guitar?"

"Exactly. Brad had to have his mom ship him another one. He's got spares but not many. Giving up one makes a difference."

Sue kept her focus forward, not wanting Adam to notice her awkwardness. The texting they'd done over the past week had felt like a game. She thought their brief date that morning would've helped her relax, but her nerves were worse than the day she'd joined the tour.

"I have to clear the air." Adam flexed his fingers against the steering wheel.

"Hmm?"

"All the texts last night. That wasn't...I hope it didn't come across as something...I know I was pressuring you, I'm sorry." Adam gave her a quick look and returned his gaze to the road. "I felt like a jerk when I called the other day and you kept inviting me to stuff and I kept saying no. I wanted to make it up to you."

"No one appreciates constantly changing work schedules like I do."

"I realized this morning that I was pretty aggressive. I'm sorry. I understand boundaries. I respect them."

"Thank you." Sue waited a beat. "I usually like your texts."

Adam smiled as they waited to turn into the parking lot. "Good." His expression fell as they pulled forward. "Wait. What do you mean, usually?"

Sue laughed and rubbed the back of her neck as the tension there finally unfurled. "Nothing, I was teasing."

Sue directed them toward her favorite enclosure when they entered the zoo. "Everyone likes the snakes and monkeys. I love the elephants. They're so serene."

"I can see how you'd appreciate calm since you go to concerts every night."

"Oh, make no mistake. I love the music." Sue took in the area, finding the clearest route to the elephant pavilion. "Balance is essential, though."

After the elephants, Adam led her to the jungle cats.

"Did you ever live in New Orleans?" Sue asked.

"Uh-uh, why?"

"Most of the people at the benefit are local or fans of the bands."

"My love for Bloody Maggots runs deep." Adam didn't hesitate.

"Says the man who missed them by three days."

"You got me. My grandmother asked me to come." Adam snapped a picture of a jaguar. "She used to be a zoo veterinarian."

"Wow! Here?"

"The St. Louis Zoo in Missouri. After hurricanes Katrina and Sandy, she donated a ton of money to help make sure the animals and their keepers were fed, housed and healthy. She has a regular monthly donation, too. The Audubon Zoo sent her a pair of tickets to the benefit as a donor gift."

"What kind of corsage are you buying her?"

Adam laughed. "No corsage. She's having hip replacement surgery in a few weeks. She didn't want to travel with the surgery so close."

"Is she upset *she* missed Bloody Maggots?"

"Honestly, I don't think she had any idea about the

music component. She'd love the little set-ups in the zoo."

"The music was inspired by the aftermath of Hurricane Katrina."

"How so?"

Sue pushed her hair back. "Jack and Amy explain it better, but tourism took a big hit, and the local musicians had to leave to make a living."

"This gives them work at home."

"Exactly. And exposure."

"This is no ordinary event."

"I'm incredibly proud of Ames," Sue said.

"Did she grow up here?"

"Nope. We're from Connecticut. Fairfield. Jack is from Cincinnati. New Orleans is their adopted hometown."

"Where do you live now?"

"My car." Sue laughed. "The rest of my stuff is in Maryland."

Adam took Sue's hand and squeezed it, filling her with a charge of electricity. Everything around her stopped for a moment as they stared at each other. Adam laid a soft kiss on her knuckles and pulled her into a nearby alcove. Sue's pulse picked up as he traced her neckline with his thumb and forefinger.

"You need a necklace," he whispered.

Sue kept her voice low. "Why?"

"To distract me from all of this skin."

Sue glanced at her chest. "You can't see anything."

"Doesn't matter. All of this is still…" He rubbed his finger along the scalloped edge of her sweater. "Alluring."

Sue stepped closer to him, putting the hand she held against the bare skin at the base of her throat.

Adam sucked in a breath.

"What if I don't want to distract you?"

Adam leaned close, his gaze darting from her eyes to her lips. She closed her eyes, ready for his kiss.

"Hey, Sue!"

She jumped, then reared back, almost hitting her head when she realized Amy was right next to them. She blinked to keep from rolling her eyes at her best friend. "What're you doing here, Ames?"

Amy enveloped Sue in a bear hug and rocked to-and-fro, forcing Sue to drop Adam's hand.

She growled her displeasure in her friend's ear.

"Spending some quality time with the animals before the big party," Amy said.

"Us, too." Sue plastered a too-bright smile on her

face as she pushed Amy away and introduced Adam.

They shook hands and Amy grinned. "I hope I didn't interrupt anything."

Sue glowered at Amy but kept her voice pleasant. "We have to leave soon for the show. You're gonna be there?"

"I wouldn't miss your guys for the world. Don't tell anyone," Amy said, lowering her voice. "Jack's coming."

Sue bounced on her feet and gave a small clap. "They'll be so psyched! They figured after the dinner last night he'd lay low until the benefit."

"That's what he wanted them to think. Jack has this little fantasy of surprising them backstage after."

"They'll love that," Sue said.

"Perfect. Well, I won't keep you. Catch you guys tonight!" Amy hugged Sue again before she left.

"Good ol' Ames. She's always had perfect timing."

Adam chuckled and slid his hand back into Sue's, lighting her up with that current of sexual tension again. "Let's eat, then go back to the club. You wouldn't want Tom to get crushed by an amplifier."

"Yeah, the guys would leave him there." Mentioning Tom had been a good reality check, but it didn't stop Sue from hoping Adam would be on the menu.

<hr>

"This was fun." Once again, Sue found herself leaning against a wall, Adam so close she had trouble breathing evenly. "You'll be back at seven?"

"Absolutely."

"Good." She glanced at his lips then away. There was nothing stopping her this time. There wasn't a reason not to finally kiss this man. "I may put you to work tonight."

Adam quirked an eyebrow. "How so?"

"You have nice long arms." Sue traced a hand from his shoulder to his wrist, noticing—and enjoying—his pulse picking up. "You can get better camera angles than me. Maybe even get a picture of the whole stage."

"You'd use me like that?"

"It would be a shame not to take advantage of these assets." She wove her fingers between his.

"If you need a good photographer, I can make some calls—"

Sue interrupted with an emphatic shake of her head. "No. I need you." Sue remembered the night in Vegas when she'd asked Adam if he had been looking for a good scoop, and he'd said, no, just her. She liked returning the sentiment. "And a few photos for Instagram, but mostly you."

Adam squeezed her hand as he bit his lower lip. "That's a hell of a way to ask for a favor."

"I need one more."

"Name it."

Sue traced her thumb lightly over his lips. "Will you kiss me after the show?"

"Then, too." Adam pulled her toward him and unleashed a kiss on Sue that stopped her brain.

She wound her arms around his neck and matched his intensity. She'd wanted to kiss him ever since she yanked the tie free from his collar in Las Vegas. The wait had been worth it. Adam broke the kiss, pressing his forehead to hers. He lifted a hand from Sue's waist to her neckline and laid it on her bare skin. Her chest tingled beneath his fingers, and she became much more aware of how tightly he held her.

"So distracting," he whispered.

She shifted, lifting her mouth to his. He kissed her again, slower. This time he threaded a hand through her hair as his other arm tightened around her waist. She felt like they were holding each other up as they traded something vital. Sue whimpered when voices drifted into their space. She pulled back gently, in a daze.

"See you at seven?" Adam asked, his voice hoarse.

"You'd better." Sue pushed open the stage door and disappeared into the club.

Sue sat at a table under the Café du Monde's signature green pergola, inhaled the chicory scent of her drink, and smiled. "I'm glad you came to the show tonight."

"I did a good job with the pictures?" Anxious, Adam scrolled through a few shots. He did okay with a camera, though he was no photographer.

"Oh yeah." Sue sipped her drink, then sat back. "What did you think of the band?"

"I was distracted."

Sue knotted her eyebrows and placed her mug on its saucer. "Distracted?"

"Photo duty, remember?" Adam hid behind his mug as he drank. He'd barely paid attention to the show. How could he when she spent the whole time touching him? Even though it'd been innocent, he'd been so acutely aware of her that it was a miracle he managed to take any photos at all, let alone pay attention to the music.

Sue straightened her posture. "That's a big dodge. Did you like them or not? Just tell me. Even if you didn't like them."

Adam leaned forward and put a hand over hers, loving the fire in her eyes. "You don't hold anything back, do you?"

"Tried that. Didn't work for me."

Adam let go of her hand and lightly traced the neckline of her sweater. The only reason he knew he liked the band had to do with the album he downloaded between Las Vegas and Austin. Her presence near him at the show had his pulse pounding so that the only rhythm he tracked came from her. She pointed out the lights on the stage, but he didn't see beyond the light she cast. She sat before him, posture stiff as his finger skirted the edge of her sweater. He followed the V-neck down and back up. Sue rolled her shoulder, edging him onto her skin. He stopped.

Her eyes were closed.

The confirmation that he wasn't the only one impacted by these light touches encouraged him. He resumed, following the edge of the fabric the rest of the way up, his finger still on her skin.

Adam skimmed her collarbone, up her neck, and stopped under her chin. He pulled her toward him, caught her bottom lip between his, and kissed her briefly. He came away breathless. What had they been talking about? How did the touch of her lips manage to scramble his brain?

He sat back and composed himself. "I bought you something."

Sue clasped her hands together and tucked them between her legs, giving her head a little shake. "I'm sorry, what?"

Adam closed his fingers around the gift. It had been burning a hole in his pocket all night. "This reminded me of you." He lifted his fist above the plate of beignets and released his fingers enough to let a rose gold necklace tumble out and dangle from his fingertips.

Sue gasped. "No."

"I had to. You need a necklace to distract me so I can focus on conversation with you. I thought this would do the trick."

Sue blushed and studied the necklace.

The gleaming chain held a round sunburst pendant. The hollow center held three small stones.

"It's gorgeous. You shouldn't have done this."

"I couldn't do anything except think of you after I dropped you off. Shopping felt productive." Adam unclasped the chain.

She lifted her hair as he leaned over with the necklace. Adam barely resisted the temptation to kiss her again before he saw the sunburst on her. He re-clasped it and rested his hands on her shoulders. When her hair swung down and brushed his knuckles, he wanted to wind his fingers into it and pull her to him. He silently counted to three and sat back.

"Perfect."

The pendant landed about an inch above the neckline of her sweater. Sue looked at it and circled her finger around the edge. "I love it."

"It's amazing on you."

"Thank you. It's beautiful."

Adam traced the outline of the charm. His lips twitched at the goosebumps forming on her skin. He liked seeing that he could affect her the way she did him.

"I shouldn't accept this."

"You have to. It was made for you."

Sue covered the pendant with her hand. "It's too much. It's our first date. I can't."

"It's our third date."

Sue shook her head. "Breakfast doesn't count, and this is all one day. One date. A really great date. But not gift-worthy." She reached toward the clasp.

Adam stopped her with a hand on her arm. "This *is* a great date. Worth more than any gift." He pulled her arm down and held her hand. "Please keep it." When she didn't make eye contact, Adam squeezed her hand. "I promise I won't give you any gifts for the next six dates."

Sue narrowed her eyes. "You think you're getting six more dates?"

"You already agreed to go to the benefit with me. I figure if I don't get you a corsage or show up in a white limo, that'll get me at least two more."

Sue laughed. "Nice strategy."

Relieved that she kept the necklace, Adam sat back and sipped his coffee.

Sue ran a finger along the chain, then she caught his eye and leaned toward him. She put a hand behind his neck and brought her mouth to his, stopping short. He held still until she pressed her lips against his. Running thin on patience, Adam pulled her closer and deepened the kiss. Sue wrapped her arms around his neck and sunk into his arms. When she finally broke away, she rested her chin on his shoulder, her fingers playing at the ends of his hair.

Ceramics crashing against the floor across the patio had her jerking out of his arms. Adam groaned quietly as she sat back in her chair.

She cleared her throat. "The beignets will get cold."

After they finished eating, Adam walked her to the hotel, keeping his arm around her. He liked holding her close.

"What else should I listen to, now that I'm into Words Fail Me and zydeco music?"

Sue chuckled. "I bet the guys never thought someone would say something like that."

"You're doing a good job of expanding their reach."

"That was a very smooth suck up."

Adam kissed her temple. "It's not a suck up if it's true."

"If you really want recommendations, I can make you

a playlist.”

“I’d love that if you have the time.”

“I’ll make the time. Are you busy tomorrow night?” Sue asked.

“No.” Adam pulled her onto a couch in the lobby.

“Will you come with me to the Echo Chamber show and the after-party?”

“Yes.” Adam took a mental victory lap that she’d asked him for the next date.

“I’m warning you, though. Everyone will be there. And I mean everyone.”

“Even your parents?” Adam gave her an easy grin.

“No parents.” Sue gave him a light shove. “Only Tom, the whole band, Amy, Jack, Robin, The Nomads. The after-party is for the people working the benefit. I have to work the room while I’m there.”

“No cater waiters?”

“Ha! The horror. No, networking.” Sue sat back and ran a hand through her hair. The low lights in the room made it and the pendant shimmer. “All the tour managers will be there. They all know people I need to know.”

“Ah. Don’t worry about me. It won’t be the first time I didn’t know anyone in the room.”

“I promise I won’t abandon you.”

Adam shifted closer, pressing a kiss to her temple.

"Still not ready to share you, but watching you work'll be a lot more exciting than going out alone."

He wasn't sure, but it sounded like Sue purred. "Perfect. Pick me up here at six-thirty."

"What about lunch tomorrow?"

Sue frowned. "Tomorrow is our biggest press day. I'll be busy all day."

"I was getting greedy anyway."

Sue rubbed her knuckles along his jawline. "I'll call if I can sneak away."

"I like the way you think." Adam leaned over and kissed her.

They were sliding down the couch when Sue stopped them and adopted a prim posture. "I shouldn't do this here. The guys could turn up at any minute."

"We can go upstairs."
"I have a roommate."

Adam kissed her below her earlobe. "I don't."

Sue sighed. "Still can't. Not tonight."

Adam kissed behind her other ear, then down her neck.

Sue shivered. "I want to, but roommate pact."

Adam took a beat to enjoy her physical reaction to him, then sat back. "Okay."

"Thank you," she whispered, then kissed him again. She jumped when her phone beeped. She leaned into Adam, pulled the phone out of her back pocket, and checked the screen.

"Gotta go. Lena, roommate, is headed back here."

Adam stood and silently offered to help Sue up. She accepted, and he pulled her into his arms for one more kiss. When he finally let her go, he said, "Goodnight."

Sue stepped back. "Thank you." She touched the necklace. "And thank you."

Adam nodded and stayed in place as she walked to the elevator. He needed distance to let her go, though not too much. He pulled out his phone and typed a message.

Call me even if you can't escape.

He watched Sue read the message as she got into the lift. She turned and smiled at him as the doors slid closed.

Sue stood outside Chris's hotel room, afraid to knock on the door. They had a long day ahead of them, and she worried it would start with having to evict another one-night stand.

"He's alone." Tom strode down the hallway, tablet tucked under his arm, and rapped on the door. "We got back at the same time last night. Apparently, the press dinner ruined his... appetite."

"Shame." Sue felt no guilt. She'd had enough of Chris's bullshit.

"You're the boss today. Tell me what to do." Tom banged on the door again.

"I need to coach Chris, so I'll stick close to him. You be the timekeeper."

"Got it." Tom held up his phone. "Calendar updated?"

"Yep."

Chris stepped out and crossed his arms as the door shut behind him. "Someone's buying me breakfast."

Sue worked to keep her face neutral. At this point she didn't give a shit if he ever ate again. Still, she needed to him to cooperate. The press at this event was too big for him to fuck around. "It's on me. We have media training to do."

"Wonderful." Chris stalked toward the elevator.

Sue checked the time and sighed. "Only four hours 'til our first break."

Tom patted her back. "You got this."

Sue returned Chris's sneer as they parted ways for lunch. They had a little over two hours before everyone regrouped for the photo shoot and the next round of interviews. Two hours for her to figure out how to get Chris to relax for the *Show Biz Tonight* cameras. Cameras she hadn't even told him about yet.

The morning had gone smoothly, but the last hour she and Chris spent together gave her a new perspective on the word brutal. He made it crystal clear that his patience had run out, and Sue struggled to keep him from snapping at reporters. She decided to forgo the invitation she had to join Robin, Amy and Jack for lunch, and hit the hotel gym instead. She knew burning off some of her aggravation would go much farther in helping her get through the rest of the day. She pounded on the treadmill for thirty minutes, missing the more physical workouts she got in her old gym, though feeling more like herself as each minute passed. As she wound down her run, she called Adam.

"Sneaking away for a break?" Adam asked.

"In a manner of speaking."

"You didn't sneak, did you?"

"Not even close. As soon as the last reporter left, I bolted." Sue reduced the speed on the treadmill from a leisurely pace to a crawl.

Adam laughed. "What're you doing now?"

"I'm on a treadmill. I had to burn off some stress."

"Do you have more stress to burn? Or can I see you after all?"

The way he asked—giving Sue an option, while making it clear which he preferred—had her lips curling into a smile. "Meet me in the lobby in fifteen minutes."

Adam talked on his phone as he paced the lobby. It had taken him five minutes to get there, so when his assistant called, he answered, relieved to have something to do. He ended the call as Sue stepped out of the elevator. Her smile hit him straight in the chest every time and brought his brain to a stop. God help him if he ever got her naked.

"Are you free for the rest of the day?"

Sue twisted her lips. "Photo shoot in the zoo in about an hour."

"I know a place where we can get po' boys wrapped to go."

"Sounds great."

Adam scanned Sue up and down. She looked refreshed—clear-eyed, a flush in her cheeks, her gait relaxed. And wearing his necklace.

He touched his index finger to the sunburst and kissed her. "Good workout?"

"It got the job done." Sue wove her fingers through his and let him lead her out of the hotel.

When they got to the zoo, they sat on a bench outside the entrance to finish their sandwiches and talk.

"I can see how coordinating an interstate news story would stress you out. Finding the right angle had to be difficult," Adam said.

"I can woo reporters all day long." Sue said. "The stressful part is getting Chris to cooperate. He's uneasy with the press, and me."

"He's uneasy with you?"

"He thinks Tom hired me because we're related." Sue rolled her eyes as she crumpled the paper her sandwich had been wrapped in. "And he thinks I'll scare away the groupies."

Adam laughed. "Groupies are an excuse. You keep moving. He'll catch up."

"No nepotism concerns?"

"I saw your handiwork in Austin. Tom would've been stupid to pass you by."

Sue looked away briefly with a small, almost bashful smile. "Thanks."

"Give Chris a beer before his interviews. Loosen him up a little."

Sue laughed and checked her phone. "When we have more time, I'll tell you why me giving Chris beer won't work."

Adam leaned forward and kissed her. "When will we have more time?"

"Maybe tonight." Sue kissed him, then sat back. "The next photoshoot's in ten minutes."

"You still want me to pick you up for the concert?"

Sue stood. "Yep. Sixty-thirty. Room four twenty-seven. Thanks for lunch."

Adam rose with her, his pulse racing like he'd won the lottery because she volunteered her room number. "My pleasure."

"Oh, it was a shared pleasure." Sue gave him a wily smile.

Adam's heart skipped a beat again and he hugged her, taking a moment to memorize her smell—that woodsy rose scent—and savor the feel of her in his arms. "I hate letting you go." He took one more inhale of her, kissed next to her ear, then pecked her lips before turning her loose.

Sue looked surprised and backed up a few steps. "Six-thirty. Then you can hang on for a while."

Sue cursed quietly as they wrapped the photoshoot a few minutes before six. The afternoon had been a huge success, but she didn't have time to rest on her laurels. After confirming the airtime for the *Show Biz Tonight* segment, as well as the story that would air on the local news in Ann Arbor, Sue focused her attention on the clothing racks designated for Words Fail Me. Despite a successful day, her mind still whirred at breakneck speed. She needed the print stories to be as good or better than the television stories. She needed to get the stories to the record label, and she needed to keep the momentum going to increase sales. Plus, she wanted to take a night off for Adam. Then she worried he was a distraction.

"A reward," she mumbled. "Adam is a reward for all this bullshit." She pushed more hangers aside and checked the shoe bags.

"You know, the wardrobe people will come back and re-do that for their inventory." Robin leaned in the doorway, arms and legs crossed.

"I know. I want to make sure their personal stuff is out, and my mind is going nonstop, so I need to keep my body moving."

Robin put his hands on Sue's shoulders and turned her to face him. "Your guys are home free. Their show last night rocked. The photoshoot is over. You got them on *three* news casts. Today is a huge win for you. Relax."

Sue blew her hair off her forehead. "Can't."

"Sue," Robin said with a scolding tone.

"I know, I know. There are so many details. The guys are done, but I'm not. I still have to follow up and read the articles from the interviews yesterday and get Tom and Brad's tuxes back and make sure Darryl doesn't get laid, and it's a lot to keep track of."

Robin pulled her to him in a bear hug and laughed.

The rumble of his laughter against her cheek frustrated her more. She had too much to do to let him slow her down. "It's not funny."

"Yeah, it is. You have to make sure Darryl doesn't get laid?"

Hearing someone else say the words finally clicked in her brain. "Okay. Yeah, that's funny, but I have more problems."

"Such as?"

"I asked Adam to pick me up at six-thirty. It's five after, and not only am I far from the hotel, I still don't know what I'm gonna wear to the concert."

"I can solve both of those problems." Robin held her at arm's length. "Let's get my car, and we'll talk about clothes on the way. Also, you're wearing your leather pants tonight. It's an Echo Chamber show. Those pants were born from one of our shows. It's required."

"Okay, that's half the outfit." As she climbed into Robin's car, Sue pulled her new necklace away from her collar. "But no T-shirts. I need to show off this gift from Adam."

Robin let out one of his signature whoops then shouted out one outfit possibility after another. His rabid energy had Sue doubled over with laughter. By the time they arrived at the hotel, her long to-do list sat firmly on the back burner.

Sue chatted with Lena as she fixed her hair and makeup and took out her clothes. She ducked into the bathroom when she heard the knock on her door. Lena let Adam in and talked with him until Darryl arrived.

That gave Sue the extra time she needed to wiggle into her pants and a lavender wrap top. She sat to put on her shoes, then stilled, giving herself a few more seconds of quiet. Her mind had finally calmed when she stepped out of the bathroom.

"I'm sorry I made you wait. The photoshoot went a little long."

Adam turned to face Sue. "Wow, I need to change."

"No, you look perfect."

"I feel like I need something edgier." Adam wore jeans and a dark fitted tee.

Sue took a few steps toward him and stroked her hands across his shoulders, something she'd wanted to do ever since she met him. "This is perfect."

Adam slid an arm around her waist and pulled her against him. The worries that plagued her disappeared, replaced by the sensation of his strong arms around her, his chest against her, the steady thump of his pulse in her ear. This man against her body was better than meditation. She held his embrace, even when her phone rang. She groaned and buried her head into his chest.

"Ignore it."

"I wish." Sue kissed Adam, lingering for a moment, then shuffled across the room to retrieve the phone. "It's Tom," she said before answering. "What's up? ... We have time in the schedule tomorrow for another interview. Can they wait until one? ... Yeah, that's perfect... No... No. Relax, Tom... They don't have to go to the show. No one'll care. He has to come to the party after. If Chris wants to disappear for a few hours until then, it's fine." Sue perched on the edge of the bed and waited for Tom to stop ranting. Fitting that he had to interrupt her moment of peace with bullshit about Chris.

"Tom. Tom! Don't call Amy. She's busy. Tell Chris he can skip the show, but he has to be at the party, and if he needs a ride from wherever he winds up, then he should call me. I'll come get him. Seriously, Tom, it's fine." As Tom worried more, Sue wished she had the key to calming him. "I'm sure. Tom, Adam is waiting, I have to go... Yes, it's *fine*... Yeah. See ya later." Sue ended the call and smiled at Adam, who sat on the bed across from her. She appreciated his patience and how damn good he looked sitting there.

"Tom's a detail man, huh?"

"Oh yeah," Sue said.

"Chris is skipping out?"

"Not likely. Jack Ragnar is one of his idols. I doubt Chris will miss the show. He's fried from today and mentioned calling a girl or taking a nap and Tom lost it. It's miscommunication."

Adam stood and held out a hand. When she dropped her phone into it, he raised an eyebrow.

She stood and spun slowly in front of him. "No pockets in these pants. Will you carry it for me, please?"

Adam slipped the phone into his pocket, then reached for her. "You had to turn."

She slipped out of his grasp. Almost at the door, Sue shot him a grin. "Yeah, I did."

Echo Chamber played at a venue double the size of the one Words Fail Me had rocked the night before. The place was still small given Echo Chamber's fame, and renowned for both its sound and the excellent stage view throughout.

As Sue steered them toward the stage, Adam took in the frenetic energy. The crowd was obviously pumped and ready for action. Adam hoped Sue was looking for Words Fail Me and would direct him to one of the balconies. Tension coiled up his spine when they stopped in the middle of the pit next to Amy and Tom. The women embraced, acting oblivious to the chaos that bubbled around them.

Adam surveyed the room as he greeted Tom. "How's the crowd?"

"Easy going right now." Tom swept his gaze past Adam. "Gotta wait and see."

"Don't worry, it's gonna be great!" Amy giggled and told them stories of some of the Echo Chamber concerts she'd been to over the years.

When the lights lowered to signal the opening act, wolf whistles and cheers rose from the crowd. On the surface it didn't seem unusual, but it felt feral. Adam put a hand on Sue's hip and scanned the room again. There were a lot of excited faces, though nothing that matched the tension in the air. Adam watched the show, staying alert, waiting for something to tip the scales and send the audience into overdrive.

When the set ended the crowd shifted forward, Adam winced at Tom, who appeared to share his concern. Amy and Sue carried on an animated conversation. As they talked, more people pressed into the floor area, making the space tighter. Guys stripped off their shirts and tucked them into their waistbands as they bounced on their feet, already sweating. Every few minutes the tide of people pushed another step or two toward the stage, driving the tension higher.

Adam had a silent conversation with Tom, nodding and subtly pointing out areas where the fans appeared to be instigating the people around them. Adam wrapped one arm around Sue's waist while Tom positioned himself to block Amy from both the back and the side. Adam maneuvered himself and Sue so that the women were side by side and Adam stood halfway behind Amy, his hands firm on Sue's hips. Like at the championship fight, Sue maintained a calm and unconcerned demeanor. How was beyond Adam. This was her world, sure; she was used to it, shouldn't she sense the danger brewing? Instead, Adam half listened to her and Amy chattering, more concerned by the extra security guards lining up in front of the stage.

When the house lights dimmed again, a primal roar erupted, bristling the hair on the back of Adam's neck. Amy's giggling frustrated him. How could she laugh when the pressure kept building? The stage lights came on exactly as the music started, and Adam found himself curling around Sue to protect her from the mosh pit that sprang to life. They both got pummeled despite his efforts to shield her. He mostly blocked her from the blows, but they were pushed all over the floor. At one point they nearly toppled over. Somehow, he managed to keep them on their feet. Sue put a death grip on his arm even as she moved with the tide.

As the first song wrapped up, Adam leaned into her ear. "You okay?"

She nodded.

"You wanna move back?"

Sue shook her head, then leaned against Adam's shoulder, speaking into his ear. "It'll calm down. I'm good."

Adam exchanged a glance with Tom, who looked like he'd had a similar conversation with Amy and gotten the same results. They had another silent conversation and squared themselves as the second song built.

About halfway through the song, Sue finally leaned against Adam. She linked arms with him and yelled, "Get me out of here," into his ear.

He lifted her so her feet no longer touched the ground and pulled her backward through the pit, bulldozing out.

Tom did the same thing with Amy, moving toward the opposite corner.

Adam pulled Sue all the way to the sound booth and gave her a quick once-over. "Are you hurt?"

"No. Are *you* hurt?"

Adam shook his head.

Sue threw her arms around his neck and pressed her entire body against him. "Thank you."

It was enough to let him forget where they were for a moment. Adam rubbed her back, then reluctantly let go. "Tom's trying to get Amy out, too." He indicated the area where he had last seen Tom and scanned the crowd.

Sue pointed toward the far-right corner of the stage. Amy and Tom were close to security, but not close enough. It looked like Tom had gotten hit in the forehead; blood trickled down his face near his eye as he still pulled Amy toward the edge of the pit. Adam couldn't tell what Amy yelled at the people around them as she shoved them away.

"I see them. Stay here." Adam left Sue next to the sound booth and pushed through the throng.

"Hey!" Jack shouted in the middle of the song. "Let them out!" He pointed to the area where Amy and Tom were, and the entire crowd surged toward them, making it impossible for the security guards to get there. "NO! I said let them out, fuckers!"

Adam had made it about halfway through the crowd when Jack dove off the stage toward Amy. His fans caught him and set him on his feet. Security guards quickly flanked Jack and got him to Amy. Jack wrapped his arms around her and pulled her toward the stage with him. People in the crowd tried to touch him, but the security guards pushed them back, making a path.

On stage, the band kept up the song, and Robin took the main microphone, getting people refocused on him.

During the temporary confusion in the mosh pit, Adam got to Tom. He grabbed Tom's arm and followed security, skirting the crowd until he got Tom back to the sound booth and Sue.

Sue hugged Tom. "Are you okay?"

"I'm good."

"You're bleeding!" Sue pointed to his forehead.

"No, I'm not." Tom wiped his forehead, then paled when he saw blood on his palm and wobbled.

Sue forced him to lean against the railing of the sound booth.

"Hang on." Adam navigated the few steps to the bar and got a bottle of water and a bar towel for Tom.

Sue mopped the blood off Tom's face, then held the rag against the cut and tried to pour water into his mouth before Tom grabbed the bottle and gulped it down.

Jack stalked back on stage with Amy in tow. "This is my wife! You guys can't fucking slam her around!"

People shouted from the pit.

"When I fucking tell you to let someone out of the fucking pit, do it!"

Jack pulled Amy to the side of the stage. They each gestured broadly as they spoke. After another minute or so, Jack hugged Amy, then stormed to center stage, shouting something at the band. "You assholes are lucky she wants a show."

Echo Chamber immediately shifted to a more aggressive song. A triumphant roar rose from the crowd, and everyone leapt into dance. Jack eyed the pit as he screamed the lyrics.

Sue didn't even bob her head when the music resumed. She remained calm and focused on Tom despite the hardcore concert happening around them. When she took the rag off his head and the cut didn't bleed, she visibly relaxed. Tom gave her a crooked smile, shoved the cloth in his back pocket, and turned toward the stage, jumping to the music. Sue's chest rose and fell as she took in and released a huge breath. She turned to Adam and tackled him with a tight hug.

"Are you okay?" She asked, still holding onto him. Her pulse raced, but her breathing was steady, as though she was calming herself.

"Not even a scratch." He rubbed her back as he held her.

"You pulled me out of a mosh pit."

"Yeah."

Sue curled her fingers into the hair above his neck. "That's pretty badass."

Adam chuckled and tightened his arms around her, appreciating the compliment. "Just doing what I was told."

"Still badass. You saved me from being trampled, and then you went back for Tom. And you totally didn't have to."

Sue's breath against his ear made it difficult for Adam to focus on anything aside from her and her body against him, the thump of her pulse now matching his. "Can't leave a wounded man behind."

"You barely know him."

"He's one of your people."

"Mmm, my very own badass." Sue hugged Adam tighter, stepped up on her tiptoes, and kissed him.

Yeah, he'd brave mosh pits for this woman daily if this would be his reward.

CHAPTER 35

People swarmed Sue as soon as she and Adam arrived at the after-party in Amy's backyard, making one introduction after another. Adam gave her space to network, appreciating the moments when she'd make it back to his side before getting pulled in another direction. Sometimes she'd bring Adam with her, other times he'd recognize someone and go in his own direction. He talked with the Nomad guys, hung out with Robin and Amy, and eventually made it over to Tom, who re-introduced him to Chris and Justin.

"You've been seeing Sue?" Justin asked.

Adam searched the party for her. "Been trying to. You guys keep her pretty busy." Justin's question seemed innocent enough, but Adam braced himself for another grilling, similar to when he met Tom the day before. *Clients*, he reminded himself. These guys were her clients.

"Duh, she's here to work." Chris dropped his beer can to the ground and stomped on it.

Adam held up a hand. "Relax. Obviously, I'm not crowding her."

"Don't mind Chris." Justin shoved Chris's shoulder. "It's his turn to be resident asshole on tour."

"Whatever, man." Chris rolled his eyes. "She

shouldn't even be here. She should be working."

Adam lifted an eyebrow. Did this guy even under-stand his own circular logic?

"She is," Tom said.

"Okay." Chris pursed his mouth.

Tom flicked Chris in the ear. "Do you think she's talking to Barry's twin for fun? I bet she'd rather talk to you."

Chris scowled as he rubbed his ear. "Barry's twin?"

"Yeah." Tom gestured toward Sue. "That guy she's talking to is Carlo's PR agent and about as friendly as a block of wood."

"That guy's a tool," Adam said. "Her phone's been going off since we got here. Either she's got a lot about to print on you guys or people are sending her messages as she meets them."

"How do you know?" Chris asked.

Adam held up Sue's phone, alerts flashing across the screen too fast to read. "She doesn't have pockets."

Justin and Tom laughed while Chris rolled his eyes

"I know her lock pattern. I can shut it off for you." Tom gestured for the phone.

"Thanks. She has it on vibrate, or I wouldn't have noticed."

Tom unlocked the phone and studied the screen for

a moment, then scrolled through the messages. "Shit. These people are scared of her."

"What do you mean?" Justin asked.

"Look at these emails." Tom held the phone between him and Justin. "Reporters are basically offering to write whatever she wants."

Again, Adam quirked a brow. He never offered the people he covered anything aside from the occasional advance copy.

Justin read the message Tom queued up. "Wow, she has them by the balls."

"Right." Chris reached for his crushed can.

Adam kicked it away.

Chris glared at him, toed the can toward himself and picked it up.

"Why would I lie?" Justin took the can from Chris and tossed it on the bar.

"Whoa." Tom continued to scroll through the messages. "She's got you built up like you're Elvis or something, Chris."

Chris crossed his arms. "What the fuck are you talking about?"

Tom cleared his throat and read aloud. "Ms. Douglas: *Craft of Sound* would like to feature Chris Lorenzo in our September issue. We understand as an up-and-coming band, reputation is critical. Therefore, we are willing to offer full approval on all photography.

In addition, we will submit all questions prior to our interview and allow Mr. Lorenzo to designate whether the article will appear in a Q&A format or as a full profile."

Chris pushed down Tom's hand with the phone. "So, they gave her full approval. She's always had that."

"She has?" Adam asked. Sure, music and entertainment had different rules than sports, but journalism didn't. What kind of writers gave up story control? *Craft of Sound* was a renowned publication with a stellar reputation. If they were offering approval, it meant one thing: Sue's reputation was at least as good as theirs, and they believed her when she said Chris was an important get. Impressive.

Chris sneered at Adam. "Yeah. We've been reading interviews since Indie Showcase, and she had me approve quotes from that dinner thing the other night."

Adam ignored Chris's attitude in favor of giving Sue credit where it was obviously due. "Everyone has granted approval?" Adam waited for confirmation before he spoke again, making the awe in his voice clear when he spoke. "She really does have them by the balls."

"Dude! *What* are you all talking about?" Chris barely keep his voice below shouting level.

"Chris. There are a few things reporters never do." Adam ticked items off, starting with his middle finger. "They never pay for stories. They never skip fact checking. And unless the person they're interviewing is at the same level as, say, the Pope, and probably not even

then, they *never* give final approval away. Not on photos, not on copy, not on anything. Ever." Adam dropped
a hand on Chris's shoulder and squeezed a little too
tight. "Sorry to break it to you, you're not even close to
being a big deal." He mentally punctuated his statement
with *asshole.*

"But she's turning you into one," Tom added.

Justin laughed. "You so owe her."

"Bullshit," Chris cursed.

Adam scanned the party for Sue again. She didn't
need to put up with any more of this douchebag's shit.

"She could sell you out for the asshole you are, and
she's making people think you're a mad scientist with a
guitar. You owe her." Justin took a swig of beer.

"Justin's right," Adam said, enjoying Chris's dark red
color. Whether it came from anger or embarrassment
didn't matter, as long as it meant the guy wasn't happy.

"You guys are all fucking high." Chris scrubbed a
palm over his head and stepped away.

"Hold on, Chris." Tom pulled something up on the
phone and showed it to Justin.

Justin whistled. "*Holy shit.*"

Adam leaned over to see the screen and laughed.
"Sue's a badass."

Justin grinned. "Yeah, she is."

"What the fuck?" Chris stomped his foot.

Tom gave the phone to Chris, a photo of their *Rolling Stone* write-up front and center.

All the color left Chris's face, and his hands shook. "That's not real."

"Real and on newsstands Tuesday." Tom gave Chris a smug smile. "They sent her preview copies of the issue. She brought them to band practice the other day."

Justin smacked Chris. "Shit, that would've been a great meeting, and you fucked it up. Way to go, asshole."

"Sue started it with that *Sound Spectrum* bullshit!" Chris's voice cracked on *spectrum*.

"Don't even try to pass that off on her." Justin sneered. "You seriously fucked up."

"What bullshit?" Adam asked. Clearly Chris piled on whatever garbage he could. Why? Sue was doing an amazing job.

Tom shook his head. "Later."

Adam furrowed his brow, then let it go. "Here she comes."

"Perfect." Justin grinned and shoved Chris. "You can apologize and maybe get her a flower arrangement that isn't half dead and stolen from a patio table."

Adam looked at Tom again.

"Don't ask."

Yeah, he'd definitely be asking later.

Sue smiled when she joined the group, but it quickly flagged. "Why do I feel like I'm walking into a trap?"

Chris spun and faced Sue, shoving the phone at her. "When are you gonna get us an *actual* interview with *Rolling Stone*?"

"When you stop being an asshole to reporters."

Once again, Adam admired how Sue cut to the chase. He needed to get her alone to *really* admire her.

"Fucking! Ugh! What the fuck!" Chris balled a fist at his side and pounded his leg.

"If you want a *Rolling Stone* cover story, you need more than 'fucks' and grunting, Chris."

Adam put a hand on Sue's hip and pulled her toward him. He growled in her ear. "So hot." He took pride in her resulting shiver.

"What? Why... Ah! Fucking hell!" Chris stormed away, his complexion shifting from white to red to purple.

Justin laughed. "It's fun watching her spring the trap on the guy who set it in the first place." He turned toward Adam. "And I'd know. I laid a super creepy leer on her day one to see what she was about. She set my ass straight in all of three seconds. No one fucks with Sexy Sue."

Adam lifted an eyebrow. He loved that she didn't let anyone fuck with her, but Sexy Sue? Where had *that* come from? "Sexy Sue?"

She blushed. "Yeah. I spring their traps on them, yet I can't shake that nickname."

Justin raised his beer bottle as if to toast her. "Own it, Sue."

She pressed a hand against her forehead and looked toward Tom. Adam followed her gaze; he had all kinds of questions for the tour manager. The man kept a stoic front.

"I was only gonna stop the vibrating, then Chris pissed me off." Tom shook his head. "I promise I only went through work stuff."

Sue dropped her hand. "It's okay. I don't have anything to hide from you." She regarded Adam, her smile subdued. "I thought I had it on silent. I'm sorry."

"No problem. It was incredibly entertaining." Sue shutting down Chris's fuckery had been one of the highlights of the night.

"Sue." Justin gripped her shoulder and gave her a small shake. "You got us into *Rolling Stone*."

Sue looked to Tom again; after he nodded, she answered. "It's only a blurb for now. They like you guys. We can get more. I'm sorry I kept it from you. I wanted to tell you all together."

"Don't ever apologize for getting us good press." Justin gave her a fist bump. "I won't tell Darryl and Brad, but you may want to send a text before Chris gets to them."

"Good idea."

Adam put an arm around her waist. "Do it now."

"Yeah?"

"Hell yeah." Tom wagged a finger at Sue's phone. "Send them that photo and the newsstand date."

Sue grinned. "I like it." She tapped away on the phone, then exhaled. "Done."

Justin and Tom's phones dinged with the message.

"My mom is gonna be so psyched." Justin grinned as he brought the photo up. "D's, too. I gotta find him. Excuse me."

"I'm forwarding this to Annabelle." Tom swiped his phone screen. "Between this, *Show Biz Tonight*, and the local news, she's gonna be on a high for a week."

Adam squeezed Sue's waist. "They were on *Show Biz Tonight*?"

She turned Adam's arm and checked his watch. "Maybe right now."

"Why aren't we watching it?"

Sue furrowed her brow. "We're at a party."

"So?"

"They're sending me the link."

Adam took her hand and stepped away from Tom. "Come on."

"Where are we going?"

"To watch your TV segment." Adam pulled her to a quiet area near a chaotic wall of trees, shrubs, flowers and fairy lights at the back of the yard.

"I don't want to leave the party, and there's no TV out here."

"We have the internet in our hands." Adam pushed Sue into a little metal chair and crouched next to her. "What station?"

"*Show Biz Tonight* is on cable. There's a package on NOLA 4 and the CBS station in Ann Arbor. The Ann Arbor broadcast will show some of the *Show Biz* clip."

Adam squeezed her knee. "Sue, you got your clients three news segments in one night in three different markets, and you're not watching them?"

Sue gestured toward the house. "This is a great party. And I already previewed the *Show Biz* and NOLA clips."

"You're killing me. Do you know what we do in my office when one of our stories gets picked up on TV?"

She shook her head.

"We get champagne and good scotch, and we crowd around the televisions and celebrate. Why aren't you celebrating?"

Sue put her hand over Adam's. "*Sports Mecca* getting a pickup is a hat tip to how good you guys are at finding great stories. Me getting my clients on the news is doing my job."

"You're doing a kick-ass job. Flaunt it."

"Don't need to. My work speaks for itself."

"Your confidence is damn sexy." Adam pulled Sue toward him and crushed his mouth to hers, almost pulling her off the chair.

Sue laughed and wrapped her arms around his neck. She kissed him again. "Shut up and show me my news clips."

Sue double checked the sizes on all the pieces of Justin's tuxedo before zipping the garment bag and giving it to him. "All set."

"Your dedication knows no bounds, Sue." Justin swung the garment bag over his shoulder.

"They sent the wrong pants for Tom, and Brad's coat sleeves were too long. Better safe than uncomfortable." Sue's phone went off with a unique alert tone. She rubbed her forehead and sighed. "And I'm avoiding my room. That's Robin; he's already been there twice today."

"He still trying to buy you a dress?"

"Oh yeah." Sue pulled out her phone and unlocked the screen. "Look at the selection." She thumbed through half a dozen photos Robin had sent that morning, each gown more stunning than the last.

Justin put his hand over Sue's. "Wait. That red number has possibilities."

Sue glared at him. "Don't." She slid the phone into her back pocket.

"Stupid question—you have a dress, right?"

"Oh yeah, picked it up this morning."

Justin grinned. "Does Robin know you only picked it up this morning?"

"Hell no. I've been telling him I had it since I got to New Orleans."

Justin chuckled. "You and Robin are too much." He re-situated the garment bag. "Brad has his?"

"Yep."

"All right. See you in a bit."

Sue settled in on the couch. Naturally, Chris would be last to pick up his tux. Normally she'd be annoyed, but with everything else done, she sat and texted with Adam, enjoying the rare quiet time.

When Chris finally showed up, Robin followed, almost running him over.

"Finally, I find you!" Robin rushed toward her.

"What do you mean *finally*? You've been calling me all day." Sue made a point of occupying herself with the tags on the pieces of Chris's tuxedo. The last thing she wanted to deal with was Robin smothering her.

"You can't wear the black dress from the fight."

"I know."

"Why?" Chris asked.

"It was on TMZ," Robin said.

"So?" Chris flopped on one of the beds.

Sue turned to Chris. "There's gonna be a lot of photographers tonight."

Chris bristled.

She held up a hand. "Don't worry. Interviews are over; it's only the red carpet." Sue put an arm on the garment rack, pointedly not looking at Robin lest he see it as an invitation to talk more. Not that he ever needed one.

Robin paced in and out of Sue's line of sight. "Since she wore the black dress to another public event, she needs something fresh for this one."

Sue put a hand over her heart as though taking an oath. "I will not wear the black dress tonight. Promise."

"Are you wearing black at all?"

"Why the grand inquisition, Robin? Don't you trust me?" Sue made a showroom model gesture toward Chris's tuxedo.

He stayed sprawled across the foot of the bed. Naturally, he wouldn't just take the fucking tux. Instead, he'd let this be as awkward as possible.

"Yes, I trust you." Robin sighed. "But you're wearing baggy jeans and a tour shirt again, and this is the perfect night to dress like a girl."

Sue's heart softened for a beat. Robin always protected her. His intense, over-the-top concern about her dress was his way of looking out for her. She should've been straight with him from the beginning—this wasn't only a big event for Amy and all the bands, it was a big date for her and Adam. Maybe their last, considering the demanding tour. She wanted Adam to remember her on her terms. And Robin, God love him, wanted her to feel fabulous. She didn't need his fancy clothes. Their deep friendship always made her feel like she could achieve anything.

"Huh?" Chris pushed up on his elbows.

"She's been dressing like you guys, and I have Ames in an *incredible* gown. If you two are gonna be seen together, Sue, you can't be wearing a tux like the rest of the guys!" Robin put a hand on top of his head and resumed pacing.

"Why do you even need to go to another party? You and Amy need more excuses to binge drink? Don't you have work to do?" Chris asked.

Robin's eyebrows knit together, and he stepped toward Chris.

Sue held her hand up, stopping her friend. "I'm going to babysit you, Chris. We don't need any more pissed-off reporters." She turned away from the daggers Chris shot at her and faced Robin. She wanted to hug him to reassure him, but she held her ground, preferring to save her emotions for when they didn't have an audience. "I promise I will not wear a tuxedo. I have a dress. A girly one."

Robin turned to her, smile bright, eyes glittering, hands on his hips. "Describe."

"I have to be ready by eight. It's six-thirty now. You want to trust me and let me get ready, or guarantee disaster by standing here and killing more time?"

Robin narrowed his eyes. "We've known each other too long, my dear. You stole my line." He lifted his chin, closed his eyes, and pointed at the door. "Go get ready."

"Thank you." Sue crossed her arms and gazed at Chris.

He groaned and rolled off the bed. "I only need like five minutes to put this on." He pulled the tuxedo off the rack and slunk out of the room.

"Let's go. I'll help you into the dress," Robin said.

"Not a chance." Sue gave Robin her sweetest smile and sailed out of the room.

At 7:45 p.m., Sue went back to Tom's room and covered her stumble with a wolf whistle. The guys looked amazing. Even Chris. How could she get them in tuxes more often? "This is quite a sight."

Brad gave Sue a bright smile as the rest of the guys turned toward her.

Chris snorted and wiggled his index finger at Sue. "Robin's gonna love this look."

Sue had applied flawless makeup, but big rollers pulled her hair off her face, and she wore a black button-down, jeans, and flip-flops.

"Is it feminine enough?" Sue held out her arms to

show off her outfit.

Chris nodded. "He'll totally be into your 'do."

He snickered as she fluffed her hair and posed.

"They're joking together. Is that a sign of the apocalypse?" Darryl asked Justin.

"Gotta be," Justin said.

Sue lined them up and checked each man from head to toe. She adjusted a few ties and tightened Tom's vest, then stood back and took them all in. For once, Tom had tamed his hair and bore a striking resemblance to '50s-era movie stars. Justin's honey-colored hair hung in a neat ponytail at his neck, while Brad left his long silky jet-black hair loose. Darryl traded his usual killer spikes for smaller, flyaway spikes. Chris looked like himself, but his posture was straighter, his chin up, and his Doc Martens had been polished.

Sue put her hands on her hips. "You guys all look fantastic. Lady killers, every one of you."

"My mom would be so proud." Darryl brushed his arms down his sleeves.

"Oh! I almost forgot! Brad," Sue called to him as she took out her phone. "I promised Annabelle I'd send pictures."

"You hear that, Chris? Annabelle's gonna check you out." Justin gestured as if to hit his high hat.

"Shut up," Chris sneered.

Sue held up her phone for the picture. "Be nice!

Everyone strike your favorite *GQ* pose."

Each man picked a different cheesy pose, except Tom, who stood at the end of the line with his hands in his pockets and looked at the rest of the guys as though they were absurd. Sue seized the moment and took several pictures.

Chris took his phone from his pocket. "Now let's take a picture of you and send it to Robin. I wanna see how long it takes him to get out here and yell at you."

Sue rolled her carefully made-up eyes. "Let's not and say we did."

Darryl straightened his tie. "I'm going to get Lena. You jokers coming?"

"It would be cool for her to get picked up by five handsome guys," Sue said.

"Perfect, let's do it." Darryl opened the door and gestured to Sue to walk through.

They filed out of the room and crowded into an elevator. Sue used the ride to check Chris's cuff links, which earned her an especially dirty glare.

When they got to Sue and Lena's room, Darryl knocked on the door.

Lena opened it a crack. "Where's Sue?"

"Right here!" She slipped into the room and found Lena's zipper had caught in the delicate fabric of her dress. She eased it free it and zipped the gown the rest of the way, gave her friend a once-over, and clapped.

"You're so pretty!"

Lena blushed and gave Sue a quick hug, then went to the door.

"Wait, let me out first." Sue left the room, keeping the door close to her. She shot Darryl a huge grin. "Knock again."

Darryl knocked, then stepped back when Lena came out.

Sue held up her camera and captured the amazement on Darryl's face.

"Wow."

Lena was statuesque in a Grecian-style pink dress. The light shade set off her tanned skin. She'd pulled her hair back from her face in a half bun with some of her hair smoothed into a wave behind her shoulders. Her simple makeup had a hint of shimmer.

Justin ogled. "Jackpot, D. Jack. Pot."

Darryl slapped Justin in the gut. "Get your own date." He touched the small of Lena's back and beamed at her. "You ready, gorgeous?"

Lena blushed. "Yes."

Sue snapped to attention. "Okay, the giant fancy bus is waiting out front. It'll go straight to the zoo. Someone will meet you there and direct you to the staging area."

Tom tilted his head. "You're not riding with us?"

"Nope. I'll take the next bus."

Chris smirked. "Can't compete with Lena, huh?"

"What the fuck is wrong with you?" Tom asked.

"Everything," Justin said.

Sue snapped her fingers. "That reminds me!" Like hell she was going to let that asshole think she cared about his opinion. Darryl and Lena had stepped away from the group, and Sue focused on them again. "Before you go, I need a picture of Darryl and Lena together."

Darryl gave Sue his phone, and she snapped photos with both her phone and his. Then she had the rest of the guys flank the couple for a group picture.

Sue clapped and grinned. "Okay, go. Don't get into any trouble before I see you again."

Justin saluted and led the way to the elevators.

Sue sent Adam a text.

S: Finished with the band stuff for now. I'll be ready in 10 minutes.

A: Last chance for a corsage.

S: NO corsage.

Sue went into the room and got her emerald-green gown from the closet. She studied it for a moment, inspecting the alterations one last time and checking the zipper to make sure she didn't catch anything as she put it on. Once clothed, she finished her hair and put on lipstick. The mirror in the room cut off above her knees, so to get a full view, she stood in the hallway outside the open door. She twisted and made sure the fabric draped right all around.

Originally, she'd planned to wear an understated cocktail dress, her focus on the band standing out. Then Adam had turned up. She liked him a lot, even though her job made a relationship impossible. As she twisted in the mirror, she hoped her instinct had been right and this dress would etch itself into his brain. She may not be able to keep him, but she could keep the memories of this night.

When the elevator at the end of the hall dinged, she went into the room for her clutch. She and Adam stepped into the hallway at the same time.

He stopped, providing the opportunity she'd longed for in Las Vegas. She hadn't wanted to get caught staring that night. Now that they were alone, she savored it. His jacket tapered in just enough at the waist to highlight his broad shoulders. His vest had a subtle, tone-on-tone chevron pattern. He'd also worn it when they met in Las Vegas, and it confirmed for her that he owned his tux. His pants were fitted at the hip with tailored legs, instead of the boxy fit the band wore. Unlike Las Vegas, Adam wore a satin tie with a Windsor knot rather than a bow tie. The long tie suited him.

Sue closed the distance between them and smoothed her hand along the edge of his lapel. "I love that Amy made this a formal event. Men in tuxedos are the *best*."

"Damn." Adam leaned back and looked Sue up and down again.

"Is that good?"

He stared for a long moment, during which Sue struggled not to fidget or fiddle with her dress.

"It's amazing."

She relaxed and smiled, then gazed at the gown and flounced the skirt. "Thank you."

Adam pressed his fingers to his temple. "I'm speechless."

"That's exactly what I was going for."

"I want to kiss you, but I don't want to mess anything up."

"Makeup is easy to fix." She moved closer, wanting his kiss. She wanted to bask in this moment and lock it into her memory.

Adam put a hand behind her ear and leaned in, unleashing a soft, slow kiss.

She gripped his arm as her knees wobbled, then pulled back, dazed. She hadn't expected his kiss to throw her off-kilter. "Sorry, I don't want to wrinkle you."

"I don't care about wrinkles." Adam kissed her again, trailing his hand down her arm and twining his fingers in hers. "We have to go before I beg you to stay here with me."

Sue rubbed her lips together, the idea of skipping the benefit sending steamy flashes across her mind's eye. She reminded herself that this was still a working date and followed him into the elevator.

Adam pulled his phone from his breast pocket.

"Everything okay?"

"Yeah." His gaze swept over her again. "No way am I letting you ride a bus to the benefit."

"It's more of a tall stretch limo."

"Still not happening." He rubbed the chain that led to the starburst pendant, his barely-there contact giving her a tiny shiver. By the time they'd gotten to the ground floor, he'd arranged for a town car.

"Usually the band gets the town car and the publicist has to fend for herself."

"Right now, you're not a publicist. You're my date, and I'm doing it right." Adam pressed a firm kiss to her lips. "You're so stunning, I almost forgot this." He gave Sue a white rose with a clipped stem. "After all my corsage talk, I couldn't show up empty-handed."

"Thank you." Sue accepted the flower and used it as an excuse to kiss him again.

"My sisters say rose colors mean something. I didn't care about the color. I wanted to give you one with perfect petals."

She twirled the rose under her nose and inhaled, delighted and overwhelmed by his sentiment. "What did I tell you about gifts?"

The town car pulled up, and Adam opened the door for her. "You'll have to give me another date to make it up to you."

CHAPTER 37

Brad waited at the edge of the tent where the bands waited to enter the party. He liked watching the arrivals, guessing to himself who made bids on which auction item. When the town car pulled up between two of the fancy buses, he elbowed Justin. "This might be Jack and Amy."

"They're not already here?"

"I don't know. Isn't everyone else staying at the same hotel like we're in a sitcom? Amy and Jack would be coming from their house, right?"

Justin buttoned his jacket. "I guess."

"Jack's here?" Chris stepped away from Darryl and Lena and joined Brad.

"Maybe?" Brad said.

"That's not Jack and Amy." Justin tugged Brad's arm. "Come on."

"How do you know?" Brad shook off Justin as a man circled the car, opened the door, and held out a hand.

"Oh, shit." Chris rubbed a palm over his head. "I'd know those legs anywhere."

"What do you—" Brad stopped when Sue's head emerged from the car. "Oh," he huffed. "Damn."

She wore a brilliant green dress with a fitted bodice. Thick straps hit her right on the edge of her shoulders, making a pronounced deep V-neck that closed in a flat knot at her side. The skirt flared when she walked, with a slit that made it look like the dress had run out of fabric at mid-thigh. If not for the flash of leg with every other step, she would've looked like she glided away from the car. Her hair was down, with big loose tendrils curling away from her face. Brad wasn't sure if the sparkle came from the dress or Sue herself.

"Robin had to get on her case." Chris jammed his hands in his pockets and shook his head. "She couldn't wear black and blend in. Fuckin' aye."

Justin pulled on his cuffs. "She cleans up good."

Brad hit Justin's arm. "Fucking understatement of the year."

Chris raised his eyebrows and turned away from the line of arrivals. "I'm gonna go find Robin."

Brad's emotions threatened to suffocate him. Yeah, he'd overreacted with Justin. Hell, his response to Sue had been over-the-top from day one. He closed his eyes so he didn't have to keep watching Sue and Adam fawn over each other.

"You okay?" Justin asked.

"I don't know." Brad rubbed his temple. Was this frustration? Disappointment? Defeat?

"It's only a dress."

"No. It's everything about her. And then that guy

shows up and she looks at him like he's the fucking master of the universe. Is he a dick? No. He's nice. Chris googled him. He doesn't only write for that website, he owns it. He's fucking loaded. What the fuck?"

"I thought you were getting over this," Justin said. "What's going on?"

Brad had no idea how to respond. Even if Justin would believe it, he didn't want to lie to his best friend. He stared out the tent window. Thankfully, Sue and Adam had moved well out of his line of sight. "If I understood why I like this woman so much, believe me, I would've harnessed that shit and won her over from the beginning."

Justin dropped his hand, his expression rapidly changing until his face turned to stone. "It was never gonna happen between you two. You have to move on."

"Sure."

"Hey!" Justin forced Brad to look at him. "Get. The fuck. Over it! This shit is old."

Brad glared. "You have no idea what you're talking about."

"I don't? I haven't seen you mope for a month? I haven't watched you make an ass of yourself? I haven't given you daily pep talks?"

Brad crossed his arms. "Putting a fifth of bourbon in my hand is far from a fucking pep talk."

"Whatever. I'm done."

"You're done? Done with what?"

"With this." Justin flicked a hand toward Brad. "You're a lost cause." Justin sneered his disgust.

Surprised by the vehement response, Brad grasped for the last argument he had. "Sorry I'm not into one-night stands like Chris."

"It's not about that. It's because you couldn't charm her like you do everyone else. You think you lost. Well, sorry. It's too bad you can't move on." Justin walked away.

Brad turned to say more as the doors opened and Sue sailed into the room.

CHAPTER 38

"All right, guys. You walk the red carpet after The Nomads." Sue turned to Darryl. "I need you to pose with the band. Lena can follow, and you two can enter the party together."

Justin tugged on his cuffs. "I didn't know there'd be a red carpet here, Sexy Sue."

"Carlo says there's a red carpet wherever they can get celebrities to congregate," Sue said. "But don't worry. This one is short."

Darryl pulled at his cuffs. "Will we get any questions?"

"If you do, they'll be light. You and Brad take them." Sue looked to Brad, who kept his focus on the other people walking the red carpet. "Brad. You can handle a few quick questions, right?"

Brad kept his eyes on the entrance to the party. "Yeah, I got it."

Sue frowned. Brad had separated himself from the group, much the way he had before their interviews in Austin. His hands were in his pockets, making it impossible to tell if he was playing air guitar, a nervous tell that seemed to calm him. She hoped he was pulling himself together. She faced the rest of the guys. "Okay. Easy. Walk out there, strike a pose, go into the party.

Done and done."

"Are you walking the carpet, Sue?" Lena curled her arm around Darryl's.

"No. Tom and I will follow discreetly."

"Actually..." Adam slipped his hand into Sue's. "Tonight, you *will*. As my date."

"You told them I'm your grandmother, right?"

Adam chuckled. "Maybe I'll try that at an event that isn't being run by your best friend."

One of the event coordinators signaled to Sue, not letting her linger on the delicious yet hopeless idea of attending another big event with Adam.

"You guys are up. Have fun—this is your practice for the Grammys!" Sue shepherded them toward the door, with Tom and Lena close by.

"The Grammys?" Chris squeaked as Sue put him between Justin and Darryl.

"Yeah, you guys deserve a few Grammys. But don't worry, that's in February. Practically a year away. Relax and enjoy tonight."

The coordinator gave the sign that the band should take their turn on the carpet, and Sue pushed them out before Chris could ask any more questions. "Yeah, that Grammys comment was really poorly timed."

Adam stood behind Sue and put his arms around her waist. "At least he's not worried about tonight now."

A broad pavilion in the middle of the zoo served as the main area for the party. Attendees had the option of visiting the rest of the zoo, but most of the action happened in or near the central area. Even though the band scattered as soon as they stepped off the red carpet, they all stayed in the pavilion.

Sue kept a close eye on Chris—she needed him on his best behavior. Still, she stayed with Adam, taking him to the dancefloor. Yes, technically she was at a work event. She was probably on her last date with Adam, too. She planned to enjoy every moment. After a few songs, Adam got them drinks while she found their group's table. The room wasn't particularly loud, but Adam leaned close to her when she spoke as though her words were intimate. She took advantage, and more than once, she pushed his silky hair over his ears and let her fingers run down his neck and rest on his shoulder.

Amy graced the stage between the salad and main courses to announce the silent auction winners. Sue admired her friend, glowing in a 1940s style sapphire-blue, satin gown with spaghetti straps, a sweetheart neckline and a flared hem.

"Isn't she pretty?" Sue asked the table with a proud smile.

"She does look lovely." Lena sipped her wine. "Robin is a brilliant stylist."

"You say that like you need his help." Tom grinned.

Darryl put his arm on the back of Lena's chair. "How many times do I have to remind you jokers? Lena's *my* date."

Lena blushed as Darryl beamed and kissed her cheek.

Sue chuckled to herself. D was the farthest thing from possessive or jealous, making his regular reminders that Lena was *his* date comical. As Sue sat back in her seat, the stage caught her eye. "Guys! I forgot!"

"What?" Justin asked.

"Amy wants you to present your items to the winners. You don't have to talk or anything, just go on stage, look pretty, and shake a few hands."

"Piece of cake," Darryl said.

Chris fidgeted in his chair. "When do we go up?"

"Your stuff is after The Nomads. When those guys are on, you go to stage left," Sue said.

As the guys left, Sue grabbed Chris's arm. "Whoever wins, don't talk to them."

"What?" he asked.

"Don't talk to the winners. You can say congratulations and thanks for supporting the zoo. That's it."

"Seriously?"

"Seriously. I'm working on something, and I need you to be the strong, silent type tonight. Okay?"

"Whatever." Chris took a few quick steps and caught up with the guys. Before he disappeared behind the stage curtain, he glanced back at Sue, then followed everyone.

Sue grabbed Adam's hand under the table and squeezed.

"What's the matter?"

"I need Chris to do what I asked." Sue bounced their hands on her leg.

"You don't think he will?"

"Generally, he does the exact opposite of what I want."

"I used to do that to my sisters," Adam said.

"Why'd you stop?"

"Because they were usually right."

Sue smiled and tapped her head to his. "As hard as Chris's head is, I doubt we'll ever reach that point."

"His loss." Adam gave her a soft kiss that warmed her but didn't entirely soothe her nerves.

"More like my headache."

"No. He's competitive. Everyone else'll get press, and then it'll be his pride and vanity fighting it out."

"Sounds painful." Sue returned Adam's kiss, hoping to encourage him to keep the distractions coming.

"Probably is."

Tom cleared his throat.

Amy was announcing who won the Words Fail Me items.

Sue tightened her grip on Adam as Chris shook hands with the winners. He murmured what looked like "congratulations" to each of them, then backed up. He'd actually followed her instructions.

As the guys and the winners left the stage, Amy explained that the final items, all donated from Echo Chamber, would be awarded in another hour.

Sue squeezed Adam's hand. "Let's dance."

Adam guided her to the dancefloor, pulling her close as they took their positions.

Sue was mid-spin when Amy goosed her. "Having fun?"

"Apparently not enough! You look gorgeous, Amy."

"Thank God for Robin. If he didn't find this dress, I might've shown up in a zoo T-shirt."

Sue chuckled. "Perish the thought!"

"Anyway, Bloody Maggots is gonna call you."

"They are?"

"Yep. They're the band anointed by Jack. And your boys brought in more bids and more money at the silent auction."

"Jack playing Brad's guitar after their show helped."

Amy tilted her head. "If you take out the guitar, Words Fail Me still commanded more money."

Sue raised her eyebrows. "Really?"

"Yep." Jack nodded. "They're relying on their label to get them exposure. They're getting good marketing stuff, but the label is hoping the marketing goes viral."

Sue shook her head. "That's not reliable."

"Yeah, so I gave them your card."

Sue stopped moving, momentarily frozen in shock. Amy referring her was normal, but Jack? That endorsement surprised her. "*You* gave them my card?"

"You get results."

Sue blinked hard to fight back tears. Jack didn't tip his hat often. "Thank you." She hugged Jack until they were interrupted by a society photographer.

Sue and Adam posed with Amy and Jack, then Amy checked a delicate watch.

"Time to announce the Echo Chamber winners!"

Amy and Echo Chamber made the final presentation of auction winners a fun highlight of the evening. They ramped up the energy, getting everyone on the dancefloor as they announced the final tally. Amy was so overcome with emotion that she hugged Jack right on stage, then sobbed her thanks into the microphone. When she revealed that the amount of money raised would fund the projects planned for the next three years, Robin whooped and grabbed the microphone from Amy.

"Let's dance!" He leapt onto the dancefloor and led the party.

Sometime after midnight, Adam took Sue away from the party and to the tent that had been used for the staging area. The only illumination came from a few foot lights near the door and a small chandelier hanging in the center of the tent. Adam pulled her into his arms again, one hand at her waist, the other holding her hand against his heart.

"Slow dance with me."

"You're not tired of dancing?" Sue wrapped one arm around his shoulders and nuzzled into his neck.

"Not when I'm dancing with you."

"You're quite the charmer." Secretly glad he wasn't ready to let her go, Sue tightened her arm around him.

Adam spun her around, pulling her closer as they moved.

"So, this necklace."

"Is amazing on you." Adam glanced toward it, then kissed near her ear.

Sue's stomach fluttered every time he dropped those small kisses on her. "The woman in the dress shop recognized it."

"Did she?"

"Yes. You shop Chopard often?"

"I saw it in a window. It looked like you."

"The Tiffany's window?"

"There isn't a Tiffany in the Quarter." He continued dancing them around the tent.

"Adam, this is too much."

"No, it's perfect."

"I can't—"

"Shhh. I already threw away the receipt."

"Lame."

"Yeah."

She shouldn't accept such an expensive gift, especially when she eschewed them from everyone else, but relief swept over her. She wanted to keep the necklace. It was the first gift she'd ever received that had stunned her. "This is at least a tenth-date gift. Maybe twenty."

"Okay."

Sue furrowed her brow. Maybe she'd had too much to champagne, or maybe she hadn't slept enough—or both—but his easy acceptance of her limit confused her.

"We'll have ten more dates."

She rested her chin on his shoulder, making sure not to let him see her smile. "You are devious."

"Only when I want something."

Sue put her mouth right next to Adam's ear and whispered, "You could've had the dates without giving me *any* gifts." And now she *knew* she'd had too much champagne. Who were they kidding? He'd be tired of her schedule after one more date, if they even got that far. She knew from experience—as soon as he saw how seriously she took her work, he'd be gone, regardless of the diamond necklace or how many dates either of them wanted.

Adam squeezed her. "Where are you going next?"

Another response she hadn't expected, and a question she didn't want to answer. Her schedule barely had time for dating, let alone pining over a charming man who kissed her like she was his addiction. She sighed. "I don't care. I'm enjoying this moment too much."

He nudged her chin up and kissed her.

She held him tighter; his kisses were laced with hunger and made her feel like she'd spent her evening in a fairy tale.

"Please, humor me. Where to next?"

Sue pulled her thoughts back to reality and her schedule. The change was unpleasant, and her tone shifted to business. Better to deal with rejection that way. "Tomorrow afternoon we leave for Oxford, Mississippi. Then Birmingham, Panama City, Savannah, Atlanta—"

"Atlanta," Adam interrupted. "When?"

"Next Saturday."

"Want to see the Braves?" Adam asked.

Sue's heart soared with the idea that he'd meet her in Atlanta, though her mind stayed firmly in reality. How exhausting would it be for them to date while she traveled almost nonstop? Sure, they'd find time here and there and maybe revisit the fairy tale bubble, but another night like this? Another stop with enough time for a proper date? Who knew when that would happen? Would either of them be satisfied with half-assed meet-ups here and there? She reluctantly pulled her head off his shoulder to look him in the eye. "I'd love to see the Braves with you. Does it fit in *your* schedule?"

"I'll already be in Atlanta for business. Plus, we're talking about a Saturday."

This Atlanta date was probably a fluke. She chose not to question it. She wanted to see him again. She knew accepting his invitation was prolonging the inevitable, and that was fine for now. "Okay, we'll see the Braves next weekend."

Adam rewarded her with another of those small kisses she loved. "Thank you. I'm pretty sure it's an early game Saturday. Do you know when you'll get into town?"

"I have my car. I can get there whenever I want after the Savannah show." She wasn't ready to reveal as much, but she wanted to be in Atlanta the moment he got there.

"Good to know. Where else are you going?"

She bit back the sigh. She wanted to bask in their current date and dream about the next one, not worry about how he'd run for the hills when she gave him her itinerary.

Adam squeezed her waist, prompting her answer.

"After Atlanta we go to Myrtle Beach, Columbia, Raleigh, and Charlottesville. We get a three-day week-end off, so I'll drop my car at home in Hagerstown. Then I join everyone on the bus, and we hit Pittsburgh, Akron, Philly, Syracuse, and Brooklyn." Sue waited a beat before continuing. Had Adam caught that she'd soon be living on a bus with six men—Tom, the band, and Luther, the bus driver? "Then we have a week off before we go to Europe."

"When are you in Charlottesville?"

"The Thursday after Atlanta." It felt like a lifetime yawned ahead of them, even though it was barely two weeks away.

"You like steeplechases?"

Yes, *Sports Mecca* covered all sports; that didn't mean he personally covered them. "Adam."

"What?"

"Will you be covering Fox Field, or just going because I am?" She wanted him to say he was going for her. It would be hot as hell. Again, reality crept in. Sure, he was the boss, but she wasn't available enough for him to cover random events as an excuse to see her. Plus, that was a shitty thing to do to his staff. She didn't want to turn this nice guy into an asshole boss.

"How do you know the steeplechase is Fox Field?"

Adam asked.

"My friend Emily went to UVA. We go together every Spring."

"Will she mind if you go with me instead?"

Sue let instinct guide her rather than logic. "She'd better not."

"Then yes, I'll be covering Fox Field."

Adam wanted to see her again and planned to follow her up the East Coast to do it, something no man had been willing to do for her thus far. Even as warmth flooded her, her doubts wouldn't be silenced. How long until coordinating schedules became a burden?

Adam kissed her cheek. "What?"

"This is incredibly flattering, but you making schedule changes for me..." Unsure of what to say, Sue shrugged. "It's too much. I can't make changes for you. It's not fair to your writers to change up your schedule all the time." As much as she loved the idea of him meeting her on the road, it was more fantasy. It couldn't last.

"I can't cover the Triple Crown this year. My team has known this was coming for a while. Plus, we constantly have to make on-the-fly changes. Flights get canceled all the damn time."

"Why can't you cover the Triple Crown?"

"My grandmother's hip replacement. I'm checking on her after."

"She lives alone?"

"Yes. My parents and my older sister will be there for the surgery and about a week after. I'll drive up once they all leave," Adam said.

"That's very sweet."

Adam kissed her. "You're not the only woman I change my schedule for."

Deciding not to worry about what she couldn't predict, Sue resolved to simply enjoy the moment. "A guy who loves his grandmother is pretty hot." She rested her head on his shoulder and let Adam waltz her around the tent until the music coming from the pavilion stopped.

As he walked her to the town car, Adam casually offered, "Café Du Monde?"

Still holding his hand, Sue twisted their arms to read his watch. "It's too late for caffeine. I'll never get to sleep."

Adam quirked a brow, then pulled her hand to him and kissed her knuckles.

Grateful for the cover of darkness, Sue let her cheeks burn. She didn't want to sleep. She had to see through her commitment to Lena, though, and she liked Adam way too much to have sex with him and never see him again. Yes, they had another date set for next week, but a lot could happen in a week. When this night ended, she needed to return to the real world—work—with no regrets or distractions.

She let Adam lead her through the hotel lobby, declining another coffee invitation. Each step was one closer to "goodnight" and the end of her dream date. She blamed Darryl for looping her into his personal stuff and keeping her from staying out all night, and she blamed Adam for being so damned engaging. Robin and Amy had encouraged this madness. What had she been thinking to even entertain this? She should've stayed focused on business. She silently berated herself even as they boarded the elevator.

Adam stood against the opposite side, staring at her. "You okay?"

Sue nodded, holding his gaze, then she mentally peeled away his tuxedo and got acquainted with the muscles she'd felt every time she trailed a hand along his arm, danced with him, or hugged him. She considered whether she'd explore his chest with her fingers or her tongue first, how he'd touch her while she memorized him. Would there be more light kisses? Remembering the pressure of his firm lips and imagining them...*everywhere* overwhelmed her. Sue dropped her gaze.

Adam hit the stop button and pounced on her, kissing her with such intensity that she would've sunk to the floor had it not been for the railing.

"I want to send this elevator back to my floor and take you to my room." He dragged his lips from her ear down her neck, then back to her lips.

Sue arched with the shiver that ran through her, smiled against his lips, and kissed him back, glad she wasn't the only one wishing this night would end differently. She decided the best way to recover her wits was to throw him off balance, just as he had her. "Too late, Adam. Sorry." She reached behind him and pushed the release button, still kissing him. Once the doors opened at her floor, she broke away and ran down the hall.

Adam stayed one step behind her. When they got to her door, he grabbed her elbow and pulled her to him. She wrapped her arms around him and let herself sink into his next kiss. He gently pushed her against the wall next to her door and trailed kisses along her jaw, down to her chest, and across her shoulders. He skimmed a hand from her hip to her knee and lifted her leg, hooking her knee at his hip. He trailed his fingers lightly along her calf, stoking her lust, until he had her shoe. He pulled it off and looked inside it, then back at her, confused.

"Where's your key?"

Sue rumbled a deep chuckle. She slid her leg down his, pulling his hips against hers, and gasped at the contact before she kissed him again. She desperately wanted to get his pants off. Instead, she tapped him with her clutch, then opened it and took out her key.

"At least I got your shoe off."

Sue laughed again, quietly. "Yes, but..."

"What?" Adam asked as he kissed her skin along the chain of her necklace, his hips still pressed against her.

"Lena said she'd be back here by three. Last time I checked, it was twenty 'til." Sue knew she should untangle herself, yet she couldn't bring herself to do it.

Adam lifted his head and looked her in the eye. "Come to my room."

"Can't."

The lust in Adam's eyes flashed to frustration.

"It's not that I don't want to. I do."

"Then let's go." He pressed against her again, this time pushing her legs apart and adding pressure against her bare thigh.

Instinctively, she rubbed her leg along his and licked her lips. They were so close, she almost licked him. Sue groaned. She needed to stop moving. She kept making this fun, sexy moment worse. She closed her eyes to clear her head. "Her brother-in-law made me the protector of her virtue." She opened her eyes to see the shock in Adam's.

He put a tiny bit of space between them. "You're kidding."

"I wish."

"People still do that?"

"Most of her family is in Brazil. Victor's looking out for her."

Adam pressed his forehead to the wall, forcing them closer together.

She groaned with him as all their pressure points met. There was too much clothing—and obligation— between them, but the contact still tempted.

"I *hate* brothers-in-law."

Sue shifted her arms around him for a hug. "Me, too." She kissed him again, her passion restrained.

He shifted his hand from her waist to her ass and squeezed as he pulled her lower lip between his teeth.

Sue hummed her desire while she silently damned her ridiculous curfew.

"Why is my chest vibrating?" Adam asked.

At one point in the night, she'd lost track of her clutch and tucked the phone into her dress. She enjoyed the wonder on Adam's face as she pulled it out of the bodice, the levity helping to rein in her lust.

"How'd you get that in there?"

"Magic." She checked the message and sighed. "Lena's on her way."

Adam frowned and took the room key from Sue. He opened the door and gave back the card and her shoe. This time when she crossed the threshold, he followed and wrapped an arm around her waist. When he kissed her, Sue put an arm out to grab the wall, needing it to keep one foot in reality while the rest of her clung to him and the fairy tale. When he finished kissing her, he didn't let her go right away. They held each other until her phone went off again.

"I hate Victor so much," she said.

Adam stepped back and pushed a bit of her hair behind her ear. "Breakfast?"

“Yes.”

“I’ll be back here at nine.”

“Don’t be late,” Sue said.

CHAPTER 39

After lying awake for three hours, Sue got up and quietly put on workout clothes. She slipped out of the room and tapped the door closed. Just because she couldn't sleep didn't mean Lena shouldn't. The temptation to text Adam loomed. She checked the time. A message as the sun rose would wake him. Sue took the stairs to the main floor and padded to the small gym as she fiddled with her earbuds and selected a playlist on her phone.

She stumbled then stopped when she got to the line of windows looking into the gym. Adam lifted free weights. Despite wearing a ball cap and standing with his back to her, the way he moved and the glimpse of his mouth in the mirror made her certain it was him. The damp patch between his shoulder blades proved he'd been there awhile. He lifted weights from his waist to his shoulders. Captivated by how the muscles in his arms rippled through each rep, Sue pursed her lips to stop a gasp when he lifted the weight over his shoulder and did triceps curls.

She slipped into the gym, sat on the floor next to the door, and watched him do a few more sets. She held still when he replaced the weights on the stand and pulled his phone out of his pocket. A moment later, her own phone vibrated.

A: You awake?

"Yes," Sue said.

Adam looked left and right before he turned, then smiled.

Sue waved and stood. "Couldn't sleep. I was gonna hit the treadmill."

"Me, neither." He closed the distance between them and kissed her cheek. "How long have you been here?"

Sue glanced away, fighting the heat rising in her cheeks. "Biceps."

Adam chuckled and twined his fingers with hers. "Hungry?"

"So hungry." For him. This little trip to the gym had wound up being a reward in itself, and she was more than ready to thank him for it.

"Let me put on dry clothes, and I'll take you to breakfast."

Sue curled a fist into the hem of his shirt. "I don't mind this."

Adam lifted an eyebrow, then kissed her, keeping space between their bodies. "This is not how I want to get you sweaty," he whispered low and rough.

She looked him in the eye. "Let's go get me sweaty."

"*A Tree Grows in Brooklyn* is one of your ten favorites?" Sue rolled over, using one hand to shield her eyes from the sun. She lay next to Adam under a group of trees in Armstrong Park. The weather and the company were ideal, but this was not how she thought she'd spend the morning. "Was it required reading in high school?"

"Nope," Adam said.

"Did a girl have something to do with it?"

"Why are you surprised I like that book? It's a classic."

"Yes, and I want to know what prompted you to read it."

Lying on his side, Adam put his hand on her stomach and rubbed his thumb back and forth against the edge of her top. "It was a girl. My younger sister read it and talked about it incessantly. I wanted context. One chapter in, I was hooked."

"I love that you read it for your sister. It's a great book."

"It is," Adam whispered, then kissed her cheek.

She turned to kiss his lips and smiled. "I'm sorry about before."

"Stop. You have nothing to apologize for."

But she did. Sue had no control over when and where Chris's hookups were going to show up, nor could she control the public fit this particular woman had thrown. However, Sue was capable of taking herself out of the situation, and she'd chosen not to this morning. Chris hadn't even been there. She could've left it to security.

Instead, she caved to her sense of duty, and rather than escaping into Adam's room and finally, finally exploring his body, she'd agreed to answer "a few" questions from security. For almost an hour. When she texted Adam that she was finally free, he hadn't responded. She trudged to her room, where Lena still slept, quietly berating herself through a shower and as she dressed. This was why she had yet to maintain a long-term relationship. She put work ahead of everything. She consigned herself to the idea that like most people, Adam didn't want to come in second and she should let him go.

About ten minutes later he knocked on her door, sheepishly explaining that a call from his mother had kept him from seeing Sue's text right away. They walked the city, eventually settling at the park, lazing in the shade and playing the "top ten" game Adam had tried to start when they were in Las Vegas. They traded lists of their favorite things, falling into colorful conversations that ignited Sue's brain in ways that made her both grateful and disappointed that they'd never managed to make it to bed.

She was grateful because she was afraid to get too attached, but disappointed because the more they talked, the more Adam turned her on. And he kept touching her. A hand on the small of her back as they left the hotel. His fingers running down her arm, teasing her hip when they finally sat. The touches were light but enough to keep her keenly tuned to his body. On top of all of that, he was freshly showered and smelled like grass and sunshine. The man had each of her senses in overdrive.

"This is a business trip for you. Our jobs are more complicated on the road. I get it." Adam rubbed a circle against her abdomen. "I'll take your spare time." He kissed her again.

Prince's song 'Kiss' bubbled up in her mind, and Sue finally gave in. This man put a song in her head and was willing to run the gauntlet that was her life on tour. Not only did he deserve a shot, she wanted to give him one.

Sue scrubbed a hand over her face, ready to see where this would take her. "We have a noon checkout, and I haven't finished packing."

Adam checked his watch. "It's almost eleven. Do you have a lot to pack?"

"Hard to say." Sue stretched. "Robin and I did a lot of shopping. I may have to make a few trips to my car."

Adam rolled onto his stomach and caught her eye. "You could use a luggage cart."

"There's no challenge in that."

Adam kissed her forehead, then her mouth. He sat up and pushed his fingers through his hair. "What time are you guys leaving?"

"Darryl and I take Lena to the airport at four. We'll hit the road from there."

"I don't want to be away from you."

She sat up facing him and twined her fingers through his. "You'll see me in a week."

"It'll be weird not seeing you every day."

"Are you saying you aren't even gonna call until next Saturday?" Sue kept her tone light and feigned a pout.

Adam grinned. "Maybe I want you to call me."

"My mother taught me that a lady never calls a gentleman."

"That was a terrible lesson."

"I don't know. My mom is pretty smart." All Sue thought about was *not* talking with Adam, even though she loved his banter.

He kissed her again, this time deeper than the last.

She slid closer and wrapped an arm around him, forgetting where they were and what they'd been talking about, and focused on how he'd lit a fire in her that she didn't want to put out.

They sat in each other's arms for a few minutes before Adam stood and pulled her up. He kept her hand in his as they walked back to the hotel.

They arrived at the same time as Justin. He climbed out of a cab, tuxedo rumpled and missing his tie, the vest unbuttoned and his shirt untucked.

"Does this mean Amy won the bet?" Sue asked.

Justin grinned sheepishly. "I'm not sure."

"Amy said you'd have a sleepover, right?"

"Yeah." He stretched out the word. "Did she bet that

I'd sleep *with* someone? Or *near* someone?"

"Spill." Sue sensed a story brewing. "Money is riding on this."

Justin took off the jacket and vest and draped them over his arm while they waited for the elevator. "You guys saw how much my girl drank."

"Yeah, I felt bad for you," Adam said.

Justin grunted. "Thanks. She tossed it as we were getting out of the Lyft at her place."

"Gross." Sue blanched. She'd dealt with more vomit since meeting these guys than she had her entire life before them.

Adam rubbed the small of Sue's back. "Game over."

"Yep." Justin pulled the elastic out of his hair. "Except she didn't think so."

Sue shivered as they stepped into the elevator. As far as she was concerned, puke was a deal breaker for at least a few hours. "How could she not know that?"

Adam pushed the button for Sue's floor. "You're the kinda guy who walks a lady to the door, especially if she can't walk herself, huh?"

"Sure am." Justin leaned against the back of the elevator.

"Oh no. She thought you were still interested," Sue said.

"I honestly don't know what she thought. She threw

up two more times. I think she ate at least as much as she drank. She passed out on the floor in the bathroom."

"Where did you sleep?" Adam asked.

"On her couch. It had a view of the bathroom. I should've left." Justin pushed his hair off his face. "I wanted to make sure she was okay."

"That was nice of you." Sue patted his arm.

"Too nice. When she saw I was still there this morning, she pounced."

"Amy wins after all," Sue said.

"No." Justin shuddered. "I don't know about other people, but once I see what a woman's had to eat for the last week, I want to make sure she's all settled down. And this chick still couldn't walk straight even after a shower."

"You showered with her?" Adam asked.

"Hell no. She found me on the couch when she got out."

"Did she drop her towel?" Sue enjoyed Justin's story a little too much. Sure, she was sympathetic to his date gone wrong. That didn't mean she couldn't also appreciate the tale.

"Uh, kinda? It slid a little when she sat on the couch." Justin stopped and sighed. "Fine. She has a nice rack. She also didn't brush her teeth in the shower, and she was slurring her speech. I kept my distance."

Sue giggled.

Justin frowned as the elevator doors opened on Sue's floor.

"What happened after the nip slip?" Adam asked.

"She went to the benefit with a friend, and they had a bet." Justin paused when Sue opened her door and let them into her room. He sat in one of the chairs. "The friend has a high tally, and my date wanted to prove she could keep up."

"Yeesh." Sue did a quick sweep of the room to make sure she hadn't left any underthings out. Lena's suitcase sat near the door, and two tuxedo bags hung in the bathroom doorway. She cringed when she noticed the beds were still unmade. Most everything else had been put away, though, so she perched on Adam's lap and focused on Justin.

"I told her she should move at her own pace," Justin said. "But there's no reasoning with a woman who's still drunk."

"What did you do?" Adam ran his fingers back and forth along Sue's arm.

The light touch revved her imagination again and had her wishing they were alone.

"I told her I wanted to wash up and locked myself in the bathroom. She lives on the third floor, so it took some doing, but I climbed out the window."

"You're kidding," Sue said.

"Yeah, I am."

Sue punched Justin in the arm. "What did you do?"

"I did go to the bathroom to think. I asked her if she had any coffee. While she fumbled around in the kitchen, I ditched my boxers by the shower and made a beeline for the door."

Adam laughed and offered Justin a fist bump.

"Wait, you ditched your underwear?" Sue asked.

"Sure." Justin thumped his foot. "I don't mind helping her with her friend."

Sue laughed so hard she almost slid off Adam's lap. He snaked an arm around her and pulled her close. She made a concentrated effort not to sigh. "Most people would've bolted. The underwear was a nice touch."

"I do try to please the ladies." Justin tugged on his cuffs. "One way or another."

"Do me a favor," Sue said.

"What's that?"

"Hang those pants up for me before I take them back to the tux shop."

Justin laughed. "You got it."

"I'm still a little annoyed." Sue pursed her lips.

"Why?" Adam asked.

"I bet on a sure thing, and I still lost. What the hell?"

Justin laughed again. "Sorry, Sexy Sue, I can only please so many ladies per day."

Adam squeezed Sue's waist when the nickname crossed Justin's lips.

She leaned back and kissed Adam's cheek. "Next time, embrace the debauchery and bone the girl so I can finally make some money off Darryl." She went to the vanity and gathered up the few toiletries she'd left out.

"You got it." Justin saluted, then ran a hand through his hair and made a face. "I reek. I'm gonna finish this walk of shame." Justin ambled to the door. "You want me to bring back the tux before checkout or meet you in the lobby?"

"Here, please. The sooner the better. Can you bring Brad's, too?"

"Yep." Justin waved and closed the door behind him.

"You guys bet on everything, huh?" Adam said.

"Seems like it."

"What wagers do you think they have on us?"

Sue gave Adam an impish smile. "Probably the usual. Did we or didn't we. They'll all be waiting a long time to cash out."

Adam smacked the arm of his chair. "You sound awfully sure."

"Lena and I made a pact. We're not telling anything. If neither of us talk, the guys have to get their own proof. And I can be very cagey." Sue took her duffel bag from the closet and dropped her toiletries into it before she put the bag on the counter.

"Like hiding your room key in your shoe and your phone in your bra?" Adam prowled toward her and boxed her in against the counter. He leaned so they were eye level with each other.

Sue wasn't sure what prompted him to crowd her space. She liked it. She ran her fingers through his hair before she rested them on his neck. "You don't wear a bra with a dress like that," she said in a low voice.

"What about with a shirt like this?" Adam dragged a finger up her spine, beneath the soft cotton of her blouse. He stopped when he got to her bra strap.

She arched against him. Would he unclasp her bra? She wanted him to. She held his gaze for a moment before he flattened his hand against her back, holding her against his chest as he kissed her with the same amount of unfulfilled lust she'd felt most of the week. Sue tightened her arms around his neck, and he grabbed her waist and pulled her away from the counter.

Before she could fully comprehend what happened, she was on a bed with Adam on top of her, kissing her jaw, then along her neck. She couldn't take a deep breath, and she didn't care; his weight on her was the thing she'd wanted all week. She was done resisting him. She'd deal with any regrets that followed later. This man, his attention, the fire he lit in her—she wanted it all. Now. His hands slid under her top as Sue danced her fingers down his back, tugging at his shirt. She wanted his bare skin against her body. She wrapped a leg around him and tilted her hips against his. He groaned and nipped at the pulse in her throat, making it beat even faster.

With painstaking slowness, Adam pushed her top up, his fingers crawling along her skin. She wished he wore a button-down shirt so she could rip it open. Instead, she had to settle for letting her hands roam beneath it as he teased her stomach with his fingers and her lips, neck, and chest with his mouth. He'd finally pushed her blouse above her bra and kissed the tops of her breasts, bringing her nipples to attention when a knock came at the door.

"Go away, go away, go away," she whispered, pulling Adam's mouth to hers.

"Tuxedo delivery!" Chris called through the door.

Adam groaned and dropped his head onto Sue's chest. "Totally forgot about that," he mumbled.

She lay perfectly still. "If we're quiet, maybe he'll go away."

"Yeah," Adam whispered, then softly kissed her neck.

Chris knocked again. "I know you're in there! I passed Justin in the hallway."

Sue fisted her hands. "I hate him."

Adam rolled off her. "Ditto."

Sue got up, yanking her clothes back into place. She only ran a hand through her hair to give Chris less bullshit to talk about it. She took a few steadying breaths before she opened the door.

"Bringing back the tux. Like you wanted." Chris wiggled his eyebrows and pushed past her, throwing a garment bag on the bed. "Whatchu guys doing?" He gave Sue a Cheshire Cat grin and fell into a chair.

"Packing." Sue focused on tempering her glare. She knew Chris lived to piss her off; she didn't have to let him see how successful he'd been this time.

"Yeah." Chris picked at his fingernails. "Checkout's in like half an hour."

Sue put her hands on her hips. "You ready to go?"

"It takes me like four seconds to pack. I'm not worried about it."

"I'm not concerned about your bags, Chris," Sue said.

Chris batted his eyes as though he had grown wings and a halo. "Unlike some people on this tour, I behaved last night."

"Ha!" Sue practically barked. Chris had been on the prowl after the auction. It'd been obvious. And after the raging shit fit from one of his jilted lovers that morning, the woman who'd ruined Sue and Adam's plans, the last thing she needed was to deal with another of Chris's clingy one-night stands. "That's unusual."

Chris flushed a bright red.

"Lena and I were here all night." Sue ducked into the bathroom to make sure she hadn't left anything behind.

"I know. Darryl and I drank until they opened the

breakfast buffet. And then we ate."

"So when I called you earlier, you were...?"

"At the omelet station."

Adam coughed and turned away from Chris.

When Sue caught his eye, they exchanged an amused look.

"How are you awake now?" Sue asked.

"Tom called me," Chris said. "Plus, I slammed a bunch of energy drinks."

"How did Tom know you weren't in your room?"

"Beats the fuck out of me. He said I need to empty my room and quote 'check the fuck out on time.'"

"I knew I liked that guy," Adam said.

Sue beamed at him, finally letting some of her tension go. "Do me a favor?" she addressed Chris as she went through the shopping bags Adam pulled out of the closet, deciding how to consolidate them.

Chris gestured for her to continue.

"I have Darryl and Tom's tuxes; can you go get Brad and Justin's?"

Chris sneered. "You want me to fetch tuxedos?"

"Yes. Or at least send the guys up. And make sure your stuff is packed and ready to go."

"That's two favors."

"Chris!" Hands back on her hips, Sue looked at the ceiling, willing herself not to let him get to her.

"I'm going, but I'm leaving the door open."

Before Sue could respond, Chris bolted out of the room, pulling the night latch out to keep the door from closing all the way.

"That was actually a good conversation for us." Sue pulled on her hair. "Now we get to see if he sends the guys up."

Adam rubbed her back. "He'll do it."

"Doubtful."

"There was a witness. He'll do something resembling what you asked." Adam bent over and picked up something that fell out of the dry-cleaning bag Sue emptied into her duffel bag. "Why would you get a headband dry cleaned? Wait. A scarf? No. What the hell is this?"

Sue took the shiny fabric from him. "It's a skirt. I had it dry cleaned because I didn't have time to hand wash it."

"That's a skirt?" Adam took the fabric back, shook it out, and held it up, studying it. "There's no way that's a skirt. Maybe a top?"

"It's a skirt." Sue reached for it.

Adam held it out, away from her. "That can't cover you."

"What can't cover her?" Justin asked, letting himself back into the room. He wore fresh clothes, and his damp hair smelled of shampoo. He carried two tuxedo bags.

"This." Adam held the skirt.

Justin hung the tuxes next to the others, then turned to Adam. "It covers her. Barely. But it covers her." He picked up the garment bag Chris had thrown on the bed and hung it as well.

Adam turned to Sue. "When did you wear this? Why wasn't I there?"

Annoyed and uncomfortable with the line of questioning, Sue gave the simplest answer she could. She'd had enough of men fussing over her clothes. "Robin bought it for me. We all went out with him, so I wore it."

"Does it have an attachment or something?" Adam asked.

Justin laughed and shook his head.

Sue closed her eyes before she answered. "No. Please give it to me."

"Come here."

Sue narrowed her eyes.

"Just come here."

Sue walked around the bed and stopped next to him.

Adam held the skirt in front of her waist and frowned. "I don't get how it covers you."

"You're putting it in the wrong spot."

"Show me."

Sue lowered his hands so the fabric rested at her hips.

Adam raised his eyebrows. After a moment, he turned to Justin. "You were there when she wore this?"

"Yep."

"Verdict?"

"Smokin'."

"Justin!" Sue quickly laid the skirt in her duffel bag.

"What? I have eyes."

"Oh my God." Sue turned away from both men and busied herself moving shoe boxes into one bag. When she'd initially tried on the skirt, she knew it'd get tongues wagging. She hadn't anticipated how awkward it'd be hearing *these* men talk about it.

"We're not going to a ball game next week, Sue. We're going someplace where you can wear that."

Sue shook her head. "No. I want to go to the game, and you and Justin aren't allowed to hang out any-more."

CHAPTER 40

Sue fumbled getting her phone from her pocket, answering it before she missed the call. "Hello?"

"I'm calling you first. If I ask you to call me back, does that keep you in compliance with your mother's rule about calling a gentleman?"

Sue smiled. It hadn't been ten minutes since she and Adam had parted ways with a tentative plan for the next weekend. "It's a gray area, but I'm willing to take the chance."

"Music to my ears."

"There's something we need to discuss before this goes much farther." Sue had made her decision to lower her barriers and see if a relationship with Adam was possible; now she wanted to make sure there wouldn't be any petty arguments as they got things off the ground.

"If this is another attempt to scare me off with your tour schedule or exotic piercings, it won't work."

"Exotic piercings?"

"I was trying to throw you off the tour-schedule topic. You got any?"

Sue smirked. "I have tour schedules for the next three months, easy."

"I know. That doesn't scare me. What about the piercings?"

"You'll discover that on your own."

Adam hummed into the phone and set her on edge. "That sounds promising."

"It is." Sue took a long pause as she thought about Adam searching her body and about her searching his. "Now, my concerns."

"They're not about the tour?"

"Nope."

"Bring it."

"Any team allegiances I should know about? Any deal-breaker rivalries? Do you ever foam at the mouth over games?"

Adam laughed. "I do not foam at the mouth." He laughed again. "I love that you're asking this."

"And I'll love it if you answer. What if I show up in a rival jersey?" For the first time since their first date, Sue felt legitimately nervous. As much as she liked sports, she had no firm favorites. Aside from soccer, she didn't follow anything regularly, and even soccer didn't get her undivided attention. She was on the move too much. Would that bother him?

"Impossible. I'm a journalist; I have no favorites. But if I thought you were headed down the path of sports heartbreak, I'd persuade you otherwise."

She wasn't sure she totally believed his answer.

Someone who built their life around sports had to have some preferences. She decided to give him the benefit of the doubt for now. Discovering his sweet spots could be fun.

"And you?" Adam asked. "Any music I should never play around you?"

She loved that he didn't ask her about teams, switching to the world she lived in. "Nothing comes to mind. But if you go off track, I'll persuade you otherwise."

"Perfect."

"See you Saturday?" She had to end the call despite not wanting to. The longer they talked, the less she'd want to hang up. And she needed to. She needed to get back to business.

"Yes. Sue?"

"Yeah?"

"I'm not afraid of your schedule," Adam said.

His declaration was one of the sexiest things anyone had ever said to her. She crossed her fingers that it was true, not bravado. "And I'm not afraid of yours."

"You haven't seen mine."

"I searched *Sports Mecca* for your byline. I have an idea."

"You searched my site for my byline? That's so hot." His voice dropped as he spoke.

A thrill shot through her. Still, Sue was determined

to keep her head. "Okay, Mr. Mecca. Check your ego. It was strictly for research purposes. Your schedule isn't printed on a website like mine is. I needed an idea of the logistics."

"And?"

"I'm not scared."

"Good." Adam cleared his throat. "Sue, I'm willing to do the work to be with you."

Her heart beat faster. This was the first time a man had told her he was up to the challenge. She wouldn't let him regret it. "So am I."

"Good. I have to turn in the car. Call me back?"

"As soon as your plane lands."

PANAMA CITY, FL

Darryl trotted across the parking lot toward Sue as she stashed her overnight bag in the trunk of her car.

"What's up, D? You ready to get out of Florida?"

"Yeah. Mind if I ride with you today?"

"Fine by me." Sue closed the trunk. "As soon as Justin comes out, we can go."

Darryl squeezed the back of his neck. "I asked him if he'd trade with me. He's already on the bus."

"Chris bragging too much about another conquest?" They had all grown tired of Chris shooting off about his girl du jour. Ever since meeting Lena, Darryl had gone from ignoring Chris's boasts to openly challenging the guy to shut up.

"I need to make a few phone calls, and I don't want the guys all over me."

"Okay." Sue texted Tom about the change of plans, then she shot Adam a text that they were about to hit the road. In the few days since New Orleans, they'd been texting more often and talking once a day or so. Adam put most of her concerns about their complicated plans to rest by sounding genuinely happy to hear her voice whenever she answered his calls.

"So you know, I suck at that car game you and Just play. I can point out old cars and sports cars, but I know fuck all about 'em."

Sue laughed. "Want me to give you some pointers so you can beat him one day?"

"Then I'd have to remember that shit, and I have too much going on in here for that." Darryl tapped his head.

"Everything okay?"

"Yeah."

Sue narrowed her eyes. "It's unlocked." Darryl had always been pretty open with whatever was on his mind. One-word answers were unusual for him.

Darryl climbed in and slammed the door. He faced Sue as she got in and put on her seatbelt. "I need another favor."

"Shoot."

"You absolutely cannot tell anyone what you hear. It's top secret."

More secrets? Nope. No. No. Sue kept enough secrets on this tour. "Are you sure everything's okay?"

"Pretty much."

She plugged her phone into the car charger. "What does that mean?"

"I'm going to Brazil." Darryl navigated through the screens on his phone.

Sue dropped the keys as she tried to put them in the ignition. Brazil wasn't a tour stop. Was Darryl bailing early to run away with Lena? "What?"

"During that week we have off between New York and Europe. I need to meet Lena's parents."

"She's taking you to Brazil to meet her parents?" Sue recovered the keys, slid them into the ignition, and turned over the engine. "That's intense and awesome all in one."

"Lena has no idea I'm going. That's part of the reason I need you to keep it a secret. I haven't told Tom or the rest of the guys, either. Want it all official first."

Sue pulled onto the street. "Are you surprising Lena?"

Darryl blew out a breath. "Sort of? I'm going to ask her parents if I can marry her."

Sue slammed on the brakes, lurching them both forward. She pulled into a nearby gas station, stopped the car, and flexed her fingers on the steering wheel. Her last boyfriend dumped her when she didn't want to move in together. She'd had to convince herself that Adam wasn't a fairy tale. She couldn't fathom marriage. Marriage was for more established people. For parents. For people who weren't her. "Did you say married?"

Darryl grinned. "You're a little skittish there, Suse. Don't worry. I wanna marry Lena."

Sue laughed at his wry grin and let some of her inner panic out. Then she basked in how right she had been about Lena. "I knew that night in Austin she was it for you. I figured you two would shack up first."

Darryl shook his head. "Nope. Shacking up leaves room for excuses. When we're married, there won't be a question of whether she should tour with me or whatever. She'll belong there. She belongs here now."

Sue blinked back tears. Maybe that's why the idea of marriage freaked her the hell out. Until Adam, she'd never met a man so clear with his intentions toward her. They were all pretty clear on what they wanted in their lives, but never what they wanted specifically with her. She could've been traded out with another willing female, and the guys she'd dated would've carried on just the same. She'd been so swept up in the whirlwind of Adam. A deep pang of worry churned her stomach. She didn't want to be interchangeable to him. She forced herself to focus. This wasn't about him. It was about Darryl and Lena. She cleared her throat. "Lena's the love of your life."

Darryl raised his eyebrows and flashed a smile. "You know it."

Sue pushed away the longing she felt for her own life and focused on her excitement for Darryl. She'd designed the life she was living. She didn't need to long for anything. "Why haven't you told Tom about Brazil?"

"I don't want him to try planning it for me, and I'm going no matter what he says."

"He does love to plan. And he'll get over it." Sue pulled the lever to open the gas door. "Let's top off the tank."

Darryl climbed out of the car and walked around to the pump. Sue met him there and slid her credit card into the machine. She hoped he didn't notice her hands trembling as she entered her information. She shouldn't be shaking anyway. Like he said, D was marrying Lena.

She hit the button for eighty-seven octane, and Darryl pumped the gas. "You know what's really stressing me out? If her parents say okay when I go down there, I'm proposing as soon as I see Lena again. Chances are my mom won't be able to meet her first."

"You and your mom are super close?"

"Dad died when we were little. Mom is it. She taught me everything; she gave me everything. I hate that she might meet Lena *after* I put my ring on her finger." Darryl frowned and his shoulders sagged.

"Can your mom meet you in Austin?"

Darryl shook his head. "She can't get the time off. Plus, I don't want to tip Lena off."

"What about Brazil? Lena won't be there, but she'll meet the family."

Darryl put the gas hose back on the pump and looked at Sue. "Gotta do this man-to-man. If I bring my mom, it's like I'm begging for their approval."

"She'll understand."

"I know. She's awesome like that. We already talked about it when I called her for my passport."

Sue beamed at Darryl. How she'd wound up with a group of rockers she mostly liked spending time with was a mystery she truly appreciated. "I can't wait until we get to Ann Arbor. I want to meet all these women—your mom and sister, Brad's sister. I can't wait."

Darryl chuckled. "They're gonna love you, and that will freak Chris the fuck out. It's gonna be a good time."

JACKSONVILLE, FLORIDA

More than halfway to Savannah, their convoy pulled into a rest stop. Sue climbed out of the car to fill the tank.

"Gonna use the bathroom and grab a drink. Want anything?" Darryl asked.

"Water?"

"You got it." Darryl crossed the lot to the convenience store and disappeared inside.

Sue's phone rang loudly through the open car window. She adjusted the pump to automatically fill and checked the screen. Unknown number. She finished filling up, replaced the pump, and got the service station squeegee, slopping water on the back window. As she pulled the rubber edge across the glass, her phone rang again. She finished her task, figuring it'd be the same mystery number. When she got to the front of the car, her suspicions were confirmed. The third time it rang, Sue answered.

"It's about damn time. You killed my story, now you

think you don't have to talk to me?"

"Julie Griffin," Sue said. "You're not calling me from a *Sound Spectrum* number."

"I'm not working on a *Sound Spectrum* story."

The hairs on Sue's neck rose. "I can kill that story at another pub, too."

"Oh, don't worry. This is a new story."

Nothing about the way the woman said those words gave Sue comfort. She held steady knowing Julie couldn't handle facing a cool head. "What's the story?"

"Yesterday I met Chris's son. He's gonna be a big brother soon."

Sue scoffed. Truly this woman had spun a fantasy. "Chris doesn't have kids."

"You sure about that? I have a picture of a toddler who looks a lot like him and an awfully interesting story from the baby mama."

"Do you really want to be known for trash stories?" This woman gunning for Chris made no sense. Yeah, she had an axe to grind with Sue, but there were different and better ways to do that. "It all makes you look *more* jilted."

"Funny how I was the one who jilted him."

"Yet you're acting like it was the reverse." Done with the conversation, Sue considered hanging up. If the woman hadn't been sitting on a fairly accurate smear piece about Chris's pickup lines, she would have.

"Listen, Sue. This isn't gossip. I have three women who said they got herpes from your boy, a kid who looks just like him, and a baby mama who says the record label offered her an abortion."

Sue's blood ran cold. She kept her voice steady. Even if this was all fabricated—and Sue was confident it was—she'd have to tell Chris. "Prove it. Give me names and numbers."

"Sure. As soon as I get an exclusive from Chris."

"You're funny, Julie. He has no comment. And know this—after I prove this is bullshit, you won't even be able to write for the *National Enquirer*."

Julie let out a cold laugh. "Oh, Sue. You have a text incoming."

The line went dead. A few seconds later a photo message came in. Sue clicked it open and looked into the face of a little boy who couldn't be more than three years old and looked exactly like Chris.

ACKNOWLEDGEMENTS

This book has been a long time coming and its very likely that I'll forget to thank some important people. For this, I am deeply sorry. Please know: if you ever let me talk your ear off about writing, read passages, helped me figure out plot points or offered me support and encouragement, I am eternally grateful. This book never would've seen the light of day without all the amazing support I received.

Thank you to my writing and critique partners, especially the Canton Writing Circle and the Lowcountry Romance Writers; and my beta readers, especially Alyssa, Brigid, Colleen and Sita. Patricia and Angela, thank you for beating as many bad habits out of me as you could and doing it with love and compassion. You both have made me a better writer. Suzanna, you made me cry happy tears at least twice with your amazing cover designs. Andrea, bless you for answering my random questions via text and phone. Kayelle, you have always been generous with your time and knowledge and have helped me leap forward. The Shark Sprinters and the Sharks Writing All the Words answered so many questions, cheered me on and kept me going when they had no idea how much I needed the extra push. I can't wait to return the favor.

Matthew, Amy, and Mandy who are probably so tired of hearing about this, but had my back anyway. Mom, Dad and my sibs, I can't find words big enough for you. Crawfedos rule.

To my oldest, who was so impressed that I wrote

a book, that I couldn't not see it all the way through. Finally, to my husband. Thank you for making it possible for me to sneak away and write. For letting me be in my head so much and for cooking dinner a lot. I promise not to complain out loud the next time you want to plan a Disney trip.

ELAINE REED

ABOUT THE AUTHOR

Elaine lives in South Carolina's Low Country. When she isn't writing, she can be found exploring Charleston, taking in live music and searching for shark teeth on the beach with her family.

www.elaine-writes.com

Sign up for her newsletter:
https://www.elaine-writes.com/newsletter/

Facebook https://www.facebook.com/elainereedwrites

Twitter https://twitter.com/_elainewrites

Instagram https://www.instagram.com/writeelaine/

If this book made you feel something, whether love or hate, please consider leaving a review on Amazon, Goodreads, your blog, or other book site. Share your thoughts on Facebook and Twitter. If you believe the book has value and is worth sharing, would you take a few seconds to let your friends know about it? If it they like it, they'll be grateful to you. As will I.

Chapter 1

Sue: We need to talk as soon as we get to the hotel.

Chris: Call me now.

S: You're gonna want privacy.

C: These guys know all my shit.

S: They don't know this.

C: Doubt it.

S: Would you tell them if you had herpes?

C: Probably. But I don't have anything like that.

S: A reporter says you do.

C: Im-fucking-possible.

S: You sure, fuckboy?

C: Fuck you.

S: Meet me at the hotel.

Of course he had to make everything difficult. That was the way with Chris. Why take the easy way when you could beat the shit out of yourself and everyone around you to get there first?

Sue let Darryl play DJ for the rest of the drive to Savannah. She made mental lists as she drove. Who to contact, how to respond, whether any of this was even worth a response. How could she best protect Chris? Was it true that the record company was offering women money to end pregnancies? If it was, did she need to tell the guys? If she told them, would Tom's secret about her contract also come out? The list kept growing, but she kept adding to it, trying to turn over every possibility. She needed to be prepared for it all so if the shit really did hit the fan, they would get as little on them as possible. Not for the first time, she wondered why Chris had to fuck his way across the country. Couldn't he hit pause for a few stops?

This tour was a series of leaps from one hot mess to another.

Sue and Darryl made it to the hotel a few minutes before everyone else. She texted Chris with her room number and a gory threat for him to meet her there as soon as he got off the bus.

When he finally showed up, a good thirty minutes after the bus had arrived, Sue was ending a call with Emily, her friend and attorney. She'd handed part of her list to Emily to help figure out how the hell this reporter had pieced together this story.

"What do you want?" Chris stormed over the threshold as soon as Sue opened the door.

"That reporter from Austin who wrote the smear piece dug up some dirt." Sue closed the door and moved to the window, closing the drapes.

"I don't fucking have herpes."

Sue faced Chris and noted the vein throbbing at his temple and his set jaw. "Right, but she has evidence of other things."

Chris contorted his face in aggravation. "What things?"

Better to rip off the bandage fast, right? "She said you got a woman pregnant."

"Untrue and I have the condom receipts to prove it." Chris balled his hands into fists, his face growing red.

"And that the woman is pregnant again."

He threw his hands up. "What woman? In Texas? This was my first fucking trip to Texas. We got a few weeks before anyone pops a positive pregnancy test."

Sue winced, wishing she had better news to give him. "There's more."

"Of fucking course." Chris leaned against the dresser, arms crossed, a lethal glare aimed at Sue.

"According to Julie, the woman went to the record label to find you. When she told them she was pregnant, they offered her money for an abortion."

Chris kicked over a chair, his body vibrating, the furious look on his face a sign that it took a monumental force for him not to do more. "Did she accept?" he said, his voice low, warning.

"No." Sue slid her hands into her jeans pockets. She hadn't expected such vehemence, but she understood his reaction. As far as she knew, no one in the band or on tour knew that someone had been looking for Chris. And instead of the record label passing along a message, they offered to pay the woman off and shoo'd her away. Sue didn't even try to understand the logic.

"Was she even looking for an abortion?"

Sue swallowed and shook her head. "She just wanted to contact you."

Chris ripped the phone out of the wall, threw it across the room, walked over to it, and repeatedly stomped it. Plastic pieces flew up around him.

Sue flinched and moved toward him, but backed away when she realized he was lost in his anger. Chris pulled a lot of shit and had earned his obnoxious reputation, but this was different. As much as she wanted to fix this for him, she recognized that he needed to work through the tidal wave of shit. She perched on the edge of the dresser and held her head, wondering how long to let him rage before she called Darryl.

"What kind of asshole offers a random woman money for an abortion." Chris looked up from phone with a disgusted expression. "What kind of asshole?"

At a loss for words Sue shrugged.

"Gimme her number."

"Why do you want Julie's number?"

"Not the bitch reporter. The mother. Give me the mother's phone number."

"I don't have it."

"Why the fuck not!" Chris stomped on the phone again.

It was all Sue could do not to shrink away. "The reporter told me this. Not the label. The label would contact Tom."

"Tom wouldn't keep this from me."

"No, he wouldn't." Sue crossed her arms, fighting the urge to flat-out hug herself. She hadn't been prepared for Chris to be this angry and she was scared. Not for her safety. She didn't believe that Chris would physically hurt her, but even when they'd fought, Chris had never been this...full of rage.

He gave the bits of phone another savage stomp. "How the fuck did the bitch find her?"

"I don't know."

"Fucking find out, Sue!"

Sue took a big step away. Anger radiated off Chris in waves, his behavior becoming even more volcanic.

"I asked Emily to hire an investigator. I gave her all the information Julie gave me."

"Have you given me all the fucking information."

Sue shivered, then unlocked her phone, pulling up the photo from Julie. "Everything but this." She held up the image of the little boy.

Chris stalked across the room and ripped the phone

from her hand. He paced the length of the room, then slammed the phone onto the bed. "This is not my child. I did not abandon a child!" He gripped his skull, his fingertips turning white, his eyes glassy. "I wouldn't." His voice cracked on the last word.

Rooted to the spot, Sue did all she could to keep a neutral expression. Chris was a raw nerve and the last word Sue had expected him to use was abandon. "Okay."

"I didn't do this. Not on purpose. Not by accident. Not at all." He pointed at the phone. "That is not my child."

Sue nodded.

Hands on his hips, Chris looked away then focused on Sue again, his rage simmering rather than roaring. "Stop this story. Whoever the kid is, he doesn't deserve that." Chris stepped closer to Sue. "Kill it."

"I'll do my best."

"That's a fucking hollow promise, Sue." His jaw ticked again. "Don't do your best. Fucking stop it!"

"I don't know if I can." Sue twisted her hands together. "We can tell them it's a lie, but if the woman corroborates the story, any part of it, Julie can run it."

Chris paced the room then stopped at the dresser, pressing his hands against it, his head hanging between his shoulders. "I can prove I don't have herpes."

"You have recent test results?"

"They're a year old. I'll get tested again. Where can I get tested?"

"I'll figure it out." Sue pushed a shaky hand through her hair.

"Soon. Figure it out soon. And a DNA test."

"Only if the mother agrees."

Chris snarled at her. "I'll take a fucking DNA test."

"Okay."

Chris went to the vanity, washed his face and gargled with the hotel mouthwash. He rubbed a small towel across his face and over his head. He tossed the towel on the floor and caught Sue's eyes in the mirror. "I'll take all the tests. It'll be fine. And then I'll sue that bitch for invasion of privacy or some shit like that. Emily'll help, right?"

"We can ask her."

"Good. Do that." Chris nodded, then smiled. "This is all gonna be fine. You got this, right?"

Stunned, Sue nodded. "Yeah. It's...it's gonna be fine."

"Cool." Chris walked across the room. "Sorry about the phone. Let me know what they want to do about it."

"Yeah."

He stopped just shy of the door and faced her. "You talk to the label yet?"

"No."

"Probably better if you handle that instead of me."

"Yeah."

Chris rubbed a hand over his head, similar to how he'd rubbed the towel over it. "I need some air. Let me know when I can get tested." He walked out of the room perfectly calm, as though nothing had happened.